More Than Just
BIRYANI

Andaleeb Wajid is a Bangalore-based author who likes to write about food, relationships, weddings, not necessarily in that order. Originally from Vellore, and belonging to a conservative Muslim family, Andaleeb has worked as a technical writer, content writer and food writer for several years before quitting so she could write full time.

She is the author of *Kite Strings*, *Blinkers Off* and *My Brother's Wedding*. Her Young Adult trilogy is set to be published by Bloomsbury India. Andaleeb is married and has two sons, who unwittingly add a lot of colour to her vocabulary.

More Than Just
BIRYANI

Andaleeb Wajid

AMARYLLIS

A
AMARYLLIS

Copyright © Andaleeb Wajid 2014

All rights reserved. No part of this book may be used or reproduced, stored in or introduced into a retrieval system, or transmitted, in any form, or by any means, (electronic, mechanical, photocopying, recording or otherwise) without the prior written permission of the Publisher. Any person who does any unauthorised act in relation to this publication may be liable to criminal prosecution and civil claims for damages.

Andaleeb Wajid
asserts the moral right to be identified
as the author of this work

This edition first published 2014

AMARYLLIS
An imprint of Manjul Publishing House Pvt. Ltd.
7/32, Ground Floor,
Ansari Road, Daryaganj, New Delhi 110 002
Email: amaryllis@amaryllis.co.in
Website: www.amaryllis.co.in

Registered Office:
10, Nishat Colony, Bhopal 462 003, M.P., India

ISBN: 978-93-81506-40-0

Printed and Bound in India by
Replika Press Pvt. Ltd.

To my parents

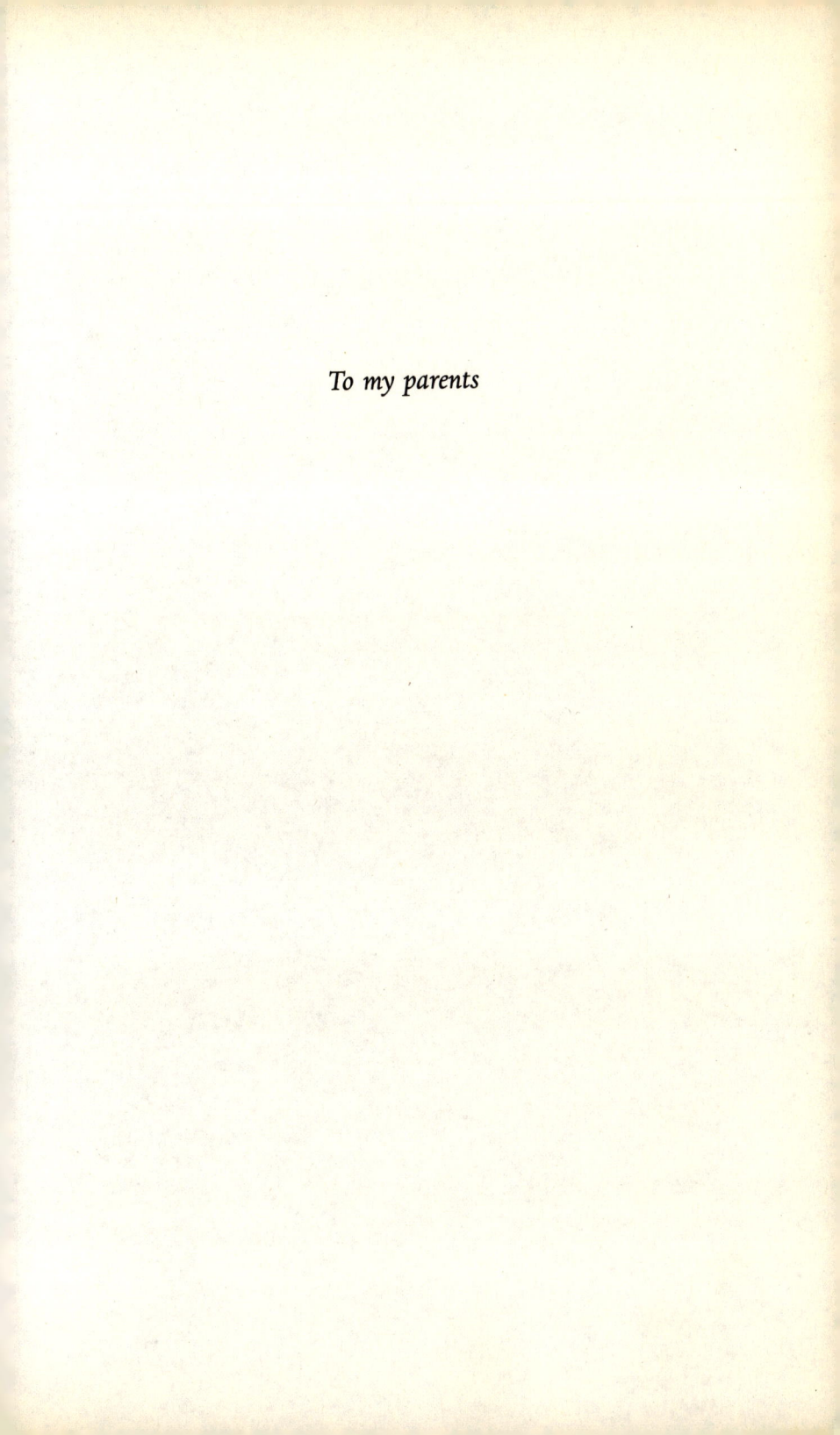

Contents

Prologue	ix
Part One	1
Part Two	93
Part Three	197
Part Four	245
Epilogue	357
Acknowledgments	359

Prologue

THE doors of the elevator creaked open and I stepped out, inhaling the peculiar smell that often lingers in the hallways of most apartment buildings in Hong Kong. I knew which apartment she lived in; yet I shot a glance at all the other doorways scattered down the narrow corridor. There was a sporting equipment store and an Indonesian restaurant. The rest didn't have any name plates to indicate whether they were homes or business establishments.

I turned to her apartment and stopped in front of the door, feeling a little surprised when I noticed that her door seemed a little more ornate than the others. There was some pretty mosaic work done on the tiles around the door. They were dark grey and yellow in colour, and exuded warmth and grandeur without looking oppressive.

I shifted my handbag from one shoulder to the other and reached out to ring the doorbell. I sensed some shuffling on the other side before the door was opened. I smiled at the woman standing at the door and she smiled back. Was this her? I took a quick look behind her and saw a messy dining table with a large bag of groceries placed on it.

'Yes?' the woman asked, still holding the door.

'I spoke with you on the phone yesterday. I'm Sonia, from *Don't Go Hungry* magazine.'

The woman's eyes widened slightly in recognition. She nodded and opened the door wider.

'Come in,' she said shyly and I stepped inside, feeling a mix of awkwardness and excitement at the same time. No one had assigned this job to me. No one told me to take off during my lunch break and hop on to the MTR from Central to Tsim Sha Tsui, and hunt down this woman's apartment. No one had told me that it would be a crazy mission because it seemed like no one even knew about this woman's existence. But somehow I felt like I was sitting on a time bomb, and I wanted to be the first one to be there when it went off.

Her apartment was small and slightly cramped. The dining table I had seen from the door seemed to be a dumping ground of sorts for everything that was lying around. There was a slightly blackened pot kept in the centre and it was emitting an aroma that immediately made my stomach clench and mouth water. I wish I'd had lunch before coming.

The table also had a stack of mismatched plates, a jug of water, some glasses, a box of crayons, a tattered colouring book, and a small plate of soggy looking French fries. Near the plate, a little boy peered at me, and I stared back amazed. He had the darkest pair of eyes I'd ever seen. I lifted my hand and did a small wave as if to beckon him. The child shook his head ever so slightly and sank down further in the chair.

I turned to take in the rest of the apartment. There was a small living room with a sofa, an LCD TV and a centre table that was surprisingly clean and bare.

'Come!' the woman beckoned me further. I slipped my feet out of my beige suede pumps and flexing my toes, walked towards her. I could see there were a couple of rooms on one side of the hall. Both doors were closed. It was slightly stuffy in the room and I straightened my shoulders hoping that my white shirt would un-stick itself from my shoulder blades.

'Can we sit down and talk?' I asked.

'Sure,' she smiled and I looked at the dark brown sofa on one side of the wall. We both sat down and I could sense the awkwardness billowing between us.

'What do you want to know?' she asked shyly.

'Everything,' I said, and realised how strange that sounded.

'But...,' she looked confused.

'Look, I know this will take time. But you don't have to do it all now,' I said, shifting a little uneasily on the sofa, trying to find a comfortable spot.

'Amma?' the boy spoke.

We both turned towards him as he pushed the plate away.

'I'm hungry,' he declared and immediately hid his head under the table.

I smiled. 'He's shy,' she explained and I nodded, but to my dismay, she got up and walked towards the dining table.

'Why don't you come and join us for lunch?' she asked, turning around. 'I haven't eaten either.'

I was tempted. She lifted the lid off the pot and the heady aroma wafted towards me, inviting me until I got up from the sofa feeling some of the awkwardness dissipate.

'What's for lunch?' I asked, as I sat down at the dining table.

'An old favourite. Biryani.'

Part One

1

Tahera Bilal had no idea that in less than three months, she would become a widow. It was 26th January and the children were at home, upsetting her schedule and driving her crazy with their incessant fights and arguments. She stood still in the heat of the kitchen, pressing a finger to her throbbing temple as she bellowed to her children.

'Zubi! Rishaad! If...' she paused. They didn't hear her over their squabbling. Looking determined and furious, she stepped outside the kitchen and stopped for a moment when she saw her five-year-old son pulling at her nine-year-old daughter's hair viciously. Her daughter's face was unrecognisable, eyes closed and mouth open in a wail. Tahera rushed forward and pulled the two of them apart. Rishaad had yanked out quite a few strands of Zubi's hair and she was crying so much that Tahera felt as though her head would split wide open.

She dragged her daughter away to the bedroom and admonished her.

'You are not leaving this room until I tell you to!' she shouted at her while Zubi rubbed her scalp tearfully.

'Why isn't he getting punished? That...that...' she burst out crying and shut the door in her mother's face.

Tahera pushed open the door and had to yield against it with her shoulder because Zubi was pushing it from the other side, refusing to let her mother come inside. A brief image of herself playing this awkward tug of war flashed before her eyes and she shook her head, not amused.

Finally, Tahera pushed her way through and staggered inside. A cowering Zubi was sitting behind the door.

'You are not to lock the door to your room,' Tahera reprimanded her but Zubi's eyes flashed with subdued fire. She looked away, while continuing to rub her scalp with her tiny hands. Tahera was torn between pulling Zubi towards her, massaging her head and telling her she was sorry, and going outside to see what Rishaad was up to.

'I...' she started, but Zubi looked rebellious. These days she could hardly recall how Zubi had looked when she was a baby, soft and sweet smelling, her plump arms waving in the air as she dribbled spit everywhere. This Zubi was not the same person. This red-faced Zubi was like a map she had to navigate all over again.

Sighing, Tahera backtracked to the hall where Rishaad was watching television.

'Why were you fighting with your sister?' she asked, sitting down beside him, resting her aching back against the sofa. She closed her eyes momentarily and thought of a warm summer, mango-tinted and blue. A Vellore summer. Everyone else hated it, rebelled against it by going away to cooler cities like Bangalore, but not her.

Summer was still three months away.

'She always calls me "stupid boy",' complained Rishaad, taking his eyes away from the Republic Day parade that was being shown on the television.

'So? You pulled her hair?' Tahera asked, opening her eyes and sitting up.

'She started it first,' he whined, and looked straight ahead. Getting up to the sound of the marchpast and drum beats, Tahera shook her head and walked into the kitchen. The day was still young, and she had so much to do before it got over, before she could lie down, curled next to her husband's ample body. Her stomach tightened and her heartbeat quickened when she thought of him but she pushed those thoughts away and concentrated on making lunch for her two brats. He had said that he'd be home for lunch early that day, which meant she had to work faster, but that wasn't a problem. She always worked fast.

As soon as breakfast was done, and he was about to leave for his shop, Rishaad clung to his legs and Zubi started yanking at his shirt.

'Don't go, Abba! It's a holiday!' Zubi had squealed when he laughingly swung her around in a circle.

'Arrey! Don't do that, ji!' Tahera had said when he picked up Rishaad and swung him around too.

'Don't listen to Ammi!' Zubi said, boldly making a face at her mother, because she was standing in her father's protective shadow.

'How about I come back early this evening?' he asked, pretending to look thoughtful. He always did that when he was kidding with them.

'No, don't go!' Rishaad insisted.

'Or, how about I come home for an early lunch and don't go back to the shop?' The children jumped happily. His eyes met hers over the dark heads of their children and she turned away, feigning not to have seen the look in his eyes.

Smiling to herself, she re-entered the kitchen and pulled out the semi-thawed chunks of mutton from the sink. She pulled at the still half-frozen pieces and trimmed the fat before proceeding to chop them into smaller pieces.

Humming to herself, she measured chana dal in her fist, washed it and put it in a kadai.

'Ammi?'

She turned around to see Zubi standing at the door, looking uncertain.

'Yes?' she asked, and opened the cupboard where she stored the spices.

'What are you doing?' Zubi asked, as she sidled inside.

'Making lunch,' Tahera answered as she pulled out the bottle of garam masala powder. Her movements were quick and efficient as she washed a handful of fresh coriander and dropped it into the kadai that now had the chana dal and mutton. She peeled an onion swiftly, chopping it into little chunks that found their way into the kadai.

'What's for lunch?' Zubi asked, propping herself on a stool.

Tahera turned to her daughter and smiled. 'Come, I'll show you what I'm making.'

Biting her lower lip uncertainly, Zubi slipped down from the stool, walked over to her mother, and peered into the kadai. She made a face. 'What's all this?'

'This,' her mother said as she uncapped a bottle of adrak-lehsun and spooned out the pungent paste, 'is how shaamis are made.'

Zubi looked impassive as she watched her mother put ground coconut, a pinch of salt, some haldi and two big green chillies in the kadai. She poured water until it just about submerged the meat and the dal.

'Watch the magic now,' Tahera whispered and pulled Zubi close to her for a quick hug.

'Magic?' Zubi asked, her eyes widening.

'Yes. How else do you think something as boring as chana dal, some mutton and all these spices come together and become shaamis?' Tahera ruffled her daughter's hair, unknowingly soothing the pain that Rishaad had caused a while back.

Zubi closed her eyes momentarily and when she opened them, the contents of the kadai were bubbling. Tahera stirred it with a wooden spatula while dreaming of another day, another time when she had just got married and was living in Vellore. Her mother-in-law had handed over the responsibility of the kitchen to her as she preferred to stay in her room, reading the Quran. Tahera had been making shaamis one afternoon, just like today, but oh, so different.

The heat in the kitchen had been oppressive and unbearable. Sweat ran down her spine in tickling trickles and she fanned herself with the pallu of her saree when she felt large warm hands settle on her exposed waist. She gasped and then relaxed back into the huge frame that belonged to her husband.

'How are you back so early?' she whispered to him as he leaned forward and nuzzled her collarbone.

'Just like that,' he whispered back and rubbed his thumbs on her skin in circles.

'Stop! Amma can come in here any moment,' she warned, pushing his hands away and straightening up.

'What are you making?' he asked her, standing upright and looking very proper as he popped a piece of coconut that was lying on the kitchen slab into his mouth.

'Your favourite. Shaami. Now go!' She shoved him out of the kitchen and he left, laughing.

'Ammi!' Zubi cried, startling Tahera out of her stream of thoughts. 'I think it's burning!'

Tahera stirred the kadai frantically, turning off the gas and then placing the kadai near the window where it could cool.

'Good you told me!' she praised Zubi and rewarded her with a smile. Yes, that little baby was still there inside somewhere.

'What's your brother doing?' asked Tahera. Zubi scowled, not bothering to answer as she stormed out of the kitchen.

'Wait! The magic is just beginning!' Tahera called out but Zubi had already left. Sighing, she popped out of the kitchen briefly. Rishaad was still watching TV.

The magic no longer hung in the air as Tahera methodically cooled the dal and meat mixture, scooped it into a mixie and switched it on, holding on to the lid tightly.

When she brought the mixie to a halt a minute or two later, Tahera lifted its lid and instinctively sniffed at the contents. Her nose curled a little in distaste. The hot motor smell of the mixie had crept inside and she shook her head, remembering the sil-batta at her mother's home in Vellore.

She cleaned the mixie carefully, all the while thinking of how her mother would hunch before the grinding stone, rhythmically moving the oblong batta up and down, crushing the onions and green chillies, mixing the dal and meat into one unified, irregular mass. *That* was indeed magic. Not this smooth mixture here.

A little later, when the doorbell rang, Zubi ran to open the door. Tahera's husband stood there, affectionately tugging at Zubi's ear who had immediately started complaining about how Rishaad had pulled her hair and how Ammi was blaming *her*.

Rishaad scrambled down from the sofa, looking angry and embarrassed and Tahera watched the two of them squabble with their father. Her work in the kitchen was done and she just had to fry the shaami. She'd been waiting for her husband to come so she could serve them hot.

'*Aapki kya shikayat hai, begum?*' he asked as he sank down into the single sofa adjacent to the one she was sitting on. He was smiling but his eyes were tired.

'Is everything alright?' Tahera asked, worry darting inside her. The two children were climbing on either side of the sofa and no amount of rebuking worked.

'I'm fine,' he answered, rubbing his temple with his finger.

'Why don't you take a nap after lunch?' she suggested. He smiled slowly and shrugged.

'Only if you agree to give me company,' he said in a low voice. Tahera looked at the children, a little horrified as she felt her face heat up. Thankfully, they hadn't heard him.

She opened her mouth to say something and then changed her mind.

'I'll serve lunch now.' She got up, knowing her husband's eyes were on her back.

She tucked a few stray strands of hair behind her ears as she passed a mirror on the way to the kitchen.

She placed a kadai on the stove and poured oil into it generously. Oiling her palms, she deftly pulled out small walnut-sized rounds of shaami from the mixture and rolled them between her palms until they were slightly oblong in shape. Then she pressed her palms together so that a diamond shape resulted. She fried the shaamis in the oil briskly, hoping they wouldn't disintegrate. Thankfully they didn't.

When she served lunch, Zubi and Rishaad started arguing about how many shaamis they could each eat. The four of them sat down at the table, her husband at the head. He poured dal over his rice, broke off a piece of a shaami and put it in his mouth. Tahera waited anxiously as he closed his eyes and shook his head.

'Perfect,' he announced and she smiled radiantly at him.

There were many elaborate meals that she had cooked and would cook in the future. But that day, with the simple white rice and the humble dal, the shaami with its crisply fried edges and warm, soft body inside added a sheen to the afternoon that was hard to replicate. Tahera didn't know it yet, but every time she needed comfort, she was going to reach out for the chana dal and the gently thawing frozen meat chunks.

2

The phone rang in long bursts and Tahera opened her eyes, a little confused. Only STD calls rang that way, prompting her to hurry from the bedroom to the hall where the phone was. It was still early in the morning, and the kids were sprawled on the mattress on the ground. Her husband was also asleep on the bed. The kids had their own room but they refused to sleep there and had taken to sleeping on the mattress. It was almost dark outside and since she hadn't even heard the Fajr azan, she knew it was not even five in the morning.

Shaking her head slightly, she picked up the receiver and said 'Hello' breathlessly.

'Tahera?'

'Ammi! Is everything okay? How come you have called so early in the morning?' Tahera gasped, squinting in the near darkness of the living room, shivering a little in the cold morning. She rubbed her arm absently, trying to allay the prickly feeling caused by goosebumps.

'Yes, yes,' her mother responded. 'Why are you sounding so worried?'

'I...it's not even five a.m.! Of course I'll be worried, thinking of you and Abba!' Tahera exclaimed, walking around the sofa to sit on it, curling her toes and tucking her legs under her knees. She wrapped the curly wire around her finger absently as she leaned back.

'What to do? I don't get any sleep,' said her mother.

'Hmm,' Tahera replied, shutting her eyes. The urgent worry had evaporated from her voice and she briefly wondered how the day would go. It was Sunday and maybe the kids could persuade their father to take them all out somewhere.

'We're coming to stay with you for a few days,' her mother announced and Tahera sat up, blinking her eyes.

'Really?' she asked, unable to contain the joy in her voice. Her parents rarely came to stay with her, choosing instead to live with her brother in Madras. Despite the number of times she'd asked them to come Bangalore, they had steadfastly refused.

'Yes,' her mother replied, and Tahera closed her eyes, imagining her mother sitting on the bed, her hair covered with the pallu of her saree. No, her mother couldn't possibly be sitting on the bed if she was on the phone. But the image stuck nevertheless and it evoked the quiet smoky fragrance of attar that clung to her and her gently lined face.

'Is everything alright?' she asked. Had something happened between her brother and his wife? His brother's wife Amina was a virtuous woman who took care of her parents as though they were her own but Tahera had always felt that there was a certain amount of subdued resentment in her. Had it flared finally?

'Yes, everything is alright, ma. We just thought it's been days since we saw you and the kids. How are they?' Ammi asked.

'Fighting every minute of the day as usual,' Tahera replied, with a grim smile. 'Aslam bhai and I never fought like this when we were young.'

Ammi didn't reply to that. Instead they spoke some more

about this and that, and the weather and the quality of water – two major points of contention for women who had lived most of their lives in Vellore.

'I can't wait to come and drink that sweet water,' Ammi said. She always claimed that the water in Bangalore was actually sweeter than its Madras counterpart.

'Well, you know we've always asked you to come and stay with us,' Tahera countered.

'Now we are. Next week by Brindavan Express.'

'Inshallah,' murmured Tahera, mentally counting the number of days till she would have her parents with her.

'Your father has requested you to make your kali mirch ki phaal for him when we come,' Ammi spoke suddenly and Tahera smiled.

'Of course.'

Her father was not a fussy eater but there were some things that he liked just so. Kali mirch ki phaal was one of them. Even his wife didn't cook that as well as Tahera did, he always claimed.

'I'll send him to pick you up from the station,' Tahera remarked, just as her mother was about to end the call.

'No, no! Why are you giving him trouble? We will come by auto, na!' her mother protested.

'No. He won't hear of it. You know he loves both of you just like his own parents.'

'Yes,' Ammi responded, 'We were very lucky to find him for you, Tahera.'

Tahera smiled at that and noticed with a start that the sun had risen.

'Ammi! You made me miss Fajr namaz!'

Both of them said their goodbyes after that. Tahera sat still, absorbing the meagre sunlight before she sighed and got up. She stretched her arms while mentally tabulating the day's menu. She went back to the room and saw that Rishaad was stirring. He was the baby of the family, for everyone except Zubi. He hadn't woken up or else he would have been screaming for his milk, which he wanted every morning. No amount of cajoling had made him understand that he needed to brush his teeth first.

Tahera prepared his milk, left it covered on the table and went on to read khaza namaz and then the day's Quran. She heard the rough thud of the newspaper as it landed outside the door and she bounded forward, a little excited because it was a Sunday.

She loved reading the weekly horoscope section for some reason, even though instinct and intellect told her not to pay too much attention to it. She marvelled at how some woman named Tiny could look into the future and tell her that her week ahead was going to be just great. It could turn out awful and she wouldn't hold anything against her, but she felt a minor connection with her as she read the horoscope for Sagittarius, her sun sign.

She opened the door and saw the neatly rolled newspaper lying on the ground along with the day's milk, left by the milkman. She went back inside, unrolled the paper, smoothed it out on the table and pulled out the weekly supplement first. She cast a glance at her horoscope and smiled wryly.

'*Unusual disturbances will trouble you this week* – that would have to be Suman,' she spoke aloud.

'Badmouthing Suman again?' her husband asked and she whirled around. He was yawning and stretching and she smiled at him.

'You know how it is,' she replied and he shook his head, mouthing 'women' as he went to bathe.

Suman, her brother-in-law's wife was indeed garrulous, and every sentence of hers was peppered with something patronising aimed at the other person, something that pushed up her own worth consciously. For instance, last month when they had met at a family dinner Tahera had organised at her home, Suman smiled at the chicken qurma and shook her head.

'Bhabhi, you make very good qurma, but you should taste the butter chicken I make! It is excellent! My husband says it tastes better than the ones made at hotels!' she commented.

Tahera smiled and replied, 'We wouldn't really know, because we hardly eat out.'

The point struck home and Suman was silenced momentarily; it was a family joke that many restaurants nearby had become rich overnight only because of Suman. She wasn't a bad cook, just a lazy one. For some reason, Zubi really connected with her and that disturbed Tahera. Tahera may not be college educated like Suman but she had wanted her daughter to look up to *her*, not her restaurant-butter-chicken-quaffing aunt.

'Oh well, I should probably call and speak to her,' Tahera thought as she folded the paper and went to the kitchen to prepare breakfast. There was no tearing hurry to make sure the children were ready for school and neither did she have to worry about packing her husband's lunch.

From the cupboard, she pulled out a jar which held raw peanuts and roasted a handful. When they had cooled, she rubbed the peanuts briskly, blew off their skins and ground them in the mixie with some grated coconut, a couple of red chillies, salt and a bit of water. With the peanut chutney ready, she set water to boil on the stove and measured the rice flour that she kept in a large tin in the store room.

When the water started boiling, she added some salt, and then the rice flour, stirring briskly till it became a thick mass that seemed to absorb her wooden spoon. She let it cool and then kneaded the mass, sprinkling dry rice flour over it until it became a pliant dough. She pulled out small portions from it and rolled each one of them on a floured board until they became smooth and round.

Just as she was going to start rolling out thin rotis, she heard a scream. Shutting her eyes briefly, she took a deep breath and ran to the room. Rishaad stood at one side of the bed, looking sheepish but with a devilish glint in his eye. Tahera walked around the bed to the other side where Zubi had been sleeping on the mattress and she stopped short.

The sound of running water ceased from the bathroom and her husband stepped out, a towel wrapped around his waist.

'Who screamed?' he asked, water dripping from his shoulders.

'I did,' Zubi replied, and then he turned to look at her.

Rishaad had drawn a generous moustache on Zubi's face, and thick caterpillar eyebrows for added effect, all using Tahera's kajal pencil. On seeing her face in the mirror on the cupboard, Zubi had flopped back screaming.

For a split second, Tahera saw the humour in the situation and her lips quivered as she tried not to smile. She scratched her temple and bit her lower lip and then turned away for a moment. When she turned to her husband, she noticed that he didn't look amused.

'Are you punishing him, or should I?' he asked grimly. Zubi got up and stood next to him, holding his hand possessively. Rishaad looked at Zubi and then his father and ran towards his mother, crying.

'Oh typical! He's such a brat but you won't see that, will you?' Zubi asked, challenging her mother who was startled at the animosity that she displayed. 'It's better if Abbu punishes him.'

'Fine. It's decided then. Come here, young man. And you, Zubi, go and wash off the kajal from your face.'

Tahera looked at her husband as he spoke the words authoritatively, wondering if he would really hurt Rishaad. Yes, he ought to be punished, but...

'Rishaad and I are going for a little walk. And we're going to be very hungry when we return. So I hope breakfast will be ready by then,' he said, as he walked past her, almost rubbing his roughened thumb across her cheek.

'Walk?' Zubi peeked out from the bathroom, looking enraged. With half the kajal washed off her face and the remaining half running down in black streaks, she looked even more comical.

'Why does he get to go for a walk? I want Abbu to....'

'To hit him? Spank him?' asked Tahera, as she folded the sheets and kept them in a drawer that slid out from beneath the bed.

'Yes,' Zubi folded her arms across her chest.

'You wash your face first,' Tahera told her as she dusted her hands and went back to the kitchen.

An hour later, the four of them sat down to a breakfast of steaming hot rotis that were soft, fragrant and golden with ghee.

'How did you punish Rishaad?' Zubi asked sceptically, eyeing him as he dipped a piece of roti into his chutney.

Tahera looked at her son and noted that he looked a little embarrassed as he lowered his eyes.

'I...I'm sorry,' he said, looking at Zubi who still looked miffed. 'I won't do it again,' he added and averted his gaze quickly.

Tahera shook her head, amazed. 'What did you tell him? I mean, I usually have to scream and shout just to make him hear me sometimes.'

Her husband unleashed a brilliant smile and shook his head. 'Trade secret,' he whispered, as he leaned across and ruffled Rishaad's hair. The only one who still looked put out was Zubi who felt that Rishaad hadn't been punished at all.

'Okay, how about we go to Cubbon Park this evening? And Zubi can have an extra ice cream,' he raised his eyebrows at his daughter. People said she had a striking resemblance to him but he was positive that he had never been so stunning.

'No. I mean, no, I don't want an extra ice cream,' Zubi replied, looking almost mollified. Tahera hoped she wouldn't notice that there was still a faint line on her upper lip.

'How about we go to your Suman Chachi's house afterwards?' Tahera asked on impulse and Zubi's eyes lit up.

'Yes!' she looked almost happy and Tahera rued about the strange connection Zubi had with this aunt.

'Okay, but first we need to check if they are free or if they are planning to go out to some restaurant for dinner,' she couldn't help adding. Her husband cocked his head and grinned at her, shaking his head.

'I mean, I don't want to go at a time when they've gone out or ordered something for dinner,' she mumbled, only making the situation worse because her husband started guffawing.

'We'll come back and eat at home. Or *we* could also eat out,' he said and stopped her protests as he reached out for her hand. 'But it doesn't matter, because you should know by now, Tahera,' he continued as he lifted her hand towards his lips, 'that there really is magic in your hands.'

He kissed her fingers, looking at her in that intense way that made her stomach do the strangest flip flops even *now*, ten years after marriage. She blushed furiously and pulled back her hand, hoping that the children hadn't seen them. What she didn't notice was Zubi looking at their exchange with a strange expression.

3

About two years ago, Adil had come to his brother's house, looking a little guilty but defensive. He hadn't bothered to stop and play with Rishaad as he always did; Zubi, who always clung to his legs, was annoying him with her rendition of 'dil da maamla' because she called him Dil Chacha. 'You have no idea that that's what has brought me here,' he thought grimly as he gently pulled away her grubby hands from his trousers and went on to meet Bilal in the hall.

Tahera Bhabhi looked pleased to see him. She always insisted he stayed for a meal and he would inevitably agree. Her cooking skills were known to even the extended family. She may not know how to make exotic food, but she could turn even the simplest and humblest of ingredients into a meal that could bring tears of joy to one's eyes, especially if you were the sentimental type who loved wholesome home-cooked food. Or if you were the type who couldn't understand why the feelings that coursed through your body as you looked at the heavily laden table were more than hunger.

'You're staying for lunch,' she announced when he walked into the kitchen.

He shook his head slightly. 'I just have to speak to Bhaiya and then I have to go, Bhabhi. Next time,' he promised.

'But you love khatta sherva!' she persisted. Adil lowered his head slightly. She was right. He loved the way she made the piquant mutton curry and whenever he stayed overnight, she made sure it was ready for breakfast with piping hot chawal ki roti or cheela.

'I...I don't...think...I can,' he trailed away, adjusting his collar nervously. Tahera stared at him suspiciously.

'Is...everything okay?' she asked.

He looked up at her swiftly, a moment where he wished he could confide in her about what was plaguing him. She turned on the gas and placed a cooker on the stove, adding a generous lashing of oil. When it became hot, she sprinkled mustard seeds and curry leaves into it.

'Yes, everything is okay, Bhabhi. But I have something important to discuss with Bhaiya,' said Adil, watching her with fascination as she sliced an onion thinly and dropped it into the cooker. She stirred it with a wooden ladle and then looked up.

'Well, good for you that your brother is at home today. Actually, since the children's summer vacations started, he tries to be at home during lunch on most days,' Tahera spoke warmly. The steam from the cooker was emanating a rich fragrance of fried onions.

She scooped out half a teaspoon of adrak-lehsun paste from a bottle and added it, stirring as she watched the golden-yellow paste turn into shades of brown. Adil shifted from one foot to the other and then walked out of the kitchen, because the domesticity of the scene, the aroma of the food being prepared and the sight of Tahera as she cooked so serenely, reminded him uncomfortably of his mother.

'Adil!' she called out, surprised at his sudden exit. She turned off the gas. Feeling a little worried, she followed him to the hall where her husband was watching TV with the children.

They chatted for some time and Tahera lingered on the periphery of the conversation, trying to understand what was wrong. When Bilal asked him about his job, Adil winced a little because he knew how disappointed his brother had been when Adil had decided against helping him out at the shop. Adil hadn't wanted to step into the unknown, and almost hazardous territories of a family business. He wanted comforting reality, to be paid at the end of each month for work that he had done properly.

'It's going well, Bhaiya,' he replied and knew what would follow. Every time he came to visit them, Bilal would start talking about how he needed someone trustworthy to help him in the shop and Adil would just sigh and pretend that the comments were not meant for him. Before his brother could launch into that, Adil decided to start talking.

'I'm getting married,' he announced and everyone looked up. Rishaad, who was a three-year-old, also felt it was important to stare at Dil Chacha as though he were sprouting weeds instead of hair. Zubi who had been humming stopped abruptly and Tahera clapped her hands to her mouth in shock.

'But...' she started and then stopped when she saw the look on her husband's face. She quickly came and sat down on the sofa.

'Let him finish,' Bilal spoke slowly, his eyes narrowed.

'I...I'm getting married to Suman,' Adil said, lowering his eyes to the ground. When there was silence all around him, he looked up nervously.

'Suman?' Bilal repeated, almost sarcastically.

'Yes, she's a Hindu girl. We were classmates in college and we've been in love with each other for the past two years. We want to get married,' Adil managed to mumble, almost miserably, avoiding his brother's gaze.

'A Hindu girl?' Tahera squeaked and then, straightening her back abruptly, she took the children to their room.

'Go play!' she ordered them and hurried out. Unknowingly, she used the pallu of her saree to dab the tears that had sprung to her eyes. She should have paid heed to their relatives and got him married to a proper Muslim girl earlier. But how was she to know? She looked up for a brief moment, as though her vision took in, not her cream-coloured ceiling but that of the heavens from where she was sure her mother-in-law was looking down upon her with horror. Her father-in-law too. She walked back to the drawing room, feeling uncertain and wretched, wondering how they could turn the situation around. But the situation had already turned around.

'Sit,' Bilal beckoned to her. She sat down beside him nervously. Adil still looked guilty although there was a measure of relief on his face too.

'She is converting to Islam,' Bilal told her, and sat back. Tahera looked at him, mystified.

'So? How will that make her one of us?' she shot the question without realising that it could be considered insensitive.

Her husband looked at her, startled. He hadn't expected such antipathy from his wife.

'If she's going to convert, what more do you want?' he asked her, cradling his head in his hands that were clasped around his neck.

Tahera looked at him, annoyed. What was with him? How could everyone in their family accept this…this Hindu girl in their midst? So what if she converted?

They argued back and forth for a while and then Adil got up, excusing himself.

'I have to leave,' he said, confusion writ large on his broad, square features.

'Leave for where? Sit down. You're having lunch with us,' Bilal ordered. He turned to Tahera and spoke in an exasperated tone.

'If she won't know how to conduct herself in our gatherings, then teach her, na? I don't have any problem with who he gets married to, as long as she's a Muslim.'

'But...people will talk and they will...'

Bilal shook his head and sat straighter, motioning Adil to sit down. Adil sat back, looking resigned and observed a rare heated exchange of words between his brother and sister-in-law. The perfect couple, who almost never fought, was at loggerheads because of him. But there wasn't much he could do about it.

'Bhabhi, what's your problem?' he interrupted finally. 'I mean, you agree with Bhaiya on everything he says. His word is final for you. So, why are so upset now, even though he has given us his blessing?'

Tahera glared at him. 'Because only I will be answerable to your mother when I die,' she exclaimed, her voice wobbling with emotion.

Adil rolled his eyes and the action irritated her further. She got up and almost ran all the way to the kitchen.

'It's better if I leave,' Adil murmured, looking towards the kitchen, feeling a little distraught himself.

'No. Stay,' his brother spoke softly, the command in his voice making Adil slouch back in the sofa. 'When are you planning to get married?' he asked suddenly.

'I...we...err...next week,' Adil nearly stammered, looking down, feeling shame flood his face. Shame for some reason had chosen to arrive in his head now and refused to leave. He had the distinct feeling he was being selfish, but really, there was nothing he could do.

His brother nodded. 'Don't worry. We'll come. I can't say I'm happy about this though,' he said, looking thoughtful. Adil chose to keep quiet and his brother continued. 'See, we all have certain expectations from life and the people in our lives. When those are not met again and again, we can't help but be disappointed.'

Adil shut his eyes briefly. This was a double whammy. Now he had let down his brother twice. He made to get up but his brother's firm hand closed around his and he sat down again.

'Tahera worries about the uproar this will cause and how people will talk. It's natural. You ought to be worried too. The kind of ugly things people might say could possibly scare off your Suman too. Are you sure she's willing to go through this?' he asked.

Adil nodded.

'And her family? Are they aware about this?' Bilal asked, his eyes fixed on his brother. 'There could be a serious problem from that side.'

'I…yes…there is a problem. Her parents are not happy at all. But we have anyway decided to go ahead. I can't believe that you are willing to accept her, Bhaiya,' Adil spoke, looking down again.

'Look at me,' Bilal spoke curtly. 'I'm accepting your decision because it's a decision, not a choice I have to make,' he said to Adil's cautiously raised face.

Sudden sounds of pots banging and clanging in the kitchen startled them both and Bilal motioned his head towards the kitchen. 'Go talk to your bhabhi. Tell her everything will be alright.'

Adil got up, somewhat grateful to have been spared by his brother; yet he felt nervous.

In the kitchen, Tahera had lit the stove but she was standing near the sink and the pressure cooker seemed to be burning up. Her eyes changed imperceptibly when Adil walked in and she twisted her mouth in distaste at him.

'How could you?' she whispered as she turned away to the sink, huge chunky tears rolling down her cheeks.

'I...' Adil rushed forward to the pressure cooker and stirred its contents briskly. 'What do you add next?' he asked and leaned forward to sniff appreciatively. She glanced at the mutton kept on a plate, washed and trimmed. He took the plate hesitantly and shoved the mutton pieces into the cooker. The mutton started sizzling and changing colour, turning light brown from pink.

He used the wooden ladle to turn the meat pieces over and around, while in his head innumerable thoughts pulsated. He didn't realise when she had come and stood next to him. She held out her hand for the ladle. He handed it to her silently and stood by her side, watching her drop bright red chilli powder, haldi, salt and zeera-methi powder into the cooker, frying the masalas and letting them coat the meat.

'How come you don't get this powder in the market?' he asked her and looked away because he knew he was babbling and she wasn't buying any of it.

'It's zeera-methi, right?' he asked again, sighing, wishing she wouldn't give him the silent treatment. Technically he didn't need their permission or blessing but life would be so much easier if he got both. He'd been surprised, rather shocked, when his brother had nodded in approval. But he had no idea that Bhabhi would put up such a front.

Tahera didn't reply. He darted a glance at her; her eyes seemed stony and unresponsive and for a minute, Adil felt slightly afraid of her. Afraid that she might chuck something at him.

'You don't get it in the market,' she replied after a while, lifting the ladle to sniff the masala delicately.

'Then?' he asked, a little eager to keep her talking, to let the words emerge one by one.

'I make it at home,' she said, turning away from the stove to walk the two steps towards the mixie and pull off the jar from it.

She yanked it viciously and Adil had the feeling she was imagining it was his head that she was uprooting.

'How?' he asked, hoping his voice didn't betray his nervousness.

'Why? You want to do the cooking in your house because your wife won't know all this?' she asked him unkindly. Within the next second her face flushed. She handed the mixie jar to him in silence.

He took a deep breath to tell her that she was being unnecessarily melodramatic and it was *his* life, and he was free to marry who he wanted. But before he could utter a word, she started talking.

'You have to roast whole zeera and methi seeds on a tawa, cool it and powder it. That's all.' He nodded, realising that she was now adopting his way of dealing with unwanted emotions. By talking of the mundane. He was alright with that.

He uncovered the lid of the mixie jar and spooned out the contents into the cooker. It was a thick blend of tomatoes and onions that sizzled as it touched the base of the cooker, sending spurts of oil to the surface almost immediately. He stirred everything together, this heterogeneous blend of meat and tomatoes and spices, wondering how it became the unified khatta sherva that he loved so much.

'Now?' he asked. She took the wooden spoon from him.

When she didn't reply, he bit his lower lip and then his upper lip which for some reason was quivering.

'I...I'm sorry if I have hurt you, Bhabhi. But this is what I really want. I want *you* to accept her too,' he said, turning away as she covered the pressure cooker with its lid and adjusted the whistle on top.

She shrugged and looked around as if wishing there was something else to do, and Adil knew that it would be a long time before things became normal. He was only glad that he wasn't living with them.

One last attempt, he thought, and then I'll leave.

'How does khatta sherva become khatta?' he asked and she looked up.

'Why do you want to know all this?' she asked, looking irritated. 'You've never bothered to enter the kitchen before. Why this sudden interest?' At that moment she noticed her husband standing at the door but Adil hadn't seen him.

'I...I just want to know, Bhabhi. I want to know what it is that goes into this salan you make, because I want to construct it in my memory for later. I doubt I'll be eating it ever again, at least not the way *you* make it.'

Her husband shook his head and Tahera looked at him, wondering how she could possibly approve Adil's decision. And how could he, her husband, be so lenient towards his brother? What if it had been his son? Then? Would he have agreed even then?

Sighing, she twisted a lump of tamarind from a jar.

'This, Adil,' she said, 'this is what makes it khatta. And stop all this acting.'

'Acting?' he asked, a little angered and annoyed.

'Then what is all this nonsense about not eating with us again?' she snapped.

He lowered his head a little. Suddenly, the deep voice of his brother startled him.

'Come outside and sit with me. Tahera will call us when she is ready to serve lunch.'

Now, two years later, whenever they visited Suman's house – Suman's because she couldn't think of it as Adil's – she always thought back to that day when he had brought her into their lives, so unceremoniously. Somehow, all the events collapsed and the details blurred, and she could only clearly remember him asking about the sourness and where it came from in the salan. And then her mind would skip to the day, months later when she was teaching Suman how to cook it.

'Imli. It's sour and unpalatable, although most people won't agree to that last bit,' she had said importantly, as she smothered it in hot water and squeezed it rhythmically. 'But you put it in the salan, especially this one, and it changes everything,' she ended, looking at Suman's oval face, her almond-shaped eyes, thinking that *she* was the imli in their family.

4

'Bhabhi, green is *so* your colour!' Suman gushed when Tahera removed her burkha that evening. 'It's so much better than yellow or orange!' she added. Tahera glowered at her before folding her burkha and keeping it beside her handbag.

Adil smiled uneasily but didn't say anything and Tahera flashed a message to him mentally – Is your wife giving me a compliment or insulting me? But she knew he wouldn't pick it up. That part of him had disappeared somewhere in marital bliss and she missed it sometimes, especially when she would remember the easy, laughter-filled days of his summer vacations when he would visit them in Vellore. Then when they moved to Bangalore after her in-laws had passed away, he had lived with them for a few years and life had been pleasant, and even fun.

Tahera watched her husband sit down carefully on the sofa and smile a little at Mujeeb, Adil's one-year-old son, who was crawling on the carpeted floor before them. He bent down to lift him up in his arms and tickled his tummy. Soon the child was squealing in delight.

Zubi and Rishaad were also present; and Rishaad was eyeing Mujeeb's toy collection that was strewn on the ground. He slipped down from the sofa inch by inch, hoping his mother wouldn't spot him. Zubi smiled at Suman who sat down beside her and was telling her something with a great deal of relish. Tahera looked away momentarily, not wanting to watch Suman bond with her daughter in a way she never could for some reason but when she heard Zubi's eager voice asking Suman if she could show something, Tahera turned to them. What were they talking about?

Zubi had got up and was following Suman to a room off the hall. Hesitantly, Tahera got up and followed them. She stood at the door of the room, watching Suman show something to her daughter and Zubi was gasping over it, covering her mouth with her hands as though overcome with emotion.

'What is it?' she asked sharply, unable to contain the burst of jealousy that came with it.

'Ammi, Chachi and Chacha are getting me an easel and canvas board for my birthday! They know how much I love painting and....' she trailed off, her eyes drawn towards the stand near the window.

Tahera spotted the easel near the window and noticed Suman looking at Zubi in a proud sort of way; there was an element of smugness too. Now was not the time to ask Zubi about her sudden interest in painting or how her chachi had heard about it before she had. That would come later.

'You shouldn't spoil her, Suman,' Tahera said, looking in the other direction. 'Her birthday is still a week away.'

'It's nothing, Bhabhi,' Suman said warmly. Tahera felt more hackles rise within her, making her uncomfortable and unhappy.

'Come, Zubi, we should be leaving soon!' said Tahera, wondering if she ought to physically drag Zubi from there.

'Where? You're having dinner here. I'm making biryani!' Suman stated.

Suman's biryani was unfortunately like ghee rice in disguise and

Tahera often made that clear to her, most of the time unkindly. But that did not deter Suman and she kept trying, which irked Tahera the most.

The children had already eaten and Mujeeb was fast asleep. Zubi and Rishaad were nodding off in front of the TV even though Adil had put on their favourite cartoon cassette.

Tahera looked at the children uncertainly and tried to hurry Suman in the kitchen.

'We have to go home early, Suman! The kids have school tomorrow!' she urged.

'I know, Bhabhi. I'm almost done,' Suman replied, looking up from the cucumber she was dicing into irritatingly irregular pieces for the salad.

Tahera sighed, feeling a little exasperated. She plucked the coriander leaves on the counter, pulling them in rough bunches with the stalks and dropped them on a plate nearby.

'My parents are coming tomorrow,' she told Suman, because the silence in the kitchen felt awkward. Suman looked up, her eyes shining.

'Really?' she asked and Tahera couldn't help but compare how similar both their reactions had been to that news.

'For how long will they be staying?'

Tahera smiled. Suman's reaction was akin to that of Zubi's when she had told her the news.

'I don't know, Suman. I didn't ask them. They're coming here after a year. I didn't want to ask when they'd be leaving,' she chided gently and Suman nodded.

'I'm going to be coming to your house almost every day now,' Suman warned and Tahera muttered something under her breath about how horoscopes were often right.

'When do the children's summer holidays start?' enquired

Suman, oblivious to the conflicting emotions that Tahera always felt around her.

'Next week.'

'Let's plan and go somewhere. All of us! With Ammi and Abba,' Suman said eagerly, as she passed the salad bowl to her.

Tahera tried to suppress the irritation she always felt when faced with Suman's enthusiasm for everything, although she warmed to the way Suman referred to her parents as Ammi and Abba.

'Hmm…' was all Tahera said. 'Adil won't get leave, right?'

Suman's face flushed a little as she emptied the biryani into the serving dish.

'Actually, Bhabhi, he has been meaning to speak to Bhaiya for a long time. He's planning to quit his job so he can help Bhaiya in the business.'

Tahera stepped back, somewhat involuntarily. The first thought that came to her mind, irrationally was: Oh no! Not here too! She couldn't let Suman inveigle her way into their life so much.

When those thoughts settled down, she smiled a little.

'His brother will be pleased to hear that,' she murmured and then got busy with setting the table. Both brothers had been obviously discussing this very matter because when Suman called them for dinner, Bilal emerged looking ecstatic.

Tahera felt guilty for not feeling the same way about this news. She glanced at the children and saw that they were asleep. All through dinner, they discussed business and Suman's eyes danced when she saw how happy Bilal looked. And for some reason, Adil, too, looked relieved.

'Are you sure, Adil?' Tahera asked during a pause in the conversation. 'You were so sure about not getting into business. What made you change your mind?'

Adil looked at Tahera and smiled ruefully. 'Bhaiya has always been right, Bhabhi. I was just not willing to accept that. No matter how hard I work in my job, at the end of the day, it's not my own. But in business, all my hard work is translated into growth for the shop. It's making so much sense to me now,' he explained.

Tahera tooked at Suman as he spoke and wondered if she had influenced him in this decision; and for a change Adil seemed to have read her mind. 'Actually Suman was the one who convinced me,' Adil added. Bilal looked at Suman in disbelief.

'You accomplished what I couldn't!' he exclaimed.

She's looking so silly and pleased about it, Tahera thought to herself and smiled vacantly. The food in her mouth was unappetising and it was getting harder to keep it down.

'Bhabhi, you have to teach Suman how to make biryani,' Adil said. 'Like how Amma used to make. Like how you make it.'

'I'm afraid some things can't be learnt, Adil. It's not a matter of skill, but more about family and culture,' Tahera said, getting up. She didn't see Suman's white face or Bilal's puzzled and exasperated expression. She took the plates to the kitchen, not realising that with every word, she was carving new and more painful wounds.

'Suman might be a Muslim now, but if she has to learn how to cook food, she needs to remember that Muslim food is more than just biryani. If you ask me, this isn't even biryani.'

Feeling self-important although she knew that she had done something out of character by being so rude, Tahera put on her burkha and didn't meet anyone's gaze. She was already regretting the way she had reacted but she couldn't retract her words now. Maybe it was a combination of the easel for Zubi and Adil's decision to join the business that had driven her to it...knowing that Suman had been behind both.

Later that night, when the children were asleep on the mattress, and the kitchen counter was clean and sparkling, Tahera walked towards the hall where her husband was sitting, reading.

She sat down next to him quietly, not wishing to disturb him because she loved the way he looked when he was reading. He wore glasses and would often hold the book down on his lap as he read; it made him look so intellectual and important that it sent a frisson of longing through her.

'The father of my children!' the words echoed in her head whenever she saw him this way. Today, she felt nervous as she sat down next to him. He barely looked up at her. When she edged closer to him, he lifted the book from his lap and shut it. A quick glance at the cover showed that the author was some man named Alistair MacLean. Bilal then reopened the book but held it far above his lap and continued reading. This was the signal Tahera needed as she turned sideways and lowered her head and rested it on his lap. She lifted her feet, put them over the side of the sofa and looked up at her husband who had stopped reading and was peering down at her face with an inexplicable expression.

'Should I apologise to them?' Tahera asked, knowing she didn't have to explain any further.

Bilal closed the book and put it on the table by the side of the sofa. She held his hand as he tried to remove his glasses. He rubbed the side of his cheek absently and sighed.

'Why?' he asked.

Tahera knew he wasn't asking why she should apologise but rather why she had said what she did in the first place. They had a level of communication so well-tuned that they understood the gaps in their conversations and often skipped the pauses, the whys and wherefores that populate exchanges between other people.

Tahera shut her eyes briefly, darkness swallowing the image of her bespectacled husband. She lifted his hand and put it on her chest and opened her eyes again. He was smiling ruefully at her.

'That monster has to be tamed. I don't know how,' she mused.

He nodded, instinctively knowing that the monster she referred to was not Suman.

'I'll teach her how to make biryani,' said Tahera. Bilal smiled.

'Like how you taught her all those other things?' he teased, tugging the end of her saree's pallu.

'What other things?' Tahera asked, smiling as the pallu slipped off and his hand came down to knead her shoulder gently.

'Ask Adil. He keeps wondering why food never tastes the same when she makes it,' murmured Bilal, removing his glasses and lowering his head to kiss her.

'But you only said that there's magic in my hands!' Tahera protested sometime later and laughed when Bilal lifted her in his arms and carried her to their room.

5

Μ‎ARCH was a sensuous month in Bangalore, Bilal observed idly as he got out of his car, letting the warm breeze caress his face. There was no hurry. The train would arrive in another half-an-hour and so he stood outside, leaned against the sun-warmed door and closed his eyes. The children would be so thrilled to see their grandparents he thought, as he straightened a little later, and shaded his eyes against the bright sun to see the time on his wrist watch.

He walked with the easy grace of a man who knew his body well. He'd always had a slightly bulky body but it had never seemed like a hindrance as it only added to the quiet power that he exuded. Hands in his pockets, he crossed the road and entered the Cantonment Station. He bought a platform ticket and then walked inside, briefly wondering what Tahera would be doing.

He'd have liked it if she had come along, but he had to go to his shop as well; so he had combined a couple of other chores before going to the station. A disembodied voice crackled above him, announcing that the train would arrive shortly. Bilal ran his finger below his collar, letting the afternoon breeze cool him.

As it was a Monday, the station was not too crowded. A few coolies slept on the platform, their bodies turned towards the grimy walls, while a few others were squatting and smoking beedis. Bilal could spot the train turning around the bend. Minutes later, the dusty train stopped, steaming and smoky, and Bilal scanned the windows, a little nervously, for his in-laws.

There they were. Smiling, he walked towards their compartment, got inside and picked up the suitcase near Abba's feet.

'Arrey, no no! We'll manage!' Abba protested weakly but Bilal shook his head and gave him a one-armed hug.

Bilal turned to his mother-in-law and smiled widely. Ammi looked the same every time, he thought, feeling thankful and grateful for no reason. He hugged her and she stepped back shyly.

'Arrey, bete! You are my damaad!' she admonished him lightly but still looked up and touched the side of his jaw affectionately. Bilal smiled again, and picking up the other suitcase, he led them outside.

'Mashallah! The weather here is so wonderful!' Ammi exclaimed as they crossed the road.

The car, however, had become stuffy and hot and Bilal rolled down the windows swiftly. On the way home, they spoke about Madras, how unbearably hot it had become and why the beach offered little consolation. While they passed Chinnaswamy Stadium, Ammi muttered that they had to go to Lalbagh this time.

'It's the perfect time to see the flowers,' she beamed.

'Ammi, this is not Lalbagh. It's Cubbon Park,' Bilal explained patiently and Abba laughed heartily.

'Your mother-in-law always forgets this, Bilal. It's not just this. She forgets so many other things too. I'm only hoping she won't forget me one day.'

Ammi looked indignant when he said this but she smiled at Bilal in the rear view mirror.

'Don't listen to a word he says!' she told him.

'How's Aslam?' Bilal asked, as the car stopped at a signal. He turned a little to face his father-in-law.

The creased face with twinkling eyes changed a little imperceptibly. 'He's okay,' Abba replied after a while. Bilal stole a quick glance at his mother-in-law and saw that she was looking outside the window, seemingly oblivious to the conversation.

They reached home in a little while and Ammi's face broke into a huge smile when she saw Rishaad standing near the gate with Tahera.

'I thought they'd be in school!' she exclaimed as she got out while Rishaad came running to her outstretched arms.

'He comes back early. Zubi will be back a little later,' Bilal replied as he parked the car inside the garage. Tahera hugged her father and then she turned to her mother who was carrying Rishaad on her hips.

'Ammi! Put him down! He's not a baby anymore!' Tahera chided her. 'How could you ask her to carry you, Rishaad?' she scolded him when he slipped down, looking a little sheepish. They went inside, a quiet babble of voices and laughter.

Later, when her parents had washed up and were sitting down in the hall with Bilal, Tahera came and sat down too.

'Come. Sit. It's been so many days since we saw you!' Ammi said and Tahera made a face.

'I keep asking you to come and stay with us!' she replied.

'You've put on a little weight,' Ammi remarked casually. Tahera cast a swift glance at her husband, feeling mortified as he smirked at her.

'I've been telling her that too!' he added. Tahera sighed heavily. 'But I like her this way too,' he amended as he saw that Tahera looked upset.

Tahera wasn't too convinced though. She looked down at her lap and then in an attempt to change the subject, she spoke to her father. 'I have made your favourite!' she said, looking almost like a little girl waiting for approval.

Abba stroked his beard thoughtfully and smiled. 'Good. It feels like ages since I've tasted your kali mirch ki phaal.'

Tahera went to the kitchen. Her mother followed her after a while. The phaal was simmering in an open pressure cooker and Ammi's face broke into a smile.

'We are probably the only mother-daughter in this world, where the daughter cooks better than the mother.'

Tahera shook her head at the compliment. 'What nonsense,' she said, although she was pleased, as she poured the steaming dal from a pot into a large bowl. The rice had blossomed beautifully and she arranged it in a round serving plate. She then stirred the contents of the pressure cooker briskly, turning off the gas after a moment. Her mother observed her quick efficient movements, almost with envy.

'It all comes down to a sleight of hand,' her Ammi commented, peeping into the pressure cooker. Tahera stepped back, surprised.

'Hmm?' she asked.

'It's not just a question of grinding together the tomatoes, onions and coriander and cooking it with the meat and garam masala,' Ammi explained.

'Then?' Tahera asked, puzzled, tasting the phaal with a spoon to check for the salt. She handed the spoon to Ammi who dipped her finger in the spoon to check for herself.

'I don't know how you do it, but you seem to have the right touch. I mean, look at this,' Ammi gestured, picking up the mixie jar that had held the tomato-onion-coriander paste a while ago. 'It's never the same when I make it. The colour is different and so is the aroma. It's about how much of what you put into it. Especially phaal.'

'Ammi!' Tahera admonished her lightly. 'I learnt to cook from you. And I still miss the old sil-batta we had at home in Vellore. I loved watching the onions and tomatoes getting crushed under that heavy stone. *This* is nothing.' Saying so, she stirred it briskly one more time and tapped the spoon against the cooker to dislodge the masalas.

'It never looks or tastes the same when I make it. And when Amina makes it…' Ammi trailed off and Tahera looked at her mother, wondering at the flat tone in her voice.

Ammi shook her head and brought a bowl from the counter, into which Tahera poured the gently bubbling phaal, stirring it with a spoon to ensure that it was uniformly mixed.

'It's just phaal, Ammi,' said Tahera, wiping the side of the bowl which had a few dark brown splashes of phaal.

Ammi shook her head and smiled. 'Has that Suman learnt to cook it this way yet?' Tahera swallowed audibly.

'What?'

'Nothing, Ammi. I…we had gone to their place last night and I…I was so rude to her. Again.'

Ammi looked at her, exasperated. 'Chalo, call and tell I have come. She'll come running,' Ammi said as they took the food outside.

As they sat down together at the table, Tahera looked around, wishing for Zubi's presence too. She glanced at Bilal as he ate, the movements of his hands as they dextrously mixed the rice and the dal and brought the food to his mouth. He looked at peace, almost smug; he was noting the way his father-in-law ate the food, relishing it and lavishing praise on Tahera.

Later, they were relaxing in the living room and watching TV when the doorbell rang. Zubi stood outside, impatient and unable to stop herself from screaming with delight as she ran in and launched herself onto her grandmother's lap. Everyone laughed and fussed over her and Tahera sat back in the sofa, letting it cushion her back more deeply. She noted how happy her parents looked and how excited her children were while Bilal, she realised, was looking at her with that serene expression on his face. She decided to invite Suman and Adil for dinner and immediately felt better about the whole thing. She smiled radiantly, feeling happiness flood her heart. Life was good.

6

'B<small>UT</small>...'

'But what, ma?' Ammi asked Tahera. Tahera was sitting on the bed, her feet dangling and her shoulders drooped. Her father was rocking gently in the chair near the window, looking at the rose bushes Tahera had planted. He was involved in the conversation by mere virtue of his presence. He hadn't said a word so far.

'But I thought everything was fine!' Tahera protested, fighting an instinctive urge to fold her knees against her chest until everything contracted to just that much space. She hated knowing that the people she loved were unhappy. Not when she was very happy in her own life.

'It was. But...oh, I don't know. What is the harm anyway?' Ammi asked her. Tahera turned to look at her mother who was lying down, shading her eyes with her forearm, the way she did even when there was no need to protect her eyes.

'But the two of you, living all alone in that house? That's...' Tahera couldn't finish what she wanted to say. Her parents had just told her that they were moving back to Vellore. Their old ancestral house was there...dusty, peeling but still standing.

'It's where you were born,' Ammi reminded her gently, removing her arm from across her forehead and smiling at Tahera. 'I thought you'd be happy.'

'Happy? No. I'd rather you came and lived with us,' Tahera spoke briskly, getting up, twisting her pallu into urgent little knots around her fingers.

Her mother sat up with an effort and sighed. 'This problem with Amina has been there since the past few years and now, the two of us constantly get this feeling that we are intruding into their lives. It is as if we are stopping them from doing what they want to. But what was unsaid before is now slowly being said and we want to leave before things get ugly.'

Tahera sighed deeply. Why did men change so much after getting married? Look at Adil. And now Aslam bhai too.

'Men are such snakes,' she said with such vehemence that it startled her mother.

'What?'

'I...I meant...I hate the way they forget their flesh and blood, like moulted skin and then they just move on...' Tahera tried to explain and she turned to see her mother laughing soundlessly, her shoulders shaking.

'What about Bilal?' she asked Tahera who narrowed her eyes. Had she done the same with her husband? Alienated him from his parents? No, she hadn't done that. The credit went to both of them actually.

'No, he's not like that,' Tahera defended him. Her father turned to her just then.

'I know he's not like that,' he affirmed. 'But you have to understand, Tahera. We'd like to be independent. Especially as we have our own house.'

'But...you both are old and...' Tahera's voice trailed off when she saw her mother raise her eyebrow.

'Not so old that we can't live alone. And we have each other. But Tahera,' her mother said, 'think of how nice it will be for you to come to Vellore and stay with us during the vacations!'

Tahera checked herself from making renewed protests. Wouldn't it be wonderful if her children could stay in the same house where she had grown up? They had such an urban existence, and although Vellore was a large town, it was still a town. There was something comforting about growing up in a place where everyone knew each other…not like here in Bangalore, where even after having lived for seven years, she didn't know the names of her neighbours.

She sighed deeply and twisted her lips into a semblance of a smile.

'Okay. Maybe this is not such a bad idea. When are you moving to Vellore?'

Her parents looked at each other. 'We were thinking of going next week,' her mother said. Tahera gasped.

'But you just got here! You can't leave so soon! The children have their vacations!'

Abba sighed. 'We have already been here for a week. We thought we'd be here for Zubi's birthday and then go back in a few days.' Tahera shook her head while making some mental calculations. Zubi's birthday was on the day after tomorrow, and that didn't leave her with much time to spend with her parents.

'No. Let's discuss this later.' Tahera turned to her mother resolutely. 'I'm making gajar ka halwa for tomorrow,' she said, clearly indicating that the earlier conversation was over.

'Yes, it's one of Zubi's favourites,' Ammi added.

'I know. I was actually going to ask if you could make it,' said Tahera, looking at her mother with a certain amount of frank curiosity.

'Me? Why?' her mother looked surprised and taken aback. 'You make it so well, na!'

Tahera gave a self-deprecating smile. 'Yes, but you're the expert.'

'Now?' Ammi asked, looking a little discomfited. 'I wanted to take a nap.'

'Okay, you take your nap and come later. I'll keep everything ready,' Tahera said, walking away and suddenly remembering that she still had to invite Suman for the birthday party.

Suman had visited them only once since her parents had arrived and Tahera felt a certain amount of misgiving towards herself for having created the awkward situation. Adil, too, had visited just that one time and although Bilal hadn't said anything, she felt his gaze upon her back whenever she sat at the dressing table and brushed her hair at night.

'What?' she had asked him the previous night, feeling resentful and cornered.

He shrugged and got back to reading the book that was curled around its spine and that irritated Tahera even more.

'When is Adil joining your business?' she asked him, trying to fill the gap of silence with words.

'He said sometime soon,' Bilal replied, fixing his eyes on his book.

'I...I don't know how to say sorry,' she spoke suddenly, and he looked up at her. Her body was half turned towards him and her hairbrush was in her hand. He smiled at her ruefully and removed his spectacles.

'Have you realised that Zubi is just like you?' he asked her instead.

'How?' Tahera questioned, dropping the hairbrush on the dressing table with a clatter. She looked at him as she lifted the heavy mass of her hair, bringing both her hands together at the back as she swiftly plaited it.

'She can't say sorry either,' he remarked, watching her perform these nightly rituals with something akin to homesickness. He couldn't understand the feelings that coursed through him when he watched her pull the hair pin between her lips with her teeth and push it into her hair, or dab Pond's Cold Cream on her face in spots, which she went on to blend onto her face briskly. She switched off the light and walked towards him in the darkness of the room and Bilal was truly glad his in-laws were here. Zubi and Rishaad were thrilled to sleep in their own room because their grandmother slept there with them, telling them exciting night-time stories. As Tahera reached the bed and climbed onto her side of the bed, he pulled her towards him, eliciting a surprised gasp from her; he was quick to shush her.

'No kids in the room,' he reminded her and Tahera nodded in the darkness, giggling a little, feeling like a young girl.

Shaking her head free of all those troubling thoughts the next morning, Tahera reached for the phone and dialled Suman's number. When Suman answered, Tahera said the first thing that came to her mind.

'I'm sorry, Suman,' she spoke quickly before the words dried up and she was left with only regret.

'For what, Bhabhi?' Suman asked her warily. Tahera could hear Mujeeb crying in the background and there was that slightly harried sense of urgency in Suman's voice that Tahera was well acquainted with.

'Are you busy?' Tahera asked and she heard Suman place the receiver without any warning on the table as she must have run to Mujeeb. She came back a moment later, panting, and picked up the receiver.

'I...no...tell me,' Suman managed to say.

'It's Zubi's birthday tomorrow. We're having a small celebration at home. Please can you come with Mujeeb and Adil?'

There was a brief bout of silence after which Suman said, 'Of course, Bhabhi', but she sounded more peremptory than enthusiastic.

Both of them didn't want to bring up the apology that Tahera had begun the conversation with.

'Okay, see...'

'Reme...'

Both of them had started speaking together. After a minor tussle over who would speak first, Tahera reminded Suman about the plans she had been making for all of them to go out somewhere together. 'Abba and Ammi are planning to move to Vellore and they will leave soon,' Tahera offered the nugget of information like a conciliatory gesture and it worked.

'Really?' Suman asked, and from the tone of her voice Tahera knew that she had forgotten and forgiven. They talked for some more time before Tahera said goodbye and ended the call.

She walked into the kitchen and pulled out a plastic bag full of crisp dark orange carrots and tipped them into a large flat plate, the kind she usually used to clean rice in. She washed and scraped them and then grated the carrots into a huge mound in the centre of the plate, but her mind still lingered on the conversation with Suman.

As her fingers went up and down rhythmically against the oblong grater, she missed a little and grated a little bit of her middle finger instead, on a little triangle below her nail.

'Ouch!' she muttered and held her trembling finger under the cold water of the tap. It stung and with the cool water, she felt a tiny hot and cold sensation dart up and down her body. Shaking her head resolutely, she went back to the grated carrots and started, only to stop when she saw that the orange colour was getting a little tinged with red.

She blinked and saw that her finger was bleeding again. She

tore out a piece of cloth from an old cotton saree, burnt it and wrapped it around her finger, closing her eyes tightly against the fresh upsurge of pain. She was sure they didn't have Band-Aid in the house.

'Not today. I'll tell you about it tomorrow. Really,' Ammi fended off Zubi as she trailed into the kitchen with her. Zubi stopped whining when she saw her mother clutching her finger.

'Today, Zubi bibi is going to make gajar ka halwa for her own birthday,' Ammi announced. 'What happened? You cut your finger?' Ammi looked exasperated and Tahera nodded, a little embarrassed. She didn't like to appear vulnerable to Zubi who was holding Ammi's pallu, turning and twisting it.

'Arrey stop!' ordered Ammi. She pulled Zubi and made her stand in front of Tahera. 'Come. Watch.'

'I don't want to,' said Zubi, making a face. 'Abbu got a new activity book for me. I want to do that.'

'After this,' Ammi said firmly as she pulled a low stool from a corner and placed it before the stove.

'Leave her, Ammi. She's too young,' said Tahera and Zubi almost scampered away but Ammi caught hold of the sash of her frock.

She insisted that Zubi climb atop the stool and watch the proceedings. Sighing, Zubi did as she was told. Tahera grated the remaining carrots quickly and handed the plate to Ammi.

'Ghee?' Ammi asked in a very professional manner. Sometimes, on Doordarshan, the afternoon programmes would include a cookery show and Tahera would watch them entranced, wondering how those women had the confidence to face the cameras. Tahera didn't know that they were facing the camera. For her, it was as if those women were facing another TV on their side. For a moment, she looked at her mother with admiration. If Ammi was asked to host a cookery show, she'd do an excellent job of it.

'Ghee, Tahera,' Ammi repeated patiently.

'Huh? Yes, yes!' Tahera opened a cupboard and pulled out a jar of homemade ghee.

Ammi uncapped the jar and used a spoon to dig out some of the glistening, golden ghee. Tahera watched as she shook the spoon gently into a heated vessel where it sizzled and swirled as the grainy particles turned a deep yellow. Next, Tahera handed her a few pods of cardamom and a couple of cinnamon sticks, which Ammi broke and dropped into the vessel.

'See?' she showed Zubi. 'Watch carefully.'

Zubi made a face but lingered there as Ammi shoved the grated carrots into the vessel and stirred briskly. Tahera briefly considered inviting the family who lived in the house right next to their's but just as swiftly decided against it. She found it very difficult to cultivate a sociable attitude towards her neighbours, for the simple reason that no one smiled or even looked in her direction. Even though they had been living there for seven years, they were all strangers to her and she preferred it that way.

Tahera smiled when she observed Zubi watching Ammi make her favourite halwa. Zubi had probably thought that by standing around, she would get to taste some halwa right after it was cooked. But she would never have thought that she'd get drawn into the entire process of cooking it as well. Ammi stirred the grated carrots in ghee until they became all shiny, and then she added spoonfuls of thick khoya that Tahera had saved by skimming the malai off the milk in the degchi every day. Immediately the carrots lost their orangey sheen and the whole mass became liquid in texture. Ammi let the halwa cook slowly and she started telling Zubi about when she had first started to make desserts.

'I didn't know how to cook all these meethas until I got married,' she confessed to Zubi, who looked at her, surprised.

'Then?'

'That's another story. I'll tell you about it one day,' Ammi promised her and then added two cups of sugar to the halwa. The moment the sugar touched the halwa, it transformed once again. It became thick in consistency and that was when Zubi had asked if she could stir. Ammi refused but Zubi insisted and the moment she leaned towards the vessel and started stirring, she stepped back screaming.

Tiny drops of the halwa, hot and furious, seemed to have attacked her arms. When she came back after washing her arms with cold water, she watched her grandmother stirring the mixture, unmindful of the hot splashes.

'Doesn't your hand hurt?' she asked.

'Our hands don't feel the heat,' she sounded almost proud as she stirred the halwa. 'One day yours won't either,' she promised. Zubi wasn't so sure.

7

Towards the end of April, Suman finally organised the outing that she had been so excited about earlier. So infectious was her enthusiasm that it caught up with everyone...even Tahera, although she had been reluctant at first. The plan was to go to Nandi Hills in two cars for a day trip. Both the kids had been waiting for Sunday so they could set off. Zubi had already decided that she would sit with Suman Chachi in their car although she hadn't mentioned the plan to her mother.

Suman, Adil and Mujeeb would come to their house in the morning and they would leave together. For some reason, Bilal didn't want them to make biryani to take along.

'Just make some light snacks. That will do,' he had informed Tahera and her mother, both of whom felt a bit put out. Light snacks actually meant more work. They finally decided to make samosas, cutlets and jamuns. Tahera and Ammi spent the whole of Saturday in the kitchen, kneading stiff dough for the samosas, boiling potatoes for the cutlets, making the kheema filling for both. Finally Ammi went for a short nap in the afternoon.

While still lingering in the kitchen, Tahera touched the base of her back briefly and winced. She had been on her feet for most of the day and she felt immensely tired. They still had to stuff the samosas, shape the cutlets and keep everything ready so that she and Ammi could fry them in the morning. But Tahera, too, needed a nap and she walked to her room, glad that she didn't have to bother about the kids as they had gone to the park with Abba.

She swept the curtains towards each other to darken the room. Sighing, Tahera stretched out on the bed, wincing even more as the pain became more pronounced. She slid her foot back and lifted her knee off the bed and the pressure on her lower back eased. A sudden thought occurred to her, and she sat up swiftly, clutching her chest with her hands.

She should have realised it before. The urge to recoil when Ammi was sautéing the onions for the kheema should have been enough proof. Slowly, gently, she brought her hand to her abdomen and rubbed it gently. It was too soon to know, but she knew.

In the morning, Zubi stared at the pounding rain with a fury that matched the rain itself. But she controlled the urge to scream as another lightning bolt slashed the dull grey sky. The rumble of thunder that followed made her swallow and she looked back at her father, who shrugged his shoulders helplessly.

Ammi and Tahera had been up since five a.m. and although the day had seemed slightly cool for April, they hadn't noticed anything until around eight when the sky started darkening.

'Oh no!' muttered Ammi when she saw the rain begin.

Tahera looked at the rain from the kitchen window and was unable to understand what she felt at the moment. She was angry that all their hard work would be wasted, a little upset that they wouldn't be able to enjoy Nandi Hills, but she was also oddly, a little jubilant. Rain meant that Suman's carefully thought-out trip was cancelled. She felt guilty for having such feelings but they were there and she couldn't do anything about it.

Suman wailed on the phone. 'Bhabheeeeee! What are we going to do? Ammi and Abba are leaving this Wednesday, right? This is the last Sunday.'

'Maybe the rain will stop,' said Tahera, but looking at the torrents of rain, that seemed highly improbable. The rain hadn't abated until noon and even as it slowed down, the chances of them going to Nandi Hills seemed very slim. The roads would be slick and dangerous and Bilal, who was over-cautious in matters of driving, didn't want to take the risk, especially since Tahera had given him the amazing news last night that there were chances she was pregnant again.

Zubi and Rishaad, however, were very upset and refused to eat the samosas for breakfast. Finally, Bilal had to entice them with the promise of taking them to the fair that evening if they forgot about the Nandi Hills trip and ate breakfast.

'But Badey Ammi won't come to a fair. And what about Suman Chachi?' Zubi had pouted.

'They will all come,' Bilal had said firmly. 'I'll speak to them.'

So that evening, at about five, the whole family set out for the RBANMS grounds where a fair of sorts was held annually, and since it coincided with the summer vacation of the children, it was bound to be crowded. Tahera's parents weren't too happy about accompanying them but they came along nevertheless and once they reached, they waited near the entrance for Adil and Suman to show up.

After everyone had arrived, they went inside the teeming fairground and Zubi looked around excitedly at all the different rides. She walked with Suman, holding her hand. Suman pointed at the ferris wheel and asked Zubi if she would like to ride it. Zubi nodded and turned to ask Tahera for permission.

Tahera shook her head imperceptibly. 'Not right now,' she said when Zubi didn't seem to understand. 'Maybe a little later.'

Zubi's face flushed and she turned away, but her father was quick to hold her hand and lead her towards one of the chaat stalls. It seemed like everyone in Bangalore had converged to the fairground that evening, hoping that it wouldn't rain again. It took around twenty minutes for everyone to find a place to sit down and eat.

Tahera's father didn't look very happy with the plate of masala puri but joined in reluctantly when everyone started talking about how good it was. Zubi's was sweetened considerably with jaggery syrup and Rishaad was simply munching a few empty puri shells. Then Tahera remembered she was carrying the snacks that they had fried in the morning. She passed them around and Suman started praising the samosas.

'I always thought samosas were fat cones filled with potatoes,' she said as she bit into a crispy triangle. 'These are amazing. Ammi must have made them, no?'

No one answered and Suman didn't persist, but she saw Tahera exchange a swift look with her husband.

The kheema samosas had flaky edges that puffed up when fried in hot oil, and the grainy filling inside was succulent and moist. No one turned down the offer for a second helping and soon the paper bag was empty.

'Good you brought them along,' said Bilal and Tahera smiled. She brushed the crumbs from her burkha and stood up, when Zubi pointed to a stall that was selling gigantic papads.

'I want one,' she insisted and Tahera shook her head again. 'You just ate masala puri and two samosas. Do you want to throw up?'

'Abbu, please?' Zubi turned to him and dragged him towards the stall where the vendor was sprinkling red chilli powder on crunchy sago papads. They bought two and came back to the group. Feeling and looking important, Zubi broke off bits and passed the papad around to everyone. The effect of the chilli powder was a slow heat that lingered even after the papads were finished.

'Now ice cream!' Suman announced, hissing because her mouth was burning.

Adil went off to buy ice cream and Zubi looked at her mother, to ask if she could go on the rides now. Tahera looked concerned and there passed between her husband and her, a look that spoke a conversation of its own.

Let her go.
No!
Why?
You know why!
No, I don't know why.
But…
Fine, I'll go with her.

By the time Adil came back with the ice creams, Zubi and her father had gone to wait in the queue for the ferris wheel. Suman too had wanted to join them but since she had asked for the ice cream, she stayed back, waving at Zubi who had hopped along with her father.

The whole group moved towards the ferris wheel. Rishaad had already made a mess of his shirt. Tahera wiped the Chocobar dribble from his chin and swiped his shirt half-heartedly with a napkin. She wished that Zubi and Bilal hadn't gone, or that Bilal hadn't had that silent argument with her.

She watched them inch forward in the queue and sit in the swinging metal cars when it was their turn finally. The ferris wheel started and soon excited screams rent the air as they moved upwards slowly and then faster. The metal cars were open at the top and as Zubi and Bilal passed by them, Zubi stood up and waved.

'No!' the word barely escaped Tahera's lips but the car had already moved away for another round. Bilal had pulled Zubi back to the seat when Tahera felt Rishaad's hand tugging her burkha.

'What now?' she asked him, irritated because she wanted to keep her eyes on Zubi and Bilal. But a loud scream tore through the noisy fairground. Tahera looked up again trying to spot the comforting figure of her husband and daughter. She couldn't understand. What was happening? She felt fingers clutch her arms and she was tugged towards the ferris wheel.

'What happened? Where are they?' she asked Adil who had pulled her along, white-faced. The words seemed to stick to each other and she stopped when she saw the crowd that had gathered near one of the gates of the ferris wheel.

'I don't know what's happened, Bhabhi!' Adil stuttered, his voice breaking as he made his way through the crowd, pulling Tahera in his wake. Tahera turned back and saw that Abba was holding Rishaad in his arms and Ammi was crying.

The wheel was now moving sporadically, to help the people from each car get down.

'Where's Zubi?' Tahera asked as they reached the edge of the crowd. She stopped.

Now instead of pulling her towards the epicentre of the crowd, Adil was pushing her away. 'Go, go!' he sobbed but she couldn't move. 'Get Zubi,' he said, pushing at her shoulder but Tahera stood there, unmoving, gaping down at the body of her husband. His neck was at an awkward angle. His face was turned towards her and his eyes were open.

'He's dead!' the words registered in her mind before the rush of feelings and thoughts started crowding her head. She realised she couldn't breathe. She couldn't feel. She couldn't see what was happening. Her eyes blurred with hot tears that wouldn't fall on their own and her face seemed on fire. Adil was kneeling next to his brother's body and sobbing uncontrollably.

'Did you see what happened?' someone behind her spoke. She knew they weren't asking her because another man answered.

'No, but I heard he fell from the car when it was right at the top.'

'But how?'

'The gate was loose and it must have opened somehow.'

'Really? Tch! Poor man! He must have died instantly.'

'Arrey, paapa! See, that's his wife there!'

Tahera felt their words like angry ants on her skin and she controlled the desire to scratch her body till it turned raw. The ferris wheel was still disgorging people when Zubi ran past her and fell in a heap next to her father's body.

'Abbu! No! No! No!' she screamed as she took his hand and shook it. Adil wiped his tears, lifted Zubi and turned her towards her mother.

'Ammi!' she panted and threw her arms around her abdomen and clutched it tightly.

Quietly, Tahera prised Zubi's arms from her stomach and flung them away.

8

Beyond the clear glass, green water shimmered in the setting sun. Ferries bobbed indiscernibly in the undulating water, and around us, Hong Kong was discarding the workday stress just as it embraced it. With diligent speed.

Zubi was staring outside, a finger pressed on the cold glass, when I sat down at the table. She looked up at me and I smiled at her brightly. She adjusted the pallu of her saree so it fell in front of her other shoulder; she tugged at it to pull it down. She looked respectable but a little uneasy.

This was the first time we had met here, at this Starbucks in Harbour City. Usually, I would go to her house during my lunch hour and on getting back, I would try to note down not just everything she had said, but *how* she had said it. The last time I had gone there, I was shocked at the turn her story had taken. To me, it was an unspeakable horror. But for Zubi, she who had lived through it, reliving it for me had made it seem so real that I was afraid she wouldn't stop crying for a long time.

The afternoon she told me about her father's death, I couldn't bring myself to go back to office. Without really thinking of where I was going, I strolled inside Kowloon Park, trying to clear my head. I stopped near the pond and watched the ducks circle on the surface of the water. I tried to sort the stories and images in my head.

Deep inside, I knew that the germ of the idea I had when I first found Zubi was good. And she had lived up to it. But now, for some reason, I was getting drawn into her story, more than I had thought, and *that* unnerved me.

All my life, I'd lived in teeming metropolises. Whether it was Mumbai, London, or now, Hong Kong. At first, I couldn't reconcile the image of the sleepy Bangalore she had painted with the city that I knew. Sort of at least. But then, I also couldn't quite fit the fiery Zubi with the somewhat complacent and quiet woman she had turned out to be. In fact, once I even told her that she doesn't sound like her at all, to which she had merely smiled. But after listening about her father's death, I realised that over plates of steaming biryani, cups of ginger tea and gajar ka halwa, I had merely scratched the surface of Zubi's life. Finding it to be a teeming, whirling mass of emotions instead of placidity, had stunned me enough to step back and re-evaluate.

I didn't get in touch with her for nearly a month because, well, I was busy with work. Four new restaurants had opened up recently and there were chances that I would be asked to cover the mid-Autumn festival this year. But that was in September, nearly a couple of months away. Maybe I was just looking for excuses to avoid her.

After a few days, however, her story started plaguing my mind again. I checked my weight in the morning, like I did every week and groaned when I realised that I had put on five pounds. As I struggled to tug my skirt up, I remembered how Zubi's mother had felt when everyone had teased her about putting on weight. But that had been because she was pregnant, right?

My curiosity had been aroused. What had happened to them

after her father died? How had they survived and what did food have to do with anything? Or everything?

That was when I called her, to ask if we could meet in Harbour City instead of talking in her cramped apartment. She asked if we could meet in the evening as her husband would be at home to take care of her son and only then could she step out. I agreed.

There must have been some confusion because when I arrived at the Starbucks on the ground floor, she wasn't there. I had waited for a while and then called her, only to learn that she was already on the third floor, at the Starbucks with the view of the harbour.

'What will you have?' I asked her, getting up again after a brief and awkward silence.

'Coffee,' she said softly and I nodded. I came back with two large cups of cappuccinos and a thick slice of chocolate cake. By mutual but unspoken consent, we wasted a little time stirring sugar into the coffee, and after that, there was nothing else left to do. But talk.

Zubi held the paper cup with both her hands; it was as though she was deriving warmth from it. It seemed she too had been wondering whether to speak to me or not. Maybe this was our last meeting, I thought, feeling a little panicky.

'Even till today, I don't know what happened on that ferris wheel,' she started speaking suddenly. I wanted to ask her so many questions but strangely found myself unable to formulate even a single lucid one. So I took a sip of my coffee and nodded in her direction, asking her to continue.

'After that....' she trailed off, looking outside as dusk fell over the waters. Two Chinese men looked at us impatiently, their trays bulging with sandwiches and coffee, waiting for us to get up from the prized spot. I ignored them and prompted Zubi.

'After that? What happened?'

She turned to look at me. 'You know, you never really told me what you want to do with my story. I…I'm not sure if this is such a good idea.'

I felt my face contort slightly and I forced it to relax. 'Zubi, let's take this one step at a time. For now, let's focus on the story. The rest will fall together in time.'

She sighed heavily. 'It's not just a story, you know. It's what happened. It's my life.'

'I know,' I assured her quickly. 'I'm actually living your story through your words. Why do you think I didn't meet you for so long after our last meeting?'

She didn't reply but continued staring at me. I decided to elaborate. 'I needed some space, some time to think about what you had said and what I could do with it. Whether I could do anything at all.' I placed my coffee cup on the table and smiled at her encouragingly.

'Talk,' I insisted.

She looked around swiftly, as though confirming that there was no one there she knew, which at one level was really absurd. The coffee shop had grown crowded and noisy and I realised that it had been a dumb idea to meet her here. But I had wanted to see her outside the confines of her house, without her son's hovering presence.

'I have an idea. Let's finish this,' I said, pointing to the cake and coffee, 'and we can go somewhere else and talk.'

She nodded and shyly accepted a bite of the cake. It was dense, moist and oozed chocolate from its pores; and true to chocolate's reputation as a mood changer, our souls felt light as we walked outside, though I can't quite vouch for our butts.

'My aunt makes really good chocolate cake,' she muttered and I looked up.

'Suman Chachi?' I asked her and she nodded but her face closed up again.

We meandered outside the coffee shop, two disparate women, who nevertheless paused and stared hungrily at the impressive line-up at the Jimmy Choo store window. I eyed a pair of perfect tan stilettos while Zubi's eyes grew round when she saw the price.

'Seventeen hundred dollars!' she exclaimed, and I blinked.

'How long have you been living in Hong Kong?'

'Three years,' she said without taking her eyes off the display.

'And you're still not used to the prices?' I asked feeling a little surprised.

'Actually, we rarely come to these places,' she explained, tugging her pallu tighter and tucking it behind her elbow, feeling very self-conscious. 'I came here twice and both times we just went to Toys"R"Us.'

She probably bought knockoffs at the night market, I thought. Realising how shallow I sounded to myself, I dispensed the thought immediately. What she wore or where she bought her shoes or bags from was no concern of mine.

As we walked further, Zubi bit her lower lip apprehensively. She looked at the display on her mobile and put it away quickly.

'Do you have to leave?' I asked, feeling disheartened.

'No, I can stay a little longer. Do you want to walk along the waterfront?' she asked suddenly. I nodded after a moment and we walked along the bustling Canton Road till we reached the waterfront. Since it was already dark, lights twinkled from across the water and the Hong Kong skyline stood in majestic, beautiful contrast against the sky.

Zubi held her pallu to her nose delicately and I grinned. 'You don't like the fishy smell of the pier, huh?'

She nodded.

'Then why did you want to come here?'

She shrugged. 'I love the lights.'

We found a place to sit and wasted some more time watching tourists from mainland China chattering as they took pictures with the hand prints on the Avenue of Stars. Zubi shook her head and smiled. 'You'd think they were seeing Salman removing his shirt.'

I guffawed. 'You're like an onion,' I said without thinking.

'Huh?'

'So many layers to you,' I explained hastily in case she thought I meant she was smelly and took offence.

She grinned and for the first time, I saw a little of the Zubi she had been...or could have become.

9

I<small>F</small> she opened her eyes and looked absolutely nowhere, but straight up, she could see the ceiling fan. Since she was sure of that, she opened her eyes and stared ahead. A cobweb dangled from the centre of the ceiling fan but she didn't want to see where it led. She focused on the ceiling fan, fixing its shape and contours in her eye until everything else behind it faded. She shifted slightly on the bed and immediately dust motes danced their way upwards, releasing a scent of musty wood, hair oil and sadness.

'Ammi!'

Tahera shut her eyes quickly again.

'Ammi!' Zubi sounded hysterical but Tahera would not open her eyes. Five minutes later, she knew she was alone and once again in her old room in Vellore. The room where she had grown up, matured into a young woman and left without a backward glance when she got married. It was this room that she had returned to when she became a widow.

Widow. She repeated the word in her head again and again and again until the word lost its meaning and was just a series of sounds connected to each other in her constantly parched mouth. How could one word obliterate her existence? How could it inspire pity in others and such immense sorrow in her parents? How could it confuse her children and make them think that their life, as they had known it, was gone forever?

Tahera squeezed her eyes tightly and tears that had pooled inside brimmed over. Every tear that fell from her eyes was like a breath she took. It happened involuntarily.

It was fifteen days now since that day. Tahera knew the number of hours and if anyone asked her, she could even tell them the minutes of her life spent as a widow. If 22,800 minutes had garnered the magical ability to stretch endlessly, how was she going to spend the rest of her life? She turned her face towards the pillow, where a slice of sunlight had struggled inside. She blinked as she reached out to shut the window tighter. Something was stuck at the window sill and she couldn't push it through while lying down.

With difficulty she sat up and immediately felt her world spin around her. Dazed and unfocused, she knelt on the bed and pushed the window firmly, dislodging whatever that had been stuck and drowning the room in darkness.

'Tahera!' her mother gasped. 'Why are you sitting like that? It's not good for the baby!'

Tahera turned around quickly towards the door and felt herself fall back on the bed as she lost consciousness.

'She doesn't eat at all. If it weren't for the baby, she would have starved herself,' her mother sobbed sometime later. Tahera kept her eyes closed, hoping that they would leave.

Both her parents were sobbing and Ammi kept asking Abba, 'What will happen to her? What will happen to the children?'

'I don't know, Ruqayya. I don't know,' her father's voice was gravelly and trembled.

Tahera opened her eyes a little and Ammi turned to her. In the first few days after the accident, Tahera had let herself be poked by needles that injected intravenous fluids into her as she had refused to eat. But since then, she had eaten food sporadically, just for the sake of the baby. However, it couldn't be just hunger that seemed to stretch the vacuum inside her. She felt lightheaded at all times and in some corner of her darkened mind, she knew that she had to take care of herself. But why? Why should *she* feel pain? Why should she taste food? Why should she drink water? When he wasn't there anymore, his physical form obliterated into dust, when he had risen above the human urges and feelings and gone away somewhere without her... why? Why should she continue to live? For the children? she asked herself impatiently.

They had buried him in Vellore in the family graveyard. Tahera had refused to return to Bangalore, even though her parents had decided to come with her. Her mother had reasoned with her saying that now Tahera was in iddat, the mourning period that lasted for four months and ten days but as she was pregnant, her mourning period would get over only when she delivered the baby.

'Think of your children. How will they go to school if you stay here?' Ammi had asked. Tahera hadn't replied. She didn't want to be burdened with decisions. She didn't want to think of what she had to do and whether she could do it or not. She just wanted to lie in bed, sleep and never get up. When she was lying in bed, she just had to shut her eyes to see his face swimming before her.

Ammi had tried convincing her to return to Bangalore after the seventh day fatiha but Tahera hadn't listened, and Ammi had given up hope. She had vaguely heard Ammi and Abba talk about sending Zubi and Rishaad to Bangalore with Adil and Suman.

'I don't want to burden them but how will they go to school if she stays here?' Ammi asked. Tahera felt the familiar undercurrent of hostility whenever Suman's name was mentioned, but now, it had fed on itself, on her silence and on her devastating thoughts... it had magnified into a monster.

'My children will not live in that house,' she spoke, her voice hoarse and faint. Ammi nodded resignedly. 'Let them waste a year. It's just a year,' Tahera spoke again. 'I have years and years ahead of me to live without him...' her voice broke and she started crying again.

Tahera's mother didn't know which was worse – seeing Tahera cry or sleep in morose silence. At the moment, however, mother and daughter shared a silent look between them.

'At least come and sit outside,' Ammi blurted after a moment. 'You don't have to always keep sitting in this room.'

Tahera shook her head. Barring her visits to the bathroom, Tahera had refused to leave her room. She hadn't read the Quran and neither had she read namaz since the day her husband died. Lifting her hands in supplication seemed like a mockery. The only thing that she wanted, desperately, was something that prayer couldn't give her. So why bother?

Later that day, when Tahera's children stood at the door, she turned her face away from them, her head hurting and eyes smarting. She didn't have the energy to deal with *their* pain. She knew she was being selfish but she couldn't control it. They had lost a father but they had their lives ahead of them, unmarked territory, where they could make a new beginning, become a part of another family. Her life, however, had crashed to a full stop and she had to deal with her own pain before she could alleviate theirs.

'Ammi,' Zubi's voice, tremulous and uncertain, sounded in her ear.

'Where's Abbu?' Rishaad asked. Slowly Tahera turned to face them. She took in their faces properly for the first time since that day and was mildly shocked to see how drawn they both looked. Hadn't they been eating?

As if aware of this slender chance, Zubi caught Tahera's hands in her warm grasp and leaned closer but she hesitated. 'Ammi, I'm sorry,' she said quickly. Tahera felt a void so large in her body that she just had to inch forward for it to swallow her completely. She remembered her husband telling her that Zubi never said sorry.

She turned Zubi's hand in her own and squeezed it gently.

'Why aren't we going back to Bangalore? I want Abbu,' Rishaad spoke, his lips quivering and face sullen.

'Not now, Rishaad. Can't you see? Ammi's not well,' Zubi reasoned and led him away, unknowingly stretching and pulling apart the pain inside Tahera.

'Zubi?' Tahera called out and Zubi turned back immediately.

'Yes, Ammi?' she said eager to please and placate.

Tahera's thoughts were jumbled and she couldn't articulate them into words. She shook her head and saw Zubi's face visibly age before her as she took Rishaad's hands and pulled him outside.

'Badey Ammi made kheema with rotis for dinner. Come, I'll feed you,' Tahera heard Zubi telling Rishaad.

'Api, why doesn't Ammi talk? Why is she angry with us? Where's Abbu?' Rishaad asked, his voice tiny, like him.

Tahera wished she could make the atmosphere even quieter, make it more silent so she could hear Zubi's answer.

When she didn't hear anything, for the first time in days, curiosity got the better of her. She edged out of bed and slowly crept up to the door. It was already open and she stepped into the rectangle of light thrown by the bulb in the hallway. She focused her eyes ahead and saw that Zubi was sitting cross-legged on the floor, Rishaad in her lap, one arm around her neck like he used to do with Tahera. Zubi was tearing the rotis into pieces, scooping the kheema into each piece and feeding it to Rishaad. Tahera's chest tightened painfully and the sounds and smells of the outside world seemed overwhelming. Abba was sitting on the floor too – they didn't have a dining table in the Vellore house – and he was eating slowly. Ammi was making rotis in the kitchen and bringing them outside one by one.

Strangely, it was the smoke from the kitchen doors that beckoned her. It was not an enticing curlicue, rather a screen of dense grey smoke that hung over the heads of her children and her father as they ate.

She walked past them slowly towards the kitchen and the three of them paused, shocked almost. Zubi was about to get up but Abba stopped her. They watched Tahera enter the kitchen, each thinking of different reasons for her sudden appearance.

Inside the familiar and well-loved kitchen, Tahera stood watching her mother roll out rotis deftly and cook them over the stove on a hot griddle. Her mother looked at her startled, but she continued rolling the rotis. Without a word, Tahera walked up to the stove and started flipping the rotis mechanically. Tahera's mother looked up at the blackened ceiling of her kitchen, as though she could communicate with the one above, and shut her eyes briefly but tightly and muttered a quick prayer.

10

27 April 1992

Bangalore

By our Staff Reporter, *Deccan Herald*

A 38-year-old man died in a freak accident on Sunday at the RBANMS Grounds at the site of the annual fair.

Little did Bilal Ahmed and his family know that a casual outing would turn into a tragedy for them when they went to the crowded fair on Sunday.

Eyewitnesses claim that Bilal was trying to stand upright while the ferris wheel was at its highest point and that he fell down from the height. He died instantly from a broken neck. His daughter was with him in the ferris wheel when the accident happened.

A loose bar in the ferris wheel carriage is said to have been the cause of the accident. The police are conducting an investigation regarding the safety levels of the rides in the fair. The fair was shut down for the day after the accident. Mr. Bilal was a businessman in the city and is survived by his wife and two children.

Zubi folded the paper cutting and ran her fingers over the crease in the middle, flattening and tightening it. Her father's death had been reported in the newspaper. Everyone had been running around trying to get his body back from the hospital – where it had been sent for a post mortem – so they could leave for Vellore. By everybody, she meant Adil Chacha, Badey Abbu and Aslam Mamu, who had come from Madras as soon as he had heard about the accident.

It seemed that in one snap of some unknown but all-knowing fingers, her life had changed forever. Conversations were conducted over heaving sobs and crying sessions that didn't seem to end. When her father's body was brought from the hospital, wrapped in a white cloth with just enough space open for them to see his face, it was like he had died all over again. Zubi's pain was sharp and intense and she clutched her stomach as she saw everyone cry over his sewn up body.

Every day she looked at the paper cutting she had taken before they left Bangalore. Each day, she ran her fingers over his name, the inky words already looking blurred and unsteady. Or maybe it was because she cried so much whenever she read the news report that the words looked amorphous to her eyes.

No one had seen her take the newspaper to her room where she had run her scissors around the report carefully, through eyes that streamed tears. She had folded it and kept it with herself when Adil Chacha found her in her room and told her that they had to leave.

She missed Bangalore. She missed being in her house. She missed her father so much that she didn't know how she would live the rest of her life without him. At times she felt jealous of Rishaad who really didn't comprehend what was happening or that they would never see their father again, never hear his voice, never hold him or hug him. Rishaad kept thinking that Abbu had just gone away somewhere and would be back soon. But there were times when she felt sad for him too. Imagine not knowing the level of grief? Imagine not comprehending grief?

For some reason, all her animosity towards him had vanished since that day. Now that Ammi was in some kind of limbo, she knew it was her responsibility to take care of her brother but she wished that she didn't have to do it. Still, at nights when she crawled next to Badey Ammi, she felt her wrinkled palms on her cheeks as they wiped away the tears and held her tightly. Badey Ammi was wonderful. She smelt faintly of Cuticura talcum powder and attar and she knew how much pain Zubi was in. But Badey Ammi was not her mother and she wanted her mother back. She wanted normalcy in her life. It was a month since her father had died and she knew that life would never be the same again but she so badly wanted to start living again.

At first when they had come to Vellore, she had been a little relieved because she knew that Badey Ammi would take care of her mother. She had felt marginally comforted in the old sprawling house, where she had stayed when her mother had been pregnant with Rishaad. Those days had been idyllic and luxurious, days when she didn't have school, friends, homework or Rishaad to trouble her. Her father would visit them every weekend and when he left for Bangalore, she'd have a horde of chocolates to last her till the next weekend.

This visit, stay, whatever…was stark. Through the windows in one of the other rooms, she could see the narrow galli adjacent to their house. She sat there for hours, watching people walk, children chase each other and clamour around the kulfi man, tender-coconut sellers and the mango carts. It was the mangoes that called out to Zubi the most. Sometimes the air near the window was fouled by a stench that rose from the open gutters nearby, but whenever the mango carts passed by, Zubi would inhale deeply. The mango-scented air held so many promises, which seemed bleak the moment the mangoseller walked away.

Ammi no longer stayed alone in the room, which was a relief. But seeing her sit outside in the hall, hair uncombed, wearing the same saree for three days until Badey Ammi held out a towel, soap and fresh clothes to her, gently leading her to the bathroom, wasn't comforting either.

One day, Ammi came out of the bathroom looking fresh and clean, her hair tied in a thin towel knotted at her nape. She smelled of Cinthol soap and for just a moment, Zubi forgot everything and ran to her. She held her tightly and Ammi smiled a little before pushing her away. She had overheard her grandparents talking about a baby and she felt dismayed. She didn't want another person in their family. Not when her father wasn't there.

Ammi seemed a little better these days. She still cried, but she read namaz and the Quran although Zubi wondered uneasily what she prayed for every time she held her hands out in dua. Zubi wanted to ask Ammi if they could go back to Bangalore. School was due to start next week and she still had to get her books and uniforms.

Her mother looked at her, unable to comprehend Zubi's dilemma.

'You want to go back?' she asked, a little sharply. The quality of her voice had changed and it was always husky now.

Zubi nodded, looking at the ground. 'School starts next week.'

'But I'm in iddat,' Ammi said. For a brief moment, Zubi got the feeling that Ammi was no longer speaking to her as she normally did. Ammi was talking to her like she was a grown up. The thought frightened her immensely.

'But, Ammi, what about school?' she repeated.

'We can't leave until my iddat gets over,' Ammi said, her eyes moving back to the page of the Quran that she had been reading. Zubi watched her eyes skim the pages, right to left and back again.

'When will it get over?' Zubi asked in a small voice.

'December.' Ammi looked up at her and closed her eyes. It sounded as though she was consulting Zubi and not stating facts to her.

'December?' Zubi exploded. 'But...what about our schools?'

'We can write a letter and explain to them—' Ammi looked far away as she spoke but Zubi interrupted her.

'No school will let us take leave for so many months! They'll remove our names from the school, Ammi!' Zubi wailed.

Ammi closed the Quran gently but she looked annoyed.

'How do you know? Has anyone ever done it before?' she asked, looking straight into Zubi's eyes.

'But—'

'Ok, even if they don't, we can go back end of May. Although that would mean that I have to do an extra two months of iddat, I don't really care.'

Zubi still looked worried and slightly mutinous. 'But our school books and uniforms and—'

Ammi silenced her with a look. 'You should have thought about that before,' she said, a nasty edge to her voice.

Zubi looked at her baffled. 'Before what?' she asked.

'Before taking your father up in that ferris wheel,' her mother spat out and walked away, not knowing (or maybe she did) that she had just ruthlessly crushed any hope that Zubi might have had. Hope that she wasn't to blame for her father's death.

11

A more than generous lashing of oil. Whole garam masalas. Sliced onions. A brisk stir and then, the wait. Tahera's mother pursed her lips, and wondered how she had ended up doing this again. After so many years, she was back to cooking three times a day and she hated it. With a long-handled spoon, she moved the onions around in the kadai listlessly, watching them sweat out their lilac colour, turning an insipid pearly white as they absorbed the oil.

Her mind was not focused on the cooking and she wanted to lie down because her legs were aching. But if she didn't cook, what would they eat? When she and her husband had planned to move back to Vellore, they had never imagined the turn things would take. Ruqayya was emotional but practical as well. Her husband had saved some money and for the two of them to live there, it would have been more than sufficient. After all, living cost in Vellore was much cheaper than Bangalore. But with Tahera and the kids...she chided herself for thinking about something as mundane as expenses when her daughter...she dabbed her neck with the folded pallu of her saree. She couldn't...or rather didn't want to think about what would happen to them. Even if Tahera went back to Bangalore, how would she and the kids live alone? And make ends meet?

She stopped stirring the onions in the kadai and her eyes glazed over with the smoke that seemed to wrap itself around her head in slow suffocating degrees.

'Tahera!' she called out before stumbling and sliding sideways and collapsing on the hard kitchen ground.

Tahera came out of her room and called out to her mother. When there was no response, she looked around briefly and saw that the kids were nowhere to be seen. Feeling a little worried, she lifted her saree pleats a fraction and walked quickly towards the kitchen.

'Ammi!' she shook her mother's shoulder feeling frantic. She looked around for her father but he had gone to the masjid because it was Friday and he wanted to be there early.

Her mother moaned a little and opened her eyes. Tahera leaned forward, grabbed the jug of water that Ammi kept for cooking and splashed some water on her mother's face. Then, pouring a little in a glass, she brought it to her mother's lips.

Her mother sat up with difficulty and sipped the water but she refused Tahera's help.

'I have to cook lunch,' she said stoically as she moved towards the stove. The onions were burnt completely and she leaned forward to turn off the gas.

'But what happened?' Tahera asked, wrinkling her nose. The smell of onions frying was something she associated with each pregnancy because it became intolerable to her only then. There was something cloying about the smell that made her feel as though the centre of her chest was being trampled upon slowly and painfully.

'I don't know. Must be the heat,' Ammi replied, wiping the perspiration running down her neck with her pallu. Tahera breathed through her mouth for a moment and then shook her head as though to clear her thoughts.

'You go and lie down for some time. I'll make lunch,' she got the words out with great difficulty. It was odd that she and her mother were unable to communicate about such a small thing as lunch. A swift thought darted through Tahera's mind – that if she were in Bangalore and in her own house, then she would have simply avoided making lunch if she didn't feel like it. After all, it wasn't like her husband would be coming home, expecting food on the table. The sharp pain that the thought brought almost made her gasp but she turned to her mother resolutely.

Her mother had been thinking that if it had been just her husband and her, they would have eaten leftovers and managed. But with the kids and Tahera there, she had to make a proper Friday lunch.

'No, no! You can't tolerate the smell, na. I'll make,' she said, trying to push Tahera weakly.

Tahera shook her head and pulled her mother away from the kitchen and led her towards her bedroom, silencing her protests.

'Where are the children?' she asked her mother.

'I don't know. I thought they were with you,' Ammi said. 'They must be playing somewhere.'

Tahera nodded, a little distracted. She had felt cocooned in her grief all this time but now she could almost feel the physical tug of mundane activities that constituted life, pull her back.

'What were you cooking?' she asked her mother instead.

'It's a Friday,' Ammi answered simply.

Tahera looked at her blankly. When the meaning registered, she was surprised at how hostile she felt towards her mother. While Sundays are usually reserved for preparation of elaborate lunches in other homes, most Muslim homes chose Fridays. Friday was the day when women deliberated about cooking something special. Tahera usually made biryani on Fridays because it had seemed simplest but her heart lurched at the thought of making biryani now. If the food they ate were to reflect her state of mind, she would have made tasteless, bland dal every day.

'I was making khushka-qurma,' said her mother. Tahera glanced at her briefly before nodding and walking back towards the kitchen.

She lumbered towards the kitchen, a part of her subconscious understanding that for women, even grief could not isolate them, no matter how much they resisted it. She discarded the burnt onions and washed the pot clean with a scouring pad. She then chopped some more onions, wiping her nose with the back of her hand to prevent it from running.

She sautéed the onions in oil and then added half a spoon of adrak-lehsun paste, swallowing her saliva at the back of her throat. What was worse was that her mother's kitchen didn't have an exhaust fan either. She stirred briskly, added salt and washed mint leaves. The aromas changed; the air now had a delicate and not unpleasant fragrance that still made her want to heave. She looked around for the jug and poured water into the pot. The onions that had been subdued sufficiently reacted almost violently, shuddering and then floating on top of the water. Her mother must have cleaned the rice and kept it somewhere.

She looked around and found the rice soaking in another pot. She stood at the stove, feeling nauseous as she waited for the water to boil before putting the rice in it. Normally, she multi-tasked and would have had the onions chopped and the tomatoes blended in the mixer for the qurma while the water boiled for the khushka. But what was the point of all that efficiency? So she let lethargy take over her and she put the soaked rice in the bubbling pot sometime later, welcoming the hot splashes that greeted her hand.

She felt a presence behind her and she whipped around because it almost felt like her husband was standing there. Instead it was Zubi and Rishaad.

'Where were the two of you?' Tahera asked them. Zubi bit her lower lip and then spoke.

'We were in the house next door, playing.'

Normally Tahera would have berated them for going without informing her. But nothing was normal in their lives anymore. Belatedly she realised that Zubi was expecting her to scold them. But her mind protested and she turned away, understanding that Zubi's need for attention was getting a little out of hand.

After the day when Tahera had blamed her for her father's death, Zubi hadn't spoken to her for two whole days. Tahera didn't mind and neither did she care. But after those two days, some sort of truce had been established between them and Tahera had felt too tired to breach it; so she just accepted it with equanimity.

'What are you making?' Zubi asked, looking curious. Rishaad had seated himself on the stone steps that led to the courtyard outside the kitchen and was flicking pebbles in the dust.

'Lunch,' Tahera replied, irritated for some reason. 'Come, I need your help.'

Reluctantly Zubi peeled onions for her and then washed potatoes and peeled them for the qurma.

'Can I go now?' she asked. Tahera shook her head.

'Stand here and watch,' she ordered.

Feeling fidgety, Zubi watched her mother pull out a pressure cooker and wash it. She poured oil, dropped a few cloves, cardamoms and a stick of cinnamon in it. While Zubi had been peeling the potatoes, Tahera had chopped the onions finely. She put the onions in the cooker and stirred them, all the while covering her nose with her pallu.

'Here. Stir this,' she told Zubi as she moved away to puree

the tomatoes. Zubi pulled up a stool and stood near the stove, stirring the onions in the pressure cooker. Fascinated, she watched them change colour but when they started browning, she got a little worried.

'Ammi, they're turning black,' she called out.

'Add adrak-lehsun,' Tahera replied, switching on the mixer.

Zubi opened the lid of the jar and grimaced at the strong smell. She pulled out a heaped teaspoon and showed it to her mother who shook her head. Above the sounds of the mixer, she said, 'Not so much!'

'Then?' Zubi shouted back. She dropped some of the paste back into the jar and put the rest in the cooker. Tahera switched off the mixer and pointed to a plate where her mother had kept the washed mutton pieces.

'Put the mutton in the cooker now.'

Zubi made a face. She wasn't going to *touch* mutton! Raw meat! Yuck! And it stank too. Tahera glowered at her, still standing near the mixer. Feeling resigned, Zubi shoved the mutton pieces into the cooker, watching them turn from pink to brown. She'd never realised before that cooking had so many colour transformations that it almost seemed like magic.

'Stir,' Tahera said, still holding her pallu over her nose. She was looking out at the courtyard where Rishaad was trying to climb a tree. Her baby was no longer a baby, she thought with a pang. He was all grown up. And there was going to be a new baby. One who would have never seen his or her father.

The thought was enough to send a rush of wetness to her eyes, blocking her sinuses. She turned away. She would cry later.

'Now?' Zubi asked and Tahera pursed her lips. She instructed her to add red chilli powder and salt and stir the meat with the masalas. Zubi did as she was told. After a while, Tahera took the spatula from Zubi's hands. Tahera's ministrations were brisk as compared to the slow manner in which Zubi had been stirring the contents of the pressure cooker.

'Move,' Tahera instructed a little crisply and then she poured some curd from a packet into the cooker. She stirred the mixture, added the pureed tomatoes and mixed everything together.

'Ammi, what about the potatoes?' Zubi reminded her and Tahera nodded. She had cut the potatoes into cubes and tossed those into the cooker as well.

By now Zubi was so interested that she wouldn't have left even if her mother would have asked her to go.

'What are we making, by the way?' she asked her mother.

'Qurma,' her mother replied, vaguely amused at the way she had said 'we'.

When oil started peeping out on the sides of the frying mutton and masalas, Tahera poured water into the cooker, closed the lid and fixed the whistle.

Both of them stood staring at each other in silence as pressure built up in the cooker noisily. Tahera wished she hadn't been so harsh with Zubi that day but she also irrationally thought that she had been right. She didn't know what Zubi was thinking though as she stared back at her.

'That's all?' Zubi asked, breaking the silence. For a moment, Tahera didn't understand what she was asking. Zubi nodded towards the cooker and Tahera shook her head.

'Have to add coconut paste and coriander leaves,' she muttered and turned away to stare at the courtyard.

'Ammi...' Zubi started, but Tahera didn't turn to look back at her.

'Hmm?' she asked instead, still looking at the blistering hot courtyard where her son was playing.

'How many times do I have to keep saying sorry?'

'Never. Don't ever say sorry again,' said Tahera, her voice flat. This time she looked at Zubi in the eye.

'But—'

'Things will never be the same again, Zubi. Your apology won't make any difference,' Tahera's voice sounded devoid of any emotion. She checked the pot to see if the rice was cooked.

'But—'

'We're going to Bangalore next week. Go now. Go read namaz.' Tahera cut off the conversation there and then. A loud shrieking whistle pierced the air as the pressure cooker let out steam.

Tahera watched her daughter leave, her shoulders drooping and head bowed down. She called out to Rishaad before leaving. He abandoned his attempts to climb the tree and followed her into the house. Grief could do strange things to you. It had brought her children together in a way she had never thought possible. It had also made her into a person who constantly felt that she was inside a cramped pressure cooker, waiting for the whistle to blow.

12

The house was full of people who had come for the chehlum, the fortieth day fatiha, that was held for Bilal. The crowd made Tahera want to retreat further into the house. The sight of all the well-meaning people who had their own normal lives to lead back in their houses made her feel resentful and irritated. But she stayed in her room where she was joined by numerous relatives.

Her brother had come from Madras with his wife and children and so had Adil. Suman hadn't come along as Adil had driven down. He was planning to take them all back to Bangalore a day after the chehlum. It had been decided. Her parents would stay with her in Bangalore till her iddat got over and then...no one had been able to think that far ahead yet.

There was a distant rumble in the air and the ladies looked towards the partially shut window as though by merely looking at it, they would know if it would rain or not. Tahera sat in one corner of the bed, reading the Quran; the other women were doing the same. A quiet wind blew inside and well-thumbed pages ruffled, chiffon dupattas slipped back slightly before everything returned to normal.

The fatiha was to be held in the evening after Asr namaz but people had already started arriving even though it was just afternoon.

Many came and spoke to Tahera, offered their condolences but she liked those who didn't talk. A woman she barely knew sat next to her and Tahera glanced up at her momentarily. There was compassion in her eyes; Tahera swallowed back the despair and nodded at her. The woman took Tahera's limp hands into her own and squeezed them hard before getting up and leaving.

'Who was that?' Tahera wondered to herself. She had seen that woman a few times at weddings but had never been introduced to her. She looked around, wondering who she could ask when with a blink, the room was cloaked in darkness even though it was broad daylight. The power cut drew a collective groan from the women.

'Open the window!' someone suggested and Tahera felt a minor prickle of irritation. She was sitting closest to the window and she pushed it open with her palm. Feeble light entered the room and many women got up to go outside to read the Quran.

Tahera secured the window and tied its clasp on the sill so it wouldn't bang shut on its own. A warm breeze rushed in and Tahera let it caress her face briefly. She shut her eyes, acknowledging to herself how badly she wanted to stay here in Vellore. She didn't want to leave, knowing that he was here. Not alive, but still. He was buried here. She didn't want to go back and continue a life without him, one where gradually his presence would be obliterated. Once they were in Bangalore, the mundane everyday life would slowly eclipse this grief and she knew that it would heal it, although it was hard to imagine that happening now. She wanted the grief to be fresh. She wanted it to be real. Her life had changed and she wanted that to be evident, rather than crawl back into normalcy, which everyone else would have craved for.

Tahera felt a slight movement in her belly; she looked down, a little shocked. She rested her back against the wall and wondered how it was possible for movements to start so soon. But she recalled that with Rishaad she had felt the movements sooner than with Zubi.

She rested her open palm on her stomach and pressed it down very gently. Nothing. Maybe she had imagined it. That was when she felt the first few droplets of rain hitting the side of her face. Everyone looked surprised. It was raining in Vellore.

School had already started and Tahera realised that she was no longer the fastidious mother who made sure her children never missed even a single day. Today was their last day in Vellore and they were leaving early the next morning. The chehlum had progressed smoothly, and the house was almost back to normal except for the presence of Adil.

The children were happy to see him and he had managed to banish the gloomy atmosphere by talking to them. However, his eyes met Tahera's a few times and she recognised the pain mirrored in his. The children were a bit subdued in her presence but when she went towards the kitchen, she could hear them talking to him, a little excited about returning to Bangalore.

'I don't know how we will get our books and uniforms now,' she could hear Zubi lamenting to Adil. 'We were supposed to get them in May.'

She couldn't hear Adil's reply but she bit her lower lip and then resolutely walked into the kitchen.

'Why are you cooking today? We can manage with yesterday's leftovers, na?' she asked her mother who was bent over the sil-batta, running the oblong stone up and down.

Ammi shook her head. 'Adil is here, no? How can we serve him leftovers?' she said, referring to the food from the previous day's fatiha. These days Tahera felt irritated at the very sight of festive food, or rather anything that deviated from regular meals.

She hadn't touched the biryani cooked by the professional cook hired by Adil for the fatiha.

'So what are you making, then?' she asked her mother.

'We have to clean out the kitchen and fridge, na? There was some kheema in the freezer so I thought I'll make kufta,' she replied.

Tahera nodded, chewing the inside of her cheek absently. She had taken to helping her mother in the kitchen these days again… out of sheer boredom and angst that threatened to drive her crazy. It was odd how comforting it had become – the soothing motions of stirring onions and chopping potatoes or just grinding masalas on Ammi's sil-batta. They used the sil-batta inspite of having a mixie and Tahera had half a mind to take it back to Bangalore. However, Ammi didn't let her grind anything on it because of her condition.

Although the smell of onions frying still made her want to heave, she had tried to overcome it so she could stay in the kitchen with her mother. If she allowed herself not to think, she could almost believe it was her life before her marriage – when she had been a young girl, flush with giddy dreams of the future, sadness that eventually her way of life with her mother would end, but also excited about what the future would bring. Sitting in the kitchen with her mother, she could fool herself into thinking that a decade *hadn't* lapsed in her life. But reality crashed in…in the form of her children and she would gulp the pain and purse her lips before continuing what she was doing.

'Have you both finished packing?' Tahera asked her mother who was measuring the kheema for the kuftas.

'I'll do it once this is done,' Ammi replied.

'Why don't you go and do it now. I'll make the kuftas,' Tahera suggested. Her mother was about to protest but she nodded her head and left. Tahera sighed and breathed deeply. Tomorrow, she would be in her own house and her own kitchen. But nothing would be the same. There would be no Bilal sneaking up behind her, or calling out her name as he entered the house. There would be no one praising her effusively for what she did best – cooking. And there would be no one kissing her fingers with such intensity that it made her blush.

Gritting her teeth, Tahera dropped the kheema into the mixie jar and then in swift succession, added chopped onions, a handful of coriander leaves, some garam masala powder, a couple of green chillies, a bit of haldi powder, adrak-lehsun paste and some salt. Compared to most other dishes, kufta was easy to make, but she knew that the proportions had to be right or else it could all go horribly wrong. She saw that her mother had kept the ground coconut nearby, and she put some of it into the mixie. She switched it on, holding the top of the jar and despite the loud whirr of the mixie, her mind had already drifted towards other thoughts.

Her sister-in-law Amina had sat with her the previous night and explained to her patiently that it was all Allah's will and she should accept it.

'This was meant to happen in your life, Tahera. This was all part of Allah's plan for you,' she repeated, not backing away from the anger that had erupted in Tahera's eyes. Tahera had kept quiet throughout Amina's explanation because she didn't quite know what to say. She couldn't possibly tell her, 'Wait until your husband dies', because her husband was her brother and even if that were not the case, it would be a terrible thing to say to anyone.

Amina continued. 'I know this will be hard for you but you have to accept it and move on. You can't stay fixed in your grief. I'm sure Bilal Bhai wouldn't have wanted you to suffer like this or cause such suffering to his children.'

Tahera stiffened. 'What do you mean?' she asked Amina finally. Amina looked around at the people who were seated near them and lowered her voice although no one was paying any attention towards them.

'Have you seen how thin Rishaad has become? And Zubi? She looks like an old woman dragging him around everywhere. Your children are not yet orphans, Tahera. They have you. You have to give up this grief and take care of them.'

Tahera had wanted to lash out at Amina but she didn't. First there were too many people around who would witness the ugly scene and second, a reluctant part of her agreed that no matter how uncomfortable Amina made her with her piousness, she was right. Grief was a luxury for a mother and she had indulged herself way too much already.

Tahera switched off the mixie and prised open the lid. She emptied the yellow-brown-green mixture into a small bowl and mixed it with the fried gram masala powder that her mother had ground earlier on the sil-batta. She kneaded it into a soft dough and then put water to boil in a kadai. When the water in the kadai simmered, she made small round balls out of the dough, and dropped them into the water, one by one until all the kufta dough was over and the kadai was bubbling.

She wiped her hands on the pallu of her saree, feeling a sudden onslaught of panic at the thought of leaving Vellore. But as the panic threatened to overwhelm her, she saw Adil walk inside the kitchen to place a tea cup in the sink.

'Here, give that to me,' she said, taking the cup from his hands, avoiding his gaze.

'Bhabhi...,' he started. Tahera looked up. He seemed unsure. He, too, had aged in these forty days, she thought.

'We have to talk,' he continued when Tahera nodded. 'Here?' he asked looking around.

Tahera shrugged and sat down on the steps of the kitchen. He sat down beside her.

'I don't know how to say this, but...'

He took a deep breath and continued. 'I...You don't have to worry about anything. I'll take care of everything.' He spoke the words in a hurry.

Tahera looked straight ahead, not comprehending his words and he realised that she hadn't really paid attention to him.

'I mean, about Zubi and Rishaad and their school fees and education and everything. I'll take care of it.'

Tahera drew in a shuddering breath and scratched her right eyebrow. Her mouth felt dry. She knew she had to worry about living expenses and bringing up the children. But to *depend* upon her husband's brother, no matter how genuinely he cared for them?

There was a quick succession of thoughts in her head. The Bangalore house belonged to them. Maybe she could sell it and rent an apartment somewhere and live on the money. Or maybe they could just stay here in Vellore. But before she could expound her theories, Adil spoke again.

'Zubi and Rishaad are like my own children. You don't have to worry,' he said. 'Inshallah, even for Zubi's wedding, I'll do all I can.'

Tahera felt a weight pressing down on her chest. The different aspects to becoming a young widow were just making themselves apparent to her and they were not pleasing. She now had to depend on someone else for *her* children's future. An irrational thought occurred to her. How that Suman would gloat! But she suppressed it immediately. It was a stupid thought, fed by her own insecurity.

'Thank you, Adil. But we'll manage,' she said, getting up to stir the contents of the kadai. The water had dried up and the pale kuftas were slowly turning brown. She poured oil along the sides and scraped up the kuftas that had stuck to the bottom of the kadai.

'But…how?' Adil was standing beside her now.

'Something will come up. Allah put me in this difficulty and he will find a way for me to get out,' she said, echoing Amina's words. Strangely, they were true and despite the numerous questions and doubts that popped in her head, she felt a modicum of peace.

'It's impossible. You know the cost of living in Bangalore. At least…at least let me transfer the partnership in the shop from Bhaiya's name to yours so you can get the monthly drawing.'

Tahera continued gently working the kuftas over but letting them linger in the hot kadai so they could develop a lovely crust, the kind that Bilal liked. With that thought, she turned off the stove and turned to face Adil, who was still looking at her intently.

'As you wish. But everything else, we'll find a way to manage,' she replied, smiling lightly at him.

'Are you alright?' he asked her and Tahera knew he had reverted to behaving the way he used to during the early days of her marriage when he had found out that she was younger to him. Until then, he'd been the respectful brother-in-law, but after he discovered how young she was, he had taken to teasing her like an older brother even though he called her bhabhi.

'No, I'm not alright, Adil. I just lost my husband and my life has changed forever. Your help and offer is much appreciated,' Tahera burst out, turning back to face the kadai. 'But we need our self-respect too at this time in our lives.'

'I—'

'We'll manage,' Tahera spoke firmly.

'As you wish,' Adil said curtly before exiting the kitchen. She knew she had hurt him but since the day her husband had died, she hadn't felt this measure of motivation. She had no idea how, but she would find a way. She felt a prickle of unease, but she soothed it as she removed the kuftas, placed them in a serving dish and called out to the children.

The children, Abba and Adil sat down for lunch while Tahera and Ammi served them.

'Kufta?' Zubi asked, surprised and pleased. It had been so long since they had kufta at home. She couldn't even remember the last time she had tasted it.

Before Tahera placed the rice on her plate, Zubi leaned forward, picked up one kufta and bit into it. Tahera watched the expression on Zubi's face... so like her husband's, she thought. It was such that she almost felt it like a physical blow to her stomach.

'Perfect,' she said, echoing her husband's oft-repeated phrase whenever she cooked something he liked.

Tahera licked her dry lips and covered her mouth with her trembling hand. He wasn't really gone was he? She had a part of him, right here.

Part Two

13

'And then?' I asked her, as the doors opened in a swish and the three of us stepped inside the train. Barely seconds later, the doors shut and we quickly clutched the icy pole in the centre for support. The MTR was crowded as usual, and I did a quick scan of the occupants with whom we would spend the next five minutes... the time that it would take to reach Zubi's station.

The American tourists with their shorts and halter tops looked at ease as they shook out a map and deliberated where to go. Two pretty Chinese girls, who seemed not more than seventeen, had their heads bent over their iPhones. Those who had found seats looked distracted and only a couple of old ladies spoke to each other in rapid Chinese, gesticulating wildly and for some reason, one of them glanced at us before returning to her conversation.

I knew that no one really looked out of place in Hong Kong, and the people never bothered with what you did, or what you wore or what you were. Still, she had glanced at me, Zubi and her son for a quick five seconds.

I briefly wondered what she must have made of us. The startlingly pretty woman in a pink saree, the tall lanky woman in jeans and a white camisole and the dark haired three-year-old who was busy rooting in one of the many bags that Zubi had near her feet.

'Arrey, Abid, no!' she said, pulling his hand away from the bags and clutching it firmly as the train rocked and swayed before stopping at Jordan.

'Hmm?' I repeated my question as people flowed out and in.

Zubi shrugged elegantly. 'Then we grew up,' she said, looking over my shoulder at the blinking light near the roof of the train where the next station's name was lit up.

'We have to get down,' she announced and I nodded, feeling a little irritable. Of course I knew we had to get down at Tsim Sha Tsui. The problem with the MTR trains in Hong Kong was that they were so fast, they got you to your destination before you had time to get comfortable for the journey.

The train stopped, and the three of us got down. I helped carry some of Zubi's shopping bags and she nodded at me gratefully as the three of us clambered up the subway stairs onto Nathan Road. I noticed her son was not walking but almost nodding off to sleep.

Zubi muttered something under her breath that sounded like 'shit' and handed one of the bags to me before carrying him over her shoulder where he promptly slumped into deep sleep. We walked briskly, imitating the strides of the others around us or surely we would have been trampled. Two signals later, we turned the corner near her building. By then Zubi's trudging had become slower, her child's body seeming like a dead weight on her shoulders.

I bunched all the carrier bags together and held them in one hand, wondering what I had got myself into. It was a Saturday evening and I could have easily dressed up in something slinky and sexy and headed off to Drop but for some reason, I wasn't in the mood for clubbing. I hadn't been in the mood for a long time actually and I briefly wondered if I was growing old. I was just twenty-eight. No way. But I couldn't quite pin-point the reason for this restlessness or understand it. Instead of calling my best friend, Natalie (who was probably at Drop already), I had found myself calling Zubi.

Zubi sounded distracted and then told me that she wasn't at home. She was at the Yau Ma Tei market, purchasing vegetables for the week with her son.

'So, are you done yet?' I asked her, sitting cross-legged on my bed, fingering the fringe of my jeans.

'Almost,' she said, sounding a little breathless.

'Okay, hang on. Can you meet me at the Yau Ma Tei station? I want to talk to you. Maybe we could meet at your place?' I found myself asking her.

She sounded surprised. 'I…my…actually my husband will be at home today.'

'So?' I asked. 'I mean, he knows that you've been meeting me, right?' I bit my lower lip.

'Yes,' she deliberated over it for some time before saying, 'Okay. I'll wait for you there. Come soon.' I leapt off my bed, feeling the inertia vanish in seconds. And now here I was, lugging her groceries up the steps that led to her building.

'Uff!' I muttered as I pressed the button for the elevator with my elbow. Zubi looked at me apologetically and smiled. Her son was asleep on her shoulder and she looked more uncomfortable than me.

'Does he live in your building?' I asked Zubi, trying not to make it evident that I was referring to the man who was walking towards us. When he saw that the lift had arrived, he sprinted forward and bolted inside just before the lift doors squeaked shut.

There were times when I misplaced Zubi in my head with

my other friends and pretty much forgot that she was married, especially when I was checking out guys. Zubi, it would seem, had no vision for men because she would have *never* noticed a guy, no matter how hot he was. It always confounded me and I belatedly remembered the fact as we moved to a corner to give the man some space.

I covertly checked him out, noticing that he was tall, had a great physique and very dark eyes. For some reason, my eyes kept getting drawn to his hands. They were veined and there was some sort of quiet power about them. I quickly looked up to see his face, the details of his clean cut looks barely registering in my mind when I realised with a little chagrin that he was staring at Zubi intently.

I drew in a breath but almost choked when he leaned across and touched Zubi on her shoulder. I was sure Zubi would scream but instead she looked relieved and handed her sleeping child to him.

Wait a second. *This* was Zubi's husband?

The lift doors opened at Zubi's floor and the three of us got out, the man holding the back of Abid's head with care. Zubi took some of the grocery covers from my hand and I walked towards their apartment, feeling dumbfounded.

I had never met her husband before and a number of confusing thoughts rushed through my head. I'd expected someone more middle-aged, average looking and slightly boring. That he was the complete opposite just didn't fit. But that was mostly because of Zubi's reaction to him when he wasn't around. Like she didn't really care too much about him. Like he wasn't worth so much of her attention. Even now, there was a distracted air about her as she unlocked the doors and the three of us walked inside in complete silence.

Looking a little hesitant, Zubi introduced me to her husband who merely nodded and went inside the nearest bedroom. I assumed he had tucked Abid into bed. He emerged a little later, looking serious as he went into the bathroom. Zubi was unpacking the groceries and lining the shelves of her tiny kitchen. She passed me the bag of vegetables for the fridge. Feeling uncommonly domesticated, I opened the door and placed the bag inside. The sound of the flush was heard from the bathroom and then the door opened. He stepped outside, and headed back to the bedroom.

Two thoughts made their presence felt in my mind at that time. Zubi and her husband behaved as though they were strangers living in one house. (It really was none of my business though.) And it had been a bad idea to visit her when he was home. I doubt we would get any talking done today.

So I got up from my crouched position and straightened up. 'I think I'll go. We'll meet up another day,' I said.

Zubi cocked her head back and looked at me quizzically.

'Why?' she asked, her pallu tucked around her waist.

'I...It's just that...I wanted to ask you so many questions and...' I glanced uneasily at the room where he had gone.

Zubi shrugged. 'He'll take a nap while I make dinner. Come on inside. We can talk while I cook.'

Even though the apartment seemed smaller than it was because in my mind his physical presence was very large and intimidating, I stepped inside the narrow kitchen. I was bursting to ask her questions but I didn't know if she had realised I had been checking him out in the lift. That would be awkward.

'Can I help?' I found myself asking. She smiled and shook her head.

'Let's just talk,' she said as she measured out atta for rotis.

'Okay, so that was it? You guys returned to Bangalore and then?'

'Like I said, life happened,' she murmured, kneading the atta rhythmically. The silence in the kitchen was punctuated by the loud sounds of traffic from outside.

'Meaning?'

'My mother wanted to sell our house in Bangalore, but for some reason decided not to,' Zubi spoke up. 'That was the best decision she took, especially because of the realty prices there now.'

'Then?'

'Instead she rented out a portion of the house and we survived somehow,' Zubi added.

'What about...the baby?' I asked hesitantly.

'Oh, my brother Suhail was born in December that year. He's a completely spoilt brat,' she said, her eyes affectionate as she punched the dough and covered it with a plate.

'He must be what, seventeen or eighteen, now?' I calculated.

Zubi nodded. 'He turns eighteen this year.'

'Wow!' I was unable to say anything else.

I watched her chop onions with remarkable efficiency and she wiped her eyes with the back of her hand.

'So?' she asked.

'Uh...It's still incomplete. I mean...there are so many things I need to know about—'

'I know,' she interrupted me.

14

It was going to take a long time for her to get used to waking up every morning, looking at his face. She blinked a little in the weak morning light and observed his fine features quietly, almost afraid to breathe, in case that woke him up. They had been married for just a week now, and technically he was still a stranger.

She turned her face slowly to take in her room. It was a little plain and bland compared to the room she had left behind at her mother's house. But it had her husband, she thought shyly turning back to look at him. His breathing was even and only when asleep did he look a little less serious and intimidating, although she knew that it was only a façade. It seemed like a delicious secret that she hugged to herself whenever she thought of him.

There were times when the newness of marriage was so exciting that she looked forward to seeing him come home every evening from work; but there were other times, like now, when she wanted to bridge the unfamiliarity in their lives immediately. She wanted them to become a couple and not just two people still teetering towards each other.

If they had been more comfortable with each other, she wouldn't have hesitated from running her finger slowly across his forehead. But right now, although her finger was twitching, she held it back. She continued watching him, praying that no one would come banging on their door like they had done the morning after her wedding.

While sleeping, both she and Omar had somehow gravitated towards each other and they were startled by the banging as much as the fact that they were sleeping in such close proximity. She still blushed when she thought of how embarrassed he had looked before bounding away to open the door and snarl at his younger sister Nadira.

Oh, what the heck, she thought and ran her finger on his face just the way she had fantasised sometime back. His eyes opened immediately and she pulled back her finger as though stung.

He stared at her intently for a few seconds, although to her it seemed like endless minutes. When he spoke, he merely said two words.

'Kishore Kumar.'

She blinked her eyes rapidly, before remembering that he was picking up from exactly where they had left off last night.

'No, Dilip Kumar,' she said.

He rolled his eyes expressively; she smiled a little, wondering what he would say.

'That old fart?' he asked and she gasped. His Urdu was not like hers. For some reason, she found it a little more crude but nevertheless exciting.

'He's not old! He's only thirty-six!' she argued, 'and he's not a...a...'

'Yes,' he smiled, 'continue.'

'Well, he's not a joker like Kishore Kumar at least!' she countered, to which he frowned.

'There's no comparison,' he claimed and she nodded.

'Well, at least you got something right!' saying this, she got up, her tummy doing an incredible dance as she recalled that he had just been reaching out for her when she had moved away. Feeling a little lightheaded and giddy, she walked around the bed, took her towel, a fresh set of clothes and reached the door. It was still quite early in the morning but she wanted to bathe before the others woke up. That was another thing. Her room didn't have an attached bathroom. In fact, none of the rooms in this house had bathrooms. And she would have to go and wake up that girl to heat water for her in the kitchen which would easily take another twenty minutes.

'Ruhi,' he spoke quietly. She turned to face him, feeling a little shy suddenly. He was sitting up in bed, looking serious again.

'Come back here,' he said and she shook her head although she was sure that she would go to him if he asked her one more time.

'Please?' he asked, cocking his head in a way that was so endearing that she pursed her lips and took a step forward.

'I only want to tell you that *Chalti Ka Naam Gaadi* is a much better film than *Madhumati*,' he said with a grin. She narrowed her eyes before walking out of the room.

She turned back briefly because she had to have the last word before leaving.

'You have a deplorable taste in films. And my name is not Ruhi,' she said but was stopped because he spoke again and she didn't hear him clearly. 'What?'

'Your name sounds like someone saying he wants to vomit,' he said mildly.

She gasped in outrage, but before she could come up with a retort, he was at the door before her.

'Which is why I think Ruhi is a better name than Ruqayya. No?' he gently pushed her outside and shut the door, laughing. Ruqayya fumed as she made her way to the bathroom.

Later that morning, she stood in the smoky kitchen. Looking up at the blackened ceiling, she felt stifled. Her mother-in-law was telling her about what everyone liked for breakfast and she wasn't quite sure she would be able to remember everything. Maybe she should have brought along a notebook.

'Are you listening?' her mother-in-law asked her sceptically, looking away from the thin white semia she was squeezing out in a seemingly intricate but random pattern on a small circular straw mat.

She deftly placed the straw mat inside a huge pot while flames from a wooden stove licked its sides. She pulled over another one and did the same thing while Ruqayya hoped she wouldn't ask her to do it. It looked too difficult to do.

She fidgeted with her saree's pallu, wondering when she would be able to wear chiffon sarees instead of these heavy zari ones and briefly, her mind darted to Omar and what he would be doing. Probably lounging in their bedroom while she was being slowly steamed in the hot kitchen. Was she the only one who found it odd that she and her husband had to behave like polite strangers in front of everyone else but inside their room they could be themselves?

'Are you?' her mother-in-law repeated the question and Ruqayya looked up startled.

'Yes, yes, Ammi!' she answered, trying to look more interested but failing to really figure out what her mother-in-law wanted from her.

Without realising it, both of them sighed together. Ruqayya missed her home and her parents. She wasn't like the many women for whom their mother's homes were just a transitory phase in their lives... one they could leave at the first chance. Barely a week in her in-laws' home in Vellore and she knew that the kind of life she had lived before marriage wasn't something everyone else had experienced. Look at Nadira, she thought.

Nadira was the same age as her but she had never been to school. She had been home schooled by an indifferent teacher and she couldn't read Urdu as well as she ought to. When she saw Ruqayya reading a magazine, she had gasped, and requested her to tell what she was reading.

Her mother-in-law had sighed for a different reason. She glanced sideways at her new daughter-in-law and wondered if she had made a huge mistake. Maybe she had, but she could never let it become apparent because then she'd be the butt of jokes. She had to abide by her decision. Omar had been getting so many proposals from girls in Vellore but he had been a little insistent on getting an educated wife.

So, she had to spread the net wider and when she heard about Ruqayya from some common relatives, she couldn't quite believe it at first. Ruqayya had actually finished her schooling at an English medium school in Madras. Her first thought was, what were her parents thinking? Who wanted such an educated girl? But then, her son did. She thought of him with no small amount of pride because he was one of the very few Muslim men in town who had acquired a college degree.

Ruqayya was the only daughter of rich and well-meaning parents who had not really been too bothered about instilling in her the qualities a bahu should ideally possess.

She continued making the semia deftly and had to suppress a little stab of irritation when she remembered that Ruqayya knew what semia were, but had no idea how they were made. As she covered the pot with a lid, she sat down heavily on the kitchen steps and told Ruqayya to heat the paaya salan.

Ruqayya grimaced. She looked at her mother-in-law's face for a fraction of a second before wondering how she could tell her that she had never lit a kerosene stove in her life. Or that she didn't really relish trotter curry for breakfast.

She tapped her feet on the stone floor and wondered if someone else would come inside the kitchen and help. Surely someone could have come by now. The house was full of people even now, a week after her wedding.

Say it and get it over with, a small voice told her, but she wasn't sure. Could she tell her mother-in-law of just a week, the woman with whom it seemed she would be spending more time with than her husband, that she had never cooked before? Or that she wasn't interested at all.

No, the latter bit could come later she amended. She cleared her throat and scratched her cheek briefly before speaking.

'Ammi, I don't know how to...' she started and her mother-in-law turned to face her, staring in disbelief.

'You don't know how to what?' she asked her.

Ruqayya bit her lower lip. 'I don't know cooking at all. I don't even know how to light this stove,' she said quickly.

Her mother-in-law's eyes widened and Ruqayya just wanted to run! She didn't want to answer questions about her non-existent culinary skills or her parents, which was where all these questions eventually led to, all the time.

'Ruqayya! Wait!' her mother-in-law called out, but Ruqayya walked away from the kitchen swiftly, feeling wretched. She hurried to her bedroom and opened the door and saw Omar tucking his shirt into his trousers. He looked startled to see her. He dropped his hands awkwardly and asked, 'What happened?'

She fanned her flushed face with her pallu and sat down heavily on the bed, shaking her head, tears streaming down her face.

'What?' he repeated but she didn't speak. She had expected him to ask her again and she might have told him tearfully about how she felt but when she slowly looked up, he was gone!

What? He didn't want to know what was wrong? Or had he gone to ask his mother why his wife was upset? Maybe that was it. Feeling a little mollified, she took a deep breath and sat straighter and waited. And waited. After half-an-hour, she realised he wasn't coming back into the room. And then she heard him call out to his mother, 'Ammi, see you in the evening!'

Ruqayya stood up in shock. He hadn't even bothered to come inside to ask her what was wrong. She wanted to run after him and yell at him but common sense told her to keep quiet, considering the scene that would create.

She was hungry... her tummy felt hollow and self-pity loomed inside her. Her own husband wasn't bothered about her. Why had she got married? Why had her parents allowed her to get married into such a family?

She fretted some more and then sat down on the bed, wondering how she was going to face everyone. In retrospect, running to her room seemed like a foolish thing to do.

She noticed that Omar had discarded his night clothes on the bed carelessly and she had a good mind to leave them that way; but as though they had a mind of their own, her hands made their way towards the clothes.

Listlessly she folded them, chiding herself for being sentimental when her husband, evidently, didn't even care about why she was upset. A knock sounded on the door and she looked up anxiously. Was that her mother-in-law? Her mother-in-law came inside her room every day to inspect whether everything was in its place. Ruqayya hated the invasion of privacy but it seemed there was little she could do about it. She had to stop thinking of how things had been back home, because whether she liked it or not, this was her home now.

Tremulously she called out, 'Come in!'

To her relief it was Nadira who lingered at the doorstep, looking uneasy.

'Bhabhi, come for breakfast. We're waiting for you,' she said and walked away.

While an internal monologue played itself inside her mind, Ruqayya covered her head with the heavy pallu and stepped outside, feeling tense, angry and annoyed with herself because she was also feeling shy.

Outside her room was a large hall where breakfast had been laid out. Ruqayya tried to avoid looking at the numerous faces that looked at her expectantly. She looked down at the patterns on the woven mat, walked towards the nearest vacant place and sat down. Had her mother-in-law told everyone that she couldn't cook? Were they going to laugh at her?

The lull in the conversation stretched. Ruqayya briefly looked up and saw that the expression on her mother-in-law's face was inscrutable. Was she looking smug or angry? It looked like a weird combination of both.

Ignoring the looks everyone was giving her, she broke the steamed semia that Nadira had placed on her plate and dipped it in the fiery orange paaya salan. The already limp threads seemed to collapse and Ruqayya concentrated on eating breakfast without getting any of it on her clothes.

She had asked Nadira a couple of days back about exactly how many people lived in their house.

'They're here for the wedding, aren't they?' she had asked and felt a tiny jolt of shock when Nadira shook her head.

'No, they all live here,' she said simply.

'What? They *all* live here?' she couldn't quite believe it. Even now the idea that eight people lived in this house seemed preposterous.

None of them were even actually related to her husband. Shoving all those thoughts aside, ignoring the feeling that she was being observed as she ate, she got up quickly and walked towards the kitchen to keep her plate.

She half feared her mother-in-law would be right behind her but instead it was Nadira who was struggling to carry all the plates to the kitchen. She crouched down near a tap in a corner of the kitchen – an enclosure of sorts where dirty dishes were washed – and filled a pot with water to wash the plates.

Ruqayya observed her, feeling uncomfortable. Much as she didn't want to, she ended up thinking about her mother's house, the multitude of servants there, and the fact that their kitchen had a sink. Apparently, these people had never heard of the concept.

'Shall I help you?' she asked her despite her misgivings because she felt bad for Nadira. No one treated her with respect.

'Arrey, no, Bhabhi! I do this every day,' she protested, smiling as she scrubbed a particularly oily bowl with an untidy handful of coconut fibre. Ruqayya didn't know what was expected of her, but surely they didn't expect her to crouch wearing her expensive gold and silver filigree sarees to *wash* dirty vessels.

'Ammi wanted to ask you to make firni today,' Nadira spoke, pushing away a strand of hair that had fallen across her forehead with her wrist.

'Huh?' she asked, leaning forward carefully to take the washed plates from Nadira.

'Firni. You know what that is, don't you?' Nadira asked her and Ruqayya quelled the urge to respond with sarcasm. Of course she knew what firni was. She loved it. It was one of her favourite comfort foods. The only problem was that she didn't know how to make it.

15

Dinner that night was to be an elaborate affair. Ruqayya's mother-in-law had invited some of her relatives for dinner and had been busy all day in the kitchen cooking biryani, khatta baingan and chicken fry. As if there weren't enough people already in this house, Ruqayya had fumed momentarily before escaping to her room where she spent the rest of the day ensconced within the pages of a magazine and listening to film songs on her radio.

She thought Nadira had been joking when she said that her mother-in-law had expected Ruqayya to make firni for the evening. Ruqayya had never stepped into a kitchen so many times in all her sixteen years than she had this past one week. Briefly she recalled her mother's parting words to her.

'Be a good daughter-in-law. Listen to your mother-in-law. Think of her as your mother. Be respectful.' Ruqayya had nodded her head without understanding a single word because she was overwhelmed at the thought of leaving her parents. Many a time she had overheard other children and adults speaking of her parents with disdain. They tittered about how spoilt Ruqayya was and how one day she was going to be in a lot of trouble because of her parents. She used to feel a little outraged every time someone spoke that way about her parents but she'd ignored them. Today, she wondered if this was what they had meant.

She was the only daughter of her parents, yes, but they had two sons and she had been born many years after them. Maybe that was why they had been so indulgent although she couldn't quite imagine being treated in any other way. Look at Nadira, she thought. Her mother-in-law treated her like a resident servant. And Nadira did everything without a word of complaint.

I can't be like that, Ruqayya thought with a shudder. I don't know how much longer I can stay this way, cooped up in this room. Someone knocked on the door and she looked up feeling resigned. Was there never to be a moment's privacy in this house?

She got up from the bed, draped her pallu over her head and opened the door to find an aunt standing there, smiling at her. She knew this aunt was one of the many people who lived in this house but she had no idea what her name was even though she had been seeing her every day during mealtimes.

'Ruhi?' she asked, and Ruqayya bit her lip with irritation. That husband of hers! How could he tell everyone to call her by this new name?

'My name is Ruqayya,' she said, a little sullenly and then opened the door wider, letting the woman inside.

'I'm Omar's aunt, Shameem,' she proferred as she stepped over the threshold. Ruqayya nodded and asked her to sit down on the bed, which the woman promptly did. Ruqayya sat down in front of her and idly shut the magazine she had been reading, wondering why this lady had come.

'You like reading?' she asked. Ruqayya looked up and nodded.

'I wish I had the time to read too,' she said with a smile, pulling the magazine towards her and flipping the pages with interest.

'You *know* how to read?' Ruqayya asked sceptically and the woman looked up, surprised.

'Of course I know how to read!' she said, a little defensively. 'I can write perfect Urdu too!'

'But Nadira…' Ruqayya's voice trailed away.

'…Is a lazy girl who didn't want to study. What can you expect?' she asked with a derisive smile.

Ruqayya was silent for a few moments. 'Nadira is not lazy,' she said finally. 'She's a very hardworking girl. I could never be like her even if I wanted to!'

To her surprise, Shameem Aunty started laughing. 'No, no! That's not what I meant. She wasn't interested in studying.'

Ruqayya ran out of things to say, and wished Shameen Aunty would hurry up and say whatever she wanted to. She didn't have to wait too long.

'Apa told me that you don't know how to cook.' She let the words hang in the air, expecting Ruqayya to defend herself or say something. But Ruqayya sat feeling impassive. Great. Barely a week since her wedding and she was already ruining her reputation here.

Shameem Aunty sighed. 'It's a tradition in our house. The new bride has to cook firni. On her own.'

Ruqayya's head snapped up. 'I don't know how to,' she shrugged. She preferred being open and honest.

Shameem Aunty raised her eyes to the ceiling and Ruqayya was sure she was having all sorts of unfavourable thoughts about her, but to her surprise, she didn't say anything. She got up from the bed and Ruqayya looked at her expectantly.

'Come. If you don't know something, you should make the effort to learn. Sitting in your room looking pretty won't get you anywhere,' she added, a little disdainfully as she left the room.

Ruqayya suppressed the irritation she felt at Shameem Aunty's supercilious tone and got up to follow her. Whatever the situation with her mother-in-law and these other aunts, she knew that she liked her husband. Immensely. In fact, she had felt a strong jolt of attraction on their first night together when he had lifted the veil from her face, and sat back in surprise to see that she hadn't closed her eyes as was the tradition. He had smiled at her then and her heart leaped but she didn't say the words that had sprung to her mind. If she had, he would have laughed at her instead of being flattered. So she kept the fact that he looked quite like the irresistible Dilip Kumar to herself. Tucking the edge of her pallu behind her ears, she left her room with a smile on her face.

All thoughts of Omar and Dilip Kumar fled, however, when she entered the busy kitchen. It seemed like there were a hundred people when in reality there were just four. But they seemed to be everywhere at the same time as they chopped onions, stirred the curries and ground masalas. Just looking at the seeming whir of motion made her feel dizzy.

'Where were you, Shameem? You know you have to make khatta baingan! Where did you disappear?' an aunt screeched as she pumped a second kerosene stove furiously. Ruqayya's mother-in-law was draining steaming water from a huge pot in which she had parboiled rice for the biryani.

'Arrey! Stop looking around. Come here and help!' she remonstrated and Ruqayya jumped, feeling intimidated and very inadequate. To her relief, she realised that her mother-in-law had shouted at Shameem Aunty and not her.

It was hard to believe that they were all in the *same* house. In her room, the atmosphere had stilled, until it seemed solidified. She had felt suffocated there despite listening to her favourite songs. But here…in this kitchen, it was as if every two minutes the atmosphere was showering tiny sparks on the women and they worked with more fervour and energy.

'We're almost done here,' her mother-in-law spoke as

she layered the rice over the simmering gravy for the biryani. 'This has to go for dum and then that's it. Ruhi can make the firni then.'

All activity ceased and all eyes swivelled to her. Except her mother-in-law's who continued to arrange the yellow rice in the pot. Swallowing, she nodded and watched from the sidelines as the huge daawat was prepared meticulously by the five women in the kitchen.

Watching them as they went about their work, Ruqayya briefly wondered how her mother had managed huge dinner parties. For a moment she wished she had visited the kitchen at such times to see if the same frenzy had been there as well.

'Okay. The milk is in this lagan. You have to boil it and reduce it,' her mother-in-law informed her as she busied herself with tidying up the kitchen. The others had already left.

Reduce? How was one to reduce milk? Her query was probably etched over her face because her mother-in-law looked up at her and sighed.

'Just let it simmer and don't let it boil over. And make sure it doesn't get scorched at the bottom. You have to keep stirring or the milk will get burnt and it will be ruined,' she said before dusting her hands and walking out. Ruqayya looked around in alarm. She had thought that Shameem Aunty was going to help her out. That's what she had meant back in the room, right?

Her mother-in-law turned. 'The sugar is on the top shelf in that aluminium tin. And remember to put sliced almonds. I'll send Nadira to help you with the rice.'

Ruqayya watched her leave in dismay. She tried to recall the taste of firni but it was so simple that it was hard to capture. What went in it? Milk, sugar and rice. That's all. But in which order? And what if she didn't get it right?

She licked her lower lip nervously as she stirred the milk. When would Nadira come? And would she know what to do? Feeling tears of frustration pool in her eyes, she clamped her eyes tightly wondering why girls had to go through these ridiculous rites of passage.

She felt her pallu slipping from her head and she wiped the sweat that had beaded on her brow with the back of her hand, hoping that Nadira would come soon. Nadira came a good twenty minutes later. She looked at Ruqayya sheepishly.

'I wanted to come earlier and help, Bhabhi,' she started but Ruqayya didn't let her complete her sentence.

'Forget that! Tell me what I'm supposed to do!' she said in a fierce whisper, her arms aching from the continuous stirring.

'Firni...' Nadira started looking around furtively.

'Yes! Firni! How do we make it?' Ruqayya asked her, knowing that she probably looked ridiculous, decked in her expensive Benaras saree and jewellery, stirring milk.

'Ammi asked me to help you with the rice,' she said uncertainly and Ruqayya wondered if she was simple minded.

'So let me do that first, and then I'll tell you what to do,' she said, scooping out some rice from a container on a shelf.

'That doesn't look like rice to me,' Ruqayya said doubtfully.

'It's broken rice,' Nadira explained as she measured some and then put it to boil.

'I have no idea what you're doing, but I'm glad at least you seem to know what you're doing,' said Ruqayya, feeling slightly relieved for the first time that evening.

She looked outside at the darkening courtyard and her spirit lifted when she realised that Omar would be home soon. But when she returned her gaze to the milk she was stirring, she felt her stomach clench.

'It's no longer white!' she whispered to Nadira who just shook her head and smiled as she stirred the boiling broken rice.

'That means the milk is being reduced properly. Bhabhi, has it become creamy?'

Ruqayya lifted the spoon and saw that the milk had indeed become creamy. She looked at it in wonder and then followed Nadira's instructions. When the broken rice was cooked, Nadira scooped it into the milk and stirred steadily.

'Sugar?' Ruqayya asked, looking confused. Nadira merely nodded.

They stirred the firni in turns. Nadira lifted the now viscous firni in a spoon and tested the rice. Seeing Ruqayya's quizzical look, she tried to explain. 'It has to...they have to belong together. The rice and the milk,' she said, her face flushing with the effort of expounding a concept to her sophisticated bhabhi.

Ruqayya nodded, new-found respect for Nadira beaming in her eyes, as she watched her measure sugar in a long steel glass which was normally used to measure rice.

She shook the sugar into the firni and then stirred. Ruqayya noticed that the sugar disappeared immediately. They stirred for some more time and then Nadira spooned a bit of it and blew on it delicately, asking Ruqayya to taste it.

'See if it needs more sugar.' Ruqayya swiped some of it on her finger and brought it to her mouth. It felt foreign to her. The taste was simple and bland. She knew firni was not an exotic dessert but what she just tasted seemed like a let-down. The thoughts flitted across her face swiftly and Nadira seemed to understand her disappointment with it.

When they spoke, neither of them knew who was trying to console whom. It hadn't been a disaster, but it wasn't spectacular either.

'I'm an idiot!' Nadira spoke, dramatically slapping her forehead.

'Ammi puts sliced almonds in firni and when it cools, she adds rose essence to it!' she said excitedly.

'And that makes all the difference?' Ruqayya asked dubiously.

'Also, firni is eaten cold. Not hot,' Nadira explained.

When the two of them had finished, they covered the firni with a lid and kept it to cool near the window. It was almost dark now.

'Go and get ready, Bhabhi,' Nadira said, wiping her brow with her dupatta.

'Ready?'

'Guests are coming. You have to look like a bride, no? And do you want Bhaiya to see you like this?' she asked, a little shyly.

Ruqayya licked her dry lips and felt dismayed. She had to dress up again? But as she left the warm kitchen, she felt a slight breeze cool the perspiration around her neck. It brought with it the delicate scent of jasmine flowers that her mother-in-law had planted in the courtyard. Ruqayya glanced back at the huge lagan of firni they had just made, at Nadira's plain but friendly face and felt a tiny surge of hope rise inside. She *could* manage this. No. She *would* manage this.

16

OMAR stashed his cycle in its usual corner and called out as he always did to his mother. 'Ammi, I'm home!'

That was when he remembered that he was now married. And it wasn't just Ammi who would be waiting for him. He could feel strange sensations course through his body. He wondered if Ruqayya was angry with him because he hadn't consoled her when she had barged into their room this morning, crying.

But what was he supposed to do? He hadn't seen a woman cry, not even his mother. He may have seen some of the other aunts cry over some things or while remembering long-departed relatives, but he had never been actively included in it. What was a man supposed to do when a woman started crying?

He'd taken the easy way out by escaping outside for breakfast and then leaving for work. But now he regretted his action. He ran his hand through his pomaded hair and stopped short. Maybe she would have forgotten about it. Clearly, Omar did not have any idea about what to expect from a woman.

His mother handed him his towel and spoke, 'Wash up quickly and wear some nice clothes. Guests are coming for dinner and tell your bride to wear all the jewellery. All of it.'

He grimaced as he went into the hamam first and washed up.

He emerged a little later, shaking water drops from his head and rubbing the back of his neck with his towel. To his chagrin, his room was locked.

Feeling a little foolish, he stood outside, aware that many eyes were upon him; he knocked on the door softly. Apparently she hadn't heard. He knocked louder and then felt relieved on hearing the rough sliding of the bolt as the door was opened from inside.

He stepped in and chided himself for feeling nervous. The smoky fragrance of attar gently lifted the air around him and strangely caused his heartbeat to quicken. He saw her sitting on the edge of their bed, wearing a resplendent saree. She was fixing large jhumkis in her ear lobes, wincing as she pushed them inside.

She had not covered her head with her pallu. Omar observed her hair that she had left loose. It was dark and lustrous and the sight of it made his throat go dry. Pretending not to be affected, he walked inside, hung his towel on a hook and made for his cupboard. Aware that she was following his movements, he felt a little shy and also defensive.

'You're not ready yet?' The moment the words were spoken, he realised he shouldn't have said them. Because she just lifted one dark eyebrow eloquently and went back to meticulously wearing her jewellery.

He rummaged in his musty wooden cupboard and pulled out a fresh lungi and shirt. He wore them in quick self-conscious movements. He avoided her gaze as he picked up his comb and stood before the small square mirror on one wall.

A minute later he turned and saw that her back was to him as she swiftly braided her hair and flung it down her back. She stood up and rearranged her saree in silence, wearing the pallu over her head. Without realising, they both spoke at the same time.

'I...' she started.

'You…' said Omar.

She paused, waiting for him to continue and he felt his face flush under her scrutiny. In the past seven days of their marriage, despite the physical intimacy they had shared, he had been aware of an undercurrent…of something stronger between them, and it had intrigued him, drawing him towards her. She was like a heavily scented gift-wrapped package that he was slowly unwrapping. He was fascinated by everything about her, from her quick flashing eyes to her tinkling laugh; he even enjoyed the verbal sparring sessions they had. He was so glad she was not the kind of woman to fall in with his opinions and ideas and have no mind of her own. But this morning's actions had taken him several steps backwards.

'You were upset about something this morning,' he started after clearing his throat.

'Yes,' she said. So she was not going to make it easy for him. He imagined how things would have been if he had asked this question in the morning instead of running away. Sighing deeply, he continued.

'And now? Are you okay now?' he asked. Her lips thinned into a line and he realised he should have asked her what the problem had been.

'I'm okay now.' Her voice sounded distant, like a stranger's. Suddenly he was seized by the urge to make things return to how they were before between them, like how it had been this morning when he woke up to her soft touch on his face.

'You were saying something?' he asked, smiling at her, hoping to soften the sharp edges that had sprung between them.

She looked confused for a moment, shook her head and said, 'Nadira helped me make firni today.'

Oh. Then to his surprise, she sat down on the bed heavily; her face looked downcast. Oh no.

'What happened?' he asked faintly, hoping she wouldn't cry again.

'I don't know how to cook!' she mumbled, looking down into her lap.

'So?' he asked, a little confused.

'So, your mother and aunts think that I'm not normal!' she blurted, her face flushing.

'But you just said you made firni!' he pointed, sitting down beside her. He knew it had been almost too good to last and maybe he was going to be stuck between his wife and his mother like many other helpless men he had seen.

'I...I don't like cooking,' she admitted, forcing the words out as though saying so would make her less of a woman.

He looked at her lowered face and realised that he really didn't care. He hadn't married her so she could cook for him. Food wasn't important to him. Most of the times at least. His mother and Nadira could cook and so could the other aunts in the house.

'Well, I don't really care whether you know how to cook or if you don't like it,' he said. For the first time that evening, he was rewarded by a watery smile.

'Really?'

Bolstered by her smile, he grinned and said, 'Absolutely. I didn't marry you because I wanted a cook!'

He was amazed by the transformation on her face. 'Then why did you marry me?' she asked, a little shy, a little sly as well.

He took one of her hands and saw that it was covered with sparkling rings. He pressed it tightly and felt his heart grow lighter.

'Obviously not because of *your* taste in films,' he teased and got up laughing when she snatched her hand back in indignation.

17

I stared at the screen of my laptop, almost as if staring would help me get some new ideas. These were the times I wished I didn't have to work like everybody else. Wouldn't it be wonderful if I could just spend my time doing what I wanted to do, not what I *had* to do?

I fingered the tray of paper clips idly, conversely wishing that I was not into food-writing but rather a more active form of journalism where I wouldn't have so much time on my hands. I'd be *that* busy. But I loved writing about food and here I was.

My gaze shifted back to the screen and I knew I had to think harder if I had to present some interesting ideas at the meeting later that afternoon or Vera, my editor, would unleash her sarcasm on me once again. But even the thought of Vera's caustic tongue couldn't shake away the feeling of listlessness. Maybe it was the weather.

I angled my head and leaned back on my chair till I could see the floor-length window that graced one side of our office. It had been humid and warm the whole day although inside the airconditioned office, we could hardly sense any changes in weather. However, after lunch it had started raining and the downpour was relentless as it lashed against the building.

'You didn't bring your umbrella again?' Linda asked me as I swivelled back my chair to its original position. I shrugged. I hated carrying umbrellas at any time of the year. If you asked me, you really didn't need one. All the buildings were connected somehow or the other through walkways and there would be one which would inevitably lead to the subway. Of course, I didn't use the subway to reach home, but even so, I have to wait for just five minutes for my bus.

'But it's August. And you know how much it rains in Hong Kong in August,' she said, flipping a pen between her fingers. I shook my head, not really in the mood to talk to her. It wasn't just me. The feeling was prevalent throughout the office; people grouped together in various spots, chatting and gossiping.

It had been a month since I had last met Zubi. Her husband Khaled had made himself absent conspicuously on the two times I met her after that day at her house. On both events he hadn't returned from work and Zubi kept looking at the clock because she had to make dinner for him.

At our last meeting, I sat down with her at her cluttered dining table and watched her look at her son who was watching a Chinese cartoon on TV. It was strange, how our relationship had changed over the months. I hadn't expected much from that first impulsive visit of mine but it had led to a deep and rich collection of memories that were as satisfying as a good meal. But for someone like me, unmarried and free, ambitious and proud, Zubi struck as an oddity. Why it should be the case, I couldn't quite fathom.

I remembered her from my first visit. Hesitant, nervous and stuttering. Not that she was more confident now. But her nervousness had been replaced by a form of anxiety, as though she was belatedly realising that she was sharing too much of herself with me. She wanted to know what I planned to do with all the recordings and notes that I had made but I honestly didn't know myself. A book seemed the most logical answer, a food memoir of sorts, with recipes, but I hadn't told her that yet. What if she decided against meeting me then? I still had so much to learn and understand.

On our last meeting, I looked around her tiny apartment once more, positive that one day I would glean more from her about herself. Then I asked her the question that shook her out of her reverie.

'You do realise that these are your grandparents you're talking about?' I asked.

'What?' she laughed, her complete attention on me once again.

'All these details about their lives and everything…it's fascinating alright. But how did you get to know it all?'.

'My grandmother loved to talk,' Zubi said simply.

My laptop screen blanked out. I flicked my finger across the touchpad lazily and it came alive again. It was the month of Ramadan and Zubi had plainly told me that there was no way she could entertain me during this month.

'But why?' I had asked her. 'If you're not going to be eating anything all day, you'll have more free time right?'

She looked at me as though I were sprouting horns on my head. 'I'll meet you after Eid,' she said with a look of finality on her face. I knew it was pointless to argue further with her.

Maybe that was the reason for my inertia. The fact that I was stumbling around in this quagmire of her life, her parents' and now that of her grandparents', had changed the way I had viewed my own life's ambition. I was fascinated with her stories and her descriptions of food. Until recently, in my mind, I had always bracketed Muslim food as equivalent to something with lots of meat and rice, which was most probably biryani. But Zubi's story had me riveted. There was so much more I was learning about her world that there were times when we were talking, and I would look around, surprised to see that it was 2010 and we were in Hong Kong, not in Vellore or Bangalore.

That was when I wondered if she had any Ramadan stories to share. At times, I felt a bit like a stalker…no, worse – lover, calling her up, asking her to meet me, expecting her to make herself free for me. But this project, call it that if you will, had assumed epic proportions in my head. No one in office knew I was working on this on my own and I wasn't sure that it would be taken too kindly. But I disregarded all the thoughts as I slid my phone towards me and tapped her name to dial her number.

It rang for a few minutes and then I felt the phone vibrate as it was answered.

'Hello,' a deep male voice spoke. Oh shit. This had to be her husband. The man I had seen only once and had a stupid five-minute crush on in the elevator.

'Err…is Zubi there?' I asked, my face flushing as though he could see me.

'Yes, but she's busy right now,' he replied. I knew that he knew it was me and despite the almost six-month connection I had shared with Zubi, he behaved as though he had never heard of me.

'Oh. Could you ask her to call me when she's free?' I asked, feeling my stomach clench and unclench.

'Okay,' he said and without any prelude, disconnected the call. I stared at the phone in my hands for a moment and forced myself to relax and closed my eyes. A vague picture of Zubi formed in my head. She was so pretty but in a very unself-conscious way. Like she'd be surprised if someone complimented her. Next, I thought of her tall and brooding husband. What a catch, I thought, not without any small amount of jealousy. I don't know why, but it irked me that the two of them just didn't seem to fit together in *one* picture. You know what I mean? Like the only thing holding them together in that one single frame was a little boy with dark eyes.

In my entire life, I've never interfered in anything that wasn't my business. But given that my grandmother was a nosy busybody interested in everyone else's life in her neighbourhood back in Mumbai, I felt that I had inherited some of her inquisitiveness. Actually a lot. Why else would I have gone looking for Zubi in the first place?

18

During the first Ramzan after getting married, Ruqayya found herself reluctantly pulled into the busy activities – that had doubled in intensity – at the house.

'If we're not having breakfast or lunch,' Ruqayya wondered, 'then why are we still *cooking* so much?'

The only good thing was that in the mornings, everyone woke up a little late and they entered the kitchen only around two p.m., after Zohr namaz. But once they entered, it was like a web they were caught in, and would be stuck there till the time when the fast is supposed to be broken. Only for around ten minutes would each one of them leave the kitchen to read Asr namaz.

At first Ruqayya stayed away from the kitchen completely. She would just sit in her room, reading the Quran, wondering why time passed so slowly when one didn't have to eat. But because all the women were hovering around the kitchen, her part of the house was so silent that it began to annoy her. Every little thing could set her off these days into moody silences or tearful reminiscing of her mother's house, but she indulged in both only inside her room.

Because iftar was such an elaborate affair that required preparing a number of fried items, cut fruits, sherbet and the ubiquitous rice ganji or porridge, it took quite a bit of time for the women to prepare all of it well before everyone sat down to open the fast at the dastarkhaan.

On the first day when she ventured inside the kitchen to see what was keeping everyone so busy, Ruqayya saw Nadira grinding rice in the chakki for the ganji. She looked up at Ruqayya, pushed aside a tendril of her hair that trailed across her forehead and smiled. Ruqayya smiled back at her but the smile froze on her face when she noticed Shameem Aunty looking at her with a certain amount of animosity. What had she done to *her*?

She noticed that she was chopping onions for the dal vadai that was supposed be had with the ganji.

'Have you finished, Nadira? I have to grind the dal,' she spoke curtly. Nadira merely nodded.

Her mother-in-law had ignored Ruqayya as she stood there and wished she had not made things so awkward for herself. Though she was glad that she wasn't actively involved in cooking, especially since her husband said he didn't quite care whether she did or not, she was beginning to feel a bit guilty.

'Why are you here? Go rest,' her mother-in-law ordered her, without looking up from the tawa where she was browning the moong dal to be used in the ganji.

Ruqayya swallowed a little, and her lips felt parched. A tiny movement in her belly caused her to look down in surprise, and her actions were noticed by her mother-in-law, whose expression changed immediately.

'You felt it?' she asked, her voice down to a whisper. Ruqayya looked up at her shining face and nodded, her heart racing. At four months of pregnancy, she was amazed at the new changes in her body every single day.

'Come, sit,' said her mother-in-law, moving to make place for the girl who didn't know or want to learn how to cook, but would give her a grandson in a few months' time.

Ruqayya sat down gingerly and observed the activities in the kitchen with a surprising amount of interest. Everyone was so busy. She'd love to be doing something too. Since it was Ramzan, she wasn't even listening to film songs on the radio and neither was she reading any of the magazines that Omar brought for her.

To her utmost surprise, she found herself asking her mother-in-law, 'Can I do anything to help?'

Her mother-in-law looked bemused. She looked around as though she were searching for some work that could be given to Ruqayya...which wouldn't be that difficult but it seemed as though everyone was doing everything.

Just then, one of the older aunts, a woman who had been living in this house since the time Ruqayya's mother-in-law had been a new bride, spoke.

'Ask her to make halwa. She can't go wrong with that,' and her face split into a gummy smile.

Ruqayya felt a little frisson of fear inside her. Oh no! Why had she even come to the kitchen? Her mother-in-law felt her tense a little beside her. She seemed to be debating about whether or not the task could be trusted to her and then sighed deeply.

'Ruhi, it's not difficult. I'll tell you what to do and you just have to stir the mixture. Make sure it doesn't stick to the bottom of the vessel. That's all,' her mother-in-law spoke intently. Ruqayya licked her dry lips and nodded. Her mother-in-law's attitude towards her swung between hot and cold, and at the moment, Ruqayya knew she was feeling kindly towards her.

She sat straighter and her lower back ached a little.

'Okay,' she said and watched as her mother-in-law instructed Shameem Aunty to pass the ingredients to her.

She pulled the sugar tin close to her. Shameem Aunty counted eggs from a tray in the cupboard.

'What are we making?' Ruqayya asked hesitantly while her mother-in-law leaned across the space to pull a vessel towards her.

'Andey ka halwa,' she announced and opened the lid of the vessel. Ruqayya peered into it, and saw that it was almost full with the cream that had been skimmed from the top of boiled milk.

'Is this...?' she asked and her mother-in-law nodded.

'Yes, this is khoya. I hope you know what this is at least,' she murmured, the last bit under her breath. Only Shameem Aunty seemed to have heard it, however, and she shook her head slightly.

Refusing to feel intimidated, Ruqayya nodded. 'Yes, I know.'

'Good. Then just mix the eggs, sugar and some of this ghee in the khoya and let it cook.'

'That's it?' Ruqayya asked, unable to believe that making this would be so easy.

'That's it?' mimicked Shameem Aunty softly, before she turned away to mix the batter for the dal vadai.

'No, you have to put this also,' her mother-in-law said, dropping a few cloves, cardamom pods and a couple of cinnamon sticks in Ruqayya's palm. 'And this,' she said her voice lowered, leaning behind her and pulling out an old yellow plastic container with 'Dalda' written on it. Ruqayya's eyes narrowed.

'What's that?' she asked her mother-in-law who put her finger on her lips, as though it was a big secret. Feeling a little thrilled, she looked around and saw that the old aunty who had suggested she make this halwa had nodded off to sleep in her sitting position. Shameem Aunty was facing the other side, and Nadira had left the kitchen. It was almost like her mother-in-law was giving her a secret ingredient and didn't want anyone else to witness it.

Softly and furtively her mother-in-law unscrewed the plastic lid and pulled out some glucose biscuits from it. Ruqayya was disappointed. *This* was the secret ingredient?

Her mother-in-law only smiled and with a combination of miming actions, conveyed to her that she was to crush the biscuits and add them in the halwa mixture. And she had to do it quickly before Shameem Aunty turned.

There was disbelief writ across Ruqayya's face as she crushed the biscuits with both her palms and dropped the crumbs in the khoya. Her mother-in-law stirred the khoya quickly so that the biscuit crumbs would disappear in its rich depths. She then asked Ruqayya to break the eggs in a bowl and then add them to the khoya.

'Why not directly?' Ruqayya asked because this was something she could do. Break an egg.

'And what if even one of them is rotten? Then? The halwa will get ruined, no?' her mother-in-law asked her, shaking her head in wonder at such an elementary question.

Feeling chastened, Ruqayya broke the eggs one by one carefully into a bowl and then when she saw that none of them were tinged with red or were bad in any way, she poured them into the khoya.

'Now sugar,' instructed her mother-in-law. Ruqayya measured out the quantity and put it into the vessel. When everything had been added, she placed the vessel on the kerosene stove and lit it.

'Now your job begins,' said her mother-in-law, moving to get up.

'Wait!' the word slipped out before Ruqayya could think clearly. 'What?'

'I...how will I know that it's ready?' she asked, her voice lowered so that Shameem Aunty couldn't hear her.

'You will know when it is,' her mother-in-law said and walked away. Ruqayya watched her leave, feeling panic grip her again. What if she messed this up? The last time she had actually done anything in the kitchen had been months ago when she made the firni for the first and last time.

That wasn't a disaster, she reminded herself. In fact, one of Omar's uncles who had come for the daawat had assumed that her mother-in-law had made it and had lavished praise on her. Her mother-in-law had been surprised and a little pleased but she didn't clear the misunderstanding that *she* hadn't made it. Only Omar and Ruqayya looked at each other for a fraction of a second and Ruqayya decided to remain quiet.

That time, Nadira had been with her. She wondered if she could call Nadira to just give her company, and of course, tell her when the halwa was ready. But Nadira was in the other end of the house, in her own room, and wouldn't possibly be able to hear her. Everyone else in the vicinity would.

She looked around at the empty kitchen, wondering why everyone else disappeared whenever she was asked to cook something. But it was also a good thing. Imagine doing this with ten people breathing down your neck, she thought.

Stirring the khoya mixture for the halwa was not at all like stirring the firni, which she had done meticulously but in a leisurely sort of way. Here the halwa was already beginning to stick to the bottom and she had to hold one edge of the vessel with a rag and stir the contents furiously. Also, the khoya was beginning to solidify.

'I will never enter the kitchen again,' she whispered to herself, moving the spoon in quick turns until her upper arms ached.

While mulling over those thoughts, she stopped stirring for just a few seconds. The halwa bubbled in distant spurts. What was it that Nadira had said the last time? Everything, the sugar and the khoya especially, seemed to belong to each other. She also had a feeling that the crushed biscuits were responsible for this bonding.

So, was it ready then? She had no idea but decided to remove it from the stove anyway. After placing it on a clean spot, she lowered the wick of the kerosene stove as she'd seen her mother-in-law do, and blew it out.

She turned to her newest creation. Andey ka halwa. Hard to imagine that anything with such an inelegant name could have such a tantalising aroma. Her stomach growled in anticipation but she was fasting, even though she was pregnant.

Her mother-in-law ambled over quietly into the kitchen and leaned towards the halwa. She smiled.

'I told you,' she said, her voice, a rich texture that was half-way gloating and half-way thrilled.

Ruqayya smiled back at her, pleased that she had got it right. 'Don't forget to put nuts in it,' her mother-in-law reminded her, before sitting down in front of the stove to fry the vadais for iftar.

'And don't tell anyone about adding biscuits,' she mumbled as the others started coming in to finish the final preparations.

Ruqayya didn't go back to her room that day. She hung around, cutting apples into slices, peeling oranges and helping Nadira in whatever way she could. Omar came back early from work that day and was surprised to see her sitting in the kitchen, chatting amicably with Nadira and his mother, and his heart felt full.

She looked up to see him standing near the door of the kitchen and she smiled tentatively.

'Bhabhi made andey ka halwa today,' Nadira announced. Omar clutched his chest dramatically and everyone looked at him, shocked.

'You asked *her* to make it?' he asked, mock concern on his face although his eyes were twinkling.

Ruqayya narrowed her eyes at him and lifted an eyebrow in an expression that was all too familiar to him now. It clearly meant, 'Just you wait'.

At iftar, when everyone praised the halwa, Ruqayya sat back in surprised pleasure. She had no idea that cooking something would make her feel so happy. Shameem Aunty gave her a puzzled look.

'Bhabhi,' she addressed Ruqayya's mother-in-law. 'How is it that when I make andey ka halwa, it looks like curdled eggs? How did *she* make it just like you do?'

Her mother-in-law shrugged but Ruqayya noticed that she was trying hard not to smile.

19

The train steamed into Katpadi station and Ruqayya felt a little thrill go down her spine. She was going to meet her parents after nearly six months! Actually, her mother had come to Vellore to visit her when her mother-in-law had written to her, informing her about Ruqayya's pregnancy. But that visit allowed very few moments alone with her mother because she had come bearing so many gifts, boxes of mithai and new clothes for her and Omar that before she knew it, her mother had already gone back.

Her mother had written to her mother-in-law requesting her to send Ruqayya to Madras for her first Eid; but her mother-in-law had been reluctant. She finally relented and agreed to sending both Ruqayya and Omar to Madras but just for four days. Ruqayya had felt mutinous when she heard of these changes in plans and had argued with Omar until he had got annoyed and snapped at her.

'Fine. You stay at *your* mother's house for Eid, and I'll stay at *my* mother's house,' he told her curtly. Ruqayya didn't like the way her mother-in-law manipulated every situation to suit her but she knew that it probably came from years of living as the sole matriarch of the family.

At the moment, however, all resentment was forgotten as she felt excitement surge through her. She was travelling alone with

Omar for the first time since their wedding and that itself promised to be an experience worth remembering.

'Careful!' Omar cautioned her as she placed her foot on the steep stairs that led to the train's compartment.

Later, she sat down on the hard wooden seat next to him and loosened the hold on her chador so that it would slip down her face and she could observe his side profile without him knowing. The wind from the open window ran through his hair and he turned to her. She looked away quickly, wondering why even after six months of marriage, she was sometimes a confusing mass of emotions around him. Good emotions though.

'You know, Ammi didn't want to send you in the first place,' he spoke and felt Ruqayya tense beside him.

'Then she was thinking of sending someone along with us. Most probably Shameem Aunty,' he said slowly, waiting for her reaction, which came just as he had expected.

'Your mother...' she started, letting the chador slip down her face completely.

'...means well. She's just concerned about you and the baby,' he finished, finding her hand under the chador and squeezing it lightly. The baby! It sounded strange on his lips and even now he couldn't quite believe that he was going to be a father.

Ruqayya rested her free hand on her distended belly under the chador and smiled a little dreamily as the baby moved inside, tightening and stretching her skin in ways she had never imagined possible.

The journey to Madras was uneventful. Her father had sent one of her brothers to pick them up from the station, in their car. She sensed that Omar was impressed and despite not wanting to be, he seemed to be feeling a little resentful, as though he thought her parents were showing off.

They were both quiet and thoughtful as they sat back on the shiny seats and watched her brother instruct the driver to turn the crank before he came and sat down in the front seat. Throughout the way, her brother kept up a conversation with Omar, asking him about his work and about life in Vellore. Omar didn't speak much and Ruqayya realised that he wasn't too comfortable with the whole idea of spending a few days at his in-laws' house.

Think about me, she flashed at him mentally. This was a holiday for him, but for her, living in her in-laws' house and getting used to it were two different things. In her house, her parents and her brothers had a joyful reunion and she felt that Omar was feeling left out but she couldn't do anything about it. He went into the room that had been allotted to them and emerged sometime later, ready to go out.

'Where are you going?' she asked him, surprised and a little hurt, for some reason.

'To meet a few friends,' he replied and nodded in the general direction of her father and brothers before heading outside.

Coming back to her mother's house as a married woman was not the same as living there when she hadn't been married, Ruqayya thought. First of all, she wasn't staying in her old room. Her parents had wanted her to stay in one of the larger rooms in the house. Then there was her husband who was staying with them. She was confused because she wanted him with her but at the same time understood that his presence changed everything.

Later that day, her mother was surprised to see her saunter into the kitchen. Her mother was instructing the cooks for the iftar preparations.

'Lost your way, have you?' she asked her warmly. Ruqayya shook her head. She was observing everything carefully and differently now, mentally comparing this kitchen with the one back home. She felt a pang when she realised that she had already started considering that house to be her home now. She realised then that home for her would be whichever place Omar chose to call home.

'So, learnt any cooking yet?' her mother asked the question although she dreaded hearing the answer. She had tried to interest Ruqayya in cooking from the time she was a young girl, but it only took onions to be chopped, for her to run away from the kitchen. She wondered what her mother-in-law thought of this trait and decided she didn't want to know.

'I still hate cooking,' Ruqayya said morosely and her mother sighed. 'But I made firni and andey ka halwa!' she added proudly. Her mother looked up in surprise.

'Really?' she asked, handing Ruqayya a glass of warm milk. Ruqayya refused the milk.

'I'm fasting,' she explained, to which her mother frowned. In this condition? But she didn't say anything because she felt that Ruqayya had changed quite a bit, and it seemed like most of it was for the better.

'How were the desserts?'

'Everyone liked them!' said Ruqayya, and her mother smiled.

'You could make it your speciality then!' she suggested. Ruqayya gave her a puzzled look.

'What do you mean?' she asked her mother, sitting down on one of the chairs.

'See, every household will have a woman who is a specialist at something. So, maybe you could make desserts your speciality,' she explained.

Ruqayya was silent. She had never given a thought as to why her mother-in-law insisted that Shameem Aunty make the khatta baingan or that she herself would make biryani each and every time. Ruqayya didn't want to become like Nadira who helped everyone in every single thing, but would never be considered any sort of specialist.

'But I don't know anything yet,' she voiced her doubts. 'I mean, I've just made those two desserts.'

'Then it's a good thing you came here!' beamed her mother.

'You'll teach me?' Ruqayya asked, her eyes shining. She was thinking of how pleased Omar would be to know that she had found something at last. Something that would earn his praise every single time because he had a sweet tooth.

'As long as you promise not to run away from the kitchen,' said her mother seriously and Ruqayya started laughing.

Omar had not returned even though it was time for iftar in another half hour. Ruqayya was beginning to feel anxious. Where had he gone? And why? This wasn't how she had imagined spending time with him in Madras would be.

When he did come, just about ten minutes were left for iftar. Ruqayya followed him into the room they were sharing. He went into the attached bathroom, and emerged a little later, his face washed and looking bright.

'Where were you?' she asked him uncertainly.

'I told you, right? I went to meet my friends,' he replied before pulling out his crochet topi from his pocket and fitting it over his head.

Iftar in her house was a vastly different affair from what it was in his house and she knew he was noting the differences. For one, Ruqayya's house had a huge dining table where all the family members sat down; and they had servants to serve them. No one came in hurrying with the dishes until the last moment. The atmosphere was relaxed and quiet and Omar noticed that his mother-in-law and Ruqayya weren't sitting with them.

He knew he was being resentful of her wealth for no fault of hers and he appreciated how much she had adjusted since she came to live with them. But it was the acknowledgement of that adjustment that made him more irritable. Still, as they broke the fast, he vowed to stop being so judgmental and prickly. After all, despite the initial hiccups and her refusal to cook, Ruqayya had begun to mingle with his family, as he had wanted her and expected her to do.

Since he was the son-in-law of the house, his in-laws had gone out of their way to create a sumptuous iftar for him. There were mutton chops, two types of bhajji and dal vadai. There was spiced vermicelli, studded with little juicy mince bits and also what seemed like a mound of hot steaming puris, served with semolina halwa.

He surely couldn't eat it all! He protested as his father-in-law piled his plate and refilled his bowl with the ganji.

'No, no! You have to eat!' he said jovially, placing a couple of crispy puris on his plate and a huge dollop of the halwa.

From beyond an alcove of sorts, he could sense the presence of his mother-in-law who stood there and shyly offered the information that Ruqayya had made the halwa. Omar's head whipped up and he looked around to see Ruqayya standing at the entrance of the dining hall. Her brothers reacted just as Omar had done some days back when she had made andey ka halwa.

'No! Why did you ask her to? Should I ask the driver to keep the car ready to take us to the hospital?' Shuaib, her second brother asked.

Ruqayya glowered at him but didn't say anything and simply watched as Omar lifted the golden halwa from the plate with a piece of the puri and brought it to his mouth. He closed his eyes and concentrated on the warm sweetness that contrasted with the piping hot crackly puris. He opened his eyes and saw that

Ruqayya was staring at him intently. It felt a little awkward to see her standing there so he just said, 'Aren't you eating anything?'

She nodded and walked away, feeling disappointed. This had been a relatively easier dessert to make, but still she felt he owed her at least a few words of praise. Her mother had shown her how to delicately roast the semolina in ghee, which was then kept aside. Ruqayya had then heated some more ghee and dropped a pod of cardamom, a couple of cloves and a stick of cinnamon in it. When that sizzled, she added water and then the roasted semolina. They had stood near the stove, watching the semolina bubble and absorb the water and her mother checked if it was cooked. On confirming so, they added sugar and mixed it thoroughly. A generous amount of fried cashewnuts were stirred into it and Ruqayya smiled when she realised that there was indeed something different about making a dessert. Especially the feeling inside.

It wasn't about filling your stomach or satisfying your hunger pangs. That was for the everyday food and salan that anybody could make. A properly prepared dessert, however, lingers in one's memory and teases the taste buds. It can convert any occasion into one of celebration and Ruqayya marvelled at how little she had understood this before.

Now, however, she sat on the bed in her room and looked out of the window, feeling dejected. She didn't know what she had hoped for. Omar walked into the room and saw her sitting on the bed. She didn't turn to look at him.

He sat down beside her, picked up her hand and shook it gently.

'Hmm?' she asked, not wanting to show that she was disappointed because her reaction suddenly seemed childish to her.

'If there's one dessert I absolutely hate, it has to be semolina halwa,' he spoke and she looked up, surprised.

He nodded and continued. 'Ask Ammi. Why do you think she

has never made it all these days? I just don't like it at all!' he smiled.

Ruqayya didn't know if she should be annoyed or mortified. Opting for annoyance, she huffed, 'So why didn't you say anything? No one forced you to eat it!'

Omar shrugged. 'I've decided to change my mind,' he smiled loftily but his smile faltered when he saw that his words hadn't got the reaction he had expected. She was still looking angry.

'What's the matter?' he asked, chiding himself for feeling nervous because of his wife. He was a good eight years older to her and yet she had the ability to make him feel small.

'Well, you could have told me *before*, right?' she asked him, getting up to go to the bathroom.

'But I like it now! I like it the way you made it!' he insisted, spreading his hands out in a helpless gesture.

'Don't give me that rubbish,' she called out from the bathroom as she shut the door. Omar was mystified and bemused. Women!

20

The four days at her mother's house passed in a blur for Ruqayya. Before she knew it, it was time to go back to Vellore. Her mother was tearful and seeing her cry made Ruqayya feel oddly guilty because although she was sad about leaving her, she wasn't moved to tears. In her suitcase, there was a sheaf of papers with recipes written in careful Urdu and she felt a little excited about the prospect of trying them out.

'Don't worry, go on now,' her mother consoled her as they left the house.

'Huh?' Ruqayya was surprised.

'You'll be back in a couple of months' time for the delivery, right?' she asked her, smiling tearfully now. Ruqayya glanced at Omar.

Ruqayya nodded doubtfully. She knew it was customary for women to have their first child at their mother's house. She only wondered what her mother-in-law thought of that custom.

Since barely a few days were left for Eid, her mother had given her a sparkling green sari with pure silver zari work and a set of new clothes for Omar as well. Omar looked hesitant about accepting the gifts, and seemed taken aback when he saw that his mother-in-law had presented Ruqayya with a huge, chunky gold necklace.

On the way back home, both of them stayed silent. Ruqayya

was sitting near the window. She looked out at the verdant green fields and realised that there were conflicting emotions inside her. She realised she had actually missed the noise prevalent at her in-laws' home. But at the same time she knew that she would also miss the various comforts that her mother's house offered.

The mountains whipped past them as the train raced along and Omar pondered over whether he should accept a job in Madras and move there with Ruqayya. His mother could stay back in Vellore with her coterie and of course, there were the talks of getting Nadira married. Omar was not the kind of man who coveted other peoples' possessions but the short stay at Ruqayya's house seemed to have woken him from a stupor. They were not poor by any standards and his father had left them two other houses in Vellore when he had died. It was the income from these houses that had carried them so far until Omar had started earning. But somehow, none of it seemed enough.

Unaware of the turmoil inside Omar's mind, Ruqayya edged a little closer to him, put back her head and slept. Her face was still partially covered with the chador. Omar observed her features, imprinting them on his mind, without being aware of what he was doing. When the train stopped, she was still sleeping and the chador had completely slipped away from her face. Omar had a wry smile on his face as he nudged her gently and woke her up.

'Get up, Dilip Kumar's biggest fan!' he whispered and pulled out their trunk from under their seat. Ruqayya rubbed her eyes, cracked her knuckles and rearranged her chador properly before standing up in the still-vibrating train.

Ruqayya was keen to try out something from her mother's collection of desserts for Eid, but she was a bit wary about approaching her mother-in-law. Her hesitation was also compounded by the fact that her mother-in-law was rarely alone and Ruqayya didn't want to speak to her about this in the presence of the other aunts.

On the day before Eid, there was a lot of frantic running up and down from the terrace from where they were hoping to see the moon. They weren't letting her do any of the running around though and she sat placidly on a straw mat, her gaze fixed on the sky. When Nadira came and sat next to her, Ruqayya pressed her hand gently. Nadira was the closest she ever had to having a sister. It also helped that Nadira looked up to her with a reverence that almost bordered on obeisance.

'Has Ammi decided what dessert she will make for Eid tomorrow?' Ruqayya whispered to her, after noting that there wasn't anyone else on the terrace.

'What's there to decide, Bhabhi? Ammi always makes sewayyan for Eid,' Nadira said, looking surprised.

Ruqayya was disappointed but she tried not to let it show. 'I...I was hoping to try out something I learnt from my mother,' she admitted at last.

'Oh!' Nadira's mouth took on a round shape. 'W-what were you thinking of making?'

Ruqayya bit her lower lip, wondering if she should tell her what she had been thinking.

'Kaddu ka halwa?' she half-stated and half-asked.

Nadira made a face. 'No one likes it at home,' she said. 'But maybe...,' she added quickly, '...maybe they will like it the way you make it.'

Ruqayya pursed her lips. She wanted to do this but at the same time didn't want to bring attention to herself.

She vaguely recalled seeing a long bottle gourd in the kitchen earlier in the day. Her mother had been very amused when she saw that Ruqayya was entranced by the idea of making desserts from seemingly insipid vegetables.

'You mean you can turn carrots, beetroot and even bottle gourd into a delicacy?' Ruqayya had asked her in disbelief.

'Look! There it is! The moon!' Nadira piped up and ran downstairs to tell everyone. Ruqayya muttered the prayer that she had been taught to say whenever the Eid moon was spotted. She then glanced at all the aunts who had come upstairs and her mother-in-law who had trudged up last, clutching her aching knees.

The sounds of 'Eid mubarak' rang up in the air and immediately her mother-in-law started conferring with Shameem Aunty about the menu for the following day.

Ruqayya carefully listened to their plans about how much had to be cooked and what each one of them would do. It seemed that they would be up even before dawn so they could start rolling out and filling samosas with a spicy kheema mixture and then frying them. Breakfast was going to be an elaborate affair with not just the samosas, but rotis and paaya salan and a number of other dishes. There was also the sweet sewayyan that her mother-in-law wanted to make that very night but Shameem Aunty told her they could make that too during the early hours the next day.

Ruqayya knew that now was the moment to tell her mother-in-law that she wanted to make the dessert for Eid but she couldn't bring herself to speak. Not with Shameem Aunty sitting there. One of these days she had to ask someone what it was about her that Shameem Aunty just couldn't stand. She had seemed friendly enough in the beginning.

So she got up quietly with everyone else, her slow movements at odds with her mind that worked rapidly as she wondered what she ought to do. If she gave up now and didn't do anything of her own, she would become like one of the many women in this house. She pitied their subservience to her mother-in-law and although she knew that her mother-in-law was not a bad person, she, Ruqayya, was too much of a free spirit to be shackled by her conventions.

The more she thought about it, the more she understood the dynamics of this house and it almost fascinated her. There had been no such hierarchy in her mother's house. Not that she knew of. Here, right after her mother-in-law was Shameem Aunty and then another aunty and then the old lady who had been living in this house forever. Last of all was Nadira and she herself came even below Nadira because of her reluctance to enter the kitchen.

Later that night, Omar was stretched out beside her sleepily and his hand strayed towards her belly, rubbing light, lazy circles. The baby moved inside but she couldn't concentrate on either the movement or Omar's ministrations which normally would have been enough for her to turn towards him.

'What's the matter?' he asked.

She wondered if she should share her rambling thoughts with him. He would probably laugh. On the other hand, he might not.

So, hesitantly she told him of the recipes her mother had entrusted her with and that she wanted to try out one of them for Eid.

Omar was silent as he pondered over her words. He had been right. The atmosphere in this house was too cloying and if Ruqayya wanted to make something as silly as kaddu ka halwa, she had to think so much and worry about whether her desire would end up upsetting his mother or aunts. But he didn't tell her about the thoughts that he had been having about going and living in Madras.

Instead, he said, 'What's stopping you? You should make what you feel like. It's your home after all.'

Ruqayya sat up slowly, surprise etched on her face.

'What?' he asked, feeling a bit defensive. 'My mother is not a monster.'

'I never said she was,' Ruqayya replied indignantly.

'Then go make your kaddu ka halwa. Who's stopping you?' he asked, turning around to sleep. She thought he was angry but he wasn't.

She got up from the bed and opened the door slowly. Outside it was dark. Despite her various misgivings about comforts in this house, she was thankful they had electricity. Even then, it was something that was used sparingly and she didn't even bother looking for the important-looking switchboard that had been placed on the wall sometime earlier this year, according to Nadira.

She made out dark forms sleeping on straw mats outside their room and wondered which one was Nadira's. She felt extremely excited at the thought that she was doing something which almost seemed illicit.

She clutched her chest when she suddenly saw one of the sleeping figures get up and look at her.

'Bhabhi?' Nadira asked, puzzled. 'Where are you going?'

Hot relief flashed down her body and feeling almost dizzy with it, Ruqayya lifted her finger to her lips and shushed her.

'Can you come with me?' she asked, bending down towards Nadira. Someone stirred nearby and Ruqayya felt wary once again.

'Where?' Nadira asked while getting up.

Together they walked along the dark corridor that led to the kitchen. There was a small open courtyard near the kitchen where the sil-batta and the chakki sat, like fat, solemn guardians, glistening in the faint moonlight.

'What do you want to do? Do you need to go to the toilet? Or do you need some milk? Are you hungry?' Nadira asked. Ruqayya shook her head at her, almost angrily.

'God! How much you talk!' she admonished her and immediately regretted the outburst because Nadira's face fell. The poor thing had been trying to merely help.

'I'm sorry, Nadira. I didn't mean to hurt you,' Ruqayya spoke quickly. 'I really need your help for something. Only you can do it.'

Nadira was immediately mollified. A watery smile formed on her face. 'What help?'

'I can't do this without you. I need you to help me make kaddu ka halwa', Ruqayya spoke softly. Nadira gasped.

'Now? You mean now?' she asked, her voice trembling. 'Ammi...'

'Yes, that's why. I want to make it now itself,' Ruqayya spoke, looking around furtively.

Together they walked inside the kitchen and Ruqayya switched on the light. The bulb that hung from the centre of the kitchen ceiling crackled and glowed and Nadira looked at it, worried. During day time, they always worked by the daylight and towards evening, they always lit the lanterns. Only on rare occasions was the bulb used.

'Okay, what help do you need?' she asked, darting glances at the bulb again. If someone found them out here, there was no saying what would happen.

'First get the ingredients together,' Ruqayya parroted from memory. That was her mother's first rule. No hunting around for things at the last moment.

Nadira brought the bottle gourd to her and Ruqayya instructed her to peel it, cut it into half and remove the pulp from inside. Meanwhile she got the rest of the ingredients ready. Sugar, ghee and the most important of all – khoya.

'Now?' Nadira asked her, looking around, hoping no one would walk inside, demanding to know what they were doing. She wondered why there was so much secrecy to this whole act of making halwa, as though they were doing some nefarious activity like black magic. Shuddering at the thought, she glanced around quickly and uttered a dua to dispel the possible shaitans and jinns that could be roaming around at this time.

Ruqayya handed her a grater; Nadira started grating the bottle gourd quickly. She passed the plate to Ruqayya who had lit the stove and placed a large vessel on it. In the vessel, Ruqayya put the grated bottle gourd and then added the sugar. She stirred and kept referring to the recipe which she had in her hand.

'What do you want me to do now?' Nadira asked her. Ruqayya pointed towards the cashewnuts.

'Chop them up roughly,' she instructed and her gaze went back to the stove. She stirred the mixture perfunctorily, feeling panic edge its way inside her. What if it turns out to be disaster? What if someone walked in now?

'Ya Allah!' Ruqayya murmured a litany in her head when she saw that the sugar had dissolved and the bottle gourd seemed to be shedding copious amounts of water. The whole thing looked like a watery mess to her.

'Here! Stir this!' she told Nadira while she angled the paper towards the bulb to read it clearly.

She took over from Nadira once more, feeling a little relieved. Apparently this was supposed to happen. She lowered the flame and kept stirring until the water dried up. Finally, she added the khoya with a little bit of misgiving. Her mother-in-law had probably kept this aside for the sewayyan, she thought, wondering what she would think of her nocturnal activities.

Ruqayya stirred the khoya into it briskly, and then cooked it for some time, watching the khoya do the mingling act with the grated bottle gourd that seemed to have lost its green colour and emerged as a glistening mass that emitted sugary steam into the air.

'Mmm!' Nadira murmured as she looked into the vessel. 'It smells delicious.'

Ruqayya smiled at her and when the ghee started leaving the sides, as was mentioned in the recipe, she removed the vessel and placed a kadai on the kerosene stove.

She fried the cashewnuts in ghee and then quickly fried a few cardamom pods and a couple of cinnamon sticks as well, and put all of those in the halwa. She layered the glistening halwa with fried nuts and both of them ate a couple of spoonfuls, the hot halwa burning their tongues.

'This is really very tasty!' Nadira whispered to her and Ruqayya nodded happily. Nadira helped her clean up the bit of mess they had made and then switched off the light in the kitchen.

Ruqayya went to sleep, a quivering mass of emotions. The following morning, she would know what her mother-in-law thought of her idea of cooking the halwa in the night.

Morning came, accompanied with a couple of brisk knocks on the door. Ruqayya sat up with a little difficulty. These days she couldn't move about as easily as before.

Nervously she opened the door, but not before covering her head with her pallu. Her mother-in-law stood there.

'Tell Omar to take his bath and go for Fajr namaz. Eid namaz will follow soon after that,' she spoke brusquely.

Ruqayya nodded, feeling relieved and disappointed at the same time. Just as she was shutting the door slowly, her mother-in-law spoke again.

'Ruhi...' She seemed torn between admonishing her for her little stunt last night and ignoring it at the same time.

'Did jinns visit our house last night?' she asked, finally opting for sarcasm.

Ruqayya's thoughts were frantic and jumbled but she took

a deep breath and reordered them in her head before speaking.

'I don't know, Ammi. If you want, I'll find out.'

Her mother-in-law seemed taken aback by her audacity. 'Next time just consult me before doing anything,' she muttered before walking away.

Ruqayya shut the door and leaned against it, her hands on her chest and a smile on her face. Omar was awake and looking at her, puzzled.

'What happened?' he asked as he yawned and got up.

Ruqayya shook her head but couldn't stop smiling for the rest of the day.

21

By the time the summer of 1959 had rolled around, much had changed in the world. But none of it mattered to Ruqayya because she was in a cocoon, the interior of which was a bit like the movies she loved to watch. All soft focus and no sharp edges. If her world seemed hazy, she knew whom to blame. Her three-month-old son, Aslam. She couldn't quite recall the last time she had slept at night and woken up in the morning without getting up in the middle even once.

But there were many other things that she couldn't recall now. Like how blissful life had seemed in those early days of marriage. Or how she had made a big deal about *not* wanting to cook. Somehow, with a squalling infant by her side, everything else had receded.

At first things hadn't been so bad. She had returned to her mother's home for her delivery and everything went smoothly. Even after Aslam was born, he was perfectly well-behaved for almost all the forty days she had stayed there. Of course, it could also be that every time he cried even a little bit, there was someone who would take him away from her, soothe him and bring him back to her only when he was asleep. Unless he was hungry, he was hardly with her so she hadn't known what it would be like to be entirely responsible for a baby.

To Ruqayya's relief, her mother had planned to send a maid along with them to help take care of Aslam. She was beginning to feel a mild sense of panic at leaving her mother's house after being there for nearly two months. Omar would visit them once every two weeks. The two of them had brought this little baby into the world, but strangely, the process had somehow stretched them apart. There was no longer that easy banter between them and somehow, everything seemed to be revolving around the baby. For both of them.

When it was time for her to go back, her mother-in-law had come with Omar and a few of the aunts. Nadira hadn't yet seen the baby and would, only when Ruqayya went back to Vellore.

'Ammi, you should have brought Nadira along with you,' Ruqayya said.

Her mother-in-law turned to her and shook her head but didn't say anything. When it was time for them to leave, her mother-in-law frowned upon seeing the maid getting ready to come along with them. She insisted that they didn't need her.

'My grandson won't be looked after by servants,' she said importantly. 'We have many people in our house to help Ruqayya.'

Ruqayya had looked at her mother helplessly and then at Omar, who seemed slightly bewildered. The moment they stepped on the train, Aslam started crying and everyone looked at her, flustered. Throughout the journey he cried, refusing the bottle that her mother-in-law offered him and even though he was barely two months old, it seemed apparent that he was rather stubborn. When they got off the train at Katpadi, a slight breeze lifted the dust off the ground and as though slightly mollified by it, Aslam calmed down.

But it seemed that he was no longer the quiet infant that he had been at her mother's house. By the time he turned three months old, Ruqayya didn't know why people chose to have babies. She said as much to Omar, who looked shocked. She hated that he slept outside their room now, in another hall. During nights, Aslam's crying kept him from sleeping. Omar didn't want to go to work red-eyed and sleepy. So it had seemed the most logical solution to him.

He was in the room only when he needed to pick up his clothes.

'What do you mean?' he asked, as he slipped his arm into the sleeve of his shirt and turned to do the same on the other side. Ruqayya watched his simple movements with a combination of aches and desires and turned her face away briefly, afraid he would see it.

'Nothing is the same anymore,' she whispered. 'You're not the same anymore.'

'Neither are you,' he replied as he tucked his shirt inside his trousers.

She looked up instantly, her eyes flashing fire as she mentally recounted the pain she had to undergo while giving birth. As if he knew.

How she wished for their easy intimacy of just a few months back. Two months before Aslam was born, she had begun to make her mark in the kitchen as the one to turn to when it came to desserts. Her mother-in-law had started relying on her to make the sweet dish every Friday or Sunday and each time, she had tried out something new. It seemed as though her mother's recipes were fool-proof. She had never slipped up even once. Even when she had made something that no one had ever eaten in this house, like caramel pudding, the desserts turned out perfectly.

Each dessert was a victory for her, one that she guarded in her heart with glee. But it had all changed when her parents had come to take her away for the delivery.

'Yes, I've changed,' she admitted, looking down at Aslam who was sleeping peacefully. Omar came and sat down beside her and she felt gratified when he took her hand in his and squeezed it lightly.

'I can't believe you're not sleeping in this room with us,' she admitted finally. He looked up, surprised and a little embarrassed. 'I mean, *we're* your family. We should be more important to you than your sleep,' she continued, without looking at him. She trailed her finger down the baby's soft cheek.

Omar was quiet and looked thoughtful.

'Did you hear about the proposal that we received for Nadira?' he asked. Ruqayya stiffened. He was avoiding the topic completely! She wished she had the courage to pull him by his collar and do something drastic but she continued stroking Aslam's cheek without looking at him.

Omar cleared his throat and got up. He ran a finger around the back of his collar and continued, as though Ruqayya was interested.

'The boy's family is from Ambur. They came to see her last month when you were still in Madras. I think they have selected her. Ammi was saying that the engagement ceremony might take place next month.'

Ruqayya remained silent and Omar turned on his heels to see her reaction. She wasn't looking at him. He noted the changes in her face absently although they held no meaning for him. Her face had become slightly puffy because of water retention, but his mind could picture the beautiful, glowing girl he had seen when he had lifted her veil on their first night together.

Her body had thickened and it made him uncomfortable to see her feeding the baby. But he didn't know how to express all this to her without making her more angry. He only hoped that in time things would become better between them. There were times when he too wished they hadn't had the baby so soon. Being a parent was very different from being a husband. Maybe if he'd been just a husband for a longer time, becoming a father wouldn't have been so awkward.

'Ammi was telling us that she will need your help for the engagement preparations,' he offered suddenly and it worked. Ruqayya's head shot up.

'My help?' she asked, sceptically.

'Yes. For the engagement we have to send at least ten different types of sweet dishes to the boy's family and she was hoping you would make something.'

Ruqayya felt indignant and pleased at the same time. How was she going to find the time to make desserts when she had to take care of Aslam? But her mother-in-law had specifically mentioned her and that had to mean something.

Omar's mother had said no such thing. She had, in fact, sent for Maryam Bu, an old woman who was connected to them through various cousins and aunts; she was considered an expert when it came to making sweet dishes in huge quantities. If Ruqayya had known the amount of cooking that she would have had to do to make even one sweet dish, she would have probably strangled Omar for looking so pleased with himself.

'When is the engagement?' she asked finally and Omar smiled at her.

'Next month. We'll fix the date soon,' he assured her before leaving the room in a hurry. Ruqayya watched his departing back and swallowed a tightened ball of frustration and hope.

If Ruqayya found it odd that Nadira was the one who spent maximum time with Aslam, she didn't say anything. She was actually relieved to have some time to herself whenever Nadira came and took him outside. At first she was reluctant to give him to her because Nadira had never held a baby before. But there was such longing on her face that Ruqayya couldn't deny her the simple pleasure of holding Aslam's soft, warm body.

One day as Nadira was cooing to him, waiting to take him out, Ruqayya, while changing his clothes, spoke, 'I heard that you will be getting engaged soon. This is great news, Nadira!' Ruqayya hadn't been prepared for the way Nadira's eyes clouded and then blanked out.

'Thank you, Bhabhi,' she said quietly.

'I…You're not happy?' Ruqayya asked and again Nadira looked up surprised. She sat up straighter and adjusted her dupatta over her head, looking uneasy.

'Why? Why are you asking?' her tone seemed almost hostile.

'No…you just…didn't look very happy,' Ruqayya muttered as she wrapped Aslam in a thin shawl and handed him to her, feeling a confusing mixture of emotions inside her.

Nadira was silent. She held Aslam in the crook of her arm as she had been instructed and gently rubbed his forehead with her thumb. His eyes opened and he yawned; Nadira smiled at him, like she never had before and Ruqayya was astonished at the change in her face. She looked radiant.

'Why don't you smile more often, Nadira?' Ruqayya asked, unaware that this question would not make Nadira feel any better. The awkwardness between them increased.

'I…this is the sixth family that has come to see me, Bhabhi,' Nadira spoke and Ruqayya fell silent. Sixth family!

'What happened to the other five?' she asked cautiously when Nadira did not offer any more information.

'They came, they saw and they rejected me.' Nadira's eyes did not meet Ruqayya's.

The words stunned Ruqayya who had lived a sheltered life, one that had not included the showing of girls to families of prospective grooms.

'But...'

Nadira got up swiftly, still holding Aslam and chose to ignore further queries from Ruqayya.

'Bhabhi, can you make tea today?' she asked and left the room before Ruqayya could answer. Sighing, Ruqayya got up and went into the empty kitchen. It was the official naptime at their house and the moment the azaan sounded in the badi masjid outside, everyone would start coming in after they finished reading the Asr namaz. They would want their tea, steaming hot and ready. And they would want their glucose biscuits as well. She had never given a thought to this job that Nadira did every single day. Before her mother had finished reading the namaz, Nadira would have everyone's tea ready on the tray, in their preferred cups or glasses and a plate of glucose biscuits by the side.

Tea, tea, tea, thought Ruqayya frantically as she wondered how Nadira managed it with such efficiency. She vaguely recalled seeing her boiling water, adding tea leaves and sugar and then... she set up the pan, chiding herself for not knowing how to make tea when she was touting herself as the expert in desserts.

And Nadira? Tea was *her* specialty. Everyone wanted Nadira to make tea for them and Ruqayya had never thought that they asked so because they *liked* the tea she made. She had merely assumed that it was because making tea was a mundane job and everyone gave her the most boring jobs as she took them without a word.

As Ruqayya strove to recall who drank in which cup, she felt a hot splash on her hand – the water was boiling. Frantically she dropped the tea leaves and the sugar and watched the colour darken instantly.

Later that day when everyone sat around drinking their tea, an aunt exclaimed as she took a sip, 'Did you put water in the tea or tea in the water?' Her sarcasm was aimed at Nadira who was also having tea.

'If you make tea like this in your in-laws' house...' Shameem Aunty said threateningly as she shook her cup to slosh the tea in it. Most of it spilled onto her saucer. Ruqayya looked at each face, horrified and upset. Nadira looked calm but didn't say that she hadn't made the tea that day. Ruqayya saw her mother-in-law looking grim and she decided to confess that it was she who had made such disgusting watery tea.

'Actually, I made the tea today,' she announced tremulously and all the attention was diverted to her. They stared at her for a few seconds and went back to sipping tea as if nothing had happened. Her mother-in-law started discussing the menu for the evening with Shameem Aunty and everyone behaved as though she hadn't spoken at all.

She was baffled. She had been quailing at the sarcasm and criticism that would emerge from Shameem Aunty or her mother-in-law but no one said anything.

As people continued doing their chores and Nadira picked up the dirty cups to wash them, Ruqayya felt ashamed momentarily. The moment stretched and expanded until she got up and ran to her room where Aslam was sleeping. Nadira was no fool. A simple move on her part had shown her that she, Nadira, had a place in this house, even though it was transient. While Ruqayya, despite having the more important position of daughter-in-law, especially one who had recently gifted a baby to the family, was really no one. Even now.

22

If I hadn't been surfing the Internet aimlessly that Thursday, I wouldn't have caught the new video. But we were having a slow day in office and that often meant that we were glad that the Internet speed was fast.

I had been researching some generic food terms in Urdu, so technically I was working. Although not for the magazine. My heart did a little flip-flop when I saw the video and just like all those months ago, I felt my mouth dry up. Only now, there was anxiety coupled with excitement. And I was ashamed to admit, jealousy as well. Why was she doing this? Hadn't she promised me that she would tell her story to *me*? Actually, there had been no promise, written or verbal, and now I realised my foolishness.

Had someone else got to her? I pulled out the headset from my desk drawer and slipped it on, looking around surreptitiously as I hit the play button. No one was bothered about what I was doing, although Linda winked at me and continued with whatever she had been busy with.

Thankfully the video lasted for only six minutes and I breathed a sigh of relief when it got over. I checked the number of views that the video had; there were hardly any. Another cause for relief. But for how long?

I reached out for my phone and called her, my eyes still focused on the last image in the video. Sighing deeply, I waited for her to answer. A new thought came into my head. What if she doesn't speak to me? What if she's trying to avoid me? I couldn't stalk her and force her to meet me. But there was still so much to know.

We had met the day after Eid, just a couple of weeks back and she had given no indication whatsoever that she was planning this. In fact, I had been surprised and pleased when she called me for Eid at her house.

'Come, Sonia. It's just the three of us and some neighbours from our building. I'm doing a lot of cooking today. I thought you would like to watch.'

I thought it was sweet of her but I was covering the opening of a new restaurant and although I could have passed on the job to someone else, I didn't. It wasn't that I had lost interest. Far from it actually. But with so many people in her tiny house, I wouldn't be able to talk to her. To listen to her talk I mean.

So I visited them the next day and she served me the most delicious leftovers I had ever eaten. I made it a point to go when her husband wouldn't be at home. No, no, it wasn't because of the silly five-minute attraction. It was because I felt she didn't open up enough in his presence. She was subdued and looked a little lost. Also, new ideas were shaping in my head about her story and I was scared that they would evaporate if I didn't act upon them soon enough.

'Your grandmother's story is amazing,' I said, as I leaned back on the sofa and settled myself comfortably. 'But…I feel she had things too easy. I mean, everything eventually fell in place for her, right?'

Zubi rubbed her temple absently and a strand of hair fell across her face. She looked younger and somehow vulnerable.

'How old are you?' I asked her.

'Twenty-eight,' she responded, surprised.

'Oh! Same as me then!' I exclaimed. Funny, but we'd been meeting for so many months and we had never bothered to find out each other's age.

'I thought you'd be older,' she said, a mischievous smile on her face when she saw me narrow my eyes.

'Unfortunately, I can't say the same for you,' I offered, after a brief moment of deliberation when I wondered whether I could tell her the truth. 'I thought you were probably twenty-four.'

'No!' Zubi seemed inordinately pleased. It was a universal feeling in all women I suppose, to be happy when considered younger than they are.

'How long have you been married?' I asked her casually and noticed that she tucked the strand of her hair repeatedly even though it no longer bothered her.

'Six years,' she replied and my lips parted in amazement. Six years of living with that deliciously brooding husband of hers and she looked like she was serving a life sentence.

'Aren't you happy with him?' I asked her before I could stop myself. The change that came over her was so rapid that I quite believe I imagined it. Knowing Zubi and her propensity for avoiding topics that she didn't want to talk about, I was mildly bemused when she got up quickly as though she had forgotten something.

'How could I have forgotten!' she exclaimed as she came back, her face excited and yet slightly closed, as if to say, 'please don't ask that question again'. I decided to let her be for now. She was carrying, a plastic box, the kind that people in India usually stored sev and mixture and other such savoury items in.

She prised the lid open and handed the box to me.

I could smell the sugar even before I saw what was inside. 'What...' I was too surprised to speak.

'Some people came from India just before Eid and this came from my house,' she explained.

'Your mother made it?' I asked, peering inside the box.

'No. My grandmother did.' I pulled out one piece. It was a fluted round, like a cookie, but it crumbled in my hand when I picked it up.

'Your grandmother! She can still make all this stuff?' I asked her, sniffing the sweet delicately.

'Oh yes. Eat it!' she urged. I leaned forward and took a bite. It was like sugary sunshine that melted on my tongue. Little crumbly sugar-coated bits that dissolved slowly and I felt myself light up from inside.

'Oh my God! What *is* this?' I asked her, taking another bite.

'One of my grandmother's specialties. It's called lauz,' she explained.

My mouth was on a mission of its own. Leave me alone, it said. Don't talk. Just continue eating this.

I watched the phone ring with trepidation and when she didn't answer, I hit the end button, worry beginning to gnaw my insides slowly and surely. I couldn't concentrate on anything now. Even though there wasn't any work yet, I wanted to leave immediately.

Would Vera be pissed if she found that I took a half-day leave today? Vera was always pissed though. She had never intended to become the editor of a food magazine. It seemed as though she had put herself through a projectile, hoping to land in some glamorous fashion magazine, but had instead ended up here.

I glanced in the general direction of her office and wondered if I should call Zubi again. But I didn't. Instead, I got up, gathered my things that were strewn on the work station and dumped them in my bag.

Peter Wang, one of the photographers on the team looked up. 'Going somewhere? Need me to come along?' he asked, looking hopeful. I shook my head.

'Then?' Linda asked, and I wished she would stop being so pushy.

'I have some personal work. Have to be back home early,' I replied and strode out before anyone else could stop me. Half-an-hour later, I stood staring at Zubi's door, hesitating to ring the doorbell.

What if...but before the thought formulated, I stepped back in shock when the door opened from inside. Zubi's husband Khaled was stepping out and he stopped in surprise when he saw me.

'Hi!' I volunteered. Khaled nodded.

'Zubi's in? Can I go and meet her?' I asked, feeling stupid for asking his permission.

He looked at me squarely and then nodded again. God. It was like I had never heard him speak. Oh, I had. On the phone the other day. But still!

I had a feeling I knew why Zubi was avoiding me. I had asked her prying questions about her own life and she wasn't prepared to talk about that.

'Thanks for nothing,' I muttered as I watched him stride away in the direction of the lift. I shut the door behind me and Zubi called out from the kitchen, thinking it was her husband.

'Did you forget to take something?'

When I didn't answer, she stepped out, looking more domestic than I had ever seen her. Her pallu was tucked inside a corner of her waist and her hair was pulled back tightly into a bun. Her eyes were streaming because she had been chopping onions.

'Oh. You!' she spoke and I knew for sure that she had been avoiding me.

'No more personal questions!' I said quickly and she looked puzzled. 'Just don't start avoiding me!'

Zubi stared at me for some time, shut her eyes as though doing some internal calculations and then nodded.

'Great!' I said as I dropped my handbag on the dining table. It fell there with a thump.

'What are you making?' I asked her, walking towards the kitchen.

'Lunch,' she said without offering any details. Whatever it was, it smelt homely and yet divine.

'Zubi, I need to know if you have any more of that lauz stashed away. I can't think of anything else but eating it,' I admitted.

She looked at me for some time before her face broke into a smile and then she nodded.

'Just one left!' She pulled out the plastic box from under the kitchen cabinet.

'One!' I asked, outraged.

'Yes. Both my husband and son love it.'

I took the last piece of the sugary heaven-on-earth and bit into it gently, catching the crumbs with my other hand.

'How? Tell me how your grandmother makes this!' I said, a while later, my mouth complaining about how little it had received.

Zubi stirred the contents of a pressure cooker with a wooden spoon and shook her head smiling.

'You want the recipe or the story?' she asked.

'Both.' I was feeling immensely greedy.

23

One night in the month of May, Ruqayya went to sleep as usual with Aslam by her side. She missed Omar. Some elementary change had happened inside her and now she didn't even ask him to come back to their room. Her world now revolved only around Aslam and she could sense Omar going further and further away from her until last week, when he told her that he was going to work in Madras. He had found a job there and once he had settled down a bit, he would come and take Ruqayya and Aslam with him.

Ruqayya didn't understand at first. 'But what about the others?' she had asked him.

'What others?' he asked her, looking puzzled. Once upon a time he had to merely say one word and she would understand what he was referring to, even in the very early days of their marriage. Now, however, the two of them had grown apart, unwound from each other like the threads of a frayed string.

'Your mother and Nadira and...' Ruqayya spoke, searching his beloved face for answers. What had happened to their easygoing relationship? Why this uneasiness between them? Much as she loved Aslam now, sometimes she wished that he hadn't been born. Her life had been different and infinitely better before.

'Oh they will be here. In fact, I am going tomorrow,' he announced. Ruqayya looked up, feeling shocked and angry.

'And you're telling me *now*? When are you going to come back?' she asked through clenched teeth.

'I'll come just a few days before Nadira's engagement. The pay is good, Ruqayya,' he said, almost pleading with her to understand. But she didn't want to understand and she hated it when he called her by her name. Why didn't he call her Ruhi anymore?

'But Nadira's engagement is in two weeks. Why can't you go after it?'

'Yes, I know. But I have to start working from tomorrow or they won't take me.'

She didn't say anything but watched in silence as he dragged out a large suitcase from the top of the cupboard, dusted it and packed it with his clothes. The next day he was gone.

A week later, Ruqayya woke up to see that the house was packed with people and there was too much going on. None of it made sense to her. Would someone tell her what was happening? She hated being treated like an outsider even now, a year into her marriage.

Leaving Aslam sleeping on the bed, she went outside to investigate. In the kitchen, her mother-in-law was issuing orders to everyone; her voice was tinged with anger and anxiety.

'What happened?' she whispered to Nadira who looked scared of her mother as she flipped rotis on the tawa.

'Maryam Bu was supposed to come and make all the sweets for my engagement but...something has happened...' Nadira stretched out her neck in the general direction of her mother who was yelling at someone. '...I think she fell down and broke her hip, so she can't come. And now Ammi has to make everything at home.'

Ruqayya bit her lower lip. 'I can help,' she offered tremulously. Nadira smiled at her and shook her head. Ruqayya remembered Omar mentioning that his mother wanted her help. But since then, her confidence had taken a hit and she wasn't sure whether she could approach her mother-in-law and offer help.

Nevertheless, she lingered in the kitchen, listening to the fascinating talk about gajar ka halwa, jamun, dum ka roat and some new desserts that she had never heard of. She rolled the words around in her tongue soundlessly, testing their newness and admiring their strangeness. Lauz, rangeen lauz, badam ki jaali.

Suddenly her mother-in-law clapped her hands and everyone fell silent. Ruqayya had heard about Hitler on radio and from her parents. She had seen his grainy black-and-white photograph in a magazine and found him so funny looking that she laughed and laughed until her father told her that he had killed so many people and he was not a funny man. Her mother-in-law was not a funny woman either.

'Nadira's engagement is to take place next Sunday. By Saturday we have to finish making all these sweets. But if we start making them now, they will get spoilt. We have to start making the dry sweets on Thursday and the others on Saturday.' Ruqayya felt as though her mother-in-law was speaking into a mike.

'There are a lot of preparations to do,' she announced and spoke some more, allotting work to everyone except Nadira and Ruqayya.

Ruqayya felt her heart sink rapidly. This was the first time since Aslam's birth that she had become excited about anything. Why were they isolating her from that too?

'I'd like to help, Ammi,' she interrupted her mother-in-law before she lost the nerve. Her mother-in-law halted the stream of words and instructions and looked at her impatiently.

'Fine. You can assist Shameem,' she said. Ruqayya groaned inwardly. But there was nothing she could do. She glanced at Shameem Aunty who was staring into space as though it made no difference to her.

Three days later, just as she had suspected, Shameem Aunty left her with the most boring and mundane job of making khoya out of milk.

'Keep stirring. Make sure nothing gets stuck to the bottom of the pot and only when you have proper khoya, call me,' she said before walking away. Ruqayya watched her leave with misgiving. This wasn't what she had expected when she offered to help. Sweat pooled at the base of her neck and trickled steadily down her blouse, spreading wet patches everywhere. It was mid-May and very, very hot, and she had just had lunch, so she was feeling drowsy as well. Also, since they were reducing such huge quantities of milk, they were doing it on the wooden stove, and sparks blew from it every now and then, making her jump back in fright each time.

At one point when Aslam started crying, she called out to Nadira anxiously, asking her to stir while she fed him. By the time she returned, Shameem Aunty was back in the kitchen, looking at Nadira critically. What was this power that Shameem Aunty held over Nadira and her mother-in-law? She had to find out one day.

'I thought I told *you* to watch over the khoya,' she spoke to Ruqayya sharply when she saw her enter the kitchen.

'Yes, but I had to go because Aslam was crying,' Ruqayya replied, worrying if the khoya had been ruined.

'You should have called *me*,' Shameem Aunty insisted and stirred the khoya vigorously. The milk had now reduced completely and was at the bottom of the pot that Shameem Aunty scraped gently. She removed the pot from the fire and when the khoya had cooled down considerably, she measured it into another pot using a large cup. Ruqayya watched her apprehensively, wondering what she was doing. It was pointless to ask her.

'Are you going to just watch me or help me?' she asked, looking up at Ruqayya, whose face flushed.

'Tell me what to do,' said Ruqayya uncertainly. She was sure whatever Shameem Aunty was making, it would be terrible. She was doing it with such bad grace.

'Powder this,' she ordered, after measuring sugar into a thali and handing it to her.

Ruqayya was almost about to ask her 'how' but stopped herself in time. She walked outside to the little courtyard where the silbatta and the chakki were kept. She remembered wondering why her mother-in-law had made one of the aunts wash both vigorously with soap and hot water and kept them out to dry in the sun.

Nadira followed her and together, they made fine powder out of the sugar. The sun was no longer at its peak but Ruqayya was glad that Nadira was around, giving her company. A sudden thought occurred to her.

'What will I do after you get married?' she asked Nadira, who looked up. She had been scooping the powdered sugar into a dry plate that had been covered with paper.

'Meaning?' Nadira asked, her brow furrowing.

'You're the only person here who cares about me,' Ruqayya explained. 'You help me so much and I couldn't have managed anything without you.'

Nadira's face broke into a smile and she looked away shyly. 'You're very nice, Bhabhi.'

Actually I'm not, thought Ruqayya. I'm not half as nice as you are.

'And Bhaiya cares about you,' Nadira defended her brother gently.

Does he now? Ruqayya thought bitterly. But they were nearing the end of the job. Ruqayya quickly glanced at the kitchen where Shameem Aunty seemed busy with something else.

'Tell me. Why does she hate me so much?' Ruqayya asked. Nadira's face turned red and she shook her head.

'She was nice only on the very first day she spoke to me. After that…' Ruqayya's voice trailed away. Now was not the time to dig for information from Nadira.

Nadira looked scared and her eyes had become round. She looked around almost fearfully and Ruqayya supressed an urge to roll her eyes. Surely Nadira was over-reacting.

'Because…because she was hoping to get me married to him,' Nadira spoke and Ruqayya felt a thud inside her chest. What? WHAT?

'But he's your brother!!! What is wrong with that woman?' Ruqayya spoke in a fierce whisper and Nadira shook her head miserably.

'I am not his sister. Ammi adopted me. I am…her daughter,' Nadira said, indicating towards the kitchen with her head.

Heat rushed to Ruqayya's face as many things began to make sense and mental locks clicked into place. Nadira's plain features compared to Omar's handsome face. The way people treated Nadira in the house…almost like a servant, and the way Shameem Aunty constantly bullied her around. At the same time, a lot was still unclear.

'But if Ammi adopted you, then you *are* his sister,' Ruqayya spoke a little loudly.

'Yes, I know,' a tear ran down Nadira's face.

'After Omar Bhaiya was born, Abba died. Ammi had wanted a daughter and…and *she* had one too many. So she gave me to Ammi to take care of. Then one day, her husband got married to another woman because she wasn't able to bear him a son, and the new wife kicked her out. The other daughters continued to stay there. So she came and asked if she could live here.'

Ruqayya listened to the story with rapt attention. God! It was like something from a movie.

'But she must have seen that you and Omar were like siblings. So why did she get this insane idea to get you *married* to him?'

'I always knew that I was not Ammi's daughter. But Ammi had treated me well until she came along. She told Ammi that now that she was here in this house, I had two mothers and she needn't worry too much about me. After that Ammi got busy with other things and started neglecting me.'

Ruqayya listened in grim silence. 'When did she come to live here?'

'Four years ago. I was fourteen then. She came and started telling me things like how wonderful it would be if I could get married to…to…' Nadira couldn't complete the sentence. It seemed to choke her. Ruqayya looked towards the kitchen, now scared for Nadira.

'Okay, stop. Stop. Tell me later,' Ruqayya whispered but it seemed that Nadira couldn't stop herself now that she had started.

'She kept telling me that I should make myself eligible for him and I should learn to read and write. I told her it was not possible. He was like my brother. He *is* my brother.'

Ruqayya tucked a strand of hair behind her ear and felt anxious and wretched for some reason.

'Did Ammi know of her plan?'

'No. But she kept telling me that I should be ready for it because she would convince Ammi that it was a good plan and I…I wanted to kill myself. She was planning to speak to Ammi but one day Ammi announced that she had heard about you because you were educated. And then she went to see you and then the rest happened.

'Ammi found this proposal for me and even though she doesn't love me like she loves Bhaiya, she's taking care of all my wedding expenses,' Ruqayya murmured. 'If Ammi ever found out what plans she had, then...'

Ruqayya listened in silence, feeling uneasy. Her back prickled.

'Have you two finished talking?' Shameem Aunty's soft voice startled them both because she was standing outside the kitchen. Nadira almost gasped in shock but Ruqayya calmed herself. She had kept a constant lookout and was sure that Shameem Aunty had come and stood at the door of the kitchen just now. She couldn't have heard them speak.

'How long does it take to powder sugar?' she asked again, shaking her head as she took the powdered sugar from them.

Ruqayya followed her into the kitchen while Nadira stayed away. Good thing too, thought Ruqayya, because she needed to compose herself.

In a large pot, Shameem Aunty mixed the khoya and the powdered sugar and put it on the wooden stove to cook. She and Ruqayya stirred it in turns. After a while Ruqayya's arms started aching with the effort of moving the thick viscous liquid, round and round in the pot. The khoya and sugar had melted into each other and the result was a deep golden-coloured confection that bubbled endlessly even as they stirred it. Ruqayya was sure she would faint from the sugary steam but she kept her mind focused on the pot, trying not to think of Shameem Aunty as a devious and scheming woman. If she went down that path, she wouldn't be able to stand there for even a moment.

After some time, Shameem Aunty lifted some of the thickening mixture on the spoon, dropped it on a plate and rolled it briskly with her fingers. It came together effortlessly and became a round sticky ball.

'Okay, it's done,' she announced and together they removed the pot from the fire. Shameem Aunty stirred it further to cool it and then divided the mixture onto four large plates. She handed one to Ruqayya and asked her to keep stirring its contents back and forth with a spoon.

Ruqayya did as she was told to and watched with surprise as the molten gold turned a deeper colour and became like dough. At the end, they had four large balls of sweet sticky dough.

'I think I could eat my hands!' Ruqayya announced, forgetting that she was with Shameem Aunty, who grunted in response. They then carried the prepared dough to the hall where everyone was getting up after their naps.

Ruqayya was thankful they didn't do the rest of the work in the kitchen. A lot of noise and confusion followed as all the women sat down to help. Her mother-in-law brought out extra rolling pins that were dusted generously with powdered sugar. The women tore out sheets of old calendars and sprinkled powdered sugar on those too.

So much sugar, thought Ruqayya, feeling a little afraid to inhale deeply. She could taste the sugar at the back of her throat.

'Have you tasted it yet?' her mother-in-law asked her. Ruqayya shook her head.

'Why not? You should have tried some. Omar loves to eat it *before* we cut it out into shapes.' She pulled out a small piece from the dough and handed it to Ruqayya who was doubtful but took it nevertheless. It seemed excessively sugary to her but she put it in her mouth.

It dissolved little by little in grainy molecules and by the time Ruqayya was done with it, she knew she was a convert.

'The theory behind lauz is simple,' her mother-in-law explained, laughing at the way Ruqayya looked at the rest of the dough. 'But you now know yourself how much hard work goes into making it.'

A muscle in her upper arm throbbed as though in response. Over the next hour, Ruqayya watched all the women pull out small balls of the lauz dough and roll it over powdered sugar before rolling it out into flat elongated chapati-like shapes from which they cut out small fluted rounds using aluminium cutters. One by one these were arranged on the sugar-dusted calendar sheets and by evening, there were neatly arranged columns of lauz everywhere.

'Once they dry out completely, we shall pack them in order to guard them from ants,' said her mother-in-law.

'Wow. This is a lot of work,' Ruqayya exclaimed. She thought about her own engagement…her mother had made a few sweet dishes at home but ordered everything else from mithai shops.

'Oh this is nothing,' her mother-in-law assured her. 'We have to do this again tomorrow, not once, but three times.'

'What?' Ruqayya asked, shocked.

'We're planning on making rangeen lauz too. For that we need to cook almond and cashew paste with powdered sugar for the white layer, pista paste and powdered sugar for the green and this same khoya and sugar for the yellow.' Her mother-in-law got up and dusted her saree and her hands. It seemed like everything was covered in sugar.

'Nadira! Come and sweep this section of the house, or tonight the ants will come and make a nice meal of us,' she shouted.

Ruqayya's thoughts went back to the conversation she had had with Nadira earlier and in a way, she was glad Omar wasn't here. Even though they were hardly communicating, she wouldn't have been able to stop herself from telling all this to him.

24

In the kitchen, the events of the previous day were repeated many times over. Some time in the afternoon, Omar returned from Madras, looking slightly on edge. He walked into his room to speak to Ruqayya, just to see her, because he'd had no idea he would miss her so much. But she wasn't there. Even the wooden jhoola in which Aslam slept was missing. He looked around; then, feeling a minor burst of annoyance, rummaged through his cupboard, found his towel and clean, fresh clothes and headed out towards the hamam to bathe.

Nadira had opened the door for him and she looked subdued as usual but there was an element of fear in her eyes too. He wished their relationship had been easier and simpler like it had been when they were children. She had followed him around blindly and although it annoyed him at times, he got used to having a little sister of his own. He didn't know when the equation between them changed but felt it had happened when Shameem Aunty came to live with them.

'Nadira! Where's everyone?' he called out as he rubbed the back of his neck.

'Bhaiya, they are all in the kitchen,' she replied before walking away in the same direction.

A little while later, feeling refreshed and much more comfortable, Omar sat wearing a lungi and a vest and sipped a glass of tea that Nadira had got for him. He watched the women as they laboured over something in the kitchen. He was surprised to see that Ruqayya was completely absorbed in stirring something over the wooden fire and had not even noticed that he was back from Madras. She pushed a strand of hair behind her ear and wiped the sweat on her neck with her pallu before she returned to stirring.

Finally, his mother came and sat down next to him at the edge of the courtyard. She followed his gaze and smiled.

'Your wife is very keen on helping when it comes to sweets and desserts,' she stated but Omar kept quiet. He was working out things in his head – life in Vellore and life in Madras. It seemed that he would have to take Ruqayya soon because wherever he was, life without her didn't seem good enough. It seemed like a flashback to the time when she was living with her parents when Aslam had been born and he couldn't wait for the weekends so he could be with her.

Ruqayya had seen him but instead of smiling at him, she went back to her stirring and looked busy.

'Where's Aslam?' Omar asked.

'Right behind you,' his mother said. Omar turned around to see that Aslam was in the wooden jhoola, waving his tiny arms and legs. In the five months since Aslam was born, Omar had never felt a strong connection between him and his son. He had hoped that the moment he would see his son, the feeling of becoming a father would be ignited inside him. But it hadn't. He was still the same. But Ruqayya had changed because she seemed to have adapted to the role of a mother more easily. He realised that he resented her bond with the baby because it felt as though the two of them had undertaken a journey together and she had travelled ahead of him, while he straggled behind.

He picked up the baby as he had seen Ruqayya do numerous times with such ease and held him in the air. Aslam's chubby legs waved in the air and he smiled at Omar, a happy and gummy smile. Omar held him that way for a while and forced himself to feel proud or happy or whatever it was that parents were supposed to feel. But there was a sense of detachment and this made him feel frustrated.

He handed the baby to his mother who cooed to him and baby talked effortlessly. This made Aslam more excited and he started babbling. Omar watched the two of them and with a sense of foreboding told his mother that he planned to move to Madras for a few years with his wife and son.

His mother looked at him distraught. 'But...we just got a baby in the house. Why do you want to take him away from us?' she asked, angling Aslam's body against her shoulder and patting him to sleep.

'It's not that. This is the time when I can earn money and make something out of myself. Let me do it now, when he is small. We'll visit often and you can also visit us there.' His mother nodded but Omar knew that she was not happy. Unfortunately, there didn't seem a way by which everyone could be kept happy.

'What are they making?' he asked in an attempt to divert his mother's attention.

'We made lauz yesterday and today we're making rangeen lauz,' she said. 'And jaali,' she added.

Omar raised his eyebrows in silent appreciation. But when was Ruqayya going to be free? He ate his lunch near the kitchen, keeping a lookout for Ruqayya who had finished stirring the contents of the pot but was now doing something else equally laborious. To him, it seemed as though Ruqayya was doing all the work and that everyone else was just lazing around. His mind was unable to grasp the fact that everyone else was also just as busy as her but only Ruqayya stood out in stark relief. Everybody else faded into the background.

With an increasing feeling of annoyance, he watched her as she made large balls of the lauz dough. Right next to her, Shameem Aunty was doing the same thing with green-coloured dough. This was made with a paste of pistachios and cooked with sugar, just like lauz. When the women had finished, they emerged from the kitchen holding the lauz dough in huge plates. Shameem Aunty smiled when she saw him. She broke a piece of the green dough in her hand and brought it near his mouth. Awkwardly he took it from her and ate it, his mind unable to register the sweetness because Ruqayya was coming out now.

She looked at him but didn't smile and merely nodded as she made her way to the hall where the women would be rolling out the lauz in three layers.

His irritation levels heightened considerably as he watched her leave and then realised that there was no one in the kitchen. He felt foolish sitting out there alone and he, too, followed the women to the hall where they sat down and dusted rolling pins with powdered sugar.

Ruqayya was asking his mother questions about rangeen lauz and Omar swallowed a sudden surge of anger that made its way into his stomach, making him feel hot and uncomfortable. Was she deliberately ignoring and avoiding him? This hadn't been how he'd imagined their reunion to be. Things had changed between them but they both had to work to bring back the excitement that marked the initial months of their marriage.

He lingered on the periphery and watched the women roll

out the lauz on paper dusted generously with powdered sugar. His mother rolled out an almost perfect square, dabbed a little water on it and placed a square of white lauz on it. They repeated this with the square of green and then finished with another regular lauz square. His mother pressed all layers gently and then quickly and efficiently started cutting the rangeen lauz into diamond shapes.

Watching his mother diluted some of his anger. This was pure nostalgia, especially waiting for the scraps of lauz that couldn't possibly be rolled back into the original dough as they had different colours mixed in them. His mother, however, had become more adroit over the years and cut the shapes in such a way that there was minimal wastage.

'Ruqayya!' his mother called out. 'There's still one last thing left to make before tomorrow. Dum ka roat.' She handed a plate of soaked badams to Ruqayya.

'Remove the skins and grind them into a paste…and do it quickly,' she said. Omar felt flushed with impatience. He went inside his room to wait for her.

Now? Ruqayya groaned. She was already tired from all that stirring this morning and although her heartbeat had quickened considerably when she had spotted Omar sitting with his mother outside the kitchen, she hadn't spoken to him. She'd been hoping she could go to her room after dinner.

'I've already soaked the suji in milk. We're just waiting for the badam now,' Omar's mother informed Ruqayya, who sighed and got up.

Ruqayya sat down cross-legged and started popping the skins of the almonds, which she then kept on a plate. Nadira helped her and together they finished the entire lot in ten minutes.

'You stay here. I'll go make the paste and give it to Ammi,' Ruqayya told Nadira when she got up to go to the chakki. She glanced back at her room and then quickly walked towards the courtyard where she sat down, made a paste of the badam, transferred it into a bowl and gave it to her mother-in-law.

Her mother-in-law mixed the ground badam, the soaked suji, a few large dollops of ghee, sugar, khoya and a generous pinch of saffron and stirred them together for a few minutes.

'Did you get the banana leaves?' she asked Shameem Aunty who nodded and handed a few cleaned banana leaves to her. She arranged the leaves at the bottom of a large metal tray and then poured the dum ka roat mixture on it. She covered it with a lid and then placed it on the fire stove with a few burning coals on top.

'Why banana leaves?' Ruqayya asked, a little curious.

'So that it doesn't stick to the bottom of the pan,' her mother-in-law said, without looking up.

'And that's it? No stirring?' Ruqayya was relieved.

'Why? You liked stirring khoya?' her mother-in-law asked as she got up.

'No, no! I just asked,' she said, wondering if she, too, could leave but her hopes were dashed when her mother-in-law asked her to watch over it.

'The top should get slightly burnt,' she said and Ruqayya nodded, her shoulders drooping. It took nearly an hour for that to happen after which her mother-in-law came back to check if it was done.

'Good,' she murmured as she lifted the lid and inhaled. Ruqayya's fatigue and irritation were dispelled momentarily by the wholesome aroma that emanated from the pan. While the sweetness was slightly cloying, it also released a wave of nostalgia inside her. For some reason, she couldn't quite understand why she was feeling that way.

Her mother-in-law took a knife and used it to gently scrape along the sides of the tray. She then cut a small piece for Ruqayya, watching her reactions avidly. Ruqayya ignored the throbbing in her shoulder and placed the sweet in her mouth.

It did not melt instantly and *that* was the magic. It released its flavours in layers. There was the richness of saffron and almonds, the delicate aroma of ghee and the grainy texture of suji that had blossomed and blended seamlessly with the khoya.

'Is it good?' her mother-in-law asked her. Ruqayya could barely nod. She couldn't speak. For some reason, dum ka roat was reminding her of her mother and she missed her terribly.

She was still sitting in the kitchen when Nadira came to make dinner for everyone.

'What happened, Bhabhi?' she asked, looking concerned. 'Are you alright?'

Ruqayya didn't know. It seemed as though everything was getting too much for her all of a sudden.

'I don't know! I can't understand it,' she said, horrified to discover that her voice was breaking and she was on the verge of tears. She cleared her throat a couple of times and got up to go to her room.

'Bhabhi, ask Bhaiya to come for dinner in a little while,' Nadira called out. Ruqayya nodded lamely.

Omar was sitting on the bed, reading a magazine when she came in; he wished he could say everything that he'd been meaning to since he'd returned, but for some reason, the words got stuck.

'What?' she asked, as she sat down on the bed and levelled her gaze at him.

Several things ran through his head and he wasn't quite sure what he ought to begin with. He settled for the banal, however.

'Where's Aslam?' he asked. Ruqayya sighed and looked away.

'Outside. Sleeping,' she replied and lifted her feet onto the bed. She rested her head on her bent knees and Omar wished she would look up and talk to him.

'Is...is everything alright?' Omar forced the words out of his mouth. He was really hoping she wouldn't cry.

'Why? Why are you asking?' she asked him, or rather mumbled, her head was still bent low.

Omar thought of the many different things he'd been meaning to tell her. The past two weeks in Madras had been good but they had also raised a level of self-awareness in him. He knew what he wanted. Well, almost.

But just as he was formulating his thoughts, a strange analogy crept in his head. He wondered what she would say if he told her. Only one way to know.

'You know what we are?' he asked her. She didn't look up and gave no indication that she was listening.

'We're like rubberbands,' he continued. Was she asleep? No. She lifted her head slightly and looked at him through the corner of her eyes.

'What?' she asked in complete bewilderment.

'Yes, we're like rubberbands. The more you pull and stretch us apart, the closer we're going to get to each other.' He was excited with his theory.

She stared at him for ten seconds before she burst out laughing. 'You're mad!' she blurted out and continued laughing. 'I have never heard anything more stupid than that!'

'I mean it,' he said, still excited although not that sure anymore. She shook her head.

'We've grown apart,' she said. 'And we haven't got closer. I don't think so.' She looked a little sad as she said it. Omar caught hold of her hand and squeezed it.

'No. Even I didn't know it until right now,' he said. 'Or the fact that I missed you terribly when I was in Madras.'

'But even when you were here, you didn't really care much about me,' Ruqayya countered lightly, wishing her heart wasn't beating so fast.

Omar was silent for a moment. 'I don't know. It's just that this parenting thing took me by surprise. And I realised that there's so much I want to do for you and for that I need to earn more money. And I need to stay in Madras too.'

Ruqayya looked down and nodded. Omar tugged her hand and she looked up surprised. He tugged her harder and she fell towards him, surprised and shocked. He hadn't touched her this way since the baby had arrived.

'What...'

'Shh...' he said, placing his finger on her lips and then tracing them lightly. 'I've decided that the three of us will move to Madras as soon as we can. We'll make a new beginning there.'

Ruqayya's eyes leaped up to his and she looked at him intently. 'Do you mean it?' she asked, afraid to believe it was true. Imagine living on her own with just her baby and her husband!

'I do. I told Ammi already.'

'And? What did she say?' she asked him, a frown on her forehead.

'Nothing,' he shrugged.

'This doesn't change anything yet, you know. Something is different and we need to work it out,' she said seriously.

Omar felt a little irritated. Yes, he knew that much had changed but hadn't he accepted it and wasn't he trying to make amends? Why did she have to keep *talking* about it?

'Let's not talk about it,' he said and her head snapped up. She had been snuggling close to him and she stopped.

'What do you mean?' she asked.

'See, this is what I meant. Let's not talk about it and make it into something more than what it is,' he said, tracing a finger down her back. She moved away from him and sat straighter.

He sighed in frustration. 'How does talking about it change anything?'

'Since we're not going to talk about it, I really wouldn't know.' Saying this, she got up and walked out of the room.

When outside, Ruqayya realised she was smiling. She was angry at him and yet she wanted to laugh at his theories. She also felt really overjoyed at the thought of going to Madras where she could meet her mother more often.

She went to the kitchen and helped Nadira make rotis. 'You know, you're the bride. You shouldn't be here doing all this,' Ruqayya told her.

'No, no! It's okay. I like doing it,' said Nadira. Ruqayya smiled and shook her head. She could never understand some people. Like Shameem Aunty, she thought. In the smoky kitchen, she momentarily put aside her resentment of the woman and actually felt sorry for her. But it lasted for just a moment. And she was surprised to realise that thanks to Nadira, she actually had something that she could use against Shameem Aunty if the opportunity ever arose. What a pity they were moving to Madras!

With all these conflicting emotions doing the rounds, the family sat down for dinner. Ruqayya noticed that her mother-in-law still had some of the white lauz in a covered bowl.

'I thought we were done with all this?' she asked when she spotted her mother-in-law.

'We still have to make badam ki jaali,' her mother-in-law said and indicated to her that she should fill Omar's glass with water.

Rolling her eyes slightly upwards, Ruqayya did so and watched him drink it. He had finished eating, so he got up, washed his hands and went back to their room.

When dinner was cleared, her mother-in-law sat down with the white lauz and started rolling it. Ruqayya watched her as she cut out a large fluted circle, like four or five times the size of a regular lauz and kept it aside. Then she did the same with another round in which she started cutting out intricate designs.

'See? That's why it's called *jaali*,' she explained, showing the almost intricate lace work that seemed to have emerged on the round of white lauz.

'Oh!' Ruqayya exclaimed, unable to say anything else. Everyone was watching her mother-in-law as she applied a paste of saffron and water on the first unmarked round. She then lifted the latticed round with the paper below, slid it on top of the earlier one and readjusted it gently so that the two rounds were aligned and the orange bits could be seen peeping from inside.

Once she had done them all, Shameem Aunty arranged them on a large plate and took them to the kitchen. Following Ruqayya's gaze, her mother-in-law explained that Shameem Aunty would arrange them on the fire to be roasted very lightly.

'Beautiful!' Ruqayya murmured when Shameem Aunty returned with one and showed it to her mother-in-law. The jaali work had been delicately browned from inside, and the orange stood out against the dull white. Some of the smaller pieces that had been cut out from inside had also been kept to roast and her mother-in-law gave one piece to her to taste.

Ruqayya took one piece and held it in her hand. She didn't know what had surged through her when she had tried the dum ka roat. She had been happy and sad. She didn't want to feel that way again, *now*. Just happy thoughts would suffice.

She felt the slightly hardened piece in her hand, still warm from the fire and hesitantly she put it into her mouth. She was instantly surprised and captivated. How could just a little fire change the texture and taste of the lauz? The sugar had caramelised slightly and it did not dissolve as easily in her mouth as before. But it was just as amazing.

I have one for you, Omar, she thought as she chewed it slowly and looked towards her bedroom, where he was probably sulking at her for walking away. She looked at the crusty and sugary piece of almond-infused sweet in her hands and thought of how much he would laugh when she compared them to lauz. Well, it was better than rubberbands, at least.

25

KHALED looked extremely displeased to see me. I know I did turn up at their house once too often and I stole Zubi away for long chats but today he looked visibly angry.

'We're going out,' he announced, his voice tight, as he held the door ajar.

'Umm, yes. I know that. I'm coming along!' I said, a little brightly. His expression changed for a fraction of a second before a mask of resignation slipped over it and he opened the door wider.

Abid ran towards me, babbling about how Ria from the park never gave him a chance on the swing. He had taken to me only recently, apparently having decided that if his mother spent so much time with me, I had to be someone special.

At first I didn't know how to handle him because I was pretty wary around kids. But he talked to me seriously almost always, telling me about what had happened at his playgroup or about his visits to the park. I'd even met Zubi and Abid in the park on a few evenings and it had all stretched into a loosely knit fabric of comfort that managed to wrap us all in its warmth. Excluding Khaled, of course.

He looked back at Zubi who was shoving a packet of biscuits into her handbag. She looked at him a little apologetically and then smiled at me.

'We're ready. Just about to leave,' she said as she stuffed a bottle of water into the bag as well. I could sense that Khaled wanted to talk to her alone because he'd had no idea I was going to accompany them. As far as I was concerned, it was no big deal. Zubi had called me up this afternoon to ask if I wanted to go to Victoria Peak with them.

Zubi had been living in Hong Kong for nearly four years now and still she liked doing touristy things. There were times when I wished I had retained that sense of wonder as well but since I could no longer appreciate the nice things, maybe I could just enjoy them vicariously and so I agreed.

'Is Khaled coming along?' I asked her before she hung up.

'Yes,' she replied, and I felt my brow furrow in surprise. Zubi knew that Khaled didn't like me much and she also sensed that I was not comfortable around him. So why was she doing this? I had no time to ask her as she ended the call, leaving me to wrap up work early so I could join them.

Actually, I was getting slightly bored now. I mean, her grandmother's story kind of petered out after they moved to Madras and that was where Zubi's mother was born. I wanted to know more about Zubi though. When was she planning to tell me about how she got into cooking? Maybe today?

'Maybe Abid and I can wait downstairs while the two of you lock the house and come?' I suggested and Abid promptly put his hand into mine. Khaled glanced at our clasped hands and held his breath as though waiting for Zubi's answer.

'Okay. Just wait for us downstairs,' Zubi said. I almost ran towards the elevator, wondering what was in store that evening. Why had Zubi called me today when her husband was taking her out to the Peak? God! Was she using me as a buffer?

Feeling somewhat miffed, I kept my eyes on the elevator and

a little later, the two of them stepped out. For the first time since I saw the two of them together, Zubi didn't look that lost. She smiled weakly at us and together we commenced our journey.

'Your office is in Central, right? Why did you come all the way back here just so you could go back the same way?' Khaled asked me as we waited for the train to arrive in the MTR.

I was a bit taken aback. First of all, this was the longest sentence he had spoken to me, ever. Second, he was right. What had I been thinking? A part of me had probably forgotten the outing and I just left as I usually did to meet Zubi.

He shrugged when I didn't answer. The train slammed into the confined space and we stepped inside quickly, getting off a little while later at Central. We walked towards the Peak Tram Lower Terminus on Garden Road and stood in line to get our tickets.

Zubi pointed out all the historical paraphernalia that had been arranged along the walls on the sides of the tunnel where the Peak Tram would arrive; Abid, however, didn't really seem too interested. I watched the two of them and then Khaled, standing at a slight distance, and I sighed. Where was the super glue that binds families?

When the tram arrived, there was the inevitable rush to get in as tourists aimed to sit on the right hand side, just to get the perfect view. I wasn't bothered but I sidled into one of the seats and watched Khaled point out something to Zubi, who had managed to procure a seat on the right hand side of the tram.

I watched her as she pulled out a handycam from her bag and started recording the journey, capturing, what brochures and websites liked to call 'breath-taking vistas' of Hong Kong on our seven-minute journey to the top of Victoria Peak.

I'd been here a few times, sometimes with friends and sometimes with a boyfriend but I had no idea what to expect on this trip. I rubbed my palms on my jeans and watched tall buildings whiz past as the tram dragged us up towards the Peak.

Once we were there, it seemed obvious that we would go to the viewing gallery where we could look out across Hong Kong and all those majestic buildings. Abid kept up a lively chatter but the three of us were mostly quiet and I began to think that maybe I shouldn't have come.

Khaled barely looked at us as he stared out at the buildings that were just beginning to light up. The air was cold and I shivered slightly. I watched the mist float in the gradually darkening sky.

Zubi turned towards me and started speaking, telling me something about a new recipe she had tried out. No matter how hard I tried, I couldn't concentrate on what she was saying. Moreover, I was not interested in her new recipes. I wanted to know the old things, what she had left behind, and yet, those which hadn't left *her*.

I watched the play of emotions on her face as she spoke animatedly and realised that Khaled was also watching her intently. I felt embarrassed for some reason.

'Let's go for a walk,' Khaled suggested and although Zubi didn't look too enthused, I thought it was a good idea. I wasn't really in the mood to listen to Zubi today. Maybe it was the cold wind or probably just the strained atmosphere. I made up my mind never to agree to something like this again. It was just too weird.

We made our way downstairs and Zubi kept looking at the darkening sky.

'What?' I asked, following her gaze.

'No. Just that it's getting dark. And the walk that he wants to go on, goes right around the Peak. It's too long and Abid will get tired.' Khaled heard us and turned around.

'I'll carry him,' he said. It seemed like we were walking against the tide of people who were moving towards the viewing gallery.

'Not that many people want to go on a nature walk,' Zubi muttered and I rolled my eyes. I loved this walk. It was called the Hong Kong Trail and could easily stretch to an hour. We just had to walk and circle our way back to the starting point, and there were some magnificent views along the way. Victoria Peak was one of those places from where you could easily see most of Hong Kong's beautiful skyline. After my initial hesitation, I realised I'd missed doing this, even though I had disdainfully thought of it as touristy stuff. Of course, all the tourists were thronging the viewing gallery and not many had the endurance to go on this quiet and very romantic walk.

We started out and walked towards Lugard Road where the trail began. I strode along purposefully, thinking that a walk this long would help greatly in losing all those extra pounds I had piled on. I decided to ignore the three of them and walk ahead on my own, although that would prove to be difficult.

I glanced back after ten minutes and saw that Zubi and Khaled were walking together, and Abid was perched on Khaled's shoulder. They were talking softly and I suddenly realised what I was. A most foolish intruder. Khaled and Zubi had obviously done this walk before and Khaled had probably wanted to take Zubi to this place because he'd wanted some time with her alone, in a romantic setting. Zubi, on the other hand, had invited me to go along with them and I had gleefully become the *kabab mein haddi*. What an idiot, I thought, feeling ashamed of myself. What had happened to me? Ever since I had met Zubi, there seemed to have been an elemental change in me, something I just couldn't understand.

I bit my lower lip and walked faster, feeling mortified when I heard Zubi call out to me.

'Sonia! Wait!'

I turned back slightly and saw that Khaled was ambling along quietly, with Abid still perched on his shoulders, and he walked past us while Zubi and I followed slowly. She had probably realised that I was feeling left out and had decided to give me company.

'Zubi, why did you call me today?' I asked her as soon as Khaled was out of earshot.

She looked at me startled. 'I...'

'I know I promised you that I won't ask personal questions,' I said and quickly added, 'but this seems like a special occasion for your husband and you've dragged me along. I feel really awkward.'

Zubi opened her mouth to say something and then shut her mouth again. 'I...actually...' She sighed and then continued walking, shaking her head.

'I don't know, Sonia. You're my friend. In fact, the only friend I have here. You're the only person who knows so much about me. I just felt like having you come along.'

I understood what she was saying and yet I felt a flash of impatience.

'I want to know *your* story, Zubi,' I said gently, wondering when I would be able to coax it out of her.

'I know. But I'm scared.'

'Scared?' I asked, surprised.

'We'll discuss this later,' she said and walked faster towards her husband who had stopped to admire the view. She took Abid from him and walked ahead of us, without looking back.

Hey! I wanted to shout at her. Why was she doing this? Why did she have to run away every time I tried probing something even remotely personal? I was a journalist and I knew how much people loved to talk about themselves if given even half the chance. And if *I* felt so frustrated, I wondered how it was for Khaled to be married to her.

Almost as if he sensed my thoughts, Khaled walked in step

with me. I looked at him and nodded and he nodded back. Then I could hold it in no longer.

'How do you put up with her?' I asked him.

He shook his head, a quirky smile on his face. Man! This was the first time I had seen him smile and it created the most amazing change in his personality. He looked younger and boyish almost.

'It's our anniversary today,' he said and gave me another heart-stopping smile.

'Whoa. No wonder you were pissed off to see me. This Zubi!' I said, feeling embarrassed and shocked. Which sane girl would drag along a third party to her anniversary outing? Especially when her husband was so dishy? O-kay. I dragged my thoughts back...glad it was dark and he couldn't see how my neck had started turning red.

We spotted Zubi walking ahead resolutely in the distance, Abid walking by her side.

'Happy anniversary!' I said, smiling at him, a little uncomfortably.

'Thanks,' he said warmly and I marvelled at how unequal their relationship was.

'Arranged marriage, right?' I asked before I could stop myself. Why was I even asking? *Obviously* it was an arranged marriage.

So I was shocked when he shook his head.

'What?' I whispered, not willing to believe that theirs had been one of the proverbial love marriages that were becoming so common in India, and yet, not that common in their community.

'Actually, Zubi *thinks* it's an arranged marriage,' he said, his head dropping a little.

'You mean....?' I left the words hanging in the air. He looked up and met my eyes, but this time when he smiled, it was tinged with sadness.

Part Three

26

WHY is it that we always want that which we can't have? Or desperately yearn for something that is beyond our reach? In his two-bedroom house in India that he shared with his two brothers and a sister, Khaled had dreamed of and yearned for solitude. An hour, or even just half, spent without people banging into tables or chairs, shouting at each other, and throwing shoes in the air, would have been wonderful.

There were times when he wondered how he had managed to become an architect. He was hard pressed for time and space in his house and although one of his brothers had moved to a hostel in Manipal where he was studying to become a dentist, the house was still small for him.

From the time he'd been a young boy, Khaled had been very dexterous with his hands. Whether it was making neat and precise drawings or sculpting with clay, he was the one that teachers looked at with utter surprise because of his seemingly effortless achievements. As he grew older, he wanted to get a job where he could continue his passion for making things with his hands and although ideally he would have loved to become an artist, he chose architecture, because buildings seemed to have acquired that special quality of almost breathing.

When he got a job, he wanted to move out from their tiny house in the small congested locality where he had grown up. He wanted to get a place closer to his office and in his search for a suitable house, he rang up a real estate agent who asked him to reach Langford Town and look for house No. 75. Apparently, the house owners were willing to rent out a section of their house and were looking for prospective tenants.

So, ten years ago, he got off his Yamaha, tucked his helmet under his arm and looked around the seemingly posh locality. Apartments had sprung up everywhere but there were a few independent houses left. He thought of how it would be to live here, to even own a place in this area and he knew it was not something he could accomplish with ease. The real estate market was shooting up like a meteor on steroids. He should know. At his new job, they were building more and more apartments and most of them were around the outskirts of the city. A house in this central location would probably cost the moon.

Putting those thoughts aside, he looked around again at the tree-lined road and the houses that seemed to have been set back a little from the road. His eyes ran over the numbers and stopped at No. 75.

He walked up to the door and rang the doorbell, hoping the people wouldn't mind renting to him because he was a bachelor. This house would be perfect, he thought. It was barely ten minutes away from his office and he almost relished the thought of the peace he could get by living alone. His mother had been appalled to know that he wanted to move out even though he had found a job in the same city; but he had ignored her protests.

The door was opened by a little boy, barely seven or eight years old. He was dressed neatly in a T-shirt and jeans and he smiled shyly at Khaled.

'Can I speak to your parents?' asked Khaled, smiling back at him. The boy shook his head and then as though he'd had a second thought, invited Khaled in. Khaled was a bit taken aback.

'No, I'll stay here,' Khaled persisted, looking around uncomfortably, wishing that the man or woman of the house would come outside soon. The boy shut the door and then after two minutes opened it again.

'Come inside and sit. Ammi will be here soon to talk to you,' he said. Khaled noticed that there seemed to be an impish twinkle in his eyes. Khaled was a little wary immediately. Was he at the right house? Were these people renting at all?

'No, no! I'll wait right here,' Khaled insisted, wondering whether he should come back later with the real estate agent.

'No, please! Ammi will be angry if she sees you standing here. Come! Come!' he grabbed Khaled's hand and dragged him inside.

Khaled was surprised and a little shocked. What was this little fellow up to?

'Hang on! Let me remove my shoes at least!' Khaled muttered as he leaned against a wall and pulled off his shoes while resisting the tug of the little boy's hand. Something was wrong here and he probably should be heading back to the real estate agent's office. He allowed himself to be dragged towards a hall where there was the usual set of two sofas along with a longer one, on which a girl was asleep. She was wearing a white churidar that outlined her calves and fell in tightly clustered folds around her ankles. He couldn't see her face but he found himself staring at her feet that dangled slightly from the edge of the sofa. He was mesmerised by them.

His lips parted slightly as he continued staring at her pretty feet. From the folds of the churidar, he could see the sparkle of an anklet. He then forced himself to look at the little boy who was eyeing him with a great deal of interest.

'Zubi di, get up! Someone's come to see the house!' the boy said, tugging at the girl's arm. The girl woke up immediately and she sat up, sleep and confusion in her eyes. He noted her flushed face and then bit his lower lip to stop himself from laughing out.

She had no idea. She arranged her dupatta around her shoulders and got up. She was blushing. Khaled saw the little boy giggle and he raised his eyebrows at him sternly. The boy lost his composure for a moment and then continued to talk to the girl who was now fully awake and clearing her throat.

'Are you a bachelor?' she asked, her voice still husky from sleep. Khaled looked beyond the dark kajal lines that had been drawn on her upper lip, the exaggerated eyebrows that met in the middle and he felt something tug at his chest. He ignored it, however, and wondered how he could tell her without making her feel mortified.

'I…yes,' Khaled replied, looking down. That was best. If he continued looking at her face, he might start laughing. But his eyes connected to her feet and he sort of forgot what he had meant to say.

'We…we usually rent out to families,' the girl continued and Khaled nodded, looking at her feet.

'My mother will be back in ten minutes and you can talk to her although I know she won't agree. Please sit down.'

'Okay,' Khaled replied and sat down at the edge of the sofa.

'Why don't you go to the bathroom before Ammi comes?' the boy asked her.

The girl frowned and dragged her brother towards the other end of the hall where Khaled could hear her admonishing him about letting strangers inside the house.

'What were you thinking?' she whispered. 'How can you let some person into the house like that? Especially when I was sleeping!'

'He looked liked a nice man,' the boy countered.

'You idiot! Don't you dare open the door again!'

'I just thought it was Rishaad Bbhaiya,' the boy said, making a face. 'It's time for him to come back from school, na?'

The two continued a whispered conversation while Khaled looked around uncomfortably. If this wasn't going to work out, it was a waste of time for him to hang around here. He ought to ask that estate agent for other options nearby and if nothing worked out, he was just going to have to stay put in his house with his family.

The doorbell rang. Maybe it was the mother. He wondered how she would react when she would see her daughter's face.

'Suhail, no!' the girl shouted out when the boy ran again to open the door. A tall, lanky boy stood there, a school bag hanging from one arm in a carefully careless manner.

'How many times have I told you not to open the door?' the girl said, moving forward and stopping short when the tall boy started laughing.

'Oh my god! You really did it, Suhail! Not bad, champ!' and the two brothers high-fived. The girl looked stricken for a moment and then ran somewhere inside. Minutes later, Khaled heard her screaming when she saw what her brother had done to her face.

Khaled couldn't stop grinning, although he tried to keep a serious face. The older boy stopped short when he saw Khaled.

'Who are you?' he asked, his voice at that odd juncture between adolescence and manhood.

'I think I'd better leave,' said Khaled regretfully, and got up. This would not work out anyway because the girl had said her mother would not entertain bachelors. He wished she'd come out so he could see her face properly without the moustache and the furry eyebrows but she was probably too embarrassed to come back.

The two boys stood looking at him as he left. Khaled turned back to wave at them.

'Don't play too many pranks on your sister!' he admonished them lightly as he exited the gate. A middle-aged woman was getting down from an auto. She went inside the house giving him a curious look on her way. That was probably their mother.

On an impulse, he turned back to speak to her. The woman held the edge of her black scarf hovering near her mouth as she looked at him, almost fearfully.

'Yes?' she asked. The boys had shut the door when he had left and the woman looked around, probably wishing they would come outside.

'I heard you're renting out your house and I came to see it,' said Khaled. The woman assessed him, looking up and down and did some mental calculations before shaking her head.

'We're looking for a family. Not bachelors,' she said, confirming what her daughter had said. Khaled nodded his head brusquely and walked out of the gate. He could hear loud voices floating towards him when the woman opened the door. This wouldn't have worked anyway. It seemed like just another noisy house. But as he straddled his bike and slipped his helmet over his head, he glanced at the house and his thoughts strangely flickered between the prettiest pair of feet he had ever seen in his life and the girl whose face he wasn't likely to forget.

27

'You fell in love with her feet?' I asked him sceptically. Khaled shook his head but looked embarrassed.

'Maybe a little,' he conceded with a smile. I felt a little incredulous but swallowed further questions when I spotted Zubi sitting down on a bench with Abid, waiting for us to catch up.

I looked at Khaled and wondered what had made him open up today because he'd never really deemed to speak to me before.

It was pretty late by the time we finished the walk; everyone was quiet and subdued. Abid fell asleep. I said my goodbyes at the entrance of the MTR and left because I lived on this side of the town in Wan Chai.

I reached home – a two-bedroom apartment that I shared with my friend Karen, a girl from mainland China. She often went back to her home-town on weekends, giving me free rein of the house and that was when I would do all this writing. The weekend hadn't arrived yet, but I was a little eager to get back to writing Zubi's story.

There were times when I would stop mid-sentence and wonder what I was doing. What could I accomplish with this book? But then I would just go to the link which I had bookmarked months ago when I had come across Zubi on the Internet.

I'd been craving for biryani then, and I wasn't quite happy with the Pakistani or Indian versions available at the restaurants in Kowloon. Out of frustration, I'd started looking up recipes on blogs even though I knew I wouldn't actually make biryani on my own. That's when I stumbled across Zubi's videos.

She had posted a total of four videos on the Internet in which she demonstrated how to make biryani. She'd split the file into four videos. I clicked on the first one out of sheer boredom. I still don't remember how I landed on the site but I played the video because it seemed better than going to yet another Indian restaurant that had recently opened in Kowloon.

When the video started loading, I smiled a little derisively because the girl in the video seemed unsure and didn't seem confident. But then she started cooking and it was like she knew there was someone on this side, watching her, and not just a camera. She seemed conscious and yet she was completely unself-conscious as she spoke in measured tones and showed how her mother made the best biryani ever. It was something to do with her eyes. She looked serious but there was a slight smile on her face as well. What arrested me was her on-screen presence.

As a food writer, I was disdainful of most food show hosts who possessed a vocabulary of just three or four words to describe everything – from food to ingredients to aromas and flavours. Either they said it was 'gorgeous', 'beautiful' or 'lovely' and they thought their deed was done.

This girl, however, kept up a monologue about her mother's cooking in a way that captivated my attention without making me want to roll my eyes in frustration. I watched each subsequent video with more interest than I had for the previous one and when it ended, I wished I could speak to her. Just like that. She seemed to be holding herself back and I wanted to know more.

Sometimes it's hard to explain how instant connections are made. You really don't know how or why, but when you see someone, you know they're going to play an important role in your life. Or maybe you, in theirs. That was how I felt when I saw Zubi's video. It was raw and *she* was raw. But with a bit of fine tuning, I was positive she would be perfect.

In one of the videos, Zubi had casually mentioned living in Hong Kong and that was when I knew that I had to do this. She lived right here. I was going to find out where her house was and I would meet her.

I had no idea what I would talk to her about, until I landed at her doorstep for the first time. In fact, after meeting her, I was disappointed because in person, she seemed a paler version of her screen self.

Anyway, after all these months of speaking to her, letting her draw out her experiences, I was convinced that we had a book in the making *and* a bunch of videos in which Zubi could demonstrate the recipes mentioned in the book. Of course, I hadn't divulged my plan to Zubi but I knew that I had a winner. Also, I needed to know if there was a market for something of this sort. The book would be a companion to the video recipes. I was sure that people would love to hear the stories behind each of the dishes.

I'd been looking around for a literary agent to whom I could sell the idea but it wasn't easy because, one, the book wasn't yet complete; two, I needed Zubi to make a few more videos; and three, I needed to do all this without freaking out Zubi...most importantly I needed to know Zubi's story. Who knew where this could take us? If things worked out, chances were that both Zubi and I could become rich and famous.

This was why I didn't want too many people to see her videos. I was a bit afraid that if people started sharing it on social media, it might go viral and would lose the surprise element for publishers. Of course, the positive side to that would be that publishers would know that this could actually work. But I was selfish and I wanted Zubi to myself for some more time.

I was in the food writing business. I knew how magazines like mine worked. We depended so much on advertisements and every month we had to do what seemed like the same thing again and again. But I'd become dissatisfied with my work even before I met Zubi. I mean, how many times could one describe the décor of a restaurant as 'tasteful'? Or the food as 'tantalising'? I had been on the verge of giving up and finding another branch of journalism when Zubi happened and I was glad because I realised that come what may, I loved writing about food.

So this whole thing was obviously not just for Zubi. Nobody is that selfless. But I wasn't too concerned about those details yet. What I really wanted to know was Zubi's story and how she found her personal connection with food. What had prompted her to make a video of herself preparing biryani? Why had she done it? Unless I had the answers to those questions, the book couldn't be completed.

I yawned and shut down my computer. Outside, a police car zipped by and a man shouted in the street. It was late in the night and yet, true to its reputation, Hong Kong never seemed to sleep. I ignored the sounds as I climbed onto my bed and switched off the lights but I couldn't get any sleep.

Imagine falling in love with a pair of feet! I turned around, pummelled my pillow into a more malleable shape and closed my eyes. Khaled's strong voice resonated in my head and almost as if on cue, my phone buzzed. I picked it up and saw a new number flash on the screen. The message below said – Can we meet? Need to talk – Khaled.

Getting Zubi to talk was part of my self-assigned job. But being Khaled's agony aunt was not in the job description, I thought with a huff as I typed 'Okay'.

28

Every evening at exactly four o'clock, the peon would go around the office with a tray, handing cups of tea to everyone along with a plate of biscuits. On some days, Khaled declined the tea; instead, he would go and prepare a cup of tea for himself in the electric kettle later during the day. The reason for this was that the electric kettle was located near a window that looked across two nearby lanes. And in one of those lanes was the house where he had almost become a tenant.

So he liked to stand there at around 4.30 p.m., looking at the two lanes from his perch on the second floor of his office. He'd watch autos milling around, people walking about and the two naughty boys, but never the pretty girl. In fact, it was nearly a year later that he saw her standing on the road, looking for an auto.

He stood at the window, leaning forward, cup poised in his hand, almost holding his breath. He couldn't make out her features from so far away; in fact he wasn't even sure if it *was* her. But she flagged down an auto and went back towards the gate from where an old couple emerged. They sat in the auto and there was plenty of waving happening before the auto finally moved away. As Khaled watched, the girl's mother joined her; they looked at the disappearing auto for a while and then went inside.

More Than Just Biryani

He wished he'd been able to find another house on that lane but things hadn't worked out and he had to settle with living in his own house, much to his mother's relief.

'I can't imagine you'd want to pay rent to someone when you have your own house in the city!' she argued. Khaled had kept quiet. But he kept a lookout for the girl, every other day. Sometimes he even had dreams in which she would actually enter his office, looking for him.

So one day when he was bent low over his table, blowing the pencil shavings away so he could look at the layout properly, he lifted his head and saw her standing near the reception. His heart began thumping; he looked around, wondering if anyone had heard it. What was she doing here?

'No, you can't meet Mr Narssimhan without an appointment,' the receptionist was telling her. Khaled looked around again and saw that no one else was interested. Was she looking for a job, he wondered.

'May I help you?' he found himself asking her as he walked up towards the receptionist's desk.

The girl looked at him, a little startled and then she smiled shyly. She hadn't recognised him.

'No, thanks. We're looking for a chief guest for our annual day function in college and I thought we could ask Mr Narssimhan to be one because he's such an acclaimed architect,' she said, tucking a strand of her hair behind her ears.

Khaled kept quiet. Narssimhan was an acclaimed architect, yes, but he would bore the hell out of a bunch of students, especially if they belonged to a girl's college.

Acting on an instinct, he bent towards her and whispered. 'Don't.'

The girl stepped back a little and nodded. She probably thought he was some sort of psychopath. She had a strained smile on her face as she walked towards the door. Khaled watched her leave with some sort of trepidation. He had no idea what he was doing as he cast a cursory glance at the receptionist and quickly stepped outside the doors.

'Hey!' he called out and the girl stopped. She was already on the stairs. She looked up at him and didn't say anything but she fidgeted with the strap of her handbag and bit her lower lip.

Khaled bounded down the stairs towards her and smiled quickly.

'I think you misunderstood me. Narssimhan is a really good architect, but he's a very boring speaker. That's why I said....' He trailed off when he noticed a look of recognition on the girl's face.

'I...I think I've seen you before,' she murmured. Khaled didn't elaborate because he didn't want to embarrass her so he looked down. He noticed that she was wearing a pair of thin, strappy white sandals that made her feet look even prettier.

'Thanks, anyway,' she said and made to leave. Khaled knew that if he asked her name or which college she studied in, it would just complicate things, so he smiled, kept quiet and waved his pencil at her before heading back to his office, with a heavy feeling.

'Umm...excuse me?'

He turned around immediately. She was still standing on the stairs, with a confused expression on her face.

'Have we met before? You look very familiar but...'

Khaled knew she would be mortified if he mentioned the time he had come to her house and so, he shook his head. She didn't seem to be the kind of girl who would laugh over it even after so many months. But feeling a little encouraged by her continued presence and her seeming reluctance to leave, he smiled back at her and spoke.

'Why did you want Narssimhan for your annual day?' he asked.

She shrugged. 'I'm studying at a fine arts college and we're looking for someone related to design. Also our chief guest cancelled at the last moment and we're desperately looking for a replacement.'

He nodded and she turned to leave. Khaled suppressed the urge to call her back; instead he headed back upstairs, went to the window near the electric kettle and waited till she came into view.

29

The heady aroma of coffee lingered in the air, its richness percolating every molecule in the atmosphere as I sat down at the Pacific Coffee Shop on Hollywood Road, waiting for Khaled to turn up. This was our second…umm…clandestine meeting after that trip to the Peak where he had revealed to me that he'd been in love with Zubi for years before he married her. It was strange listening to his side of the story because he was unveiling a side of Zubi I didn't know at all.

I tore open the sachet of sugar over my frothing coffee and stirred it, feeling a bit listless. Well, okay. This was good, getting to know Zubi from all possible angles. But I still didn't know what made her tick. My book needed some depth and it could only come from her.

I spotted Khaled as he walked through the door. He nodded at me before coming and sitting down. He looked different in his formal work clothes. More distant and more appealing. Right.

'Coffee?' I asked, wondering if he'd leave soon. He worked in an architecture firm nearby and this was his lunch break. It also happened to be my lunch break and I knew I had to hurry up if I didn't want to annoy Vera again.

'No, thanks,' he said as he sat down opposite me. He had a

faraway look in his eyes and I had to clear my throat a couple of times to get his attention.

'You wanted to meet me?' I prompted him finally. He sighed.

'Yes. But…I don't know why I started telling you all this. I mean, no one…I repeat, no one has heard any of this from me before. And you say you're writing a book about Zubi and her cooking and all that. I don't know how I feel about it.'

I kept quiet. He continued.

'Also, shouldn't you have asked Zubi's permission before writing a book about her life? I don't think what you are doing is right.'

I felt a sinking sensation in my tummy. 'I…I had discussed it with her…but nothing was clear until I started writing it.'

'Can I see what you've written so far?' he spoke suddenly and I straightened my back.

'I…it's still the first draft and there's so much I need to know,' I said somewhat defensively.

He picked up a paper napkin that had been lying on the table and I watched him shred the napkin into bits while I took a sip of my coffee.

'Even after six years of marriage,' he started and I leaned a little towards him, 'I still don't know where I stand with her. And I don't know why.'

I remembered the time I had called Zubi an onion. I had no idea how many layers I'd peeled already.

'Anyway, I don't think this is a good idea. You and me meeting up like this,' he said. I took a deep breath.

'It wasn't my idea. It was yours,' I reminded him, expelling my breath forcefully.

'Yes, I thought…I don't know what I was thinking,' he mumbled, shoving the torn napkin to the centre of the table.

'You and Zubi deserve each other,' I said, draining my cup of coffee before getting up.

'I don't want you meeting her again,' he said without looking up at me.

'You can't be serious!' I was shocked. He couldn't forbid me from meeting her or vice versa. Or could he?

'Every time she comes back after meeting you, she's more withdrawn and it takes a lot to cheer her up. I'm confused,' he admitted. I sat down again.

'What do you mean?'

'I thought her meetings with you were good for her because she doesn't have many friends here,' he looked at me squarely.

I waited for him to continue.

'But I don't think you're really her friend. You're just being an opportunist, trying to advance your career through her.'

'That's ridiculous!' I said, feeling my face heat up. There was some truth in what he said, but I wasn't being an opportunist.

'Zubi will benefit from it too,' I said, the words getting blocked inside my throat.

'How?' he looked sceptical, 'how will it help her when everyone reads about her life?'

'You don't get it at all!' I exclaimed, feeling desperate. 'This book is not just about her life.' I struggled to find the right words. Odd for a writer, really.

'It's about food and how it's more than what you eat just to satisfy your hunger. It's about how food changed her mother's life and even her grandmother's. I know there's an elemental story in there about Zubi as well, but she just won't let me get any closer.'

Khaled looked thoughtful. 'You're saying that you're trying to capture the journey of these three women through food. While that's a lofty idea, what's this crap about making Zubi do videos?

Sounds really shoddy, something that marketing people might do,' he said derisively.

'It's not like that. Haven't you seen Zubi's videos? The ones she uploaded on the Internet where she's preparing biryani? She's awesome. She's a natural. Why can't we utilise that to sell the book?'

Khaled looked taken aback.

'You haven't seen her videos?' I asked, surprised. That was when I realised that Zubi had kept Khaled completely in the dark. Why? I watched him intently as he tried to compose his face and keep his expression neutral.

He blew out a breath and cracked his knuckles loudly. 'All this is pre-emptive. You're saying that Zubi has no idea about what you're planning. She just won't agree.'

'Maybe you don't know her that well!' I snapped at him. This was getting too much. I had come here hoping to hear some more about their alluring romance and instead he was cutting me to shreds with his blunt opinions.

'Yeah, I guess you're right on that count,' he said, looking resigned. 'I don't know her at all.'

I realised I was breathing a bit heavily.

'I'll back off,' I found myself telling him. 'I won't contact her again and I won't write the book.'

He nodded. I got up and left.

30

On the weekend after my meeting with Khaled, I went to Macau with Natalie. I was depressed...as though I'd suffered a heart break. Natalie's solution for it was bright lights and lots of gambling although the real reason for her visit was the Macau Grand Prix that had started the previous week.

'Formula 1 drivers are the hottest,' she announced as we entered our hotel room. I made a face. Yes, I knew that.

'And think of all that male yumminess out there!' she trilled and I rolled my eyes. Natalie and I had found each other within the very first week of my landing in Hong Kong. Both of us had been sitting at the same communal table at a noodle shop and I was watching a group of Chinese men slurp noodles rapidly. It seemed like the bowl, the fork and the chin had become one being as they came together in noisy communion. I caught her eye over the others and she smiled when she saw that I was looking at my bowl of noodles with apprehension. We struck up a conversation outside and then after a couple more random meetings, we'd discovered numerous common interests. As a matter of fact, Natalie had been the one to help me get my current job and the one before that.

That was about five years ago. She was half-Chinese, half-American. She was tall, had the longest legs I'd ever seen and silky straight hair. In short, she was beautiful. It was also the reason why she was hardly ever single for more than two weeks.

She wasn't seeing anyone when she dropped in at my place the day after I met Khaled, and we were both feeling morose. She suggested we should go to Macau. I hadn't been too keen but Natalie was on a mission that seemed unstoppable. I hadn't told her much about Zubi because although she was my best friend here in Hong Kong, I couldn't tell her without having her ask the same question that Khaled asked. 'Why?'

So I agreed and the two of us left on a windy Saturday morning for the ferry terminal from where we would leave for Macau. An hour or so later, we reached the Macau terminal. I remembered coming here the first time, also with Natalie, but I'd been so excited and happy then. Now, it just felt like someone had died.

I ignored the colourful brochures that advertised the upcoming races or the regular casinos that heavily made-up women handed to me as we walked outside the terminal. Natalie had pulled a few strings and booked us a room in a moderately priced hotel, although I was pretty sure she didn't have plans of staying there, at night.

Coming to this noisy and colourful city was probably not the best plan of action I ought to have taken but I'd let Natalie take over because I was too exhausted to protest. At the hotel, however, I refused to go out with her.

'Maybe in the evening,' I said, shaking my head resolutely. 'We'll go and check out MGM and the other casinos if you want.'

She left in a cloud of spicy perfume and a loud huff. I drew the curtains, plopped myself on the bed and started ruminating over my last conversation with Khaled.

Maybe Khaled was right, I thought. Maybe I *was* trying to find a way out for myself through Zubi's life. But why was I really doing this? Because I was stuck in a dead-end job and wanted to do something more fulfilling? Or did I really think that Zubi could become an Internet sensation through her videos and give Nigella Lawson a run for her money? I snorted at that thought.

I drifted into sleep with those thoughts. Natalie returned around six; she switched on the lights, insisted I change into something slinky and blingy, and then the two of us left for a walk around town.

Macau was poised between two extremes – on one side it was the epitome of old world charm with its historical buildings, gardens and mosaic-lined pavements that lifted my heart a little; and on the other was the louder and more garish side that tourists loved to explore. I often marvelled at Natalie's sense of wonder that hadn't diminished over the years. She was itching to head towards Lisboa, one of the most seizure-inducing neon-lit casinos in Macau while I stalled outside the ruins of St. Paul, gazing at its greyed façade, feeling melancholy bubble inside me.

'Babe, you're *so* not dressed for this historical tourism thingy. Let's move from here!' Natalie pushed me on and I followed her reluctantly. A normal night out in Macau was pretty high on adrenaline but when the Grand Prix was on, the energy on the streets was something else. We did a round of the casinos and in each place, I saw some people celebrating wins and others having that slight edge of disappointment and defiance on their faces when they lost but...I just felt detached.

In another life, I would have gambled a bit of my money too, and watched the wheels spin in apprehension and anticipation. I would have dissed the Indians who came in search of excitement, shaking my head at their naiveté. I would have smiled back encouragingly at the attractive American who raised a glass towards me and maybe sidled up towards him in the smoky bar lounge of one of the casinos. But I was living this life. And damn you,

Khaled, for making me think. For making me *want* to understand my own motives.

Whatever it was, I had to figure it out before I could probe further. I had promised Khaled that I would not pursue Zubi anymore. But I didn't want to stop because I'd come too far and because I knew that this was a form of catharsis for me. I frowned at the word. Catharsis? Really? Was that what it was?

31

Six years ago, a young couple sat in a crowded hospital, waiting for their chance to meet the busy gynaecologist. The man would go up to the receptionist every five minutes or so and speak to her, gesticulating desperately before sitting down next to his wife again. Each time, he would take her hand, press it lightly and whenever the young woman winced, a spasm of pain would pass through his features as though he felt it too.

The wife looked very young and she was in tremendous pain. She clutched her stomach and squeezed her eyes shut every two minutes. She seemed to be around four months pregnant. The man looked at her, bit his lower lip, got up, paced the room and went to the receptionist again who looked at him, exasperated. Finally, she let the two of them go inside to meet the doctor. The man held his wife's hand, as she got up awkwardly. A tear rolled down his cheek and he wiped it away before more fell rapidly. The girl was in too much pain to respond but I felt a spasm just then and I winced.

She was having a miscarriage, just like I was. I sat on the uncomfortable chair, wishing there was someone who would go and fight with the receptionist for me. I had been two months pregnant and while I wasn't excited or jubilant about it, I had accepted it eventually. I did feel that getting pregnant six months after getting married was a bit ridiculous but then, who got married at twenty-one anyway?

I had, and look where it got me. I was sitting alone in the hospital, waiting for my husband but he had sent me a text, saying he would be late.

'Try and see if you can manage on your own,' he said when I had called him. I dropped my phone into my handbag and refused to answer it when it rang again, and so, here I was in the hospital, most probably losing the baby I hadn't really wanted in the first place. A part of me understood the physical pain, the tearing away of the foetus from the walls of my uterus, and the spasms that seemed like period pain multiplied ten times over. But a part of me was hurting somewhere else too. Or maybe it was just the hormones acting up, making me feel sad and…yes, just very sad.

The young couple emerged sometime later and a nurse led the wife upstairs where she would probably get a D&C. The man looked serious and he held his wife's other arm.

'How many months was she?' a woman next to me asked and I shrugged, ignoring the flooding feeling I was getting at the bottom of my stomach.

'I think she's five months along. Imagine having a miscarriage so late! That's too bad!' the woman answered her own question, running her hand over her ample stomach. From the corner of my eye, I glanced at it with curiosity, and I actually saw her stomach move up where the baby must have kicked.

'You?' she asked me and I shook my head, unable to answer.

'Oh, so you're just here to meet the doctor, ah? You look too young to be pregnant anyway.'

I continued ignoring her and she continued talking to me until it was my turn to go inside.

I got up slowly, placed my hand on the small of my back and walked up towards the door, feeling more blood rush into my pad and I knew that it was gone. My legs trembled a little and I managed to walk inside the consulting room where I sat down, my forehead sweaty and my stomach, a mess.

'What's the matter?' the doctor asked, looking concerned, and I told her.

'Why didn't you come immediately?' she asked me, walking me towards the examining table where I sat down breathing heavily.

'I...I didn't know it was happening,' I said, feeling foolish.

'Well, you must have had some indication?' she asked, checking my pulse and then my B.P.

I shrugged. 'Where's your husband?' she asked.

'I'd like to know that too,' I wondered aloud and she looked at me sharply.

'At least call your family,' she said.

'They don't live here. It's just me and my husband,' I replied.

'Well, it's a small procedure. It looks like you've already miscarried but we have to do a D&C to clear up your uterus,' she said frowning and turning around.

'The young couple who came some time back?' I asked her and she turned back to face me. 'Are they having a miscarriage too?'

She rubbed her forehead and shook her head.

'They lost the baby. But it's not a miscarriage. It's an intrauterine death. We're going to induce labour so she can give birth to the baby.'

I stared at her in shock. 'Give birth to the baby? But didn't you say they lost it?'

'Well, yes, but their baby was already completely formed and then died inside. So, yes, she's going to have to give birth to a dead baby.'

I rubbed my eye and felt myself sniffle as I left the doctor's room. She had asked me to wait upstairs where she would come and do my D&C but she had to attend to the couple with the dead baby first.

The two hours that I spent in the waiting room with the young husband pacing and alternately sobbing, would count to be some of the worst in my life. When the doctor emerged outside, she shook her head tiredly and informed him that the baby had finally been delivered. He sank down on the ground and cried loudly. She patted his shoulders awkwardly and made him get up whereupon he went inside the labour room to be with his wife.

When it was my turn, the doctor didn't say a word. She was too swept up by the events of just half-an-hour back when they'd had to release the dead baby to the almost-father who took it and went to bury it. I closed my eyes and tried to think happy thoughts but it seemed as though I'd never have another happy thought in my life ever again.

I tried to conjure up my husband Nitin's face but I kept seeing the crying father's face and I shut my eyes in pain when the doctor started the procedure. When it was done, she said I should wait for a few hours before going home. She transferred me to a room where I turned to the wall immediately, refusing to look at the other patient in the room. It wasn't that girl who had lost her baby. It was another pregnant woman who was being monitored closely; she had nurses coming in to check the baby's heartbeat every fifteen minutes or so.

I shut my eyes, wishing I could shut my ears to the rapid and loud sound of her baby's heartbeat and in the haze of pain, physical and emotional, I realised that although I was just twenty-two, I felt years older. When I went home finally, Nitin was watching TV. He looked at me and shook his head.

'You'd have saved yourself this trouble if you'd listened to me and got it aborted in the first place,' he said, not moving from the sofa. It was crazy to compare my husband with a complete stranger but I couldn't help thinking of that man who had cried when he had seen his dead baby. I gulped and found that my throat was too dry.

I sat down on the sofa opposite Nitin and tried to remember everything that had made me want to get married to him. He had been my senior in college where I was doing my Masters in Journalism and Mass Communication. We'd worked together on various projects, and for some reason, we had been the perfect team. I don't know when the teamwork translated into something more and it had become an unspoken thing between us. When Nitin graduated and left, he jokingly proposed to me and I foolishly I agreed. And although he seemed surprised, we went ahead and actually got married.

Here we were now, just six months after getting married, knowing that it was one of the biggest mistakes we had made. Nitin was working crazy hours as a rookie journalist and I was still studying. When I found that I was pregnant, he had said it was a good idea to let it go but I felt strongly about abortion and I refused.

He had that look of 'I told you so' on his face and I pursed my lips, thinking of the other couple who would probably deal with their loss together, as they were supposed to. I could have done with a hug at least. But he continued watching TV, sipping on his beer and smiling at some joke cracked by a skimpily clad woman who was hosting a comedy show.

I took a deep breath and told him that I wanted out. He looked at me surprised, leaned forward to place his bottle on the coffee table and cocked his head.

'Are you sure? Is everything alright?' he asked. I resisted the urge to laugh at his stupid question.

'Yes, I'm sure and no, everything is not alright,' I said slowly, getting up to leave.

At the time, it had seemed like a great deal, getting divorced just six months after marriage. But it was probably the best thing I'd done. After completing my Masters, I tried my hand at various newspapers, finding to my horror that I wasn't even vaguely interested in hardcore journalism.

I moved on to magazines and then finally landed at a food magazine where the slow pace of life and the promise of good food seemed to revive me tremendously. Textures spoke a unique language to me, and tastes revealed themselves to my tongue with sudden alacrity.

So how did I land up in Hong Kong? It was actually pretty simple. One Friday, my colleagues and I had got together at a friend's house for a few drinks and gossip, and everyone had got drunk. People started talking about what they really wanted from their lives and how they were stuck in their jobs and I realised that I didn't feel that way at all. I loved my job. But their attitude had worried me. I was the youngest there and I realised I didn't want to feel this way when I grew older. The only way to counteract it would be to do something reckless and foolish, now, when I could.

So I came to Hong Kong. I'd planned to move along to other places and explore the world but then I fell into the very trap from which I'd hoped to escape. I fell in love with this explosive city and decided that my recklessness and foolishness could halt right here. Also, I had run out of money already. How I managed to get a working visa in Hong Kong and everything else is another story, one that I don't really want to get into now.

Did I understand my motivation to write Zubi's story now? Not really. Things were still not clear but I had a vague idea that it was connected to the early losses I had suffered. The miscarriage and the marriage. Maybe by writing Zubi's story, I was trying to even out the rough edges in my life, a bit like rolling dough around so that there were no cracks and jagged edges.

32

I deliberated for two days before calling Khaled and telling him that I was willing to show him what I'd written so far. I procrastinated because I wanted to be sure of my motives but even after all the introspection, I couldn't put my finger on it. Finally, after deciding that not everything should necessarily have a reason, I called him up.

'I saw her videos and she's good,' he admitted gruffly.

'Does that mean you've changed your mind about—'

'No,' he cut off my question as though it was a given.

I was getting annoyed with him.

'How much of Zubi do you know?' I asked and there was silence on the other side. 'I mean, do you know about her life as a child? Has she told you any of that stuff?'

I could hear him take a deep breath and exhale slowly.

'Yes, she has,' he said and I closed my eyes. 'What makes you think that she would have told you stuff that she wouldn't tell *me*?'

'Because she's Zubi,' I countered. There was a pause in which I weighed my options carefully.

'Okay,' he admitted and I shook my head in relief. 'I want to read what you've written.'

'I'll email it to you. But on one condition. You will let me continue meeting her.'

Once again there was a pause and then he spoke. 'Okay.'

I emailed the half-written manuscript to him, not sure if it was the right thing to do. He called me after an hour, asking if we could meet at the same Pacific Coffee Shop where we had met the last time. Wow. That had been quick.

However, I had some work to complete before I could venture out. Vera had asked me to compile a list of the Michelin-starred restaurants in Hong Kong because it was a part of our cover story for the next month. This was the part of the job that I hated because it meant being stuck to the computer and sometimes to the phone, finding out dry facts and details when I would have loved to actually visit a Michelin-starred restaurant for a change.

While I was a complete Indian at heart, a huge part of me had readily adapted to international cuisine with no qualms whatsoever. I enjoyed gourmet food, its subtle highlights, the pleasing colours and sensations. I loved experimenting with new cuisines too and Cantonese was a hot favourite. But I let my mind wander as I gazed at the website of one of the restaurants which had the picture of a plated dessert that took my breath away. Delicately tinted pink mousse, topped with a thin sheet of raspberry gelatine, with raspberry coulis dribbled along the sides. O-kay. If not one of those, I needed something sweet right now.

I texted Khaled if he could come and meet me at the café in twenty minutes and he agreed. I planned to go a bit early so I could probably wolf down their blueberry cheesecake before Khaled turned up.

I dropped the list of restaurants with all their details on Vera's desk and told her I needed to do a quick errand. She was texting slowly and painfully on her iPhone, her delicately shaded, perfectly manicured nails, tapping on the screen, wincing each time she typed a wrong letter.

She looked up, surprised, and opened her mouth to say something to me while I rushed out as quickly as I had gone in.

'Hold on!' she called out and I paused. She came and stood at the door of her office.

'Where are you going? It's way past lunch time now!' she had her hands on her hips and she looked angry. I bit back a retort and backtracked my way towards the elevator.

'I won't take long. I promise!' I said, waving at her before stepping inside the elevator.

At the coffee shop, I stood at the counter and placed my order when I spotted Khaled walking in. He saw me and walked up, waving a hi. I nodded and just as I paid for my cheesecake, he leaned forward and spoke to the young man behind the counter in near perfect Cantonese, asking him for a latte. I was impressed and irritated because I was impressed. Khaled smiled at me ruefully before pointing in the general direction of one of the booths where I sat down with my cheesecake.

'I read it,' he said before I had even dug my spoon into the dessert. I looked up to see his expression and faltered because it seemed blank.

'I knew her father had died in an accident at a fair. But there were so many details that....did you make them up?' he asked me sharply. I shook my head.

'I had no idea she blamed herself or that her mother blamed her for it,' he said, running his hand through his hair, ruffling it.

The cheesecake had that perfect balance between smooth and grainy, tart and sweet and I ate around the edges so that I didn't finish it too soon. I didn't know what to tell him anyway.

'Reading this explains so much about her,' he continued. I was afraid to even nod. In a way, I *was* violating Zubi's privacy, wasn't I? Would she still be friends with me if she found out that I had given this to her husband to read? Or that if it was published, many more people would read it?

I brushed the alarming thought aside and asked him what I had been meaning to ask all along.

'If you met her just once after that time when she came to your office, how did you end up getting married to her?'

He stirred sugar into his coffee and continued stirring around the thick foam.

'That part was actually simple,' he said and I looked up surprised, my hand paused mid-air. Simple?

'I just made my mother send a formal proposal to her mother. At first her mother didn't agree.'

I frowned when he stopped. 'Why?'

He shrugged. 'I don't know. I ran the whole show from the back and made sure my mother didn't take no for an answer.'

I had a feeling I kind of knew Zubi's mother through Zubi and she wasn't the kind to give in easily.

'And she agreed?' I asked, sceptically.

'Actually, no,' his face flushed. 'Zubi's mother is quite headstrong. And it took a lot of convincing for her to agree to the proposal.'

'This isn't as simple as you said it was.'

He took a sip of his latte and nodded. 'I went and met her on my own.'

'You did what?' I asked, surprised. 'Tahera would have freaked out.'

He grinned suddenly. 'Yes. She was absolutely shocked. She refused to let me inside the house. But I wore her down eventually.'

I wanted to ask him more but there wasn't enough time for that.

Instead I asked him what I'd wanted to for a long time. 'Did you ever tell Zubi that you…you fell in love with her before marriage?'

He looked down at his coffee for a moment and then looked up. 'What do you think?' he asked me.

Zubi was the link between us. She was the reason we were sitting here. I had a vested interest in her story, but Zubi's story was his *life*.

'Even after six years?' I asked, unable to keep the surprise out. 'What were you doing all this while?'

'You know she doesn't communicate easily,' he started. 'And I...I had been hoping that once we moved here, to Hong Kong, she'd change. She has changed. But not for the better. If anything, she's become more withdrawn,' he said, sounding bitter.

'Where did you learn such fluent Cantonese?' I asked him, trying to change the subject. I didn't want him to blame me yet again for the change in Zubi's behaviour.

He made a face. 'I'm an architect living in Hong Kong. Not only do I know Cantonese and a little bit of Mandarin, I've had to learn Feng Shui also. It's part of my job.'

I nodded.

'If Zubi talks to you about herself, would you be able to finish the book?' he asked. I stared into the distance, and then at him, absently noting the stubble lining his jaw.

'Yeah, maybe,' I said. 'But I don't see that happening.'

'We'll think of a way,' he said and I looked up immediately. His eyes had an intense look in them and I had to replay this sentence in my head, about a hundred times, '*He's Zubi's husband. DO NOT hit on him, no matter how sexy you find him.*'

'How?' I asked instead, stepping back mentally from the situation and wishing like hell that Khaled had been balding or at least had a paunch.

He pursed his lips together and then shrugged. 'Next month, I have to go out of town for a weekend on business. Maybe you could stay with her because I was worrying about her staying alone anyway.'

'Wow,' I couldn't stop myself. 'From not trusting me, you've gone pretty far ahead, inviting me to *stay* in your home! Why's that?'

He nodded and then spoke, 'I know I've been rude to you in the past. But that was before I read your book. The book you are writing is about *my* wife. If you're going to be decoding her, then I'd sure as hell want to give you a helping hand!'

I snorted. 'Yeah right.'

33

I decided that the only way to get Zubi to talk would be to tell her the truth. Except maybe the part about meeting her husband because she may just misunderstand it. I don't know. I was confused but I went ahead and called her, asking her to come to the McDonald's on Nathan Road near her apartment.

It was a Friday evening and McDonald's was crowded as usual with young chattering girls and boys and harassed-looking mothers with their children. Zubi had got Abid along with her today. I smiled at him and got up just as she came and sat down at the booth.

'Ice cream cone for him and coffee for us?' I asked her, making my way towards the counter. Zubi nodded. I returned some time later and handed the chocolate-dipped cone to Abid, in a way glad that Zubi was not one of those mothers who didn't let their children eat anything cold or sweet. Anything enjoyable, that is.

Just to get the conversation started, I voiced my thoughts loudly and she chuckled.

'Imagine having a childhood without chocolates?'

'I know!' I said, lifting my cup, spotting two Chinese girls smiling at Abid. They kept pointing at his curly hair and making beckoning motions with their hands.

Abid looked serious as he demolished the cone slowly and I

was startled to realise that he looked a lot like Khaled. 'Your son is going to break many hearts some day. Heck, I think he's doing it even now!' I said to Zubi, pointing out the two girls to her who looked disappointed as Abid hadn't walked over to them.

Zubi laughed at that and I noted how different she looked when she laughed this way.

'Zubi, I have something important to tell you,' I told her and her face became serious immediately.

'What is it?' she asked, training her eyes on me with intensity.

'I...I have been writing a book about food. Actually,' I said, wiping my sweaty forehead with the back of my hand. 'It's a book about the food that you make. You, your mother and your grandmother.'

Zubi nodded. 'You had told me about it once...' she said, '...but I didn't think you were serious.'

'Well, actually, I'm very serious,' I told her, wishing that I would stop perspiring so much.

'I...I have a plan.' I quickly outlined what I had told Khaled – about the book and the videos.

'Videos?' she asked me, her brow furrowing. 'And the book will be a recipe book, right?'

Err, no. This wasn't like a recipe book. I didn't know how to tell her without alarming her.

'Actually, no. It's going to be like a food memoir. A foodoir is what they call it these days. And you will be demonstrating the recipes in the videos. Believe me, it's going to be a hit!'

'Memoir? Foodoir?' she asked, her eyes narrowed. 'You're going to be writing about my life?' Oh boy.

'Well, yes. I mean, there are plenty of food books out there. Our book has to have a USP, a unique selling proposition. But in fact, this book will have two USPs. Your story *and* your videos.'

I waited for a reaction but there was none. Zubi emptied a sachet of sugar into her coffee and stirred it intensely, as though her life depended upon it. She took a sip, winced and tore open another sachet. I waited patiently for her to finish and glanced at Abid who was done with the cone. He had a white and brown moustache over his lips and he smiled at me.

'Fries?' I asked him. He looked at his mother who shook her head.

'Ice cream was enough. He eats too many fries and he has to go back and have dinner too.'

Okay. She spoke, but it was nothing to do with what I had said.

'Zubi?' I finally prompted her. She sipped her coffee and looked at me.

'What?'

'What do you think?' I asked her.

'Had you planned this before?' she asked me suddenly, taking me by surprise.

'I...no...I saw your video on the Internet and I contacted you because...for some reason I could connect with you. I just felt like there was so much more to you and I needed to know it. There's a certain quality about you that intrigues the people you meet and...' I stopped talking.

'Why are you doing this?' she asked, leaning forward and staring at me.

'I don't know,' I said, sighing and pushing my cup away tiredly. 'I really don't know why I'm doing this. I just know that it's something I have to do.'

'I understand,' Zubi said slowly. I looked up at her surprised.

'What do you mean?' I asked her, leaning back into my chair.

'I understand that there are some things in life that we just have to do. Why do you think I posted those videos?' she asked me with half a smile.

'Exactly!' I was so excited and shocked to know she could get what I meant. She got it faster than Khaled, who I'd had to lure with the promise of letting him read the manuscript. And here was Zubi who didn't even ask to see it.

'So? You'll tell me your story?' I asked her, unable to keep the tremor from my voice.

'Have you done this before?' she asked me, a frown on her face.

'Done what before?' I repeated stupidly.

'Writing a food…foodoir?' she replied.

'No, never. The longest I've written is just 2,500 words for a cover story in our magazine.'

'Then how will you know if you've done a good job? Let me read it and see,' she said, steepling her fingers together. Well, well, well. This Zubi was not a fool.

'Of course, I'll let you read it,' I said, stalling for time. 'But first I want to finish writing it. And for that I really need you to tell me a little more about yourself.'

'My life is so boring. What do you want to know?'

I stayed silent and counted till ten in my head. For some reason I was dying to tell her that Khaled had asked me to stay with her and Abid in their home for a weekend. But if I did, she might clam up completely and refuse to talk to me.

'I…I need more time with you. These few hours in coffee shops and restaurants won't do. I might have to come to your place and stay for a few hours to speak to you.'

Zubi's brow cleared suddenly. 'You know what? He was telling me that he has to go out of town next month for a weekend. Maybe you can come over and stay with us? What do you think?' she asked, looking a little excited.

I felt guilt suffuse my face in an unbecoming blotchy red. I nodded and then asked the most inane question that made her frown again. 'He? Who's he?'

34

The Christmas craze was building up to a frenzy in Hong Kong and I had so many important events to cover. Vera was always snapping at everyone, almost as if some dormant gene in her had got activated the moment 1 December arrived. I put aside Zubi's manuscript because I knew that if I made too many gaffes, Vera could even fire me and I wasn't ready for such consequences yet.

One Thursday, Zubi's number flashed on my mobile. I cautiously answered her call.

'So, you're coming to stay with us this weekend, aren't you?' she asked.

I looked at the calendar on my laptop screen and nodded. 'Yes. Saturday morning.'

'Oh. But he's leaving tomorrow night,' she said and I rolled my eyes. I realised I'd never heard Zubi call her husband by his name. Surely she wasn't *that* old-fashioned?

'Who's *he*, Zubi?' I couldn't resist asking her as I swivelled in my chair. Then catching sight of Vera glaring at me, I straightened up and said, 'Okay, okay. I'll think about it.'

On Friday, I went back to my place, packed a bag with some essentials and left for Zubi's house. I carried my laptop along with me because I realised that I wanted to be able to write whenever inspiration struck.

Zubi and Abid were at the door the moment I rang the bell. She looked very excited. I looked around cautiously, hoping Khaled had left. He had. I let out a deep sigh and sat down on one of the sofas.

'Why don't you put your bag in the room and get comfortable?' Zubi sat down next to me and smiled. Abid was jumping up and down and it almost seemed as though Zubi would start jumping too if I told her to. I grinned at their excitement until I had a disturbing thought.

'Are you always this happy when Khaled goes off somewhere?' I asked and Zubi's face changed immediately.

'Oh don't shut me off, Zubi. Not now!' I added quickly, flexing my toes above the ground and then folding my legs on the sofa as I did at home.

'I…no, it's not like that,' she explained slowly. 'We're not happy because he left. We're just happy that you're here!'

'Well, that's great. I hope we can finish up this weekend so I can complete the book soon. I want to do it while I'm still interested in your story.'

'You mean there are chances that you'll lose interest?' she asked me in a mock serious manner and I laughed.

'I just want to get to know you. As you were. As you are. Not this façade you put in front of me and others, even your husband. And I want to know about the food you cook.'

'Wow. In a big hurry, aren't we?' she said, getting up to go to the kitchen.

'Yeah, sort of!' I replied, watching Abid switch on the TV. He was remarkably smart for a three-year-old.

When I said that aloud, she laughed over her shoulder and

replied, 'He's been doing that since he was a year-and-a-half.'

'So, was he born here? You said you'd been here for three years and he's three years old so...'

'No, but we came here when he was a few months old,' Zubi said, coming back from the kitchen with a plate. Steam rose in a curl above the plate and I shook my head, almost in despair.

'Zubaida Banu, do you know the number of kilos I have *piled* on since I met you?' I asked her, although my eyes were focused on the plate.

She smiled and handed the plate to me. Cutlets. This was a seemingly generic food type not restricted to any one culture because not only did my mother make them, Anna's half Anglo-Indian mother made them too. Anna had been my best friend in school by the way. The cutlets smelled delicious and I used the fork she'd kept beside them to cut off a small piece. The bread crumb coating was brown and crisp and the kheema with the potatoes inside was moist, to the point of being juicy.

It was also very hot – I realised that as I placed the first piece in my mouth, juggling it around on my tongue. I looked at her and she looked like she was trying hard not to laugh.

'Are you always this impatient?' she asked me. I shrugged.

'Never take a chance with good food,' I told her.

The apartment had darkened as the evening wore on. Zubi switched on the lights and I instantly felt homesick. I wasn't too comfortable staying in anyone's house. It had to do with the lights actually. For some reason, white light reminded me of hospitals and overly bright places that were fake for some reason. White lights were too stark.

Zubi could sense my discomfort but we had started talking about her childhood and other things so I didn't want to stop the flow.

'So when did you realise you liked to cook?' I asked her, hoping that she would give me a long story that would be really useful for the book.

'I don't know. I wasn't really into it when I was a young girl. I guess it just grew on me over the years.'

'Then why did you do the cooking video?' I asked her. She didn't reply immediately. I had removed my jacket and now I felt a slight chill because of the breeze from the window. I clamped my teeth down a little to stop them from chattering. Damn! Wasn't she feeling the cold at all?

'I...I can't really explain why I did it,' she said, looking down at her hands.

I felt dismayed but instead I asked her to shut the windows because I was feeling really cold now.

'So sorry, Sonia! I'm such a terrible hostess,' she said, jumping up to shut the window.

I rubbed my forehead slightly, wondering how I could get Zubi to talk.

'Zubi, are you thinking about the book?' I asked her and she looked away for a moment before nodding her head. I knew it. The idea that her story was going to be read by others was probably terrifying her.

'For now, please, please stop thinking about it. Just ignore the fact that it's going to be a book some time in the future,' I said, getting up and walking around the confined space of her living room.

'I don't know what to do!' she said, flinging her hands in the air, looking desperate.

'Okay. Here's what we'll do,' I told her. 'I'm going to change into something more comfortable and warm. And then you and I can talk while you make dinner. Like how we used to before.'

Zubi nodded, looking a little lost.

I went inside the spare bedroom and changed into a sweatshirt and track pants. I rummaged in my bag and found a pullover, which I wore, and stepped out.

To my surprise, the horrible white lights had gone. Instead, Zubi had lit a cheerful yellow light in the centre of the living room. I'd never noticed its presence before but then I had never been here so late in the evening. Immediately her apartment looked more warm and inviting.

'This is nice!' I said, walking into the kitchen. Zubi was stirring the contents of a pot on the stove briskly. The aroma of frying onions in the confined air gave my senses an instant high.

'What are you making?' I asked her, feeling a sense of déjà vu as she turned to me and smiled.

'Your favourite. Biryani.'

Part Four

35

In 2004, when Zubi's wedding was finalised, her brothers took almost insane pleasure in taunting her by telling her that her husband to be was fat, balding and had a protuberant nose.

'He's also got the thickest lips you've ever seen, Zubi di!' Suhail said, looking at his older brother for support. Zubi refused to listen to both of them but when Rishaad said, 'He'll probably swallow your lips when he kisses you,' Zubi got up and ran after both of them with the closest thing she could find. A long-handled broom.

Her mother found the three of them running around the house, Zubi looking fierce and her brothers were easily outrunning her as they dodged her every now and then. She flung away the broom and stomped back to her room angrily, looking a little startled to see Suman Chachi following her inside.

'Those boys are becoming really, really unruly these days. There's no one to keep them in control,' she muttered as she sat down on Zubi's bed. Zubi sniffled and wished she wouldn't start crying but Suman Chachi looked sympathetic and to her horror, Zubi found a fat tear running down her cheek. She wiped it quickly and turned to her chachi.

'When did you come? I didn't see you at all,' she said, smiling at her.

'If your father had been here today, he would have walloped those two boys for behaving this way with you. Not only is Rishaad a trouble-maker himself, he's turned Suhail, too, into a little monster!' Suman said. Zubi didn't say anything. She normally didn't like to talk about her father.

'What are you doing these days?' Suman Chachi asked her when Zubi stayed quiet for an uncomfortable length of time.

'Nothing. College got over and there's nothing for me to do these days. I just help Ammi with cooking and I'm doing some painting.'

'Good, good!' Suman Chachi said, looking pleased. 'I'm so glad you joined an art college instead of doing a regular course.'

Zubi nodded but didn't tell her that her heart wasn't in it. Her instructors had told her that she could practice and practice and become good someday but she wasn't talented. She didn't possess that raw energy that could manifest itself through her paintings. She was going to be a mediocre artist at best. Their evaluation had shattered Zubi because she'd considered herself to be good. Different from all the girls in her family, but yes, she thought she'd be really good.

'About this boy your mother has chosen for you...' Suman Chachi started and Zubi looked up immediately. She knew he couldn't possibly be all the horrible things the boys had said he was.

'I have a photo,' said Suman Chachi, her eyebrows arching up rapidly noting Zubi's interest.

'How...' Zubi didn't continue.

'I cannot imagine how Tahera Bhabhi expects you to get married to a man without even seeing his photo. This is the twenty-first century!'

Zubi kept quiet and looked outside her room's window. Her mother had merely informed her that she would be getting married this year to a man named Khaled Ahmed. He lived in Bangalore with his brothers and his mother. He had a sister who was married. That was it.

'So when, this morning, she came to show the photo to your Adil Chacha, na, I asked her for the photo,' Suman Chachi beamed triumphantly. 'She wasn't willing to give it to me at all, but then I made her give it.'

Zubi was all ears but still pretended to seem interested in the view from the window.

'I'm not going to show the photo to you unless you look at me and ask at least one question about him.' Zubi let out a sigh and rolled her eyes simultaneously.

'Does he have thick lips?' Zubi asked, looking a little worried.

'What?' Suman Chachi looked startled. 'I...no...I didn't notice his lips,' she said, pulling out her mobile phone and adjusting her spectacles.

'The photo is in your phone?' Zubi asked sceptically.

'Of course,' Suman Chachi murmured as she scrolled the photos on her phone. Zubi continued looking at her expectantly because Suman Chachi was the only one in their family who had a mobile phone with a camera. Rishaad had been begging their mother to get him one but Ammi had naturally refused.

'Here,' Suman Chachi said and showed the phone to her with glee.

Zubi took the phone from her, a little dubiously, trying to make out the blurry picture on the screen. There was a shadow on the face, probably from when Suman Chachi had taken a photo of the photo. She turned the screen towards the light to see it clearly and felt a tiny jolt of recognition.

She knew this man. She had seen him numerous times on his motorcycle around their house and realised he was the same man she had spoken to when she had gone looking for a chief guest at the nearby architectural firm. She was sure it was him. For a moment, she felt weird. Surely this was too strange to be a coincidence. But she hadn't even told him her name and he couldn't have seen her near her house.

'Isn't he quite good looking?' Suman Chachi asked.

Zubi looked at the picture again and had to agree although she didn't say anything. There was a quiet kind of intensity to him that was very appealing. Zubi felt a little tug inside her heart knowing that she had spoken to him already. He wasn't a complete stranger.

'How are the kids?' Zubi asked because Chachi was looking at her very carefully. 'Have they come too?'

Chachi nodded and made a face. 'They've already got into a fight with Suhail and Rishaad. You'd think Rishaad was too old for this stuff…but I can't believe that he's almost what…nineteen?'

'No, no, Chachi! He's going to be seventeen this December,' Zubi protested, although she knew that Chachi was right. Her brothers had become too rowdy of late and it seemed as though Ammi had no control over them.

'Where's Aliya? Has she joined the boys too?' Zubi asked her Chachi about her ten-year-old daughter.

'No, no! You know how she likes to run behind your mother, na? I can't figure out why she's so attached to your mother though,' Suman Chachi said, taking the phone from Zubi's hands. Zubi knew that her mother would laugh if she heard how puzzled Chachi sounded. It was almost as if fate was playing tic-tac-toe with them. Just as she had idolised Chachi when she'd been Aliya's age, Aliya was doing the same to her mother. *Her* mother! At times, even Zubi wondered guiltily what Aliya saw in her mother.

'So, you're happy now?' Chachi asked her, looking at her carefully.

'I...I don't know,' Zubi admitted and together they got up to go outside.

'Have you got everything ready?' Chachi asked her in a swift change of subject and Zubi had only moments to realise that Chachi was asking her about the ingredients for the chocolate cake.

'Oh yes. Everything is ready,' she said and walked towards the kitchen. Chachi had promised to teach Zubi how she made her special chocolate cake. Zubi felt a momentary surge of enthusiasm and a feeling that everything would be alright. Almost everything.

Zubi wondered where her mother was because the boys were sitting down to play a game of Pictionary and there was no sign of her or Aliya. Suman Chachi shook her head and made her way towards the kitchen.

'How's Adil Chacha?' Zubi asked her, hoping to divert her attention.

'He's fine. You saw him just yesterday, na?' Chachi asked and then added a little more amicably, 'He's coming to pick us up in the evening.'

Zubi didn't say anything because she was busy collecting the necessary ingredients and utensils and placing them on the kitchen counter.

'I've made this cake so many times,' Zubi started, looking back at her aunt as she sieved the flour with cocoa and baking powder. 'But I still don't get it the way you make it. All dense and without all the spongy holes in it.'

Suman Chachi smiled a little smugly and for a moment Zubi could understand why her mother didn't like her much. But she put aside that slightly disturbing thought and handed the sugar and butter to Chachi.

'Okay. It's not a top secret or anything but the trick to making your cake dense is making the batter runny,' Chachi disclosed.

Zubi nodded. Chachi had attended some fancy baking classes a few years ago although she never made anything except chocolate cake. Zubi had a faint suspicion that she decided to make chocolate cake her speciality because it was popular and also seemingly easy to make.

'So how do you make your batter runny?' Zubi asked, her brows puckering.

'Tch! Don't frown like that. You'll get lines on your forehead,' Chachi admonished her as she creamed the butter and powdered sugar. Zubi thought about her mother's forehead with the numerous lines and wondered how much frowning her mother had done to merit those.

'Give me half a cup of milk and half a lemon,' Chachi ordered her and Zubi got them ready for her. She watched as Chachi squeezed the lemon in the milk and let it stand for some time.

'Won't that curdle the milk?' Zubi asked doubtfully.

'Precisely,' Chachi replied, and she continued beating the batter for the cake. She added the eggs, the essence, the sieved flour and cocoa and then she swirled the soured milk in the cup before pouring that into the batter.

'But...'

'Don't ask me the science behind it,' Chachi admonished her. 'I only know that adding sour milk makes my chocolate cakes fantastic.'

'O-kay,' Zubi nodded as she went to preheat the oven. Later when she unmoulded the cake onto a plate and cut it into slices, Zubi watched Chachi as she arranged the pieces on another plate. Before she could formulate her thoughts properly, she asked her, 'Did you ever regret it? Marrying Chacha?'

Suman Chachi paused and looked at Zubi, a little puzzled.

'No, never. Why do you ask?'

'No...I...it's just that you knew Chacha before you got married,' Zubi attempted to explain lamely.

'So?' Chachi still had the ability to become a bit defensive about it sometimes. 'How much I have tried to adjust in your family, you can't even imagine...' She stopped when Zubi shook her head and waved her hand frantically.

'No, no! I didn't mean that, Chachi. I was just thinking about marriages in general,' she said. Inside her head though, she continued thinking of her parents and their marriage. She watched the boys come into the kitchen and wolf down three or four slices of the cake before running back outside. She saw her mother come inside the kitchen and smile at Chachi before trying out a piece of the cake and nodding her head in approval. She saw Aliya nibble at the cake, before asking *her* mother to make gajar ka halwa.

Zubi ate a piece of the cake, its warmth suffusing her mouth with a strange kind of melancholy and desperation. She hadn't expected these feelings to swamp her because when they started making the cake, she'd felt quite exhilarated. But all that had changed now.

She didn't voice any of those thoughts even though she'd wanted to. Because with sudden clarity she realised, she wasn't thinking about the cake but about marriages. She thought of her parents, Suman Chachi and Adil Chacha and her grandparents. She knew how much of give and take a marriage was. She'd always been able to interpret the glances shared by these married couples and it wasn't just the implication of intimacy. It was so much more. It was the sharing of lives, of happiness and pain and anguish in equal measure. She'd seen how they'd given up a part of themselves to form the whole unit of a couple. Almost like how the sour milk had surrendered its sourness to accentuate the softness of the cake.

But these couples had done it without a thought. She doubted though, whether she could do it.

36

The air was scented with jasmine and roses, a cloying perfume that hung heavily and somehow reached the back of her throat, making her want to clear it loudly. But she didn't. She swallowed and continued looking down at the rose petals scattered on the bed. It was her wedding night and Khaled's aunts had helped her get into her wedding ghagra.

'But he has to see you in *this* ghagra, right?' a plump aunt giggled as she dabbed Zubi's face with powder and painted her lips ruby red.

'Before he sees her out of it,' another aunt, whose hair was dyed mehendi orange, cackled and they tittered as they helped adjust her dupatta so that it hung over her face, obscuring it completely. Thankfully, they left soon, leaving Zubi alone with her thoughts and a sense of growing panic.

The panic didn't seem to recede when she heard the door open and although she was no longer sitting in the ludicrous position that they'd left her in, with one knee folded and her head tipped down over the other knee, she still couldn't see much. Her gaze followed his ornate silver slippers. Then he pulled them off and stashed them in one corner before heading towards the bathroom.

Zubi's heart beat madly and she wondered how everyone else

did it. How did they manage to connect with a stranger? How could they give themselves up completely? The bathroom door closed again and Zubi heard the definite click.

She was now desperate to clear her throat but she didn't because she was scared that he would think she was trying to get his attention. As if she needed to. She was wearing a freaking red ghagra and sitting on a bed with rose petals strewn on it in a typical filmy fashion.

What would he say to her? What would his first words be? What is your name? No, that was silly. He knew her name. Didn't he?

Zubi told herself to breathe calmly but she sensed him nearing the bed and it seemed that all at once, her mind, her heart and her senses were on opposing warpaths with each other. Each seemed hell bent on taking control. Both her knees were bent and she had looped her arms around them aiming for casualness. He sat down on the bed next to her. Zubi was sure that she had stopped breathing and would hyperventilate shortly.

Was he going to touch her? Would he talk to her first? God! What do two strangers do on their wedding night? Have sex straight away? She shuddered involuntarily and he noticed it, which apparently made things easier for him.

'Are you cold?' he asked and Zubi shut her eyes tightly and shook her head. All her jewellery from her head till her neck tinkled but to her, it seemed like it was clanging inside her head.

She opened her eyes a fraction and saw that he had placed his right hand, palm facing downwards on the bed. It was an inch away from her foot. She studied his hands carefully, noticing how well formed they were. Then to her surprise and shock, the hand moved and she felt a warm feeling grow inside her as he placed his hand on her mehendi-covered foot.

He felt, rather than heard her gasp, but his strong warm hands remained on her foot, tracing the curving arch, his finger going up and down and around her anklet. He then did the same on her other foot. Zubi felt the strangest sensations welling up as though from somewhere deep inside. And he hadn't even seen her face yet.

He then reached out and lifted her pallu, pushing it back over her head so he could see her face. She was supposed to have lowered her head but she felt foolish. She was supposed to have kept her eyes closed, but she didn't. Their eyes met in quiet approval and Zubi was shocked at the jolt of desire she felt for this stranger. This man. Her husband. So strong was her desire that her immediate reflex was to back away mentally.

'I don't know what to talk to you about,' he admitted and smiled. Zubi continued staring back at him and a change came over his eyes. They darkened a little and his breathing was short, as though he'd forgotten to take a breath.

'I'm tired,' Zubi said the first thing that came to her mind. 'I'm sleepy. I'd like to sleep, please.'

She noticed his surprise and the quick way in which he recovered his composure.

'Of course, of course,' he said politely but she knew that her rebuff had hurt him. She couldn't help it though. She couldn't possibly act on the impulses she'd felt when she'd seen his face from such close quarters. She watched him get up, rummage through a cupboard and find some clothes which he took to the bathroom with him to change.

Zubi looked around the room helplessly. It was a small room, made all the more claustrophobic by his presence and Zubi wondered if she could change into something more comfortable too. She heard sounds coming from the bathroom and before she could change her mind, she started removing all her jewellery and placing it on the bedside table. She heard the door open and her hands paused in the middle of unscrewing a heavy earring from her ear.

The two of them stared at each other briefly before they averted their eyes. Zubi had quickly noted that he was wearing a T-shirt and track pants.

'You can change inside the bathroom if you want to,' he said stiffly as he dusted the rose petals away from his side of the bed.

Zubi didn't reply. She continued removing her jewellery and when it was all done, she got up and went to the bathroom with a change of clothes. When she emerged a little later, she saw that the lights in the room had been switched off although a night lamp glowed from a corner.

She sat down on the bed, wondering if she'd done the right thing. But the biggest fear that had prompted her to behave that way was the fear of becoming like her mother. She did not want to become like her. Ever.

Half asleep, she was more responsive than she would ever be fully awake. In her mind she knew what was happening as she felt Khaled's warm hands on her body, his mouth touching her in ways that seemed to burn her up from the very inside. But her body refused to let her mind take over and they both surrendered to him eventually. Her eyes were still closed when he pulled her towards him, resting his chin in the crook of her neck, running his hands down her back and murmuring words that made no sense to either of them. She let him comfort her because she knew that in the morning, she wouldn't be able to behave normally. Shy and coy like normal brides.

She touched his cheek and her fingers felt his smile, but even then her eyes didn't open. In fact, it seemed she was drawn into a deeper sleep than ever. She knew she'd be horrified in the morning. But for that moment, it felt good.

The following evening was their valima. Zubi stayed inside her room most of the day, refusing eye contact with Khaled who seemed slightly bewildered with her. In the evening, one of Khaled's young cousins helped her get dressed into yet another ghagra. The cousin admired the mehendi on Zubi's arms.

'So, did Bhaiya find his name in the mehendi on your hands?' She blushed even as she asked the question. Zubi looked at her puzzled. She had no idea what she was talking about.

'Come on, Bhabhi! Surely the mehendwali must have drawn his name somewhere in all this intricate design?'

Zubi shook her head, the jewellery brushing her ears.

'Oh! That's so sad. Wait, show me your arm,' she said as she turned Zubi's palm upwards and then around and then hit upon something.

'See! There it is. K!' she jumped excitedly. And so she pointed out the small letters that made up her husband's name already imprinted on her body, albeit temporarily. As each letter was discovered, Zubi felt a frisson inside her. She knew it was fear. But it could be something else.

He came inside the room to get ready for the valima and Zubi averted her eyes from him, sitting on the edge of the bed, her back straight and her head bowed. She knew he was looking at her but she ignored him, or rather deeply ignored the strong vibes he kept sending towards her.

'Are you ready?' he asked. He'd tried speaking to her a couple of times since morning but each time, she literally ran in the opposite direction. Now, she was trapped. She sensed him walking towards her and felt him sit down next to her.

'Zubaida, about last night,' he started speaking, his hands automatically reaching for hers. Zubi shut her eyes tightly, not wanting to hear him speak about her lapse of sense or sudden surge in passion because she had clearly examined her thoughts since morning. It hadn't been his fault. Well, not entirely.

'I...'

'Can we not speak about it now?' she asked. 'It's getting late and you have to get ready.'

'But...' Khaled sounded almost desperate to say what he wanted to and she was just as desperate to avoid hearing it.

She stood up, dragging her hand away from his and walked towards the door.

'I'll wait outside while you get ready.'

She glanced at him as she shut the door. She noticed that his head was bent slightly and he was staring at the floor.

At the valima, most of the time they were in separate sections of the party hall and Zubi felt gratified to see her family. Especially her mother and her grandmother. She hugged them and her grandmother wiped a tear from her eye and kept shaking her head. Later when she was seated on the stage, Suman Chachi sat next to her and started asking her suggestively about what had happened in the night.

'But I'm your Chachi! Like your best friend! You should be able to tell me!' she whispered as a photographer took Zubi's photos. He asked her to tilt her head in one direction and he insisted that Zubi shouldn't speak. Zubi had never been more thankful.

Later that night, Zubi and Khaled were seated next to each

other while members of the immediate family performed different ceremonies. Tonight, Khaled was supposed to come back with Zubi to her house. She dreaded the coming night because he would definitely try and speak to her.

Thankfully, she was supposed to keep her head bowed so no one noticed her discomfort. She had, in fact, tuned out from everything that was happening around her when suddenly she realised that her brothers and cousins were chanting something. What were they saying? Lift her? Oh my god. Not in front of all these people!

She felt Khaled stiffen beside her and then before she knew it, he swung her around and lifted her in his arms. Zubi looped her arms around his neck to gain balance and she cursed the idiots who had suggested this. It was supposed to be all in good fun, but in front of the entire family? His mother? Her mother? God! She was so embarrassed that she swung her foot a little to indicate that she wanted to get down.

He put her down slowly and she straightened up with difficulty, weighed down by the ghagra and the jewellery and the flowers. Everyone around her was laughing and clapping and she spotted young girls giggling. In a flash, she felt what they were feeling. Envious and wistful and a whole lot of other things. It was strange that she was feeling it too, because they were envious *of* her. But *she* envied them, their willingness to participate in a wedding, the enthusiasm with which they would love and serve the total strangers who would be their husbands in future. She envied their raw immaturity but most of all, she envied how intact their hearts seemed to be.

She wished she could explain what she was feeling to him. But she couldn't because she couldn't understand what she felt either.

She only knew that every time she saw him, there was that spark of recognition, of desire, of what she didn't know, but she knew she couldn't give in.

She sat upright in the guest bedroom of her house. She felt strange because she was back in her own home and yet she had been given the guest bedroom, not her own room. Her brothers and some of her cousins had hidden Khaled's shoe and there had been a lot of good-natured teasing, which she hadn't been privy to. She'd just overheard what had happened through her aunts, mainly Suman Chachi, who had been very excited.

Her house was full of guests and there was so much going on... and yet she felt disconnected from it all because she was worried about what Khaled would say. It wasn't so much the physical act of talking to him that she was terrified of. Her mind was blocked for some reason and she just didn't want to listen to his justification or explanation. She pushed her foot back on the ground and she felt it connect with something soft. What was that?

She got down from the bed and looked under it to find Suhail crouched there, grinning at her.

'Not my idea,' he said, as she dragged him outside, her temper flaring more than usual. Imagine if they hadn't discovered him under the bed! Her face flushed as she glared at him.

'Whose idea was it then?' she asked him, her hands on her hips. Just then she heard the door of the bedroom open with a click and almost immediately she felt deflated. God! What would Khaled think of her brothers? That they were insane? It wouldn't be off the mark.

'I'm going! I'm going!' Suhail shouted and ran past Khaled who merely stared at him with one raised eyebrow.

'You might want to check everywhere else and see if any more of my crazy relatives are hiding anywhere,' Zubi spoke shakily, trying to ease the suddenly strained atmosphere.

She noticed the way he was looking at her, probably glad that she wasn't hiding behind the pallu. But before she could bring some order to her thoughts, he took two strides towards her, slipped his hand behind her neck, pulled her almost frightened face close to his and whispered close to her lips.

'Don't ever do this to me again.'

'Do what?' she whispered back, her eyes darting madly between his.

'Whatever you've been doing since morning. Ignoring me. Giving me the silent treatment. Not willing to talk to me,' he whispered again, tersely.

Zubi was unsure of her response. She just continued staring back at his eyes and before she knew it, he had closed the gap between them and was kissing her. Zubi closed her eyes and told herself to let go, to simply let the different feelings wash over her instead of trying to control them. But as things got intense, his hands moved to unbutton her blouse and she pushed him away. He looked at her, first startled and then angry. Zubi grabbed her nightie and ran inside the bathroom.

She was going to wait inside the bathroom for as long as it took for him to change and go to sleep. So she waited inside the cold bathroom, counting the petals on the flowers on the tiles until she felt drowsy. She had changed into her night clothes and was getting tired of holding her heavy ghagra in her hand. She opened the bathroom door cautiously wondering what she would do if he was right outside. But the room was dark and she could make out his form on the bed. He seemed asleep, his arm flung across his face.

Relieved, Zubi crept back into the room, dropped the ghagra on a chair and went to sleep, curled on the very edge of the bed.

37

ZUBI could never think of it as her house. It was always her mother-in-law's house. Or Khaled's. But not hers. Not yet, even nearly two years into their marriage. The days had settled into a comfortable routine where Khaled went to work as usual and Zubi spent time in the kitchen with her mother-in-law, acclimatising herself to a new household and its rules. She was keen to try some of her mother's recipes but her mother-in-law was neither open to, nor amenable to changes. It became quite clear to Zubi that her mother-in-law firmly believed that 'She who ruled the kitchen, ruled the house'. And she had no intention of letting Zubi take that place. Although at first Zubi resented her dictatorial ways, she let go after some time.

The evenings were pleasant when Khaled and his brothers returned from work and the friendly commotion dwarfed any feelings of melancholy that Zubi might have had after leaving her mother's house. Well, at least her brothers-in-law weren't mean to her like her own brothers.

The nights were still a matter of debate. To the world, it would seem that Zubi and Khaled were a perfect couple. They looked great together and one only had to see Khaled's face whenever Zubi entered the room to know how he felt about her. But when they were alone, Zubi barely spoke to him, unwilling to get drawn into his world. The more distant they were, the better it would be in the long run she thought.

She didn't know when Khaled's patience would snap but she wanted to be ready for it. So she braced herself, waiting for the day when he would give up on her.

On some nights, physical needs overshadowed their strained relationship; that was the only time Zubi allowed her mind to stop controlling her actions. She told herself that she could enjoy those moments, she was entitled to them. In fact, she looked forward to their intimacy because that meant she would see Khaled like she never saw him at any other time. His face tense, his brow furrowed, his shoulders tightened as he was poised above her. His dark eyes were always open, looking into hers as though he'd absorb her entirely through them. She would touch his face, run her fingers over the stubble on his cheek and in those few moments, they were truly alone, disconnected from the world, but together.

Every time, she would disengage herself from him gently and go to sleep as far as possible from him. She didn't know what the pain in the centre of her chest was, but it felt as though her heart trembled. All the effort in making sure she wouldn't care much about him seemed a waste at such moments because she knew that it was already too late.

She watched him covertly as he got ready in the mornings before he left for work. She absorbed every little movement he made, whether it was in the way he snapped his cuffs and folded them or the way he buttoned his shirt. She observed how he would run his finger behind his collar or simply the way he towelled his hair dry and she would shut her eyes and think:

I can't love you so much.

I won't.

What if you die?
I'll become a shell like my mother.
And I don't want to be like her. Ever.

Unaware of Zubi's thoughts, Khaled would pick up his laptop bag and nod in her direction before leaving.

Then, one day, she found out she was pregnant. Her mother-in-law was happy and so was her mother. For some reason, Zubi was terrified. Maybe it was the hormones or all the feelings that she had bottled up inside, but she was afraid that Khaled would indeed die soon and her child would never know its father. Just like her brother Suhail. She would see Khaled leave every morning for work on his bike and would murmur duas for his safety. Throughout the day she would think about him, sometimes wishing she could just call him to hear his voice. But she avoided the temptation and waited for him to return. She felt relieved only when she heard the gate open and his bike rev its way into the garage but she was careful never to show it.

Towards the end of her pregnancy though, something happened that changed the course of her life. She was at her mother's house for the delivery and Khaled would drop by almost every day. He never stayed the night with her and she was grateful because she felt uncomfortable in his presence, bloated and waddly as she was.

One day, her mother had made kutt and she asked Zubi to call Khaled for dinner. In the nearly three years that they had been married, Zubi had probably called Khaled on his cell phone a total of ten times. Each time, it had been to give him some important news or to merely request his presence at a family dinner like now.

He sounded tense when he answered the phone.

'What is it?' he asked.

'I...I wanted to know if you were coming tonight,' she said, looking out of the window at the darkening street.

'Maybe,' he said.

'Can you try and come?' she asked again.

'Why?'

'Ammi's making dinner...'

'And she makes it every day,' Khaled interrupted her. 'Look, I have to go for an interview at four. If I get back early I'll try to come.'

'What interview?' she asked him and there was silence.

'I've been talking about this at home for nearly a month now,' he said quietly.

'But I've been here at my mother's.'

'Wouldn't have made a difference where you were. You're never interested in what's happening in my life!'

Zubi swallowed, but kept quiet. She was always afraid to call him on the phone because he would want to talk about them. And she'd rather not. She didn't respond to that.

'Ammi's making kutt ka salan for dinner and she...'

'Whatever. I'll try,' he interrupted her curtly.

'She's taking so much trouble over it and she specifically asked me to call you for dinner!' Zubi snapped at him, surprised at the change in her tone of voice.

'You...I...' Khaled sounded very angry and then without another word he disconnected the call.

Zubi looked at her phone, surprised and shocked. How could he just do that?

She walked into the kitchen where her mother was stirring a huge pot.

'He's coming, na?' Ammi asked, looking up at her. Zubi was quiet as she observed the changes in Ammi. Since the time she had got married, Ammi had placed Khaled as the head of the family in her mind, although he was never here. *She* had changed – she had started cooking special things for him whenever he came home. Even Rishaad and Suhail seemed to be a little less wild in his presence.

'I don't know,' Zubi replied.

'What do you mean?' Ammi asked as she stopped stirring.

'He said he has an interview in some time. Ammi, how do you make kutt?' she asked in an attempt to change the subject.

'You have to watch and learn,' her mother repeated her oft-quoted phrase. Zubi sighed and sat down on a stool because her lower back was hurting. Ammi noted the change on her face and asked if she was okay.

'Yes, yes. I'm fine,' Zubi replied irritably. She couldn't understand why Ammi expected her to go through the same symptoms that she'd had. Each time Zubi entered the kitchen, Ammi would be surprised.

'Are you feeling nauseous?' Ammi asked her and Zubi rolled her eyes.

'Ammi, I'm nearly nine months pregnant. How can I have morning sickness and nausea at this time?' she asked her.

'You never know,' she muttered before she handed Zubi a bowl of hardboiled eggs. 'Peel the shells, and score them lightly on the sides.'

Zubi cracked each egg lightly and started pulling away the shell, anticipating the evening dinner when she would be able to mash the egg into the kutt, and let the darkly delicious flavours seep into the yolk, so she could scoop it up in her roti and eat it.

'God, I love kutt!' she muttered as she finished shelling the eggs.

Her mother didn't reply. She was making kuftas for the kutt. Zubi had tried asking Ammi a hundred times about the origin of this salan but Ammi had no idea. Each time, Ammi said, 'I only make it. I don't know who thought of it first.'

Kutt was dark, almost to the point of being black. But it wasn't like kali mirch ka phaal. Kutt was special because it took so long to make. First you had to boil horsegram in water and once all the flavours and colours had been leached from it, you had to throw away the horsegram and keep the water! Yes, exactly. Zubi had been so surprised to learn about that.

'Of course, people make edible things from the horsegram. But we are more bothered about this water,' her mother had said, pointing to the huge pot of dark water that swirled around inside. The water had to be reduced for hours on end and then it was thickened with a puree of tomatoes and onions and that unique zeera-methi powder and of course, imli that gave it a special kick.

But kutt wasn't just a salan that you poured on rice or ate with rotis. Kutt had kuftas, boiled eggs and halved brinjals that somehow managed to transcend their ordinariness to commune with the lentil water and touch a level of greatness that seemed impossible on a normal basis. As a final touch, the kutt salan was given a tadka of onions and curry leaves to give it that lilting aroma and seal the exotic flavour.

That day, Zubi watched her mother flit from one part of the kitchen to the other as she finished making this salan and she wondered if Khaled would come for dinner to appreciate it. She'd noticed that her mother loved getting praised by Khaled. It was almost as if Abbu had been revived somewhere in Khaled, as strange and awkward as it sounded, and Ammi thrived for that recognition of her culinary skills...skills that were wasted on her teenage brothers. Khaled lived up to her expectations of course.

At about seven p.m. the doorbell rang and Zubi peered outside the kitchen door to see who it was. Maybe it was a trick of light she thought as she saw Suhail open the door and stand there, talking to Khaled. Zubi covered her mouth with her hands as something clicked in her head. *Khaled* was the man who had come to their house when Suhail had painted her face with kajal.

She hardly heard him speak as he came up to her, the shock so profound that she couldn't process anything that was happening around her. Ammi offered him tea and he agreed, stretching his arms above his head to ease the kinks.

'What?' he asked her, when she continued staring at him. Somehow, the fact that he had never brought up the incident was a defining moment for her. Or rather redefined everything for her.

She went to the kitchen to get tea for him and stopped her mother who was in the process of straining it.

'Did you know that he was the man who came to our house some years back?' Zubi asked her mother, wishing she could jog her mother's memory faster when she looked at her quizzically.

'The time your brother drew up your face with kajal?' her mother asked and Zubi's eyes grew round.

'Of course I knew,' her mother continued. 'I recognised him right away.'

'Why didn't you tell me!?' Zubi asked her mother who looked a little uneasy for some reason. 'And why didn't the boys tell me anything?'

Her mother kept quiet and Zubi felt confused.

'I thought you knew,' she said and went outside as though to deflect further questions.

When they sat down for dinner, she remembered he had mentioned an interview.

'What happened at your job interview?' she asked him. He had closed his eyes in ecstasy, relishing the fragrant salan her mother had made, and then he opened them slowly.

'I got it,' he said simply, looking back at her. Although her brothers were seated at the table with them and her mother hovered near the kitchen doorway, for Zubi it was as though only the two of them existed. The baby pushed against her ribs powerfully and Zubi closed her eyes for a moment to regain her breath. There was the baby too.

'What did you get?' she asked him, rubbing her stomach lightly. She noticed that his eyes followed her movements and she stopped, a little embarrassed.

'I got a job in Hong Kong,' he said.

'Oh!' Zubi didn't know if she was surprised or shocked. 'When…'

'As soon as I can. But I've asked them for a couple of months' time before I join because…because of the baby,' he spoke to her stomach.

Zubi couldn't eat. He was going away? To Hong Kong? For how long? She wanted to ask him all these questions, badger him relentlessly but their code of non-communication had been built brick by brick and there was no way it was coming down in an instant.

'Once the baby is born and everything here is settled, I'll leave,' he said as he continued eating. 'I've got a five-year contract, but I'll try to make it to India once a year.'

Five years. Every year. How could she live without seeing him every day? She didn't know if she was dismayed by the news of his leaving or the realisation that she had turned into her mother already.

She put her roti down and bent her head a little forward. 'Take me with you. Please.'

He paused in the act of eating, surprise and even shock evident on his features. In fact, he didn't say anything for nearly five minutes and both of them kept staring at each other, wishing they could read the other's mind.

Zubi's thoughts were jumbled and harried. He loves me. I know that for sure. The litany reached a crescendo in her head and she knew that if he said no, she might do something really crazy like blurt out what she felt for him.

'Why?' he asked her finally.

Why? How could she tell him why?

'I'd love to see Hong Kong, that's why,' she said. 'I mean, who gets the chance to live in a city like that?' She continued babbling and his face closed up immediately.

'I don't know,' he said finally. 'I'll have to speak to the company and ask for visas for you and the baby.'

She nodded, relieved and immensely sad. He thought she wanted to go to Hong Kong because it was an exciting city. How could she tell him that she'd have gone with him even to Somalia or Siberia? Because all she wanted was him. Just him.

38

At the airport, Zubi faced regrets. Her mother was crying, wondering how they would manage without seeing her but Zubi was quite sure that her mother was going to miss Abid more than anybody else. Abid, all of six months, squirmed in her arms as she leaned forward to hug her mother. She was surprised when tears fell out of her eyes rapidly.

'He said we have an Internet connection there, Ammi. We can chat every day on Skype,' Zubi found herself consoling her mother. Khaled, who had come down from Hong Kong briefly to take Zubi and Abid with him looked calm and composed and he sidled up to Rishaad and Suhail who were laughing over something together.

'Boys, your mother is getting old. Don't get into too much mischief. I'll be getting a report from her every day as it is,' he said but smiled to dilute the effect of his words. He patted Rishaad on his shoulder and punched Suhail lightly in the arm. Both boys adored him and to Khaled, it just seemed like he'd found another pair of unruly brothers, apart from his own.

Zubi checked her handbag and made sure she had enough diapers although Khaled had told her that they had a connecting flight in Malaysia and there was a stopover of a few hours. She was nervous and scared. She'd never been on a plane before and yet, that wasn't half as scary as leaving everything she knew and loved, and going away with Khaled.

That's what love does to you, she thought frantically, as she zipped her handbag. How could I have done this? Why did I insist on going along? What was I thinking? When Khaled left a month after Abid was born, Zubi knew that she could manage without him. He called them every day and she liked the fact that they were so apart that he never brought up anything personal. He lingered only on the mundane and the routine. But barely ten days after he went, he called to tell her that it would take a few more months before he could come and get her, and she panicked. She'd been okay with him gone because she'd known that she and Abid would join him soon. But now that his return was going to be delayed, she felt despair build inside her and she hated herself for that.

She was supposed to have avoided this.

Instead, much to Khaled's surprise, she insisted that he find a way to come and fetch the two of them as they'd discussed before.

'But, Zubi...'

'I don't know. I can't stay without you,' the words had escaped her lips before she even realised that she'd spoken aloud.

'What?' he asked, his voice crackly over her mobile phone.

'Bad connection,' she mumbled before ending the call.

And here she was, six months after Abid was born, taking on the huge risk of moving to a new country and living in a place with only Khaled and their son.

It was only after they had entered the airport that she realised awkwardly that she had hugged her mother and Suman Chachi but not her mother-in-law. Her mother-in-law hadn't been too keen about letting Zubi join Khaled in Hong Kong but since it was Khaled who had informed her that he wanted his family with him, she had kept quiet. The last few months spent at her in-laws' place had been awkward and she realised how much she had counted on Khaled's presence in the house to uplift her spirits. She hadn't made a connection with her mother-in-law and she glanced sideways at Khaled as he pushed their luggage trolley.

She shrugged and turned around, waving at her family and his as they stood outside the glass wall and waved back at them.

Zubi smiled, thinking of their life ahead, feeling the slightest bit possessive about her husband as he played with Abid. He turned to look at her and she quickly looked away, trying to rearrange her features into the blank and disinterested look that he was used to seeing.

It was the sight of the numerous mountains as they landed in Hong Kong that endeared the city to her immediately. The mountains blazed and sparkled in the afternoon heat, and to her eyes, they seemed blue and beckoning and a reason for hope. She could imagine seeing these mountains in the morning, misty and clouded, still standing there, immovable and rock solid. And although they were thousands of miles away, the familiarity of seeing mountains, just like in Vellore, relieved Zubi.

Abid had been cranky and tired and she'd found a place to feed him in one of the rest rooms at the airport after they'd landed. She emerged minutes later, her feelings bordering on panic at not finding Khaled there and then, after a few seconds, she spotted him near the luggage carousel, loading their suitcases into the trolley.

A double-decker bus took them into the city and Khaled nudged her to reach the top level where she sat down right in front, facing the glass windows. As the bus lurched forward and wove its way towards the city, Zubi didn't know how many sights she could absorb, all at once. Abid had fallen asleep and she turned her face slightly to look at Khaled. He'd been in India for just a week and she hadn't had enough time to spend with him because he'd been busy getting everything ready for them to leave.

She absorbed his features hungrily, noting the familiar way his eyebrows seem to feather away at the sides, at his chiselled jawline, at his near perfect ears. With her heart full and her emotions near the surface, she turned to look outside the window at the very moment he had turned to look at her. She knew he was staring at her, observing her as she'd observed him seconds ago. But she didn't turn back to make eye contact.

At a traffic signal, she spotted a young Chinese couple sitting diagonally behind them. They were sitting close together and Zubi was shocked when they started kissing.

Khaled followed her gaze and then elbowed her lightly.

'Stop staring!' he whispered and bravely reached out for Zubi's hand and didn't let go. Zubi remembered nothing of the rest of the journey to Tsim Sha Tsui (TST) because she wanted to memorise the feel of his hands in hers.

Zubi's first impression of TST was the crowd and the huge buildings. When she commented to Khaled about the buildings, he shook his head and said, 'This is nothing. Wait till I take you to the other side.' He hoisted their luggage out of the bus and then before she had even taken a proper look at the building where they would live, he led her inside.

They waited for the lift, Abid heavy in her arms and Khaled holding on to all the luggage. Once or twice, he looked at her and smiled and probably for the first time ever, she smiled back at him. There was something about Hong Kong or maybe just being on their own, which made her feel a little reckless.

'What's this smell?' she asked, sniffing the air.

'What smell?' he asked instead, getting ready to go inside because the lift was finally on the ground floor.

'I don't know. There's been some peculiar smell in the air ever since I entered Hong Kong,' Zubi said, as she got inside the lift after him.

It was only the three of them inside the lift and Khaled pressed the button for the seventh floor.

'Have you been reading James Clavell?' Khaled asked her, a quirky smile on his face.

Zubi shook her head. 'James who? And with Abid? Where's the time? Why do you ask?'

'That smell you were asking, na? James Clavell would have you believe it's the smell of money,' Khaled said, shifting the luggage to a better position as the lift halted at the fifth floor and two African men got inside.

When the lift halted at the seventh floor, Khaled manoeuvered the luggage out and Zubi stepped out after him, realising that for the first time they were having a 'proper' conversation. Like normal couples. And it was perfectly fine.

She stopped when he stopped before a door and she stared.

'What?' he asked, looking a little self-conscious as he fished around for the keys in his pocket.

'It's so pretty!' she said, leaning forward to trace the yellow and grey mosaic work on the door while he bent his head a little to insert the key in the lock.

'Glad you like it,' he muttered as he pushed open the door. Zubi cast a quick glance at the other doors and saw that they were all plain and rather bare. How come their door was different?

'Did you…did you get it done?' she asked hesitantly as she followed him inside. He didn't answer although Zubi could see that he seemed pleased for some reason. Zubi forgot the question she had asked when she saw how small their apartment was. This was going to be their home, she thought, a little amazed but also dismayed. It was so small!

Khaled was watching her face carefully for a reaction and she was determined not to give the wrong one to him.

'Nice,' she said, as she took in the apartment at a glance.

Abid strained against her shoulder and woke up. She realised she had to feed him before she could even taken a proper look around the house. Or flat. Or whatever this was.

'I...I need to feed Abid,' she said, her voice faltering, as she looked questioningly towards a closed door which probably led to the bedroom.

'So feed him,' Khaled said without looking at her as he pushed the suitcases towards one wall. Abid had started crying. Zubi juggled him lightly and made cooing sounds without realising she was doing it, as she opened the door to a room. She stepped back surprised because it was the bathroom.

'Feed him here. In the hall,' Khaled challenged her as he sank into a sofa and watched her avidly.

'I...no...' Zubi opened the door of the next room and stepped inside. There was a bed here and it filled up all the space in the room. There was very little place around the bed. There was also a window right behind the bed, a little above, as though a painting was hanging there.

'Small, I know,' Khaled said behind her, in a rueful tone and Zubi jumped. She straightened and then sat down at one end of the bed, her heart beating wildly. Was he going to *stay* here while she fed the baby? Abid had begun crying in loud bursts now and there was no more time for Zubi to think. She turned her back towards Khaled and unbuttoned her blouse to feed Abid. Her back felt like it was on fire because she knew he was staring at it.

'James Clavell is the author of *Noble House*, *Taipan* and *Shogun* and many other books,' Khaled said suddenly and Zubi nodded, not really bothered and feeling uncomfortable by his presence.

'He wrote about Asia, and that peculiar smell you mentioned, is actually written about in *Noble House*. It's the smell of Hong Kong,' he continued.

Zubi stared ahead at the window in front of her, suddenly realising that she needed a curtain for it. How could they have a window in their bedroom without a curtain?

'Are you hungry?' Khaled asked her suddenly and Zubi turned just her head to look at him. Their eyes met and held each others' for a few moments; Zubi nodded.

'I'll make something for lunch?' she asked him and he raised both eyebrows.

'You would? I thought you'd be tired. If you are let's just go out and eat,' Khaled said as Zubi turned around to face the opposite wall again. She shifted Abid to the other side as Khaled continued talking to her back.

'Or I could just go and get something for us to eat here,' he suggested. Zubi was tempted but she was indeed more like her mother than she'd believed possible.

'Our first meal in Hong Kong as a family? I'll be making it,' she said softly as she put Abid on her shoulder to make him burp. She turned around just in time to be rewarded by the most gorgeous smile she had ever seen on Khaled's face.

39

It happened on the day of their third wedding anniversary.

It had been about three months since Zubi had arrived from India with Abid and made Hong Kong her home. She was bewildered, most of the time, by the crowds and the refined sartorial sense of the women here. But each day was an adventure, with Khaled gladly showing her around the city every evening after he got back from work. They had bought a medium-sized stroller for Abid, one that could be folded and deposited neatly inside a cupboard when not in use, and the three of them would go for long walks every evening.

Zubi was finally happy and slowly, she allowed it to show. She missed her family terribly and there were times when she would look outside the window in the hall and see other buildings around them, blocking the view of the sky...she would then remember what it was like to live on the ground floor.

She also felt a little shy around the other Indian and Pakistani women who were her neighbours and whom she met in the park. She felt like she was an intruder in their lives and couldn't really connect with their talk of schools and shopping and stuff on television. But despite all this, she had never felt more content.

Khaled and she had developed a comfortable routine during

the week where each morning he'd leave for work after a hurried breakfast. Zubi would clean the house, bathe Abid and then put him to sleep before making lunch. Khaled came home for lunch but would leave in a hurry again and then he'd return around 6 or 6.30 p.m. After taking rest and freshening up a bit, he would take Zubi and Abid on walks along Victoria Harbour or to iSquare or some of the other nearby malls. On weekends, they took the ferry to Hong Kong Island, the other side that Khaled had earlier spoken about where Zubi allowed herself to be stunned by the majestic and tall buildings that dotted the landscape. Zubi noted with quiet satisfaction that in the three years that she'd known and seen Khaled, he'd never looked more at ease or happy.

Some of Zubi's contentment came from having the kitchen entirely to herself. It was a really small kitchen, around one-tenth the size of her mother's kitchen in Bangalore. If she'd thought that the kitchen in her mother-in-law's house was small, this one made that seem like a master bedroom. But she didn't mind. They were a small family and their needs weren't that many. The kitchen had all the appliances she needed and that was enough. Zubi cooked all the wonderful, homely dishes that she'd learnt from her mother and all the calorie-loaded desserts that her grandmother had taught her.

She'd often see Khaled staring at her when he ate and once he even told her that he'd had no idea she was such a good cook. She had made one of her mother's simple dishes that immediately perked up the dining table. The only name for it was what they'd always been saying from the time she was small and she wasn't even sure if that was the right name. Chunchuni.

Boneless chunks of meat were cooked with regular masalas in the pressure cooker until they were tender. After drying the liquid, the chunks of meat were seared in a kadai with hot oil, until the masalas burned on the surface of the meat, creating a combination of soft yet crusty meat that instantly banished all sorts of woes from the dining table.

'I don't know what it is, but it seems like you have magic...'

'Stop!' Zubi halted his words, terrified. 'Don't say another word. Please!'

Khaled was surprised but he was used to his wife's irrational moods and he didn't pursue the matter. Zubi had been frightened that he was going to repeat the very words her father had told her mother so many times in the past. He even had that look in his eyes. As it is she was terrified that history would repeat itself, but to actually tempt fate?

On Fridays, she went to the Kowloon Masjid and read namaz with other women, connected to them by religion but distanced from their lives in so many ways. She wished she could make friends easily but it never seemed to happen for some reason. She just couldn't make small talk with people. Everything was too intense for her.

Abid was her best friend. Little Abid was growing into a sturdy and extremely naughty little child who toppled everything in sight and made life in the cramped apartment a nightmare. Even then, she never scolded him because it was only with him that she could love totally. And demonstrate it.

Of course the situation with Khaled had improved considerably since she'd moved to Hong Kong and even though she avoided personal discussions, they were slowly edging towards normalcy in their lives. In the evenings, they'd watch TV together, sitting somewhat like distant strangers until Khaled started holding her hand quietly. A few days later they had progressed to sitting closer to each other and then, even closer. A day before their anniversary, Khaled mustered the courage to put his head on her lap and when she didn't flinch from him, he smiled. In fact, she kept running her fingers through his hair until he stopped her from driving him crazy by pulling her down towards him.

On the day of their anniversary, Khaled promised he'd be back early from work. He'd wanted to take Zubi to a special restaurant but Zubi had insisted that she would make biryani for them.

'You give the money that you would be spending in that restaurant to me instead,' she insisted adamantly.

'You're kidding, right?' he asked her. When he saw that she was serious, he burst out laughing.

'Seriously? Why are you so hung up on biryani?' he asked her, pulling her close to him. She went willingly although she put her palm on his chest to stop him.

'It's difficult to manage Abid in a restaurant,' Zubi said, 'and you did say that I make the best biryani you've eaten.'

'Okay, okay. As you wish, but you know, you should be a little more open to trying other cuisines also,' he said, placing his hand on the back of her neck and clasping her hair.

Zubi made a face and he laughed and leaned forward and kissed her. Zubi wondered if Khaled would ever understand that she didn't want to share him with anyone else on this special day.

'We need to save money,' she reminded him primly as he picked up his laptop bag.

'Yeah, yeah, I know,' he said and left with a smart salute to Zubi. 'See you in the evening.' Zubi nodded and followed him outside, waiting and watching till he got inside the lift.

In her mind, the day had assumed great importance suddenly. They had got married three years ago but she wasn't the person she was now. She had been vague and beset with doubts and later when she'd fallen in love with him, she was confused and had no plans to let him know about her feelings. Because in her book, that's what her mother had done. She had loved her husband unconditionally and she hadn't been bothered with who saw it. When he died, it was like she had ceased to exist. That would never happen to me, Zubi had sworn to herself. No man is that important.

But this man was. Had become. Since she'd come to Hong Kong, however, her fears had seemed unfounded and childish. She was *not* her mother and whatever happened to her, she wouldn't react like her mother.

So, on the day of their anniversary, she finished making the biryani earlier in the day and then took a leisurely bath. As leisurely as Abid allowed her anyway. She dressed carefully in a pink salwar kameez that Khaled hadn't seen her in yet. She'd saved this one for a special occasion. She wore some of her jewellery and although not well versed with makeup, she managed to create a version of herself that was prettier than anything Khaled had ever seen.

And then she waited.

She still followed the rule about not calling him on his cell phone but when it was seven and there was no sign of Khaled, she dialled his number anxiously. He was probably on the subway on his way here. He would open the door any moment. Door, open please, she pleaded to it, when his phone kept ringing and there was no answer.

Panic leaped inside her when she tried his number again and no one answered it. She paced inside the apartment wondering what could be wrong because she had no idea what to do if something had happened to him. Her mind refused to consider that possibility and she paced up and down again.

When her phone rang, she jumped and when she saw that it was his number, the relief was so overwhelming that she shuddered. She answered the phone with a good mind to yell at him when she stopped. It wasn't his voice.

'Is this Khaled's wife?'

'Yes. Where's he?' she asked, panic returning and jack-knifing into her stomach.

'There was an accident at one of the construction sites and....'

Zubi dropped the phone in horror. It had happened. Then she collapsed on the ground and scrambled to pick up the phone and speak to the person although tears were running down her face already.

'It happened just as he was leaving the site. One of the scaffolds fell...'

No!!!! Zubi screamed the word in her head.

'Where's he?' she asked in a hoarse voice.

'Oh, he's right here. Getting a few stitches on his forehead.'

'You mean....he's fine?' she asked, unable to believe it.

'Oh yes. He's fine. He was already on his way out when the scaffolding fell along with three construction workers. One of them knocked him down as he fell.'

'What about...them?' Zubi asked cautiously. She still couldn't believe everything was fine.

'Broken legs and other injuries,' the man said.

'Who are you?' Zubi asked, her heart still racing.

'I'm Khaled's colleague. Your husband asked me to call and tell you he's fine and he'll be home soon. He didn't want to worry you but when we heard the phone ringing he knew it must have been you so he asked me to call back.'

'Why can't he come to the phone? Are you sure he's alright? Should I come to the hospital?' Zubi asked, standing up suddenly, picking up her purse and automatically reaching for Abid.

'No, no! He'll be there in half-an-hour. Here, you can talk to him,' the man said quickly and Zubi braced herself to hear Khaled's voice.

'Hi,' he said, his voice sounding strained.

'Are you okay?' she whispered.

'Yes. I am. I'll be home soon. Don't worry,' he said. Zubi hung on to the pause in the conversation and that was when Khaled, in an attempt to fill up the gap, said a few words, he never should have.

'Well, it's a good thing I wasn't up on the scaffolding with those men. Imagine if I'd have fallen from that height! I'd have broken my neck for sure!' Khaled said, laughing uneasily.

Zubi shut her eyes and then disconnected the phone. She changed into one of her old sarees and scrubbed her face clean. Then she heated the biryani and waited for him to come back home. When Khaled let himself inside the house an hour later, Zubi wanted to jump up and comfort him, hold him tight, kiss his jaw and never let go of him. He was probably expecting her to do all that, but she continued sitting on the sofa, staring at the TV. In fact, he stood at the door for nearly five minutes wondering what was wrong, and how in hell had their relationship gone back fifty steps when all they had taken were a few tentative ones forward these past few months.

'Zubi?' he said, finally and she looked up at him. Their eyes met and it seemed as though Khaled was pleading with her through his. She got up and took his laptop from him and kept it on the table. She did all this without looking at his face.

'Dinner's ready,' she said and walked into the kitchen, aware that Khaled was staring at her back, bewildered and a little angry.

'Right. Happy anniversary to you too,' he said, and flung himself on the sofa, wincing in pain.

40

On some days, Zubi waited for Khaled to leave for work. She would then get Abid ready and take him to Kowloon park. But on most days she simply liked to wander around aimlessly, looking at the handbags and shoes on display in some shops. Abid was now a year-and-a-half old and Zubi felt comfortable enough to walk on the streets of Hong Kong without Khaled.

There were no more evening walks because after the anniversary accident fiasco, Zubi had a headache and on another day she had stomach cramps and one day she was asleep when he came home to a darkened house. Eventually he stopped asking her.

On her own though, Zubi explored all the different streets near her apartment, all the bylanes and little alleyways that Khaled had told her not to visit. She'd passed by Chung King Mansions one day and went inside because there were so many Indians walking around that it almost seemed like India. On the first floor, she found a shop selling Indian spices and condiments. She lingered in the tiny shop, inhaling the familiar scents of elaichi and dalchini that pervaded the air.

On most days, she skipped making lunch because Khaled had stopped coming home. She and Abid ate whatever she had made for breakfast and she would half-heartedly prepare dinner before

Khaled came back. One day, however, he came home as usual, had his tea and then picked up Abid, sat down on the sofa and started putting on his shoes.

'Where are you taking him?' Zubi asked, before she could stop herself. It had become a norm for Khaled to go out in the evenings after he came back from work. Zubi never asked him where he went, what he did or whom he met. Inside, she was dying to, but it was safer this way. Safer for her sanity and peace of mind.

'You can come if you want to,' was all he said. Zubi stared at his lowered head and shut her eyes. Why was she doing this to them? He deserved someone better, someone who was not so screwed up. Before she could formulate her thoughts, she bent down in front of him and touched his hand. He leaped back as though her touch had burnt his skin.

'What?' he asked, almost harshly.

'I'll go back to India,' Zubi said. He narrowed his eyes and looked at her, anger growing in his eyes.

'What do you mean?'

'I...you're obviously not happy with me and...' Zubi's voice trailed away when he placed both his hands on her shoulders.

'I'm not happy, yes. Thanks for noticing it,' he said, sarcasm giving his voice a nasty edge.

'That's why....' Zubi couldn't continue because he kept staring at her, and his hands were still on her shoulder. Abid was sitting next to them, and leaned back and jumped forward, a new game which he had started recently.

'Why, Zubi? Why do you do this? Why don't you want to talk?' Khaled asked her, his hands moving downwards to clutch her palms.

Zubi's throat dried up. She looked away.

'We were doing fine. I was beginning to think that coming here had been the best decision I made. But...' his thumb pressed the swollen part of her palm below her thumb and she closed her eyes.

'Is it me?' he asked. 'Is it you? I deserve to know.'

Zubi shook her head, feeling angry with herself for getting into this situation. 'It's nothing,' she said, trying to get up but Khaled wouldn't let her.

'We can't live our lives like this, Zubi. Skirting around each other. Not talking,' his voice had deepened and Zubi bit her lower lip anxiously.

'You deserve someone better,' she said. He moved backwards as though she had punched him.

Without another word, he lifted Abid in his arms and left the house. Zubi was afraid that it wasn't such a good idea for him to take Abid along when he was angry, so she quickly pushed her feet into her slippers and ran behind him after locking the door.

The doors of the elevator were just closing as Zubi got inside, breathless. Khaled refused to look at her and Zubi looked down, understanding for the first time, what it must mean to be on the receiving end. She welcomed it. If he was punishing her, then well and good. She would endure it.

She had no idea where they were going but she followed them briskly, the sharp wind biting into her cheeks. Abid wasn't even wearing his woollen cap she thought with dismay but there was no point voicing that concern.

They had moved away from the main row of shops and restaurants and were now on a road where there were many more apartments. Boxy buildings with ACs jutting out stood proudly in the darkening evening and Zubi wondered if Khaled was planning to check out a new apartment. She hoped not. She had got used to theirs, especially because of its proximity to the market, the malls and the park. But again, she was afraid to broach the topic.

When Khaled turned, she saw that they were now in front of

a very tall building. He'd brought them to Elements, a spanking new mall in West Kowloon. She sighed. One more mall. She was getting tired of them now.

Without uttering a word, he went inside with Abid. She followed them and then stopped short. There was an ice skating rink right in front of them. Experienced skaters were gliding across the ice with ease while the novices struggled to get to their feet. She stood next to Khaled who had put Abid on his shoulders and watched the people swirl on the ice. She could feel tears burn at the back of her eyes.

He was right. They had to talk. But how could she bring up something that even she couldn't understand? He would most definitely think she was crazy. Khaled looked straight ahead, not blinking; her heart went out to him. Zubi knew how lucky she was because not many men would have so much patience with a woman's whims.

The tears spilled over and she turned her face away. She noticed a bench nearby, and went and sat down there. She desperately tried to control her emotions, half-hoping he would come and sit down next to her. But he didn't. He continued standing near the rink for a long time and only when Abid looked sleepy did he walk away. When Zubi realised he was leaving, she got up, feeling wretched. He was ignoring her completely and she knew that it was only a matter of time before he truly got fed up of her.

They walked back home in frozen silence and Zubi realised that they had been away around the same time that Khaled disappeared every day in the evenings. He was going to the skating rink every day? She wanted to ask him but didn't. Couldn't.

Inside their house, everything seemed cold and bereft and although Zubi knew she should get up and make dinner, she couldn't bring herself to move from the sofa. As long as he'd been trying, she had kept backing away, pushing him as far away as possible, testing his limits. Now, it seemed that something had snapped and she was almost scared of what he wanted. Or that he didn't want her at all.

She needed to talk to someone. Not her mother, but someone who would understand what she was going through. She considered her options. She had never made friends easily and the only person she could think of confiding in was Suman Chachi although she wasn't sure of her anymore. What if Chachi spoke to her mother? But it was a risk she had to take. Maybe she would ask Chachi to chat with her on Skype the following day she thought. She glanced at Khaled, as he sat at the dining table, turning around a Rubik cube without a word.

41

'I don't understand,' Chachi said, rubbing her hands over the back of her head and bringing them down her face. She already looked tired and Zubi had barely started.

'What don't you understand?' Zubi asked her, leaning a little downwards so that Chachi could see her face properly on the laptop screen.

'I thought the two of you were so happy. What are you talking about? It doesn't make any sense to me!' Chachi said, settling her chin in the vee of her palms.

Zubi was silent. 'I don't know if I can ever be happy,' she said, and briefly looked around the tiny space that had become her home. Abid was asleep on the sofa.

Chachi shook her head. Her face seemed magnified on screen, making her look a little odd.

'How can you not be happy? Have you seen the way he looks at you? He's crazy about you. Don't tell me you don't like him?'

Zubi bit her lower lip and then taking a deep breath, she said, 'I do. I...I l-love him a lot, but I've never said it to him. In fact I've done everything I can to make him believe that I can't stand him.' There, she'd said it.

'But why?' Chachi looked bewildered, as would anyone, Zubi thought.

'Because I don't want to become like Ammi. When Abbu died, it seemed as though she didn't want to exist anymore. And I had decided that I would never become like her. It would have helped if I *didn't* love him. Things would have been so much easier for us. But I do. And I'm so afraid of showing it to him. I'm afraid that I'll be tempting fate,' Zubi spoke in a rush.

Chachi's eyes went round. 'Oh my god. You really are out of your mind!' Chachi's words weren't helping her and Zubi covered her eyes with her hands. Chachi immediately tried to assuage the situation by comforting her.

'Look, Zubi. It's alright. Maybe you should visit a psychologist to try and understand why you feel this way,' Chachi spoke slowly, as if to a four-year-old.

Zubi still didn't make eye contact with Chachi, so she continued. 'I don't know much about these things but maybe you should speak to Khaled about this. He'll understand, I'm sure.'

Zubi made a face. 'You know me since I was a child. If you think I'm crazy, he's bound to think the same.'

Chachi now sounded serious as she ruminated over what to say. 'Maybe you should come to India for a little while and speak to someone here. Have you thought of speaking to your mother?'

Zubi shook her head vehemently. 'I'm not telling all this to her. And you better not too!'

Chachi expelled her breath through the corner of her mouth. 'Have you made any friends there? Speak to some people. Get out more often.'

Zubi shrugged. 'How does that even help?'

For some reason that seemed to make Chachi lose her patience. 'Well, it's better than wallowing in misery. Look at you. You're married to a good man and you're living in a wonderful city, all alone with him. Why can't you see that for what it is? Why can't you just let things be and enjoy yourself?'

Zubi told her about how things were becoming better when Khaled had his accident. Chachi rubbed her forehead in exasperation.

'Zubi, that could have happened to anyone. Was that any reason for you to distance yourself from your husband? Imagine what it must be like for him?'

'I've tried,' Zubi said, her voice breaking a little. 'I told him yesterday that...he deserves someone better and...'

Chachi's looked shocked. 'You *what*?'

'Yes and he got very angry. In fact he's still angry with me. He's not talking to me at all.'

'You crazy, crazy girl! You have to rectify this situation.'

Zubi looked away and decided to end the chat. Talking to Chachi hadn't been such a good idea after all. She was just making her feel foolish.

'Okay, I think Abid has woken up. I'll chat with you some other time,' she said and signed out before Chachi could even say bye. She slammed shut the laptop and sat staring into space, wondering what she could do about her life.

Abid was still asleep and she could do whatever she wanted, but inside, everything felt so bleak and lonely. Why had she done this to herself? Why had she made a mountain out of a molehill? Everyone died one day or the other. But the very thought of Khaled not being in the world, not breathing, not living, the *idea* of not seeing his dark eyes made her tremble. If she was already drawn in so deeply, why shouldn't she just jump in completely and let him know how she felt? Because she felt something would indeed happen to him. That was how fate screwed around with their lives.

She put her head on the table and cried. She felt miserable. Would it be so bad if she could explain this to him? That she loved him but would never be vocal about it? That she was scared to death of showing her love? She thought of his blank face that morning as he refused breakfast and went to work. He wouldn't really listen or believe her.

As she sank deeper into despair, she wished she could talk to her grandmother. She could still call her but Badey Ammi's hearing was bad and she couldn't talk to her for so long on the phone. It was a pity though. But the thought had formulated in her head and refused to leave. She was going to call Badey Ammi to just listen to her voice at least.

She picked up the phone, dialled her number and waited for her to answer. When Badey Ammi answered, Zubi felt a small smile form on her face for the first time in days.

At first, Badey Ammi had not understood that it was Zubi who was calling. Then, when she understood, she started talking loudly and Zubi stood near her dining table, shaking her head in wry amusement.

'Your grandfather has been telling me that he wants me to make gajar ka halwa for him. I told him I'm not making it until my Zubi comes and visits us. So he's waiting for you to come back to India,' Badey Ammi said, and Zubi felt the smile on her face grow bigger.

'How's your husband?' she asked. Zubi paused. How could she explain anything to Badey Ammi? There was no way she would understand it.

'He's fine, Badey Ammi. He conveys his salaam to you and Badey Abbu,' Zubi said automatically.

'Good, good. He's a good man. Take care of him. I hope you haven't forgotten how to make all the desserts I taught you. The next time I come to Bangalore, I'll make lauz for him and your mother can send it to you.'

'He would love that, Badey Ammi,' Zubi said, knowing that she had to end the call now. Just talking to her beloved grandmother made her feel lighter and less desperate.

She ended the call and then stood outside the kitchen, wondering if she, too, should make gajar ka halwa. The red juicy carrots that they had bought at the vegetable market the other day were lying in the refrigerator, and although they were not her preferred variety, she could use them.

Zubi had altered a few steps to the basic halwa that her grandmother liked to make, which happened to be her favourite too. This one took lesser time and she could do it without grating her own fingers along with the carrots. She chopped the carrots into small pieces, boiled them in a little milk and gave them a whirr in the mixer along with some blanched almonds. Then she mixed the pureed carrots with condensed milk and stirred until the mixture became unified and thick. She tested the halwa for sweetness, added some sugar and kept stirring although the halwa spurted everywhere and splashed her arms with hot droplets.

When it was finally cooked, she topped it with fried nuts and then waited for Khaled to come home. She had no idea what she was doing. Maybe he would be mollified by the halwa.

When he came home that evening, he didn't look at her. He removed his shoes and went straight to the bathroom. He emerged a little later, wiped his wet face with a towel and continued doing everything without looking at her at all. Inside, Zubi already felt herself sink deeper.

She waited until he sat down on the sofa where she would bring him his tea. When he sat down, he switched on the TV and looked very engrossed so that she wouldn't interrupt him.

Biting her lower lip to prevent herself from crying, Zubi brought the tea and halwa.

He took the tea from her although his eyes were fixed on the TV. Zubi wondered how things would have turned out if she had been a confrontational type of person. He'd have probably loved it because that was what *he* was like. He liked having things out in the open. She passed him the halwa. Only then did he pause to give her a brief look and then shook his head.

He picked up Abid and tickled his tummy until Abid squealed in delight. Zubi watched them, hating the bitter-sweet feeling that was running through her.

'I'm sorry,' she found herself saying as she handed the bowl of halwa to him again. Khaled ignored her. Zubi sat on the sofa, feeling desperate. Nothing was working. She had pushed him too far.

She felt her lips tremble with the onset of tears; she got up swiftly and went to the bedroom where she threw herself down on the bed and sobbed. She half-expected Khaled to come inside and see what she was doing but she kept hearing Abid's laughter and realised that no matter what she did, Khaled wouldn't come to her.

The thought added to her despair and she continued crying in the dark room, losing track of when sadness had turned into sleep. When she woke up, there was silence in the house. What time was it? She turned around and saw that Abid was asleep in his corner and Khaled was sleeping in his usual place, next to her. Was it midnight? She hadn't even made dinner!

She could only remember crying and then everything after that was blank. In her confused state of mind, she could understand only one thing. Khaled was here and he was sleeping next to her. She didn't really figure out that he slept next to her every day and *she* was the one who moved away as far as possible from him. At that moment, just the thought of seeing him in the darkened room, with the curtain fluttering above their heads where it hid the window, made her feel irrationally happy.

She touched his arm but he didn't move. She shook him and his eyes opened, and he looked around confused.

'Wha...is everything okay?' he asked, getting up and sitting on the bed. Since the anniversary, Zubi took pains not to look at him much, and to completely avoid looking at him below his neck. But today, she continued drinking in the sight of him and he stared back at her. He wasn't wearing his usual T-shirt.

'Everything is not okay,' she whispered and moved closer to him and embraced him. He tried to push her back and she knew he was still angry with her, so she held on to him more tightly.

'You can't keep doing this,' he said gruffly, his hands at his side.

'Please?' she said, running her palm down his bare back. She heard him gasp. He pushed her away and looked at her face, as though inspecting it for changes.

'What?' she asked him, knowing that he was weakening with every moment.

He flattened his hair with his hand, pushing it back from his forehead and shook his head. 'I'm not a toy or an object that you can play around with, as you like, Zubi,' he said, his voice rough with sleep.

'You're half asleep and yet you can think so lucidly!' Zubi teased him and planted a kiss on the side of his neck.

'What is wrong with you? Yesterday you tell me that I deserve someone better and today, you're all over me?' he held her shoulders and pushed her back. Zubi was fully awake now and so was he, she realised.

In a flash Zubi remembered why she'd been crying so much and to her horror, tears fell rapidly from her eyes. She wiped them away hurriedly but they continued falling and she turned her face away from Khaled, her shoulders shaking. She hated anyone to see her crying, but most of all, she didn't want Khaled to see her when she was most vulnerable.

She sensed him behind her and he gently turned her around, shaking his head.

'You crazy, crazy girl,' he whispered, wiping the tears from her eyes.

Zubi held on to his fingers and kissed them and said, 'You're the second person to say that today.'

He looked startled but before he could ask her what she meant, Zubi had pulled his face towards her and kissed him. Within moments, they both forgot what they had been thinking about, let alone planning to say.

Zubi let herself go completely in those few minutes, believing that nothing had gone wrong in her world and nothing would. It gave her such freedom to believe that and she wished she could believe it every single day.

Later, just as he was falling asleep, his face buried in the back of her neck, Khaled murmured something.

'What?' she asked, turning around to face him. His eyes were closed but there was a slight smile on his face.

'I said I loved the halwa.'

Zubi smiled and traced her finger along his nose until he caught it and spoke, his eyes still closed.

'Don't make a habit of this, huh? I have to go to work tomorrow.'

As Zubi fell asleep that night, she realised that they had reached a truce of sorts. But until she could speak to him and explain what she felt, that was what it would remain. Only a truce. And she knew she wasn't ready yet.

42

As the glamour of Hong Kong wore off, Zubi became increasingly homesick. There was only so much she could window shop or walk through the perfumed aisles of cosmetic shops where nattily dressed Chinese women smiled at her automatically and offered to show her their best products. Although the freedom was exhilarating, she was beginning to lose momentum. They had visited India sometime back during the Chinese New Year when everything was shut down in Hong Kong and she realised how much she missed everyone when they came back to their tiny apartment.

She actually missed her brothers and waited for the days when she could catch the entire family together on Skype but for them it seemed like it was more a case of 'out of sight and out of mind'. Abid was now a little more than two and Zubi sometimes wondered what it would be like to have another child, but would banish the thought from her mind immediately. This apartment was too small for another child.

Things between her and Khaled had progressed to becoming a little better but he was still wary around her. He was not like how he used to be during their early days in Hong Kong, openly adoring and happy to just see her. It seemed they had lapsed into a passive state in their marriage, like it had been before they came to Hong Kong, and although Zubi ached for the way things were before his accident, she knew she shouldn't ask for more. He was here, and he was hers.

One Sunday, Khaled took them to Disneyland. Abid was thrilled to see some of his favourite cartoon characters walking about there. They posed dutifully with Mickey Mouse and Minnie Mouse. Zubi later noted that only Abid looked truly happy. As the day wore on and they sat through different performances and shows, Zubi began to enjoy herself vicariously through Abid. Once, the two of them looked up together when Abid clapped loudly during a parade and their eyes met. She didn't know what he was thinking because his eyes slid down and he smiled at Abid automatically before picking him up and putting him on his shoulders so he could see better.

At the end of the day, when they made their way back to the metro station, all three of them were tired. Zubi was standing close to Khaled and she realised that he wasn't even making an effort to hold her hand. She should be glad because this was what she had wanted and although they spoke to each other with civility, it was more like two strangers living together in one house with just Abid being their common factor.

Zubi's sadness at the situation in her life, one she had brought upon herself, manifested itself into improving her cooking although she was already great at it. The only time she saw Khaled look appreciative was when he ate what she cooked. She began concentrating on making things that he liked. Like seafood, especially fish.

Zubi absolutely hated the smell of fish and she shuddered every time she thought about cleaning the scales. Khaled used to bring home fish sometimes; he would bring the whole fish which would have to be cleaned completely before she could fillet it. Zubi was extremely squeamish about it but she never let him know. She would merely nod when he would keep the fish on the kitchen counter in its plastic cover. It was always an ordeal for her but she did it anyway, covering the eyes of the fish with paper napkins, as though by doing that, she wouldn't be seeing it.

Then, she realised she could get cut and cleaned fish from the market on Haiphong road although that meant going through all the fish counters and seeing more and more dead fish. But it was still better than cleaning and cutting it herself. So on some days she and Abid would go to the market to buy fish. She didn't want Abid walking through the morass of fish scales and innards that were strewn across the smelly market floor and so, she would carry him in her arms, painstakingly choosing the right kind of fish.

Several Chinese vendors would holler at her but she would ignore most of them, keeping her eyes focussed on the fish she wanted. In some shops, the fish were actually kept swimming in a broad tank that was embedded in the counter; Zubi would fight back feelings of nausea while watching the vendor pull out a particular kind of fish that a customer would have asked for.

Why did we humans ever start eating fish, she wondered as she pointed to a seer fish from a tray where they all lay with their dead staring eyes. She asked for it to be filleted and then watched the vendor cut up the fish with expertise, although she really wanted to look away. She collected the bag of fish, headed home where she would immediately wash the fish and slather it with masala, leaving it to marinate till lunch time.

Fish fry was not her favourite but because she kept making it so often, she got used to eating it. Having fish at home was like her safety net. She could always whip up dal and rice and fry the fish – all of these put together make a complete meal. She would deposit Abid in front of the TV and then mix a paste of adrak-lehsun, salt, haldi, chilli powder and garam masala and a twist of lemon, which would be applied on the fish slices. The slices were then kept covered in a bowl and refrigerated for a while.

When Khaled came home as he did sometimes for lunch, he would be greeted by the aroma and sputtering sounds of fish frying. For someone who didn't like fish at all, having the smell hang in the air the whole day was really unpleasant but Zubi got used to it. It was worth it – just seeing him break into the crisp and succulent piece and give her half a smile before he devoured it completely.

Then one day he brought prawns. By now Zubi had become a veteran at tolerating unpleasant smells. Living in Hong Kong for nearly two years had made her accustomed to them. There wasn't an alley you could walk by without seeing a few Chinese men chomping on something. Initially, the smells had made her want to throw up but there was little that a person couldn't get used to if they wanted to. Abid had become friends with a little Indian girl at the park, Ria. Her mother was a very chatty woman who loved the sound of her own voice and as they watched the kids play, Sunita would regale Zubi with stories of the time she had lived in Singapore and then Bangkok and now, Hong Kong.

'Everywhere they are the same, these Chinese,' she said, shaking her head. 'Eating, eating, always eating. They will eat anything that walks, crawls, swims…' and Zubi burst out laughing at Sunita's expression.

'Really!' she said, as if to affirm her point and Zubi nodded. She knew. She'd seen. But it didn't disturb her. Who was she to judge the culinary exploits of a completely different set of people? If it weren't for the fact that most of their cooking employed pork and was usually cooked in lard, she would have gladly hung around trying to learn something new from them.

So, Zubi did not flinch when she was faced with the mound

of prawns. However, she hadn't made them before; so she needed to ask her mother how to make it best. She put Abid to sleep and then painstakingly shelled and deveined the prawns, washed them in haldi as she had seen her mother do many times and then called her, asking her to come on Skype. Her mother had taken to the computer reluctantly although it was the boys who usually set up the calls between them.

Zubi still chatted with Suman Chachi but she refused to tell her how things were between Khaled and her. When they had gone to India a few months ago, Chachi had cornered her and asked her if everything was alright to which Zubi mentally recalled the last time Khaled had made love to her passionately. It had been back in Hong Kong. If that was a standard by which one could judge a relationship, then it was going great. Just thinking about it though had made her toes tingle and her face heat up. Suman Chachi, however, misunderstood it, assuming that Zubi had finally told her husband about her true feelings for him.

Banishing the thoughts of Suman Chachi from her mind, she switched on the laptop and waited. When her mother came online, she seemed happy to see her but was disappointed to learn that Abid was asleep.

'What? You only want to see him?' Zubi teased her mother who nodded her head.

'Who wants to talk to you?' she said, to which both of them laughed. After the usual catching up, Zubi asked her mother about how she made prawn masala. Her mother seemed lost in thought for a moment.

'I can't believe I never once made it for Khaled when he was here,' she mused.

'Well, that's a good thing then,' Zubi said, smiling, 'One less thing for him to compare and say that your mother makes this way better than you.'

Her mother looked pleased when she heard that.

'So, the usual things go in the masala. Just remember to put more onions than tomatoes.' Zubi noted down the recipe in her notebook as her mother told her to sauté whole garam masalas in hot oil, followed by chopped onions and the usual adrak-lehsun, haldi, salt and red chilli powder.

'Then, you add the prawns, the chopped tomatoes, and coriander leaves and keep stirring it,' her mother instructed. 'When the prawns are cooked, you lower the flame and let it stay till it becomes a bit brown.'

'Finally, top it with ghee and let it simmer a little before you take it off the gas stove,' her mother finished.

'Great. Thanks!' Zubi said, capping her pen.

'Just tell me his reaction and that will be enough,' said Ammi, Zubi smiled uneasily. Ammi believed that the world revolved around Khaled. Why did she do that? Why did she have to make a man the centre of her universe? Worse was, why was *she* doing it too?

Later that day when Zubi served the prawn masala to Khaled, he looked surprised.

'I thought you would fry it,' he said, looking at the burnt orange dish uncertainly.

'Try this. I'm sure you'll like it,' insisted Zubi, putting some on his plate. Indeed, his reaction was absolutely worth all the trouble she had taken, Zubi thought with delight as he ate everything she had kept and asked for more.

'You should start teaching people how to cook…like hold cooking classes or something,' Khaled said, lifting her hand and depositing a wet kiss in the centre of her palm. Zubi pulled back her hand as though stung, and then she smiled at him tremulously.

Khaled pretended she hadn't pulled back her hand and continued in the same vein of thought.

'Seriously. You are an awesome cook,' he said as he ate and shook his head, as though in wonder.

His words seemed to trigger something inside her and she sat still, thinking about it. Could she do it? She had wanted to become an artist, but that hadn't materialised. And after getting married, she had become so obsessed with keeping her distance from Khaled that she hadn't given a thought to what she really wanted to do. It was only after her twenty-eighth birthday that she finally found out about what she *could* do.

43

Zubi's birthday was always an awkward time for her. She had stopped celebrating it after her father's death and she really didn't want anyone to make a big deal out of it. That was easy before she'd been married but just after their wedding, Khaled had asked her brothers about her birthday and they had told him that it was in March.

Each year, Zubi would feel a little embarrassed whenever he got her gifts and took her out because he assumed she was expecting him to do so. But her birthday reminded her of her father's death and they were both unfortunately tied together in her mind, even though the two events were three weeks apart.

With their carefully constructed non-communicative marriage, Zubi found it increasingly difficult to tell Khaled that she didn't want to celebrate her birthday at all. But she kept quiet and accepted his gifts each year, wishing that if in the multitudes of people in this world, just the two of them had been given the ability to read each other's mind, so much trouble could have been saved.

On her twenty-eighth birthday, Khaled handed her a lavishly wrapped box; Zubi smiled half-heartedly and unwrapped it. It was a handycam, a digital video recorder. Zubi looked up at him and thanked him. It was a nice gift, but really, what did he expect her to do with it? In the evening, he came back home a little earlier than usual and asked Zubi to get Abid and herself ready.

'Where are we going?' she asked, her heart sinking because she wasn't in the mood to get dressed.

'Nowhere special. Just a walk down Victoria Harbour and dinner somewhere quiet,' he snapped, looking up at her as he removed his shoes.

Zubi looked down and nodded. By the time they left the apartment, it was nearly eight. They would most probably miss the Symphony of Lights she thought to herself. She had seen the play of lasers between both sides of Hong Kong across the stretch of black water numerous times and it was no longer a novelty. But still, they walked together in silence and turned towards the harbour where the skyscrapers on Hong Kong Island were lit up like a pure and simple expression of happiness.

Outwardly, however, she muttered, 'Waste of power,' and she saw Khaled look at her, a little annoyed. Keep this up, Zubi, she told herself, and soon he won't want to take you anywhere. Despite all their ups and downs, she couldn't understand why he was still with her. It had to be because of Abid. Or because he loved her.

Over the years, her belief that he loved her because he hadn't mentioned the kajal incident had watered down considerably, even though a small part of her believed it with fierce possessiveness.

They found a place to sit down and watched the lasers jump over each other across the sky to the sound of music. Zubi allowed herself to feel mildly content when in a snap, her world shifted.

'Oh my god! Khaled! Look at you! Imagine running into you here!' a woman's voice screeched and before she knew it someone had barrelled into Khaled, hugging him tightly.

That someone was wearing a skimpy red silk shirt and Zubi swallowed hard when she thought that it was all she was wearing.

Below the shirt, long white legs stretched out endlessly, stopping in red flip flops. The wind moved the bottom panel of the shirt and Zubi thankfully realised that the girl was wearing extremely short white shorts and not thongs as she'd first assumed.

She felt her face heat up when she noticed that the girl wasn't moving away from Khaled at all. Khaled was laughing and saying something at the same time as he tried to push her away. Finally, the girl stepped back and Zubi saw her face properly.

'Zubi, this is Julie. She and I were the only newbies when I joined my office here in Hong Kong, but she's moved on to a lot of other stuff since then,' Khaled said, looking at the girl warmly.

Zubi didn't quite know how to react. In a flash she saw it for what it was. Khaled was looking at Julie indulgently and affectionately, more like an older brother but it was quite evident that Julie had a huge crush on him. She kept talking to him almost in rapid fire spurts, telling him about her modelling assignments and how her ex-boyfriend was making her miserable and how she should have listened to him and not gone out with that bastard and...and she ended with a wail, 'Why did you disappear like that, Khaled? I've missed you so much!' and once again, she lunged towards him.

Khaled laughed at her attempts and pushed her away gently, looking at Zubi apologetically. Zubi realised her mouth was hanging open and she stood up, dragging Abid along. This was ridiculous. A grown woman was going on throwing herself at her husband and she was standing there watching.

Inside her head, several insidious thoughts had begun forming rapidly. Khaled was a good-looking man who worked with attractive women all the time. She'd been so busy building blockades between them that she had never considered the possibility of other women showing interest in him.

'Julie, this is my wife, Zubi,' Khaled said, looking at Zubi and smiling at her. Zubi didn't smile back. She was not in the mood to smile and make small talk with this scantily clad girl who kept wrapping herself around *her* husband.

'Why don't you catch up with your friend? Abid and I will go home,' she said mock-sweetly as she tried to move away but was stopped by Khaled's hand on her shoulder.

'Remember our plans? We were going for dinner, right?' Khaled reminded her. He didn't remove his hand from her shoulder. He drew Zubi closer to him and looked at Julie with a smile.

'What say we catch up later, Julie? It's my wife's birthday and I promised to take her to dinner.'

'But you never call back and you don't reply to my texts! How will I catch up with you later?' she asked indignantly, her hands on her hips. Zubi noted that her action neatly outlined the shape of her breasts and predictably the girl wasn't wearing a bra.

'Yes, but you have to understand. I'm a busy man. I'm married and I have a family,' Khaled explained, drawing Zubi closer to him as if to emphasise the point.

'So this is your wife,' Julie said, trying to prevent them from leaving. Zubi didn't know whether to be amused or outraged at the way this girl was behaving.

'Yes, and that's our son,' Khaled said, bending down to pick up Abid who was staring at the girl with open curiosity.

'What does she do?' Julie asked, swinging her head back to let a cascade of rich black hair fall down her back. Even Zubi was mesmerised by her hair. And Khaled...she just about re-entered reality when she heard him say, 'She's just a housewife. She stays at home and takes care of Abid.' The casual tone in which Khaled said this hurt Zubi for some reason, more than the fact that this gorgeous Chinese girl was sidelining her.

'We have to leave now,' Khaled said, and together they moved away, although Julie kept pouting.

'Oh and happy birthday,' she called out to Zubi sulkily.

Zubi didn't turn around. Khaled was apparently very embarrassed by the whole encounter but he didn't offer any explanation which miffed her even more.

'So, women keep throwing themselves at you?' she asked as they turned the corner onto Nathan Road.

'What do you think?' he asked, a little amused.

'I...I don't know,' Zubi said.

The confusion was apparent on her face as they stepped inside Ebeneezers, a restaurant that they had frequented.

Khaled was looking at her avidly. 'You think this happens to me all the time? You've been living with me in Hong Kong for nearly three years and you've been married to me for almost six,' he said, picking up the menu card and shaking it open.

Zubi realised he sounded angry. They ordered the chicken kebabs and waited in silence, the only sound at their table being that of Abid's as he zoomed his fist across the table as though he had a car in his grasp.

'Julie didn't last long at the office. She wasn't even interested in becoming an architect. The moment she found a modelling assignment, she quit and I lost touch with her. I also deliberately stayed away from her because she didn't bother hiding her attraction towards me when we were working, even though she knew I was married,' Khaled said evenly.

'And you're telling me this now....' Zubi seethed.

'Because you've never been interested in my life!' Khaled exclaimed, flinging down the menu card on the table. Zubi winced.

'I would have been interested in knowing this,' she continued, finding the courage to stake her claim on him.

'You're jealous? You? Nonsense!' Khaled muttered as their food was placed on the table.

This was turning out to be the worst birthday ever, thought Zubi as she ate the food in silence, anger turning the food into tiny blocks that had to be pushed down her throat with glasses of Pepsi.

Later when they stood in their building waiting for the elevator, Zubi spoke again.

'What did you mean when you said I'm *just* a housewife?' she asked and he turned to look at her almost incredulously.

'Because that's what you are. Or have you been leading a secret life I don't know of?' he asked, his attempt at humour meeting stoney silence. When they reached their apartment, Zubi made to go to the room when he caught her arm and turned her around.

'You have no reason to be jealous of any woman. No matter how few clothes she's wearing,' he said with a smile, although it seemed that he was trying to convey a lot more with his eyes. How wonderful it would have been if she could just walk into his embrace and tell him how she felt. How liberating that would have been. And how relieving. But she just nodded and went to the bedroom.

As the days towards her father's death anniversary inched forward, Zubi realised that more than anything else, Khaled's comment, that she was *just* a housewife, still irked her. She had not started out in life this way. In fact, when she'd been a young girl, her dreams and ambitions kept changing every week. But she'd followed her dream of becoming an artist although that hadn't really worked out the way she'd imagined it would.

She surfed the Internet, looked for things that she could possibly do which would take her out of this realm of being 'just' something that she didn't want to be all the time. But what could she do? She read articles about how she could do something useful with her time but only very few of those things applied to her. Also, her interests were limited to cooking more than anything else. That was when she remembered what Khaled had said, about her starting cooking classes.

In Hong Kong that seemed like a foolish idea. First of all, there was no space in their house. Second, she didn't think she could pull it off – talking in front of so many people as though she knew them when she couldn't clearly talk to most people she knew well enough. Also, who would attend her classes?

But the idea had taken root and she didn't want to let go of it for some reason. On ruminating further, she decided that as a practice run, she could record herself while cooking and see how it turned out. Maybe then she could think about the classes.

Her first video was a disaster. She realised that she couldn't keep turning around and show her back to the camera. She had to look *at* the camera. She didn't even know what she was doing as she shot the first video, babbling to herself or rather to the camera. But when she played the recording, she was surprised at how calm and sure she seemed. In fact, she couldn't believe it was her on the screen, telling the camera how to cook shaami.

She deliberated over the video for a little while longer. For days, she kept thinking about what she could do with the cooking videos. And then the idea came to her in a flash. She would upload them on the Net. So what if anyone could see them. So what if she wouldn't make any money from them. It would be the thing that *she* did.

If Khaled noticed that Zubi was looking excited and withdrawn at the same time, he didn't comment. He was used to her mercurial moods. On the day she decided to make the first proper video, she watched him as he left and waved goodbye to him when he was about to step inside the elevator. He looked a little startled and then waved back just as the doors closed.

Zubi had seen plenty of videos by then to understand how these people managed doing everything. She had to do it fast and everything had to be within reach. She had been playing around with the handycam all these days, trying to get accustomed to the settings; she'd also checked out the accompanying software that had come with it, so she could figure out how to edit the video. After putting Abid to sleep for the day, she rubbed her hands in anticipation. She combed her hair and did everything she could to look presentable.

She had fixed the handycam on the window sill in the kitchen, atop a large and broad can but wasn't sure if it was capturing her face properly, so she hit the record button to do a quick test – it was doing the job just right. Of course, this meant that she would have to keep turning to the window as she cooked to talk to the camera. But since she also needed to show what was being cooked, she would have to pick up the camera and do a close-up as well. Doing this alone was proving to be difficult but Zubi realised she was persistent where it mattered.

She knew it was a bit brave and even foolish, if ill-advised, but she had decided that she would make biryani for her very first video.

44

'Muslims don't eat biryani for breakfast, lunch and dinner. Some of us would like to. But we don't. The idea that connects Muslims to biryani is so prominent that I wouldn't even like to call it a misconception. I agree that we haven't done much to prove to the world about the other things we cook so well either. Witness any of our weddings and people, especially our non-Muslim friends, can be seen looking slightly harried, wondering when that elusive call for lunch or dinner will come, which is again – biryani.'

Zubi dropped whole garam masalas like laung, elaichi and dalchini inside a pot as she turned and spoke to the camera. She had a slight smile on her face as she dropped a bunch of sliced onions inside the pot.

'So, biryani has two important elements. The akhni and the adann. Both are extremely crucial to get the taste right. Here, I'm starting with the akhni,' she said and stirred the onions around in the oil.

'If you're going to make biryani, you'll have to stop cringing at the amount of oil you'll end up using. Believe me, you will,' she said as she picked up the camera and pointed it towards the pot where the onions sizzled in the hot oil.

'You see those onions in the oil? They have to be practically swimming in oil, if not floating,' she quipped as she replaced the camera to its original position. 'And once they start browning, here comes the fun. I put in the adrak-lehsun, swirl it around a bit, and then the mutton or chicken. You have to keep stirring them around until the mutton or chicken pieces are glazed with oil and lose their raw look.'

She performed the actions while she spoke, and kept stirring. For some reason, it didn't feel odd to talk to the camera. She felt like she'd been doing it all her life.

'Now, add the red chilli powder and salt. Remember, no haldi in the biryani akhni,' she cautioned and stirred briskly. 'Add some yoghurt and let all these things mix well. It's smelling delicious by the way.'

'I've got the tomatoes chopped right here,' she pointed to a large bowl where she had chopped the tomatoes and kept aside before starting the recording.

'I'm going to put a little water in these tomatoes and squeeze them around a bit to get the seeds out and then I'm going to put the tomatoes in the akhni.' She made sure her back was not facing the camera as she did these things.

'One thing to remember – keep stirring in the early stages if you don't want your akhni to stick to the bottom of the pot. Add the tomatoes, keep stirring until the tomatoes soften and the akhni starts looking like gravy.'

Zubi picked up the bowl of coriander and mint leaves that she had kept ready by her side and showed it to the camera. 'Tear up the coriander and mint roughly and drop them into the akhni. Add very little water. Lower the flame a little and let the meat cook until it is tender.'

Then she covered the pot with the lid and leaned over to switch off the camera. But before doing that, she realised that her brow was dotted with perspiration, both from the heat of the kitchen and the fact that she was actually doing this. She lifted the lid, took shots of the bubbling akhni inside and then switched off the camera. She ran to check on Abid and saw that he was awake.

How would she shoot a video when he was awake? Her shoulders sagged as she realised she would have to wait for him to sleep again, which wouldn't be any time soon. She also didn't want to do this when Khaled was at home. Abid was hungry, so she gave him milk and then sat down by his side, simultaneously cleaning the rice for the adann. She felt a little guilty as she switched on the TV and let him watch cartoons while she went back inside and completed shooting the video. She only hoped that the audio in the video wouldn't be overpowered by the sounds of the cartoon show.

With everything ready once again, she switched on the camera, feeling truly happy. For some reason, this felt right. She was doing what she loved and she would soon show the world how good she was at it.

'And we're back again with the akhni almost done. This is when you have to start heating the water for the adann,' she told the camera.

She demonstrated how she had soaked the rice with a little yoghurt in it and then she lifted the lid of the akhni pot and skimmed off some of the oil from the top.

'I'm not deferring to any calorie-skimping schemes because I have plans for this oil later,' she said with a smile as she replaced the lid.

'Next, we heat the water for the adann. The water should be more than double the amount of rice that you're using. Drop in some mint leaves and a little haldi in the water.' Zubi turned towards the rice.

'Once the water starts boiling, put the rice in the water along with salt and watch carefully. This is the trickiest part because if you're not careful, you could end up with gummy biryani where you can't distinguish one rice grain from the other. It's better to stop cooking the rice even when it's a little undercooked because it can blossom later during the dum stage.' At this point, Zubi stopped talking because she knew she needed to concentrate. She had made sure that everything was visible to the camera as she drained the rice and quickly mixed it in the still-cooking akhni mixture. The akhni masala had reduced significantly and there wasn't much water left in it.

Zubi flattened the rice over the akhni, and with one hand, reached for the camera so she could show a close-up of what she had done. With the other hand, she poured the oil that she had reserved from the akhni on top of the rice.

'Now, cover this with a lid and keep something heavy on top. I usually keep the vessel in which I drained all that hot water over the lid although in the earlier days, people would wrap the lid with cloth and then cover the pot. Which reminds me, I have to ask my mother why they did that. I remember my grandmother doing it, and later I remember my mother using newspapers instead of cloth. Did they think that they were making the lid more air-tight?'

She shrugged and tucked a strand of her hair behind her ear. 'See, this is it. It's not too difficult to make biryani. It's a meal by itself although most people would say it's incomplete if you didn't have this to go with it.' She lifted a bowl of yoghurt in which she had mixed grated cucumber, chopped onions, a chopped green chilli, salt, coriander and mint leaves, and a dash of lemon.

'This is what we call dahi ki chutney,' she explained.

She paused the camera, went to check on Abid, came back and started again.

'Now, it's time to check if the dum process has done its duty.'

She lifted the lid and watched tendrils of steam curl their way across to her. She raised her eyebrows in appreciation.

'Wow!' she breathed and gently mixed the upper and lower layers, removing them both together on a plate. She arranged the dahi ki chutney on the side and lifted the plate to make it face the camera.

'I'm going now to eat this fabulous lunch with my son. Next time I'll show you how to make two of the most famous accompaniments to biryani – khatta baingan and dal-cha. But for now, I'm famished, so excuse me, please!'

She leaned forward and switched off the camera breathing heavily. She had done it. Phew!

She brought the handycam down from its perch and took it outside where Abid was still glued to the TV. She frowned and then sat down with him and made him eat some of the biryani. Later, she played back the video and although at first she felt like cringing, she watched it entirely, feeling a little pleased with herself.

Later in the day, she set up an account on YouTube and edited the video she had made. It took her quite some time to finish it and even then she wasn't sure she had done a good job. She had to split the file into four videos to upload them on YouTube and just when she was about to hit the final button, she paused. Should she be doing this? She hadn't even told Khaled that she had thought of becoming an Internet cookery show host. But then he thought that she was *just* a housewife, right? Let him continue to think that, she thought as she uploaded the videos. It was only later when she saw the date on the videos that she realised that it was her father's death anniversary. In her excitement about recording the video, she had forgotten. She hadn't even called and spoken to her mother. But for some reason, she was happy. She didn't know how, but she knew what she had done was extremely significant. She had done this…this liberating act on *this* day.

'You would have been proud, Abbu,' she whispered as she played the first video and watched herself show the world how to make biryani.

45

I rubbed my scalp and then pressed my fingers over my eyes watching starbursts and wiggly lines of light explode on the inside.

'You know the rest,' Zubi said, leaning forward as she sat on the sofa. I yawned and nodded. What a story! Zubi didn't know but I had been writing in the night and had been awake till three or four, furiously typing down everything because I didn't want to lose the intensity of her story.

'So you can finish the book now?' she asked me and I looked at her, meeting her eyes. I shrugged. I had written most of it already but I just didn't know how it was going to end. That part was still not clear to me.

'Now will you let me read what you've written so far?' she asked. I looked away, feeling a flash of guilt.

'Yes,' I mumbled but I think she was expecting me to hand my laptop over to her right then. I couldn't. Not yet. I don't know why but I was still reluctant to let her read it.

She watched me carefully for a while and I don't know what came over her, but she stood up and said, 'I don't think I can do this, Sonia.'

'Huh?' I looked at her, surprised. 'Do what?'

'I can't let you write my story,' she said, standing near the window. I felt my heart plummet.

'You....it's too late for that,' I said and she whirled around.

'Nothing was official. Just don't do it,' she said, her mouth a thin line.

I scratched my head impatiently. I wasn't Khaled to bear with her crazy tantrums.

'Why the hell not?' I asked her.

'Because it's too personal. It's *my* story and I don't want it out there!' she said passionately.

'Then you should have thought of it *before* you spoke to me,' I said, shutting the lid of my laptop with force.

'You never told me you'd do anything like this. I don't like it. I...I can't bear the thought of Khaled reading about this, let alone the rest of the world!' she said, covering her face with her hands.

I stayed silent for a while, hoping that if I kept quiet she would change her mind. She couldn't do this to me. Not now, when I had invested so much of my time and energy in the book. She had to be out of her mind.

'Zubi,' I spoke calmly. 'I was planning to change the names in the book anyway. No one has to know it's your story.'

Zubi looked at me and I couldn't see her face clearly because the apartment had darkened and both of us had been so caught up in her story that we had lost the sense of time.

'What?' I asked her. She continued shaking her head.

'But Khaled will know,' she said. 'If he ever reads any of this, he'll know and I can't face him and...'

'Too late for that,' I muttered softly. She looked up. I felt uneasy because I didn't know if she had heard me or not.

She got up and switched on the lights. Abid was asleep next to her on the sofa and I was sitting on the other single seater, my legs folded up, my toes making dents in the fabric.

'What did you say?' she asked me and I knew that she had heard me.

'Nothing,' I shrugged, feeling a little panicky inside.

'You said something about being late,' she insisted. I stared back at her face and I was torn between telling her the truth or just covering up with some lie. But her insistence that I shouldn't write the book was irking me and I nodded.

'He...he's read some of it already,' I said. Zubi looked at me, stunned.

'When? How?' her voice had risen and I realised that telling her had not been a good idea.

'Have you been meeting him behind my back?' she asked. I felt an uncomfortable flush rise up to my face.

'Zubi, it's not like that...' I said lamely.

'What's going on between the two of you?' she asked calmly. I felt my cheeks redden at her implication.

'Nothing,' I said trying to sound sincere but obviously failing because she didn't look convinced.

'How else do you explain this?'

'Explain what? We met a couple of times over coffee. That's it. He wanted to read the story and I gave it to him.'

Zubi covered her cheeks with her palms and kept muttering 'No, no, no!'

'Look, he deserves to know too. The two of you are crazy if you keep this up,' I said, backing away from her. She looked furious and I realised I had never seen Zubi so angry.

'You were my friend. How could you do this, Sonia? I *trusted* you!' she screeched and I looked at her anxiously.

'Calm down, Zubi. Nothing happened between me and Khaled and nothing ever will because he loves you too much!' That was an odd and disturbing moment for me as I realised that there had been a little truth in her implied accusations. I certainly had some feelings for him.

Stunned at the realisation, I turned away to avoid seeing her face. I needed to collect my thoughts quickly and probably leave. But Zubi hadn't noticed anything and continued ranting.

'How could you give my story to him without asking me? How? I trusted you, Sonia,' she kept repeating.

None of her words were making sense to me. I had to get out of the place before Khaled came back. He was due in another hour.

I started putting my things in my bag. Zubi followed me to the tiny room where I had slept for the past two nights. Or rather stayed up hammering out her story on my laptop.

'What happened?' she asked, the change in her tone surprising me. I turned around to look at her.

'I have to go,' I said, zipping my bag.

'How much does Khaled know?' she asked, blocking the door and crossing her arms. I recognised the defensive stance; I licked my lips nervously.

'He's just read the bit till your grandmother's story. That's all,' I said, hoisting the laptop bag over my back.

Zubi covered her mouth with her palm. Her reactions were really annoying me now.

'You wanted people to read your story and that's why you narrated it to me,' I said to her evenly. She shook her head.

'We were never clear about that, Sonia. You wanted to talk to me and get to know me and I was…I was so lonely and for some reason I could connect to you. I told you things I have never told anyone but I didn't realise that you would be putting down everything in a book.'

I pursed my lips and realised I was breathing heavily.

'What do you want me to do?' I asked her.

She was still blocking the doorway. 'Don't write my story. Please! I'm begging you!' she beseeched me. I looked down at my feet nervously and cast a quick glance at her feet, the same ones that Khaled had fallen in love with.

'What?' she asked me.

'I...I already wrote it,' I said, looking up to meet her eyes.

'When?' she asked me incredulously.

'On both nights I stayed up. I just have a couple more chapters to write.'

She kept shaking her head and looked at me in disbelief.

'You cannot publish this book, Sonia,' she said, her voice suddenly strong. 'I won't allow it. We never signed any contract so...'

I was getting really angry with her now.

'What the fuck do you think of yourself?' I asked her, my voice rising. 'You think I've spent months and months running after you and trying to make something out of your story for nothing?'

Zubi was a little shocked at the change in my demeanour and my language.

'Get out,' she said, quietly. 'I don't want to ever see you again. Don't call me. Don't come to my house. And don't try to meet my husband!' she said, moving away from the door.

I walked outside feeling miserable and wretched. This weekend had been amazing and it had ended in disaster. She watched me leave quietly and I turned to see Abid still sleeping, realising that if she had her way, I would never meet the three of them again.

I walked towards the elevator, my pace slow and a dull pain throbbing in my temples. Everything had been a mistake. I should never have started this whole thing of trying to write her story. I wouldn't have been so caught up with it and....I wouldn't have fallen in love with Khaled.

While leaving the building, I caught sight of him walking

purposefully towards the lift from the other entrance. I was glad he hadn't seen me. He looked tired and a little grim, and kept rubbing the back of his neck. What was he expecting from this two-day rendezvous that he had put me up to with Zubi? He had unknowingly unleashed many things but the pity was that he would never get to know about it. I had no intentions of showing him Zubi's story. Not because I didn't want him to know how much she loved him. But because in her eyes I had already betrayed her too much. This would be the final nail in the coffin. Despite realising that I loved him, my loyalties lay with Zubi, no matter how crazy she was. I owed it to her.

'I'm sorry, Khaled,' I whispered as I ran down the TST subway steps to catch my train home.

46

Okay, I was *not* in love with Khaled.

I think it was probably transference or something psychological or what I don't know because in the clear, cold and hard light of the day I could see how foolish it was. I barely knew him, although of course I couldn't deny the physical attraction I had felt, but that was it. It was just a crush I had and after listening to Zubi talk about him, it had just become a little stronger. That was all.

So I don't know why I kept ignoring his calls all day. Nor did I understand why I didn't read his texts. I kept on doing my work and since it was a Monday morning, we had our usual round of meetings in which I was so distracted and distanced that Vera finally snapped at me.

'Sonia, if you're not interested, please leave,' she said, anger brimming under her words. The meeting was almost over, so I shrugged, got up, and left, much to the astonishment of Linda and the others. I went back, sat in my usual place, and opened the document that contained Zubi's story, which I had amended last night.

I didn't know what I was going to do with it, but I knew that I couldn't possibly show it to Khaled. I read, and re-read it and felt

More Than Just Biryani

like weeping because it was so good and it had been a complete waste of my time and effort.

I saw his name flash on my mobile screen. I sat biting the edge of my knuckles; sighing deeply, I answered the phone.

'Finally!' he exploded and I winced.

'What did you say?' he asked me before I could even formulate my thoughts.

'Huh?' I asked, feeling panic flood inside me.

'What did you say?' he repeated the question slowly as though I was a moron.

'I...I'm not writing this story, Khaled,' I lied, because there it was, right in front of me, on my screen.

'What do you mean? And you haven't answered my question yet. What did you say to Zubi?' he repeated, his voice rising a little.

'I didn't say anything.'

'Zubi isn't talking to me at all. I mean, she's shut down completely. This morning she was packing her bags and she said that she wants to go back to India. After saying that, she sat down on the sofa and refused to move or talk,' Khaled sounded frustrated and angry and his voice shook.

I gulped. This was bad.

'I...I let it slip by mistake that...the two of us met and that you've read the story so far,' I admitted finally.

'Are you sure that's it?' he asked me. 'Because I don't understand this at all.'

I clung to my phone, recalling Zubi's accusation. A little part of me was afraid it was true. I couldn't tell him that. The situation was way too complicated already.

'And what is this you're saying about not writing her story?' he asked and I shut my eyes.

'I...I am not comfortable doing this anymore,' I said. 'Listen, Khaled, I...I'm at work and I can't talk now. Please don't call me,' I said and ended the call quickly. I realised that my heart was pounding and my palms were sweating.

I looked up at my phone as a text message buzzed through it.

`'She wants me to book a flight for her immediately'`

I shut my eyes and wished I'd never seen Zubi's video.

The days passed by rapidly and each day I was worried I would find Khaled waiting for me near the office, demanding to see the rest of the book. But he didn't know where I worked and I was thankful that I had never told him my office address or even the name of the magazine.

I wondered what had happened. Had Zubi really left? I didn't know and I was too scared to find out. I was angry and bitter about the way everything had shaped up and I stayed at Natalie's most evenings, drinking and bitching about life in general. Natalie didn't know anything about my tryst with Zubi and her life but one night I drank too much and spilled everything to her. She listened to everything in growing amazement.

'That stupid girl thinks I'm in love with her husband,' I slurred.

Natalie put down her glass and took a deep breath. 'And are you?' she asked me.

I shrugged. 'How does it matter? The two of them are the weirdest couple on this planet. Both crazy about each other and both refusing to tell the other.'

'Can...can I read the manuscript?' she asked me hesitantly.

My laptop was with me. 'Be my guest,' I said, 'Although I don't think I'm going to finish that book. Ever.'

She picked up my laptop, opened the file named Zubi and started reading. By then I'd had too much to drink and fell asleep, sprawled on her couch.

'Wake up, it's morning. And don't you have to go to work?' I felt Natalie's hand shaking my shoulder.

'Wha? Morning?' I looked around at her brightly lit apartment. Natalie lived in Quarry Bay, which is about four stops away from the subway near my home in Wanchai. I didn't have the energy to get up, go home, get dressed and face another day at work. Especially not when I had the mother of all hangovers.

Licking my dry lips, I looked at Natalie and saw that she was looking at me strangely.

'What?' I asked but didn't wait for her reply as I made my way to the bathroom. When I emerged a little later, with a pounding headache making me feel a little nauseous, she continued staring at me.

'What?' I asked her again, as I sat down on the sofa and called up at my office to tell them I wasn't coming. I threw my phone on the centre table and looked at her but before I could ask her 'what' again, she started speaking.

She shrugged. 'You're asking but you're not giving me the chance to answer,' she said. 'Because I think you know the answer already.'

'Stop talking in riddles,' I mumbled as I clutched my head.

'Sonia, even if you don't publish this story, you have to give it to Khaled *and* Zubi to read,' she said. I looked up angrily.

'Why?'

'It's their story and they deserve to read it,' she declared simply. I made a face at her.

'Since when did you become so...so...' I struggled to find the words, 'sensitive and... correct?'

Natalie shook her head. 'I'm not all fluff, you know,' she replied quietly.

I thought over it for a moment.

'And I do think that you've got some feelings for Khaled, which is colouring this whole decision for you. Why else would you not want him to read it? Don't you think he needs to know how much Zubi loves him and can never tell him? Are you hoping that he'll leave Zubi and then…'

'Stop!' I said, shutting my eyes. She was probably right. Somewhere inside I'd actually begun harbouring the hope that Khaled deserved someone better than Zubi; worse, I'd even thought that maybe it could be me. But no. It could never be me. I had seen the look in Khaled's eyes when he talked about Zubi…you don't get that kind of look in a man's eyes easily. No matter what she did or where she went, Khaled would love only Zubi. The realisation struck home and it was rather stark.

'And Zubi really considered you to be her friend,' Natalie continued softly. I squeezed my eyes shut and the action sent hot pinpricks up my head.

'What do you want me to do? You're saying I should make them read it together? She's probably gone back to India already,' I said, my words causing an odd lurching feeling inside me. It had been a week since the fiasco happened.

'I don't know. It's your call. You meet them, you talk to them and you make them read it,' Natalie piped in.

'And maybe, if they read it and understand everything, this could still swing in your favour. Zubi might agree to get it published and you could have that whole book-plus-video concept you were so excited about.'

God, that seemed so far away. I got so caught up with the story that I had completely forgotten my original intentions. I pulled at the little edge of skin on my pinky finger and yanked it with my teeth; Natalie winced.

'That's gross! Here, call him!' she ordered and suddenly leaned forward and flung my phone towards me. I caught it in time and then looked at it unhappily.

Natalie was right. There had been a chance for salvaging this situation but I had given up the moment Zubi accused me of having feelings for Khaled. Her angry outburst had unnerved me and taken me by surprise. It was time to set the record straight. I only hoped I wasn't too late.

47

I sat down on the park bench and waited for him. I hadn't told him anything, except that I wanted to meet him in Kowloon Park. In my bag I had a printout of the manuscript. I was anxious and nervous, wondering what he would say when he read it.

I noticed him walking towards me a little later, his steps slow and measured. I looked for changes on his face. Was he upset because Zubi had gone back? *Had* she gone back? I couldn't muster the nerve to ask him but he smiled at me when he sat down and I felt a bit surprised.

'Hi!' he said and I nodded. He looked steady and balanced and very much in control and his appearance was unexpected. I had thought he would come unshaven and probably on the verge of tears but he was dapper as usual and he looked good enough to eat.

'Thanks for meeting me,' I said, lowering my gaze. After Zubi's accusation, I didn't want to take my chances with Khaled. There were times when I didn't trust myself.

'Zubi has gone back to India,' he said with half a smile on his face.

'Oh,' I looked up at him. Why was he looking happy?

'She went the day after we spoke on the phone. I'm divorcing her.' I stared back at him in horror as he calmly made the announcement.

'What?' I gasped.

'What did you think? There's only so much a man can take. I have waited and waited so patiently that...' he ran his hands through his hair and shook his head.

'I deserve to be happy, you know. I can't walk on eggshells all my life, wondering what I did *now* to upset her.'

I covered my mouth with my hands, dismayed and outraged. 'How could you?'

'What do you mean? You've seen the way she treats me, right? She's crazy. *I'll* go crazy if I stay with her any longer,' he exclaimed while looking at the pond and the children playing nearby.

'Did you...did you do the talaq thing? Are you guys already divorced?'

Khaled shook his head. 'I...I didn't want to do it that way. Not when she was alone here without anyone to support her,' he said, looking down at his lap.

He still loved her, the thought formed in my head but I didn't articulate it.

'What about Abid?' I asked instead, my heart beating erratically. This couldn't be happening. Khaled and Zubi belonged together and the moment he'd said that he was divorcing her, I realised that no matter what, *this* shouldn't happen. Whatever feelings I'd had for him were nothing compared to how much Zubi loved him.

'We haven't discussed that but by right he belongs to me.' I felt like slapping him. How could he take Abid from her?

'I've got Zubi's story with me. I thought maybe you'd like to read it,' I said, rummaging inside my bag for it.

'I don't want to read it,' he stated. What?!

'But why?' I almost wailed. He had to read it and understand and...

'If I'm going to be divorcing her, I really don't need to know how or why her mind works the way it does,' he declared, cracking his knuckles and looking up at the sky. He was lying, I knew it. Maybe he was serious about getting a divorce but he couldn't just negate his love for her so suddenly.

'And what about how you felt for her? Does that amount to nothing?' I asked him, my fingers still wrapped around the pages inside my bag.

'I once read somewhere that it's better to be with someone who loves you, rather than someone whom you love. I've seen it firsthand now.' Saying this, he got up. 'Sonia, it's been nice meeting you but I have to go. I'm meeting a few friends this evening.'

'Julie?' I asked before I could stop myself and he frowned.

'How do you know about Julie?' he asked, looking troubled.

'You had better read this, Khaled. Please. I could tell it to you but you won't believe me,' I said, pulling out the pages.

With a sigh he took the papers from me, rolled them into a tube and smacked them on his thigh. 'Fine,' he said and made to leave.

'No, wait!' I stopped him.

'What?'

'Please, read it now,' I said, doubting that he might dump the pages in the nearest dustbin and leave.

He looked at me incredulously. 'Please?' I begged. He looked angry and then finally relented. He sat down and looked at the first page.

I sat and watched his expressions anxiously. At first he snorted but then his expression grew serious as he kept turning the pages. When he was nearly at the end, it seemed as though he couldn't turn them fast enough. He looked up at me when he was done; his expression was stone-like.

'This doesn't change anything,' he said and I stared back at him in shock. I couldn't believe he wasn't affected by it. He *had* to be lying.

'Why? Why doesn't it change anything?' I asked, 'Doesn't it make a difference to you to know that Zubi loves you so much?'

He was silent for a while and then he spoke. 'I've been hurt too much, Sonia,' he said, looking at me squarely in the eye. I was so glad that I had spoken to Natalie as she had reaffirmed my belief that Khaled and Zubi belonged together. Or I don't know what I would have done because a part of me was dying to give him comfort. To make his pain go away.

'Please! Give her a chance!' I pleaded, looking away from his intense stare. 'She's so....'

'Confused? Neurotic? Crazy?' he asked harshly, staring at the pond.

'Afraid of getting hurt,' I said softly. 'That's her only fault. This behaviour...it's her defence mechanism. The only way she's learnt to deal with it.'

'And what are you? Her shrink?' he asked, breathing heavily.

'No, but I'm her friend. And I think she deserves one more chance,' I said while looking down at my feet, hoping that this would absolve me of the guilt that would always be inside, clawing to get out while I kept pushing it down.

He looked down at the pages in his hands, turning them over and over again for some reason and then shook his head.

'Why didn't you give this to me before? Why didn't you give it to me when I asked you for it?'

I couldn't tell him the truth about Zubi's accusations. 'Would it have made a difference if I'd given it then?' I asked.

'Maybe. I don't know. I've tried so hard to understand her but I have no idea why she opened up to you although I am glad that she did.'

'When did you tell her about the divorce?'

He turned to look at me. 'That very day. I went back home and she was *still* sitting on the sofa and Abid was crying and I knew I couldn't go on any more. I told her that she could go back to India, that I would come back in a month and give her a divorce.'

I rubbed my cheek feeling worried. 'How did she take it?' I asked him and saw his expression falter.

'She looked horrified for a moment and then...now I understand why she looked resigned. As though she'd been expecting it all along.'

There were times when I wished I'd never got involved in Zubi's life. There were too many emotional ups and downs that were reflecting in my own life and it was not pleasant.

'What are you going to do?' I asked, getting up slowly.

He made a face. 'I don't know yet. I have to think.'

I had hoped he would say that he would go to India immediately and bring her back. But things weren't proceeding so smoothly. For some reason, Khaled was reluctant to put his heart on the line again, and although I couldn't really blame him, I was on Zubi's side.

'Please, Khaled, she loves you so much. And you love her too, right? Get her back,' I said. He stepped back, exasperated.

'Did you think this is some movie where the hero keeps chasing the heroine? I can't just go to India like that. I have a job here.'

'But...you have to speak to her. In person. You *can't* let her go, Khaled.'

'What's it to you? You wanted to write a book and you did. Maybe it's time you left us alone,' he snapped.

I opened my mouth to say something and then stopped. How could I tell him that I was interested in their story not just because of the book but for reasons I didn't quite understand myself?

'If you hadn't pursued her, none of this would have happened. Zubi and Abid would have been here with me in Hong Kong.' He looked angry. So now he's blaming me?

'Yes, but you would never have known how much she loved you. Loves you,' I amended.

'Then why did she decide to go back?' he asked. I looked down, feeling uneasy about the part I had played in it.

'I already told you. She was angry when I told her that I gave you the manuscript.'

Khaled shook his head. 'You didn't see her that day, Sonia. She was absolutely immobile. Like she'd been frozen and not just physically. You have no idea how much I tried to get her to talk, to understand what went wrong.'

'That's jealous Zubi for you, I guess,' I muttered.

'Jealous?' he repeated sounding incredulous.

'She kind of lost it after I told her that the two of us met and...' I trailed away feeling slightly embarrassed when Khaled seemed to understand what I was saying.

'What?' he snorted. 'I don't believe it.'

'You better believe it. You've read the manuscript. You know what prompted her to shoot that video in the first place,' I reminded him.

'But that was because she wanted to do something,' he said.

'Yes, but bumping into Julie was the catalyst,' I said. He continued shaking his head as though still trying to come to terms with it. Then he got up from the bench and exhaled loudly.

'What's the point of all this if she's never going to...to be able to express her feelings for me?' he asked, I closed my eyes and opened them, a little angry at him.

'Now you're just being selfish.'

'Selfish?' he snapped back angrily.

'Yes. Isn't it enough for you to *know* that she loves you so much?' I asked, collecting my things from the bench.

Angry silence stretched between the two of us but I didn't do anything to mitigate it. Poor Khaled, yes. But poor Zubi too.

'I wasn't going to meet Julie,' he called out as I walked away from there.

I turned around and made a face. 'Go tell that to Zubi' I shouted, walking away furiously.

'How do I know you haven't made this up? That this isn't fiction?' he called out again. I stopped and turned around, shocked at his questions. But I saw the pain in his eyes, desperate desire for the story to be true.

'If I had to make this up, I'd have written a different ending,' I told him recklessly and then was glad when he didn't get my drift.

'If I go to her and she...she turns me away one more time, that's it,' he murmured, while walking away slowly.

'Don't waste this chance, Zubi,' I muttered under my breath as I saw him leave.

48

Zubi wondered if today would be a good day to tell her mother about her impending divorce. It was high time she did it anyway. Khaled had said that he would come to India in a month to do it and almost a month had passed now since she'd left noisy Hong Kong for noisy Bangalore.

Well, who was she fooling? It was almost a month. It was exactly twenty-nine days since she'd come from Hong Kong and landed at her mother's house. Her mother had been surprised and bewildered. She kept asking Zubi if everything was alright to which Zubi simply told her that she was missing everyone and so had come down for a few days.

'Why didn't Khaled come with you?' her mother had asked.

'He has a job! He can't come down whenever he feels like it!' Zubi had tried to explain. When Chachi had heard that Zubi was in India, she came to visit and grilled her with questions about how things had turned out eventually with Khaled.

'So you didn't tell him how you feel?' Chachi asked as they sat down in Zubi's room after lunch one day.

'I can't,' said Zubi.

'Why not?' Chachi persisted. 'Why is it so difficult for you to face your fears?'

Zubi remained silent at which Chachi began to feel frustrated.

'You're a grown woman, Zubi. This is your life. Not your mother's. If you don't do something about your fears now, you are sure to regret it one day,' she said, squeezing Zubi's hand before leaving.

I already regret it, Zubi had wanted to say. In her heart, she couldn't believe he would actually divorce her. But she remembered the look on his face when he had said the words and what she had actually felt at that moment. Like someone had pushed her from a height...she felt everything fall away while she struggled to find balance.

She *would* survive it if he divorced her, she told herself. She knew she could. She wasn't her mother who had crumbled when her husband died. But having this self-assurance, this confidence that she could manage without him was not a comforting thought. Especially since she still loved him.

She shut her eyes because whenever she closed them, his face would float before them...although his features had already started looking blurry to her. She knew the individual parts but she couldn't put together the face that she loved so much.

Should she be expecting him then? How was he planning to do it? A part of her had wanted to read up about divorce in Islam but she didn't, unwilling to believe that it was soon to happen to her. She couldn't ask anyone else either because divorce didn't form a part of casual conversation.

Abid had been confused when they came here but slowly he was getting used to life in Bangalore. Zubi's mother-in-law had called her up, demanding to know why she hadn't come home and what she was doing in Bangalore.

This was why living in Hong Kong was so wonderful, Zubi thought irritably. She didn't have to answer all these questions and no one forced her to self-introspect. She made up a story about how she hadn't been keeping well and so, Khaled had sent her to India to get some rest.

'You can rest here too. This is your home after all,' her mother-in-law had pronounced loftily.

She came to see her and Abid the following day and insisted that Zubi come stay with them. Zubi didn't know how to get out of it without arousing anyone's suspicion. There was no way she could tell them about the divorce because she didn't want to answer any questions. Khaled wanted to divorce her, so why should she be the one to face any flak before it even happened?

In the end, there was no avoiding it and the two of them went to stay there for a couple of days. Zubi couldn't last any longer than that because her mother-in-law asked her too many questions and there were reminders of Khaled everywhere. She promised to return soon but didn't go back.

Keeping up a charade that everything was fine in her world was proving to be painfully difficult because her mother wanted to know why Khaled never called or why she never saw them chatting on Skype.

'He calls in the night and he's too busy for video chats,' Zubi lied. She winced when she thought of the number of lies she'd been spinning since the day she got here, starting with 'Everything is fine'.

Nothing was fine, especially all the arguments she had with her mother regarding Abid's upbringing. Ammi constantly criticised her parenting methods and Zubi's nerves were shot, trying to placate her mother and Abid and still manage to retain control over him as a parent. What would happen to Abid after the divorce, she thought, panic superseding her thoughts and she would stop thinking about it immediately.

'Zubi!' her mother called out. 'There's a courier for you. It's from Hong Kong!'

Zubi froze. She'd been looking outside her window, thinking of Hong Kong and what she would have been doing in her house at this time, if things had been normal...if she'd been normal. And now Ammi was saying...

What could it be, she wondered uneasily. Something to do with the divorce?

She slowly walked towards the main door where Ammi stood, holding a package.

'You have to sign,' she told Zubi without handing it to her. Zubi nodded, the sinking feeling inside building with every moment. Had she dreamt that this was how it would all end? No, never. She'd always been afraid that he would die and she would have to live without him. But this seemed much worse, she thought as she signed the paper with a shaky hand. This cold, clinical separating of two people who lived, but would never live together seemed worse.

The package was shaped like a book and Zubi felt her stomach clench inside. She ripped open the cover and saw that it was a book. Her book. Automatically her hand went to her chest and remained there for a moment. There was fancy lettering on top in gold and the cover was red in colour.

MORE THAN JUST BIRYANI
By Sonia Kapoor and Zubaida Banu

'The culinary journey of three women who followed their hearts' read the subheading.

She couldn't believe it. Sonia had got the book published! Despite Zubi telling her not to! And how had she managed to pull it off so soon? How did she get a publisher and...she turned the book around and felt the clenching inside her stomach worsen.

'You wrote a book?' Ammi asked, her eyes growing round in surprise, as she leaned forward to take it from Zubi's hands.

'No! No, I didn't! It's a mistake!' Zubi said as she moved away and walked towards her room, turning the book over and over in her hands. Something was definitely odd about this book. Although there was a blurb at the back, it didn't make any sense.

'*Lorem ipsum dolor sit amet, consectetur adipisicing elit, sed do eiusmod tempor incididunt ut labore et dolore magna aliqua.*'

That was the blurb? She opened the pages and saw her name leap out of it; she shut the book quickly. What had Sonia done?

She wanted to call her immediately but decided to calm herself down first. Back in her room, she sat down with the book and picked up another book from her shelf to compare. Something was definitely strange here. That was when she noticed it – there was no ISBN. There was no name of any publisher. There was no price.

'Sonia, you idiot!' Zubi thought, smiling for the first time in days. This was no published book. Sonia had just done a very clever printing job, got the pages cut and bound and even got a cover done to make it *look* like a book. And she'd been too lazy to write a blurb so the whole 'lorem ipsum' thing at the back now made sense. Maybe she had thought that if she simply sent her the pages or an email, Zubi wouldn't read it. She was right. Zubi wouldn't have read it.

She opened the first page – it began with the story about her mother – and started reading and got absorbed in the immediacy of the situations. When she came to the part where her father died, Zubi shut the book and put it face down on the table. Reading it had made it seem like it had happened just yesterday and the pain of losing her father, dulled into regret by now, suddenly throbbed intensely. Why had she revealed the deepest and most intimate parts of their lives to a complete stranger?

But she'd started reading and she was curious to see how Sonia had written the rest; so she picked up the book after some time. When she started reading the second part, about her grandmother, she started smiling. Sonia was a really talented writer because she had taken Zubi's ordinary words and made them into a story that was engrossing, lilting and captivating.

'Too bad this is never going to be published,' Zubi thought as she continued reading. After that, however, she had to keep the book aside and head out for lunch where Ammi was making a lot of noise about having a grown daughter in the home who didn't help her.

'Bah! Get Rishaad married and bully his wife!' Zubi muttered. Her mother overheard her.

'It's time, no? We should start looking for him,' Ammi said and Zubi rolled her eyes. Rishaad would freak out. He was just twenty-three and starting out in the world. Zubi's mind was still in her room where the book was lying, face down on her bed. She was itching to get back to it, but unfortunately it would have to wait. Ammi, too, was curious about it.

'If you didn't write it, why is your name on the book cover?' she asked her as she fried papad.

Zubi poured the dal from the pressure cooker into a serving bowl and wondered how she could escape her mother's ever-sharp eyes.

'This girl I met in Hong Kong just played a prank, Ammi. That's all,' Zubi said, as she wiped some of the dal that had spilled over.

'Such an elaborate prank? Why?' Ammi persisted.

'I don't know! I'll have to ask her!' Zubi snapped.

'But what was that about *biryani*?' Ammi continued.

'She's a big fan of biryani,' Zubi muttered, hoping her mother would stop the interrogation.

'So?' Ammi asked, clueless about Zubi's discomfort or irritation. Zubi wanted to slap her forehead but instead she gritted her teeth and explained that Sonia used to think that Muslims ate biryani all the time and how she, Zubi, had showed her that there was so much more to their cuisine.

At least that's not a lie, Zubi thought.

'Aah! So that's why it's called *"More* Than Just Biryani"?' her mother asked, her eyes lighting up.

Zubi nodded and smiled as she took the food outside.

She watched Abid munch on the papads and thought of how she took these same papads to Hong Kong because Khaled loved them so much. It wasn't fair, she thought. Not when she'd been so careful not to fall in the same trap as her mother. Why should she suffer? Why should every little thing remind her of him? And the biggest reminder was Abid.

She took Abid back to her room for his afternoon nap. He curled up next to her on the narrow bed.

'Ammi, where's Abba? Why hasn't he come? Why haven't we gone back?' he asked her, the questions tripping over each other. Zubi shut her eyes and patted him to sleep.

When Abid fell asleep, she picked up the book to continue reading. She'd been lying down and reading it but she sat up straight when she saw Khaled's name come up. She didn't recall telling any of this to Sonia. About how Khaled had visited her mother's house, about how he had seen her sleep on the sofa with kajal smeared on her face, about how he had fallen in love with her feet.

Zubi felt something push down inside her chest, as though someone or something was applying great pressure there. Had Khaled told Sonia about all this when they had met? Why had Sonia included this in the book? So Zubi would know about Khaled's feelings for her?

A part of her had been unwilling to forgive Sonia over meeting Khaled behind her back. But now, after all these days, she cringed at how she had behaved. As she continued reading the story, she forgot all about Sonia. This was too little information. She wanted to know more. She was desperate to know more actually. Why had Khaled told Sonia only so much?

But inside her head, another group of thoughts began taking precedence. Khaled had orchestrated their marriage from the beginning, *because* he was in love with her. But how would knowing that have made any difference to Zubi and her behaviour? She was still terrified of getting emotionally attached to him. But maybe if she'd known...

I'm never going to know, Zubi thought as she shut the book with a snap, finding a tear roll down her cheek. Would she have behaved differently? But if Khaled loved her so much, why was he divorcing her then?

He loves me *and* he hates me, Zubi thought, more tears running down her face steadily now. But he loved me of his own accord. I *made* him hate me.

Zubi sniffled and wiped the tears with the back of her hand and went back to the book. It wasn't a thick book but Zubi read her part slowly, savouring the way Sonia had portrayed their relationship, blushing when she read about herself kissing Khaled. And when she came to the part about his accident, she hated herself for being so cruel to him. What would he have felt if he'd read this, she thought. But why would he now? Not when he wanted to be free from her.

As she turned to the last page, however, she looked up surprised. What was this?

There was a post-it note stuck at the back – Sonia had written something on it. She peeled it off and read it, blinking her eyes.

More Than Just Biryani

```
Zubi, Call me or Skype me. Please! -
Sonia
```
Zubi just stared at the note, but then she crumpled it and threw it away.

Zubi waited for three days before logging on to Skype to speak to Sonia. She'd had to find the right time to do it, when Abid and Ammi were asleep and when no one else was in the house.

It was strange talking to Sonia across the computer screen. She looked uneasy and guilty and Zubi felt awkward because of the way they had parted.

'I'm sorry, Zubi,' she started and Zubi stopped her.

'It's okay,' she said. Sonia looked surprised.

'I...How have you been, Zubi?' Sonia looked concerned.

Zubi shrugged wondering what she could possibly tell her. That Khaled was divorcing her? That she would never come back to Hong Kong? It all sounded so final.

'What's common between a woman and her mother?' she found herself asking Sonia. Sonia leaned forward in surprise.

'Huh?'

'Every woman eventually becomes like her mother,' Zubi answered her own question.

Sonia looked taken aback. 'Really?'

'My mother was devastated when my father died. I...I'm trying not to be devastated when Khaled d-divorces me but...' Zubi trailed.

Sonia stared at her. 'You read the book, right?'

'Has *he* read it?' Zubi asked Sonia instead, afraid to hear the answer.

'Yes, he has,' Sonia replied slowly. Zubi looked up immediately.

'And? What did he say?'

'Sonia?'

'He...he didn't say anything,' Sonia said, looking away.

Zubi was quiet for a moment. Reading her story through Sonia's words had made her aware of Khaled's pain in a way that hadn't been possible before.

'Zubi?' Sonia asked her, looking worried.

'Yeah?' Zubi's mouth twisted slightly.

'Everything will be fine.'

Zubi didn't nod and she didn't say anything. She couldn't. After a long moment of awkward silence, she spoke.

'Do you still want to get the book published?'

'Not without your videos,' Sonia replied. But before Zubi could say anything else, Sonia asked her 'If...if you were given another chance with Khaled, what would you have done?'

'Another chance?'

'One last chance,' Sonia repeated.

'I don't know, Sonia. I don't know,' said Zubi, after which she signed out of Skype and put her head down tiredly.

49

In some part of her mind, Zubi was aware that she was behaving almost exactly as her mother had when she had been in iddat, the mourning period after her father died. She'd lost interest in food and she bristled at the idea that her mother might want to cook something special on a Friday or a Sunday when both the boys were at home. But her mother had a valid reason then, or so it seemed. While she....she didn't have one yet.

One Sunday, a few days after receiving the book from Sonia, Zubi walked into the kitchen to see her mother roasting all the different dals on a tawa.

'What are you doing?' she asked her, although she wasn't the least bit interested.

'You're looking somewhat depressed so I thought I'd cheer you up. Making khichda,' her mother said as she briskly turned around the dals so they wouldn't burn.

Zubi didn't know whether to feel touched or irritated because her mother had noticed. But khichda was her favourite. Even more than biryani if that was possible. She swallowed the feelings of regret that had surfaced in her when she thought of the last time she had made this in Hong Kong. Khaled had complained about how gassy it was and how it would upset his stomach but he had eaten every last bit she had kept on his plate and even asked for more.

'I'll make the khichda, you do the bhurta,' Ammi said. Zubi walked to the storeroom half-heartedly to pick up the potatoes, tomatoes and onions required for making the bhurta. Ammi was doing the job that involved more work. Zubi was tempted to trade with her so it would keep her mind off the sad situation in her life but she was feeling too listless to suggest that idea.

Ammi washed the roasted dals, let them soak a little in water and then turned to look at Zubi.

'Zubi, are you pregnant?' Zubi's eyes grew round at Ammi's question. Was she? Just like her mother had been pregnant with Suhail when her father had died? She didn't know. She couldn't remember when she'd had her last period.

'I don't know,' she said truthfully.

'Do you feel nauseous? Does the smell of frying onions make you want to vomit?' her mother asked her eagerly. Zubi looked at her, irritated. Before Abid was born, her mother had constantly related to her about how certain smells had made her queasy when she'd been pregnant and how she couldn't face the kitchen on most days.

'No. But you already know that I don't feel nauseated when I'm pregnant,' Zubi reminded her.

'You don't know how lucky you are,' her mother stated as she placed the vessel on the stove. 'Most women either have…'

'Morning sickness or nausea. I know. But I told you the last time itself that it's not necessary for me to go through whatever *you* went through.' Zubi repeated the words to herself slowly and shook her head. Ever since her father died, Zubi had tried to be different from her mother in every way possible. It was only when she realised how deeply she loved Khaled that she knew it had been futile. All the efforts to pretend to not care were just that. A pretence that she had slipped over her face and worn around her heart defiantly. She had wanted to avoid pain but here she was, separated from Khaled, surviving it even though it kept corroding her heart. She looked at her mother, her eyes shining. So had her mother, in her own way.

'What?' her mother asked, as she started cooking the biryani akhni which was the base for the khichda. Zubi bit her lower lip, wondering if she would ever be able to explain to her mother, the revelation she'd just had. It may have been an epiphany that came a moment too late, but she was glad it did.

Mechanically, Zubi peeled and diced the potatoes, chopped the onions and tomatoes roughly and threw in a few pods of garlic in the pressure cooker. She sprinkled haldi and red chilli powder, added water and closed the pressure cooker.

'Don't forget the imli,' Ammi reminded her. Zubi nodded, reaching to pull out a lump of tamarind to soak it in water. Ammi had finished with the akhni already and was cooking all the dals – tuvar, urad, chana and moong – that she had roasted earlier in a larger pressure cooker. When they were cooked, she would mash them, and mix it into the akhni. Cooked rice was also mixed into the akhni and after all that, everything was stirred together and simmered. Khichda was a mishmash, an inelegant compilation of everything that was tasty, but it was one of the best comfort foods that her mother made.

Zubi went through the process of readying the bhurta in complete silence. Khichda without this piquant bhurta was unimaginable. But her heart wasn't in it. Also she didn't know if she was pregnant or not.

She mashed the cooked potatoes, onions and tomatoes, added tamarind water to it and heated it. Finally she did the usual baghaar, the tempering with fried onions, curry leaves and mustard and let it float on top.

'The boys are going to love it,' Ammi said as she sniffed appreciatively. She looked at Zubi critically as though to see if she had some reaction to the numerous smells that were percolating in the air. Zubi made a face and walked outside, unable to understand whether she was feeling happy or sad about the possible pregnancy situation.

When she'd first gone to Hong Kong, she'd put aside her worries for a few months. In a new country without friends or relatives, it had become natural for the two of them to become close and she had reveled in it. She had allowed herself to be happy with her family and she thought that was why Khaled had the accident. As a reminder to her from fate. Don't get too happy, or I'll pull the carpet from under your feet. And now? With Khaled on the verge of giving her a divorce, what had been the point of ensuring that he would never know what she felt for him? If she was going to be heartbroken in the end, she might as well have lived those years better. They could have been happy. So happy.

Both the boys had taken Abid to the nearby supermarket and when the bell rang, Zubi thought it was them. She opened the door and her stomach plummeted immediately. What's the deal with my stomach and my emotions, thought Zubi. It's the heart that's supposed to skip or miss a beat. Maybe the stomach is indeed the most important organ because it's the route to the heart, as the cliché goes.

While Zubi was having these irrational thoughts, Khaled stood staring at her, and both were unable to move from their positions.

'Why are you here?'

'Because I missed you.'
'What took you so long?'
'I needed to be sure.'
'What will you do now?'
'Take you back if you will come with me?'

The silent conversation continued while they still stood staring at each other and Zubi knew that the moment had come. He wasn't here to divorce her. He was here because he cared for her more than he ought to, more than she deserved. He had come because he loved her.

As if in slow motion, she saw him lift his hand to touch her cheek lightly; she closed her eyes, and let herself melt into his hand. She turned her face and pressed a kiss in the centre of his palm. She couldn't think of anything that she could say which wouldn't be trite or clichéd.

The silent conversation between them picked up tempo.

'Don't ever do this to me again.'
'But you were the one who wanted the di...'
'Shh!'

Zubi looked surprised because Khaled had spoken aloud. He pulled her close and hugged her, resting his chin on her head. Zubi felt his arms tremble and she knew that this was what Sonia had meant by one last chance. Had she known then, that he was coming? Right now, it didn't matter.

'Come inside,' she spoke shyly stepping away from him. His eyes didn't leave hers as she called out to her mother who came outside, unable to believe her eyes.

'Where's Abid?' he asked.

'Suhail and Rishaad have taken him out. They'll be back soon. Zubi, why didn't you tell us that Khaled was coming?' Ammi turned to her, accusingly.

'No, no, Ammi. Zubi didn't know. It is a surprise for her too,' Khaled said warmly. His eyes had momentarily moved to Ammi but were now back, locked with Zubi's. It was as if he couldn't get enough of her.

Zubi sat down next to him even after Abid came back and the boys rallied around Khaled in excitement. Khaled kept looking at her every now and then as he talked to them and they sat down for lunch. Ammi was not too happy with herself for making khichda.

'It's such an ordinary dish. What will he think? I should have made haleem,' Ammi grumbled loudly in the kitchen.

Zubi couldn't bring herself to say anything to her mother. Her emotions were running high and something as trivial as the food they were keeping on the table hardly mattered. But she was wrong. The food was indeed important she realised a little while later as they all sat down to eat.

She saw Khaled's face as he ate while chatting with the boys animatedly, and with each spoon he took, his smile grew wider. She remembered what she had said to Sonia once. For her mother, food had helped her deal with pain. The ordinariness of everyday food that sustained them had made her mother realise that death may take away loved ones, but we had to keep living for those who lived. But for her grandmother, it had been the opposite. The extraordinariness of the desserts that she'd learnt to make had helped her carve a niche for herself, despite the fact that cooking was not her forte.

And me? Zubi thought as she smiled at something Abid was telling his father. It wasn't as complicated as it had been for both her mother and her grandmother. She loved cooking and she was going to share it with the world, through their stories and through her videos.

Khaled caught her smiling and she lowered her gaze, wishing

that everyone else would disappear leaving them alone.

'This bhurta is fantastic! The khichda would have been nothing without it!' he beamed.

'Zubi made it!' Ammi announced redundantly. Khaled looked at Zubi nodding his head.

'I knew it,' he said and in front of Ammi, grabbed Zubi's fingers and kissed them lightly. Zubi drew back her hand because Suhail and Rishaad were roaring with laughter and Ammi looked a little taken aback but pleased. But all the noise receded from her ears as Zubi looked down and let him complete the sentence he'd been meaning to say all along.

'There's magic in her fingers,' he said. Zubi closed her eyes and let the words wash over her. Maybe it was true. When she opened her eyes, she realised that her mother was looking at her strangely. Was she remembering the numerous times Abbu had told the same to her? Had she too felt euphoric on listening to those words? Maybe she would ask her one day.

Later that night, Khaled was waiting for her in the guest room. When Ammi had wondered if Khaled's mother knew of his arrival, he shook his head saying he'd wanted to surprise Zubi first. 'We'll go there tomorrow,' he said and Zubi nodded. With Khaled by her side, she no longer worried about her mother-in-law's questions.

Abid was asleep in the hall and Ammi insisted that she would take him to her room.

'You go, you go to your husband,' Ammi literally pushed Zubi towards the guest room. Zubi went inside, a little afraid but mostly relieved.

There were no precursors when she went inside. They'd already crossed those barriers through silent conversations throughout the day. He stood up when he saw her. Zubi walked faster and finally embraced him. She traced the small of his back with her fingers and realised how amazing it was to do this when they were both wide awake. To hold him and to be held, not when they were in the half this and half that world of sleep and dreams.

'I'm sorry,' she said finally, expelling a breath.

'I've lost count of all the things for which you should be saying sorry,' Khaled admitted ruefully but held her tighter, his hands untying her hair deftly.

She moved back to see his face and his expression changed. His eyes became darker if that was possible. 'I'm sorry too,' he whispered, leaning in to close the gap between them.

They didn't talk much after that because well, old habits are hard to break.

And that is how the story ended, in my book at least. I'm not quite sure if that's what happened though.

Epilogue

THE thing is, they're not telling me. Both of them. So I'm leaving it at that.

When Zubi came back to Hong Kong and met me for the first time, she hugged me so hard, I thought my back would break. She kept apologising for the way she'd behaved with me and I felt uneasy because she'd been so close to the truth anyhow. She'd never know how close though.

We're going to go ahead with the book as we'd originally decided, although we *are* changing the names as I'd suggested to her on that last day.

Zubi agreed to shoot more videos so we could sell them together as a package to the right publisher and I've been trying to get hold of an agent. Once that works out, it's goodbye to Vera definitely.

Of course, the videos are much better now and are being shot professionally by a friend of Natalie's. Natalie insists that we can pay him back when we're rich but I'm kind of guessing he's an ex-boyfriend and she's got some juicy stuff about him which she's holding out against him unless he helps us out. You never know with Natalie.

Since Zubi's apartment is too small, we're shooting the videos at Natalie's place, which is the largest space that any of us possess.

I often meet Zubi and Abid at Central. We travel back together to Quarry Bay and I keep Abid occupied while Zubi shoots the videos. She's become more professional at it and she even writes down a rough script before doing these videos. We're no longer uploading them on the Internet directly, although I do have a plan on how we could make it viral once the book deal works through.

On the days when the videos are being shot, Khaled would come to pick up Zubi and Abid and I'd let him inside the apartment, smiling automatically. The days of my infatuation are long gone although a tiny remnant still pulses a wee bit when I see him.

Khaled's face still lights up whenever he sees Zubi. It's as though he hasn't seen her for days. Seriously, what had he been thinking when he said he'd divorce her? That topic was never brought up again thankfully and I would watch the three of them leave, Zubi holding on to Khaled's hand while he put his arm around her. Oh, and she wasn't pregnant by the way.

I can see that they talked now. I can see it in the way she smiled at him and the way he joked with her.

'I hope you've got some of whatever you made back there. I'm so hungry, I could eat *you*,' I heard him say as they were stepping into the elevator.

'Abba! Don't you dare eat Ammi!' Abid said and I stood near the door with a smile on my face.

In another world, Khaled might have swept Zubi off her feet and kissed her soundly, not bothered with who was looking at them. Zubi might have responded by putting her arms around him and the two of them could have behaved like the love birds they were, glued together.

But I saw Zubi's smile as she reached for Khaled's hand, lifted it and kissed it as the doors of the elevator slid together and I knew that in this world, this was enough.

Acknowledgments

Thank you, Allah, for freeing the ink in my pen and making this book possible

Ammi, Phuppujan, Chachi and Khalajan – Your help with the recipes was without doubt the most important part of this book. Thank you for not losing patience with me.

Junaid – I wish you and I could have co-written that alternative recipe book we were planning but thanks for your support and help with the Hong Kong bits anyway.

Annapoorna – Much appreciation for your food journalism info. Thanks, buddy!

Sandhya, Uncle OT, Sidra and Anu – Thanks for reading the book as I wrote it and offering valuable insights and suggestions.

Anupama, Geetha, Shikha and Lubi – Your comments about the book have uplifted me and given me so much happiness and encouragement. Thank you.

Ayesha and Judy – For believing so much in me, I've forgiven you both for not having read it yet.

Mansoor, Saboor and Azhaan – Actually you guys didn't do anything. But since you do eat what I cook even when I'm in my book-writing haze, I suppose some thanks is in order.

Thank you to everyone at Amaryllis for having faith in me and my book and being as excited about it as I am.

Hong Kong – You constantly evolving, fascinating and baffling city, I totally love you.

Finally, all you people out there who have been equating Muslim food with biryani for years, thank you. I would not have thought about writing this book if it were not for your relentless requests for biryani at every wedding, Eid, tuck shop, picnic and the odd book launch or two.